THE MAGIC OF UNKINDNESS

THE BOOKS OF CONJURY, VOLUME ONE

KEVAN DALE

KEVAN **DALE** FICTION

Dedicated to Jean Patricia Carey Davis

I got my love of books from you - I wish you could have read these.

1

MY MASTER'S WAKE

Fate—cruel, relentless Fate—would not kill Silas Wilkes too, I decided.

His large nose—easily his defining feature, lending his forward-thrust head a distinctly birdlike air—pointed one way then another as he took in the crowds spilling onto the wharves. The ship towered behind us. Rope and spar creaked with the swells of the harbor, the water tarnished green in the late afternoon.

He hefted the trunk containing his tools, his bowed shoulders and thin arms straining under the weight. "Here we go, then, Miss Kate. Keep your eye out for fortune. I suspect we'll find it but one penny at a time."

A humid wind snapped the hem of my dress. I gave the ship one final glance and followed my master. Though I'd known him but forty-three and one-half days, I adored him. He'd never cuffed me, never once even raised his voice. He hadn't a cruel bone in his body. A lopsided smile was his face's natural disposition. He'd looked after me throughout the entire crossing from London as though I weren't his indentured apprentice, but his younger sister. Or even his daughter.

We passed between crates of salted mackerel and codfish that filled my nose with a briny bite. In the adjacent market, crowded stalls held ears of corn stacked in fragrant heaps, squashes and pumpkins of every imaginable shape. Geese pecked the cobbles within wooden pens. Shadows stretched from buildings of brick and timber, daub and wattle. I nearly stumbled. I'd seen shadows slip from corners, floating ever closer, deadlier than the sharks that had trailed the ship as we'd crossed the Atlantic. Blurs. Faint shades, twisting and slinking like drifts of fog.

Those shadows had murdered everyone in my life.

The only comfort I took as I followed in my master's wake was that I felt none of the chill that accompanied the spirits—a dreadful sensation, one which rendered me forever jumpy in the presence of a draft. Still, I knew it was only a matter of time.

With a twist in my belly, I slowed, hanging back. All I needed to do was drop the haversack and dart off. Disappear into the crowd. He mightn't notice for a minute or more. By then, I'd be racing between unfamiliar buildings, down unseen streets, leading the terrible spirits as far from Silas Wilkes as possible. The details after that were—vague, I confess.

I trailed Wilkes by a yard, then two, then four as he passed well-dressed gentlemen conferring in low voices, merchants haggling with patrons. Around the square, smiths and coopers peered out from their shops. A group of young men unloaded barrels of inks at a printer's shop, their work aprons stained, sharing a laugh. Most took no notice of me, save for those who marked the faded cloth patch I wore over the twisted, empty notch that had once held my left eye. I scanned the lanes opening off the market square, choosing my escape route.

"Oh, thank the Lord," said Wilkes—out of breath and red-faced—as he dropped his trunk with a clang. We stood before a tavern called the Atlantic Nag, tucked in among the sea-warped buildings next to the wharves. It stood low, its roof sagging, its once festive blue walls now peeled and mildewed. "Bloody arms about to fall out. I'm sorry. What say I hire us a carriage? I've a few shillings to spare. Can't make a fortune without arms, can we?"

I had no choice but to catch up with him.

"Will you be all right to watch over the trunk?" he said. "If I'm quick?"

No other master—not even my brothers, maybe not even my father—had ever given half a moment's thought to how I'd feel about a task.

I had to leave him. Soon. "Of course, sir."

Wilkes rubbed his bony wrists, straightened up from his usual slouch, and passed into the dim public room of the tavern. After he slipped from view, I stepped away from the trunks, eyeing the road away from the square as though following some instruction from Wilkes. No one paid me any mind. I was just a young woman, practically invisible, my choices controlled by anyone but me. By the time I reached the far edge of the tavern, my heartbeat galloped.

Come on, I urged Fate. *This way. You've missed your chance.*

I darted around the corner. Coils of thick rope lined one wall, strands of netting piled high next to them. Four fishing hands— stained breeches, faded shirts, cheeks and foreheads burnished by wind and sea—lingered by the side of the tavern. One clamped a briarwood pipe in his teeth and spoke around it as he noticed me. "There, young James—your wishes granted."

The bunch of them laughed, even as one grew a shade redder. I turned to hurry back the other direction, but the one with the pipe grabbed the sleeve of my dress.

"No, no," he said. "Don't let his missing teeth frighten you. Proper husband he'll make. Won't you, James?"

James—missing at least half a dozen teeth at the front of his mouth—smiled and raised his eyebrows.

"Give her a kiss," another of the men said, nodding his head at me. "Convince her."

"Please let me go."

"You don't find him charming?" the one holding me said. "The smell of the catch takes some getting used to. Fair enough."

"What's wrong with her eye?" James said.

That brought howls of laughter from the others. "Oi, now he's choosey," one said, shaking his head. "Rest of her looks fair enough. Gangly—but you like them tall, don't you?"

"He likes them with a pulse," said another. "Tall don't matter."

The man holding me shoved me toward James. "At least give him a hug."

James leaned forward and caught me as I slipped into him, the boards of the wharf slick with water and fish scales.

"Don't," I said.

He locked my wrist in a hard grip, laughing. I yanked and only managed to lose my balance. Whether it was all a lark or something more sinister, I would never get the chance to find out: the ghost stalking me, quiet for six weeks at sea, saw to that. A chill rose around me, an exhalation of deepest winter strong enough to prickle my skin, to force my belly to contract. Shadows, like a flock of twilight birds, crossed James' face. He let go of my wrist and stepped back.

"What—" was all he got out before his arms flew up in front of him, flailing at the queer darkness. It did little good. Thin dots of blood rose in pinpricks across the backs of his hands and his red cheeks.

I stepped away from him, the ends of my hair rising as though lifted by the crackle of a wool shift pulled over the head on a winter's morning. The laughter died in the mouths of the other men as James' face turned a darker red, scribed now by scarlet lines of blood. His eyes bulged, beseeching help. Before anyone could move to lend a hand, he flew off the edge of the wharf, dragged down into the foam-flecked water as though he had the anchor to the largest ship in the harbor tied to his neck. A lick of water lifted as the soles of his shoes disappeared beneath the surface. Hints of his legs showed through the murk then vanished. Nothing rose but bubbles—though was that a muffled scream I heard beneath the slap of the waves and the cry of the gulls?

His friends rushed to the lip of the wharf. I backed off. He wasn't coming up—not if the ghost had him.

Turning, I tried to dart off, but the one with the pipe blocked my way back to the street. I batted his hands away and ducked left—he followed my feint. I leapt right and spun past him, brushing past his grasp and stumbling out into the street.

I crashed into man in an embroidered waistcoat who stepped back with an annoyed "I beg your pardon."

And then there was Wilkes, looking about with worried eyes. He spotted me and put a hand to his narrow chest. "There you are. Goodness, I thought I'd gone and been the worst kind of fool, leaving you alone like that." He shook his head and the smile reappeared. "All I could think about was my mother's hundred warnings about Boston. Which I'd scoffed at, naturally. It's fine. It will be. Perfectly safe. Plenty of people here. And none look utterly terrified. I've been making sure."

I hurried back to Wilkes. "I'm sorry, sir."

"No, no. My fault. We'll stick together. Come, I have a ride for us. But we have to hurry."

Not needing any prodding, I followed him along the street past the tavern. I glanced over my shoulder more than once, but didn't see any of the fishing hands coming after me. We soon reached a stained wagon hitched to a pair of swaybacked, gray-around-the-muzzle horses. The driver wore his hair long beneath a battered tricorn, and the fellow next to him had the forearms and rough hands of a stone mason, with a bald head and a red beard.

"Hand with those trunks?" the driver said.

Wilkes shook his head, lifting the trunks one after another

into the wagon, then turning and helping me up over the side. "More than fine, sirs."

I settled myself in next to his trunks, shocked at the stench of the stained boards of the wagon—rot, old fish, and white spatters of gull droppings. The wagon lurched forward in a clatter of tack and hoof, setting off at a good clip along the streets that followed the harbor's edge. A small forest of masts caught the last rays of the sun and disappeared against the coming dusk over the harbor. My pulse pounded in my ears: how long until the ghost tired of his victim and sought me out yet again?

I glanced with pity at Wilkes. He bantered with the driver and his partner, cheerfully offering them descriptions of the storms we'd passed through at sea, recounting news from London, humbly recounting various snippets of praise his carvings had earned from this Lord or that—one a member of Parliament, no less. Evening came on as we trundled through the serpentine roads of Boston. I made note of all we passed, already drawing a map in my head. Twice, I almost leapt from the wagon—but both times I balked. Whom might I stumble into in along some narrow lane or alley? I scolded myself for hesitating. No, there were no guarantees—unless I stayed with Wilkes. Then, he would die.

I eyed loud taverns and coffee houses with rising suspicion. Nearby barbers, dyers, soap makers, and the were closed for the night. I read sign after sign: Crown and Comb, Painter's Arms, Six Sugar Loaves, Cromwell's Head, Faust's Statue, Hoop Petticoat, and more. Here and there, poles of black wood rose a dozen feet with lanterns atop, set back behind wrought iron posts connected by chains. A river came into sight before us, and the driver steered the team toward a wide dock where a ferry waited, tied to a landing.

Wilkes peered at the river. It shone with the fading colors of sunset. "King Street is across the river?"

"On both sides runs the King," the driver said. "This is the way. Convenient for us. Need to pick up those couple of headboards I mentioned. Sister-in-law will have my chestnuts if I put it off another week."

"I see."

"Boston's ferrymen are no laggards. We'll be quick, though I suppose you've had your fill of water travel."

"To be sure, sir. To be sure." Wilkes didn't sound thrilled at the prospect.

The driver said a quick word to the ferryman and tossed him a coin, steering the team and wagon onto the flat-decked boat without trouble. A thick rope stretching shore to shore ran through a pulley hooked to the side of the vessel. The ferryman chucked blocks of wood beneath the wheels of the wagon to keep it from shifting. Using a pole, he heaved off from the shore, and switched to poling from the side. Between his poling and the current, the ferry moved evenly across the river. One horse spooked, and the driver climbed down and adjusted his blinkers, running a hand along the poor beast's crest. During the commotion, I might have scrambled over the sides of the wagon and the ferry—but the site of dark water at dusk filled me with dread, especially after having seen the second of my seven masters drown in the Thames at Billingsgate under similar conditions.

"Almost there." The red-bearded companion leaned back, his feet by the reins, a short, unlit clay pipe wedged upside down in the corner of his mouth. The words were the first he'd spoken, and his voice was hoarse as though he spent much of his days yelling. He stared at the nearing shore.

"Brilliant," Wilkes said. "And can you recommend a tavern to find a hot bite?"

The red-bearded man tilted his head and nodded, but offered no particulars. As the ferry came to a gliding stop against the other landing, the wagon shuddered and the horses adjusted their balance, their feet clopping on the deck. The driver climbed back onto the bench as the ferryman kicked out the blocks and bade us well. In a moment, the team pulled us up an incline and onto a rutted lane. A grazing common extended to our left. Not much farther on, a smaller road opened, passing through an unkempt hedge that stretched between thirty-foot hemlocks. Beyond their tops, a fingernail moon rose in the east. I gripped the side of the wagon, forgotten by the men. My chance had come.

"This is King Street?" Wilkes said.

The driver shook his head. "Water Street. King is up ahead. You'll see it soon."

I glanced at Wilkes, who chewed the side of his thumb. In the deepening nightfall, it was hard to tell where the road led. The wagon jounced over ruts and stones, and I heard the knocking of the tools in Wilkes' trunks. I lifted my foot, getting one leg over the side of the wagon.

"This doesn't seem right," Wilkes said.

I paused. As the lane passed an overgrown pasture, a house came into view, striking me as peculiar even in the gloaming— the roof appeared to have given way, blackened timbers showing. Where the door had been, light shone, while above the windows on both the first and second stories, black soot rose in patterns left by fire. I recognized the bitter scent of burnt timber, for it wasn't half a year since the last two of my six brothers had perished. I found myself transported back to the morning I'd stared dumbstruck at the smoldering ruins along Stanhope Row in Mayfair, London, coming to understand that I was alone, adrift in the world.

If I hadn't been so lost in my own hard memories, I might have grabbed Wilkes by the sleeve and pulled him back. I might have better grasped the peril. I might have denied Fate its next cruel strike.

"Thought you might appreciate this, sir, being a carver," the driver said, pointing at side of the house where a few horses grazed. Wilkes lifted himself and stood behind the driver's bench, grasping the sidewalls as the wagon slowed. In that instant, the red-bearded man drew his hand up from his side, swinging his arm in a merciless arc even as he leapt to his feet. A short club connected with the top of Wilkes' head. The cracking thump sounded louder than a cannon. I didn't even have time to drop my jaw before he swung the club again. Wilkes collapsed, raising one arm, but the man grabbed him up by his collar and delivered a brutal series of blows to the back of poor Wilkes' head and neck. One of those strikes caused Wilkes' limbs to shudder as though hit by a bolt of lightning—and then he was still, the life beaten from him.

The driver pulled the horse to a stop in front of the house. "You're bashing," he said in a scolding tone.

The red-bearded man grimaced at Wilkes, his chest and shoulders rising and falling, a bull who'd just charged.

"I'm not having a good day," he said, the pipe still clenched between his teeth. He flicked his wrist and something wet hit the back of the wagon.

"Don't ruin him. Bad day or no."

I'd watched the entire murder and exchange without moving, stunned into disbelief. It had taken less than a quarter of a minute and my mind hadn't caught up to the dire reality. I saw no spirits, no shades, this time—yet there lay Wilkes, as dead as the others.

The red-bearded man—who wasn't having a good day—came at me, stepping over Wilkes' body. I scooted backward, pressing into the corner.

A figure advanced from the house, a lantern held aloft. "Raining bodies today, lads," the man said.

The driver chuckled. I lifted my hands out before me. "No, please," was all that I squeaked out before my voice disappeared, the muscles of my throat clenching in terror. The driver turned in the bench.

"No bashing," he said.

The club banged when the red-bearded man dropped it to

the boards. He pushed through my hands as though they were flowers and lifted me up, leaving me with no argument against his strength.

No one left for Fate to kill, save me, I thought, with a small, strange measure of relief.

"Fine. No bashing," he muttered in that rough voice. He reeked of sour sweat and onions. Turning me as though I was as light as a rag-doll, he fixed my throat in the crook of his right arm, and strangled me.

2

THE HAND OF A MURDERER

My descent into death seemed quick, overwhelming, and final. Angels, gates, brimstone—of those, I saw no sign. No rolling fields of cloud, nor warm embrace of the Creator. I saw neither my dear brothers, nor my parents. None of the seven masters I'd been passed to as they'd, one after another, been killed by the ghost. Not one of the others who'd met their demise due to my proximity over the prior year: not the stable-hand on Little Russell Street, crushed by a dozen hay bales as I'd stood watching; not the coachman who'd lost his head as the chandler Walter Ives—master number six—and I had crossed through the drizzled streets of Covent Garden; not the kindly Widow Bonewhite, whom I'd found drowned in her washtub; nor her husband Alastair Bonewhite—master number five, who ran a dye shop in Whitechapel and was hanged on the violet and indigo stained ropes over the vats of color; a half-dozen other strangers, each as pitiful as the last, whose only crime had been being somehow near me. Not even poor Wilkes, now occupying the end of that dreadful list, having apparently escaped the ghost only to meet the hand of a murderer.

And yet my own end wasn't writ indelibly. I suppose that my

would-be murderer—if nothing better might be said for him—
wasn't used to strangling young women. An unnoticed spark of
life remained, undetected by either the ruffians, the dark spirit, or
myself in that grim hour.

Choked free of my senses, as good as lifeless, I came to at the
bottom of unnamed black depths, submerged and confused. My
mind drifted upward where dim shapes and muffled sounds
announced the shores of life. A buzz and a rattle filled my ears,
like a furious pair of wasps attempting to escape a paper cone. I
eventually registered that it was my own throttled voice, groaning. Although my cries sounded loud in my ears, they went
unheard beneath the rumble of the moving wagon.

Inches from my nose lay Wilkes' face, scribed by starlight. His
eyes were open and unseeing, a look of dull surprise in them.
Thin lines of blood traced his forehead and the bridge of his
nose. The crown of his head was misshapen—bashed, if you will.
I looked away. A pair of bare feet extended just past Wilkes,
bouncing in rhythm with the course of the wheels, blackened
and swollen with settled blood. I realized the crushing weight on
my back was yet another corpse—and bit back a scream. Afraid
to reveal the life in me, I kept still, allowing only my left hand
to explore further. My fingers touched the cold hand of another,
then bunches of material—a dress—and the curve of a hip
beneath, barren of warmth, heavy as a bag of soil. The back of my
neck tickled with what I realized was a woman's hair. I shuddered, the source of the wagon's horrid stench I'd noticed earlier
now all too clear.

"Bloody unnatural." The gravelly voice of the red-bearded
man, my almost-killer, sent a ripple of dread through me. I
clamped my eye shut and froze.

"We've got a load of bodies. Is that natural?" That was the
driver. *Hand with the trunks?* I wondered how I'd missed the
sinister lilt of his voice.

"You know what I mean."

"There's a reason this road is a piece of shite."

Another sound registered with me, a sporadic tinkling, delicate and somehow musical. It grew louder and then faded, replaced by another sound that increased in frequency, until it sounded as though the wagon was being pelted by glass beads. In the space between me and Wilkes' face, starlit diamonds bounced off the boards: hail, stinging my face. I recalled the humid air of Boston, the warmth even at sunset. Where were we? Had I been senseless for weeks? Months?

The red-bearded man grunted. "Well I don't like it."

"No one's asking if you like it. Coin's just the same, either way, and I doubt you'll be complaining about that, will you?"

A chill wind whisked the hail and sent tufts of dark hair over my face, from the dead woman on top of me. The wagon turned and the bodies shifted. Wilkes slid toward me until his face touched my own, while the woman rolled halfway from my back. As the wagon slowed, the driver cursed, and I heard the snap of the reins. "Sodding beasts, go!"

"More frightened than you," the red-bearded man said.

"I'm the one that's frightened now?"

"White knuckled. Look at your hands."

The wagon sped up again.

"Just keep your mouth shut when we get there," the driver said. "I've dealt with him before."

I tried to wriggle free, my neck protesting, my limbs trembling. I needed to get out of the wagon.

"Imagine living here. Unbelievable."

"Not our business."

"Except we're the ones driving up here. Don't like it."

"Oh, good. Let's have that talk again." A gust of wind rocked the wagon. "There it is."

"He'll know we're here?"

"He always does. Just do what I say. Don't dawdle."

"Not bloody likely. Christ."

They fell silent. I paused, hoping I hadn't been heard beneath the creak and jangle of the wagon, the occasional 'hah' the driver directed at the horses. Before I could lift myself farther, the wagon rolled to a stop, falling silent. I lowered my hand and lay motionless.

"Mr. Swaine," the driver said.

"Gentlemen." The voice was rich and expressive, with an accent I was familiar with from London. "I trust your journey wasn't overly arduous."

"No, sir. Not—arduous. Not at all."

"And as discreet as required?"

The men got off the wagon. "Aye, course. Roads emptied before we even reached the signs."

"I meant your departure from Boston," Swaine said.

"Waited until full dark. Not much of a—" he paused. "A moon, sir."

"Don't mind my friend by the barn. His duties shall keep him otherwise occupied. But back to the matter at hand if you will— no prying eyes gave your departure a moment's glance? I'm relying on your acumen."

"Just another wagon leaving at nightfall, sir."

"I pray you're right. And am I to be pleased with your cargo?"

"Hope so, sir. We've five."

"Marvelous. Somewhat fresher than your last delivery, I hope."

"Hours fresh," my would-be killer said with a hoarse chuckle.

"Some, sir," the driver added. "Bit of luck that someone met with their misfortune this very afternoon, sir. Some quick thinking when no one was about, and we nicked them before anyone was the wiser."

The disapproval in the silence that followed was pungent.

"No one saw a thing, sir."

"My demand for circumspection above all else is not arbitrary, Mr. Flynn." An impatient edge entered the man's voice.

Footsteps drew closer, coming around to the back of the wagon. "Should as much as a hint of an inkling of a rumor catch the ears of various authorities or other persons of influence, I shall be darkly displeased, sir."

"Of course, Mr. Swaine. Understood. Fully. And not a one did see."

"Yet shall no one miss these hours-fresh, recently misfortuned individuals? I find that rather hard to believe." The wagon gate banged open with a rattle of chains. "For even in Boston, there are standard procedures for fatal calamity, are there not?"

"Fresh off a boat, sir. Alone. No one waiting for them."

"You know this how?"

"They came into a tavern there. Atlantic Nag. Heard it from the owner."

"I see."

Wilkes was pulled toward the end of the wagon.

"Attacked and done in, not two streets over. Young lad I know ran and told me. Got to them before the constables. Or the crowd. No one saw them."

"Save for your vigilant lad."

"As I said, sir—rare bit of luck."

One could hardly expect a killer to not also be a liar, I supposed. I barely breathed.

"So it would appear," Swaine said. "And these others?"

"That one there was killed by a falling stone during the repairs to the Brattle Street Church after it burned. Lightning."

"When?"

"Late spring."

"Not the fire—the stone."

"Course. Last week, sir."

Swaine shifted the corpses, bringing to mind the market Wilkes and I had passed through. "And this one here?"

"Potter from Cambridge. Died of pleurisy, is the tale. Ill-fitting clothes, anyhow. Dug him up with him not thirty hours in the grave. Dead of night. We came and left like shadows."

"Shadows with pick and shovel."

"We wrap blankets around the tools, sir. Muffles the sound of the soil being removed."

"How clever. And this?"

The body atop me slid off, dragged to the gate of the wagon. I remained as still as possible.

"Ah, woman, sir. Know you'd asked for some. Doxy she was. Strangled by an irate customer. We saved her from a cheap grave," the driver said. "One beneath her is the other from the ship. Daughter, I'm guessing."

"Youth are of little use. I was clear on the point."

"She's not a kiddie, sir. Tall one. Probably fourteen."

A poor guess. I'd turned sixteen on the crossing.

"Adults only, Mr. Flynn."

"Half the price, sir." Flynn grabbed me by the collar of my dress and pulled me toward the gate. I remained limp. "Missing an eye, it looks. But she was fit." He yanked my torso upward by the arm and shook it as though that might demonstrate anything at all in a lifeless body.

"What's that one doing?" The red-bearded man sounded angry.

"Doyle," Flynn snapped.

"Why's he getting closer like that?"

"I'm sorry for this, Mr. Swaine." Flynn released my arm and my head cracked against the floorboards. I managed by the fiercest will not to cry out. A scuffle of footsteps rounded the wagon. Beyond that, pounding thuds—something throwing itself against a wall, or a door—erupted a short distance away.

"Don't move!" Swaine called out, his voice sharp and commanding. He spoke words I didn't understand and the sound filled me with despair. Unable to help myself, I clamped my hands over my ears and opened my eye. No one noticed.

"Tell him to piss off, or I'll—" the red-bearded man yelled before half his face erupted in bloody slices. He staggered forward only to have his legs swept out beneath him by nothing visible.

"Jesus—" Flynn muttered. The horses whinnied.

"Back!" Swaine called out. "*Heold þone biscepdom!*"

The wagon rocked. A wave of frigid air crashed over me, sending my skin to gooseflesh, making my scalp tighten. The sensation of pins and needles crawled over my limbs. I sat up despite my feint of death.

The wagon stood between a weathered barn and an old manse. My would-be killer stood by the side of the wagon, clawing at the air in a frenzy even as more blood lifted up in fans. Ten paces from him stood an enormous man wearing filthy breeches and nothing else. Half his head was missing. A gurgled moan escaped the man with the red beard and he fell still. In an instant, the enormous man with half a head sprang forward, his hands in claws, his jaw opening and snapping. He strained, leaning forward like a man bracing himself against the fiercest of storms. Flesh tore and muscles rippled. A ghastly shriek peeled from his mouth as he tumbled backward, where he wrestled on the ground with what appeared to be empty air.

Flynn, the driver, shrank back along the side of the wagon. Shadows swarmed in front of him. Before he could take another step, his head slammed against the side of the wagon, snapping his neck with a gruesome cracking. Flynn's limbs danced like those of a marionette spun by a wicked child.

A yard from me stood the man who'd spoken with Flynn. With dark hair of a fashionable length and a trim beard, he wore a well-tailored coat over a white shirt and dark waistcoat. Cravat, breeches, hose, and shoes completed the markings of a gentleman. He held his hands out before him, palms facing the shadows wavering before Flynn. As I watched, he closed his eyes.

With a bang, the door to the barn opened and an old man

staggered out, wearing stained night clothes. His hair flew off in an untamed corona of white behind him as he made straight for the wagon, breaking into a sprint that stunned me coming from a man that old. He leapt onto the back of the huge man, clawing at his face, biting the back of his head. The pair crashed into the wagon, tearing at each other with hideous growls. I fell back, tripping over the legs of the dead woman. With a hiss, the old man clambered over the huge man and pounced into the wagon, bony hands grabbing at my ankles, dragging me forward. The wagon shook as the bare-chested man also reached for me. I tried to wrench myself loose.

"*Se sciphere sigelede wintres ymbutan!*" Swaine bellowed. The air before me lit up with glowing lines of blue that tugged at my innards in a frightful manner. Frost spread out around me in an instant, climbing across the wagon, the bodies, my dress. The shadows over Flynn's body burst into the air, a plague of grackles fleeing into the night. Before me, the old man loosed his grip on me and collapsed, while behind him the man with half a head ceased his attack and fell forward. His arms and torso wedged on the wall, tilting the entire wagon to that side. My heart thudded as I stared at them, both as motionless—and apparently just as dead—as the other corpses strewn around the wagon.

There I was, surrounded by dead bodies.

Again.

3

HARDLY DEAD AT ALL

I tore the hem of my dress loose from the frost that bound it to the boards of the wagon, staring at the enormous man sprawled on the wagon's edge. One eye showed nothing but a crusted hollow, dried strands of fluid browning in the opening beneath his ruined brow. I felt no kinship in our shared condition. The old man stretched out before me, likewise still. I stared at them with my mouth open. My thoughts crawled, stunned to treacle.

Swaine faced me, his palms upraised, his gaze as focused as if he were pointing a musket at my head. I flinched. He whispered. The surrounding air whirled, seizing my hair, my dress. Bright lines of blue appeared, thin as gossamer, spiraling around me, causing my stomach to flutter and my balance to go strange. I grabbed the wagon's side. After a few moments, the light faded, and the air grew calm.

"Why you're hardly dead at all," Swaine said. "Yet another critique I shall make of the services of these two reprobates. Not that I have anyone other than myself to complain to, at this point." He lowered his hands. "Alive the whole time, were you?"

"Yes—yes, sir," I squeaked out in a pained whisper.

"Broken bones? Cracked skull? Stabbed?"

I wanted to shake my head, but my neck wasn't having any of that. "Strangled."

"How unpleasant," he said, sounding more as though he were commenting on a broken shoe buckle. "You'd best get down from there."

I struggled to step over Wilkes' body on the wagon's gate. After a moment, Swaine stepped forward and offered me a hand. Alongside the wagon, the driver and the red-bearded man—what remained of them—glistened in pools of their own blood and torn flesh.

Swaine regarded them, his hands now on his hips. "Unfortunate. Ruined, but fresh. What to do, what to do? Are you well enough to help me drag these and the others into that barn?"

I gaped at him. He stared at me and raised his eyebrows. "Ah, I see. Have no fear—I shall deal with your father on my own. Too painful, clearly."

Careful not to shake my head, I raised my hand instead and forced my ragged voice out. "Not my father."

"I see. Your uncle? Much older brother, perhaps?"

"My master."

"Better yet. Then you can assist me without tears or grief, I'll take it. Well done."

Tears? Grief? I'd spilled a Nile of the former, and possessed an Atlantic of the latter. It was all I could do to keep from dropping to my knees and weeping, seeing poor Wilkes dead. I touched my throat where the skin was raw from the crook of the red-bearded man's arm.

Swaine leaned forward and looked. "Ah. I see. Come."

Without waiting, he turned on his heel and started for the manse. Two full stories in height and topped with a Dutch roof, the house wore decades of disrepair. Shutters, most missing slats, hung at imprecise angles at the windows. Paint peeled from the curved cornice above the front door, the design of which reminded me of angel wings carved into a tombstone. Ivy clung to the lower reaches. Blocking out starlight, a wide chimney rose from the haggard shingles in the middle of the roof.

Beyond the house, light from the heavens showed thick groves of trees, stretches of wild meadow sloping to a dark harbor. I spotted the remains of what looked to be an abandoned town—a hint of moonlight on fractured glass here, the bones of timbers poking through a fallen roof there. Faint ripples of illumination traced the overgrown ghosts of roads and the collapsed skeleton of a bridge over a flowing river. Silence held unbroken save for a mournful wind suspiring through the trees. No song of crickets broke the silence, no call of any wild things making unseen passage through the dark meadows. The manse and its grounds might have existed in another world, a world where August Swaine was the last person alive after the dream of mankind had expired. Unsettled by the thought, I hurried after him. He disappeared through the doorway. I followed. As my eyes adjusted to the interior, I found myself in an entryway of warped boards, the stink of mildew in the air.

"*Ignis*," Swaine muttered, a flick of his fingers accompanying the word. Six fat tallow candles in pewter holders sprouted flames. I gasped. He lifted one. "Now, now. As simple a conjuring as there is—anyone with half a wit can achieve it. Ridiculous that what amounts to a parlor trick could ever become the concern of kings and courts, laws and men. Emptying towns and valleys. But there we are, the world is full of wrong thinking, isn't it? Don't step on any of these lines."

What appeared to be a perfect circle filled the hallway floor, comprised of metal filings that glinted in the candlelight. We passed into a study. A writing desk stood along one wall, stacked with papers, books marked with placeholders, inkwells, quills, and more candles. Along the other wall stood a workbench where Swaine set the candle. Tinctures and bottles, tin boxes,

ivory-lidded containers, carved wooden boxes and drawers lined
the rows of shelves built into the back of the bench.

I froze. "Are you going to kill me?"

"Kill you? Do I look like a killer?" he said, looming over me.
Believe me, that's not a comfortable question when you're
standing alone with a tall man, having just left behind eight
corpses. Worse, with his shadow stretching up onto the wall
behind him like a wraith, I have to say he did look like a killer—
or, at least, he looked like a killer from a story. Yet I recalled Flynn
and Doyle, actual killers: the sideways glances; the way in which
they looked at me as though I were no more than a stray cat; their
unkempt appearance.

"No, sir," I whispered.

"How reassuring. Now that we've gotten that out of the
way"—he motioned for me to stand within yet another circle of
filings on the floor. "Let's have a look at you. Your eye—is that
recent?"

"No, sir. Kicked by a mule when I was two, sir."

"Resentful beasts. I never cared for them."

"Nor I, sir."

"Indeed. May I?" He motioned to the cloth I wore as a patch.
I'd grown self-conscious of my missing eye as I'd grown older but
whatever remaining pride I'd clung to throughout my troubles of
the past year had apparently been strangled straight out of me. I
nodded. He lifted the cloth. "Interesting." He lowered the cloth
again and lifted the candle. "And now for this throat of yours.
Can you tilt your head up?"

I did, with pain. He examined my neck, prodding it with his
fingers here and there, his touch delicate.

"You can swallow?"

I did, though it hurt.

"Breathing isn't constricted?"

I shook my head gently. He put the candle back on the bench
and searched through several drawers.

"You may sit," he said, motioning to a stool within the circle.

I did as he suggested, my knees trembling.

He scraped two powders into a mortar, measuring them with a flat knife. Dried leaves from a bottle. A few drops of a rust-colored elixir that smelled of sulfur. He ground it together with a marble pestle. "Not quite what any of *le nez*—as the perfumers of Paris rather pretentiously title themselves—might favor, but this will help keep the swelling down, and help your skin to heal."

When it was ready, he spread it over the front and sides of my throat. The mixture was cold and made my skin tingle even as the stench of it made my eye water.

"Wait here," he said when he'd used up the paste. "And don't step from that circle, whatever you do."

He left me alone for but a minute. The shadows in the corners of his study came alive, shifting as the candle flame wavered. A creaking sounded from overhead, and I raised my gaze. Tattered cobwebs dangled from the ceiling. As I scanned further, I saw a film of dust on the windows, and in the musty nooks. Swaine's work areas looked organized and clean, yet his need for dusting evidently began and ended with his work. The creaking grew louder, reminding me of the sounds from the ship that had carried poor Wilkes and me from London. Cracks marked the plaster of the ceiling, along with stains where the weather had seeped in. As I watched, one crack grew, marked by a fall of plaster dust. What might have terrified me a day earlier seemed barely worth noting after having seen a man's face torn off. A loud thud shook the ceiling, and a patch of plaster loosed and crashed to the floor.

Swaine returned, a pleated linen neck-cloth in hand. In his other hand he held a silver pendant on a thin chain, both tarnished. He showed me the pendant. "This is for your protection. You must never take it off. Never, ever. If you do, I can in no way guarantee your safety. Do you understand?"

I can't say I did, but after what I'd seen, I nodded.

"Excellent. Let's get this over your head, and we'll cover both it and your neck up with this cloth, and you should be more than able to assist me with the bodies, no?" He wrapped the cloth around my neck, securing it with a loose knot. "And let's hope you never run into the one who wrung your neck again."

"The man, sir," I croaked.

"Pardon?"

"It was the man on the wagon. The bearded one, sir."

Swaine frowned. "I see. And your master, as well, I take it?"

I nodded.

"Mr. Flynn knew of this?"

I nodded again.

Swaine swept up the candle and turned, not waiting for me to follow. I scurried after him, sparing one last glance at the ceiling.

"Careful," he said in the entryway, pointing again at the circle on the floor. I stepped over the circle and followed him. The sight of the bodies stretched out by the wagon had lost none of its power to disturb me.

"In Boston, or out of it?" Swaine said, not slowing.

"In, sir. I believe."

"And was it also in broad daylight? Did they gather a crowd, put out a tin cup for pence?"

"At a burned house, sir. It'd grown dark."

"They waited until dark? Remarkable discretion. And no one noticed you in their company?"

"Tavern, sir. Fishermen. Dock lads. Near the market."

"Well at least there was nothing noteworthy about a one-eyed young woman leaving in the company of a large bald thug with a bright red beard." He came to a stop before the wagon, holding the candle out. "As ever, disappointed, yet not surprised. Words are vaporous things, floating pointlessly out of mouths, dissipating the moment they're uttered. Tell me—would you think the word 'discreet' ought have much to do with other words such as 'murder' or 'kidnapping' or 'tavern'?"

I wasn't sure he expected an answer from me. "No—no, sir," I said.

"Ah, verity from the mouth of babes. You are correct and possessing more in the way of common sense than this pair of dunderheads. Well, if nothing else, you might help yourself to having the last laugh as you lend me a hand dragging them to the barn. You take that leg, I'll take this—and here we go."

4

NO CURSE ON YOU, MISS FINCH OF LONDON

O
n that first night August Swaine taught me one of the great lessons of life: how easily one can step into the unthinkable if someone else treats it as ordinary.

Drag eight corpses across into a barn, one after another? It was as simple as following Swaine's cues. *Watch the head. Fetch that missing ear if you would.* We might have been moving pieces of furniture for the utter lack of solemnity. As I struggled to keep the red-bearded man's fat ankle in my grip while I tugged him through the barn door, I guessed that it was likely the same with killers and murder. *Aim for the crown of the head. Put your weight into it. Make sure you get an artery. Yes, even a child—same principles, lad.* Otherwise, who would do such a thing? Or start a war, knowing the suffering and brutality to come? Or tamper with the unseen forces of magic? Thoughts were one thing—we all have them—but the doing was another altogether, and the key that unlocked that reality was someone else leading the way, saying *Yes, come along. You're doing fine, yes, like so.*

I found the barn a frightful place, encouragement notwithstanding. Starlight fell in through rotted boards and joists to decorate the bodies in their deathly repose. A nasty odor lingered in the corners. We dragged the two final corpses—the enormous man and the horrid old man who'd grabbed my ankles —within the confines of a curious pen: four iron rods hammered into the earth, each with a thick loop of metal on top strung through with heavy chains. The air around said chains crackled with a strange energy, the restless shifting in the moments before a lightning storm. Swaine cautioned me not to touch the metal.

Once we'd gotten the corpses settled, Swaine closed the barn door and lit two lanterns hung from the wood columns that held up the loft. No magic this time—a tinderbox did the trick. I eyed Wilkes, sprawled out next to a pair of chests. My seventh master to die. Had the murderous ghosts lifted the hand of his killer? Had they brought down the club? I hadn't seen them, not the way I'd glimpsed the shades and ethereal forms that had laid low the others—but who could say? Wasn't Massachusetts riven with the infernal? Might the spirits have been at play, seeing to it that Wilkes and I might fall in with such dreadful company?

Instead of fear, I felt anger—at myself. I should have fled more artfully, more convincingly. I also felt profound pity. It wasn't only that Wilkes' life ended, that his heart had ceased its beating—no, his dreams had been murdered, along with his satisfactions, his joys, his victories, and all future paths he might have taken. Those who knew him, or might ever have shared a fruitful moment with him—they'd been robbed, perhaps just as dearly. I glanced at his killer, not willing to believe the same of him, but confronted with the possibility.

Swaine stood at yet another large workbench, a lantern before him, tracing a finger along a line of text in a book he'd opened. He appeared to have forgotten about me. I spied a bucket of well-water hung on a hook attached to one of the thick wooden beams of the barn.

"Sir? May I?"

Swaine kept reading and spared me the barest of glances. He nodded. I went over to the bucket and dipped a tin ladle, drinking the cool water. Swaine said nothing. After watching him read for several moments, I wandered over to the barn door and, curious, scanned the packed earth. While I saw bits of detritus— crumbled oak leaves, a broken quill mashed into the dirt—I couldn't spot any sign of a circle of metal filings, as I'd seen in the manse. Yet I felt something. My gaze stopped at the post next to the splintered door, where a trio of symbols was carved into the wood, one atop the next. Each contained a thin silver spike embedded in the center. I held my hand before them. My skin tingled.

"I wouldn't touch that."

I jumped at the sound of Swaine's voice, pulling my hand back. He'd turned from his bench.

"I'm sorry, sir."

"Do you know what that is?"

"Is this like that circle, sir? In your house?"

"Very much like it, albeit a more potent example of a *glamour*. You know what a glamour is?"

I shook my head.

"Not even a guess?" he said.

"Like—a spell?"

"Like a spell. Yet different. Any conjecture how?"

I stared at the symbols, chewing on the corner of my mouth. "You don't cast it. It's already cast, sir."

"And the key element?"

I looked back at the symbols, recalling what I'd seen at the house. "The metal, sir?"

"I'm afraid that metal is just metal, isn't it? A spoon is metal. A silver pendant is metal. A coin is metal. I doubt very much, then, that it's the metal."

As my family had fashioned metal into all manner of weapons, I was familiar with the utility of steel, of iron, of copper. I recalled what my beloved father, rest his soul, had told me of metal several years prior, standing beside a glowing forge, draped in his heavy leather apron, sweat clinging to his brow: the connection between the will of the maker, and the materials at hand.

"It's the intention captured within the metal, sir?" I offered.

Swaine straightened, a look of unexpected satisfaction on his face. "You just now constructed that concept?"

"It's something my father once said. But I think it right, sir—given what you asked."

"I should agree. Bravo. And your father is whom?"

"Eldridge Finch, sir. He's dead, sir."

"Pity. Of Boston?"

"London."

"And his profession was what?"

"Weapon smith, sir. To the Crown." I paused. "Ghosts killed him."

"Ghosts?"

"Yes, sir."

"Ghosts don't exist."

"But—well. I saw them. Sir."

"You can't have. The notion that there are souls who for lack of proper directions are doomed to wander some dark corner of the world, rattling their chains, moaning to be released to some farther stop along the route of the divine is nothing but fancy. Misinterpreted noises. Overheated imaginations. Wishful thinking."

"They dragged him through his workshop, sir." The memory brought back the chill that wracked me on that awful evening. "Dark, like smudges. In the air. And they clawed at him. I watched the blood fly. They—broke his neck against the wall. Sir. Just as—well, just as what happened to the men outside, sir. I'm telling the truth."

"I didn't say I doubted you. I only said ghosts don't exist. Demons, however, do. Do you know what a demon is?"

"A—spirit, sir?" I wasn't sure the distinction mattered. Every waking minute since my father's death had deepened my life into nightmare, no matter what they were called.

"Entities. Infernal entities from other, unseen realms. Beings who prowl. Who hunt. Who kill, and worse. Might that be what you sensed?"

Sensed? Did he think I was making it up? That I was a meek little girl, head filled with tufts of nonsense, feathery words carrying no weight at all, only requiring a proper man to explain the world to me? Did he expect me to stare at the packed earth of the barn floor and nod along as he revealed I'd been carried away by my own *overheated imaginings*? I raised my eye to Swaine.

"They killed my father, sir. Then they killed my brothers. Thaddeus, with a knife while he slept. Willie and Roger choked on coal at the same time, in the cellar. Georgie was pushed from the window and broke his neck. Benjamin and Harry burned. Along with the house, sir."

He watched me carefully. "And your mother?"

"She died when I was six. Of yellow fever."

"But the rest of your family perished at the hands, if you will, of these entities."

"Yes. But that wasn't all, sir. An associate of my father took me in. Cyrus Beeden. A scythe flew across the stable and cut his head off. His neighbor put me to work in his shop, sanding staves for barrels. Virgil Pyke. Shoved down a flight of stairs, cracked his head and died ten hours later. Derrick Shepley was next, sir—he slit his own throat, even as he fought off the hand that held the knife. Right in front of me, sir. Newton Hutch put me in his print shop. Two weeks later, he was crushed in one of his presses. After him was Mr. Ives, strangled by a shadow. Alastair Bonewhite was hung, and his widow drowned in her wash. And others, sir."

Swaine took up a lantern and approached me. "All that would make you quite a fatal little companion, wouldn't it?"

"You ought to send me away, sir."

"Whatever for?"

"Well—because—"

"I'm not frightened of demons. Certainly not the sort you describe: crude, blunt, obvious."

"But they've killed everyone. Sir."

"They haven't killed me. Nor will they. Furthermore, as long as you wear that pendant, they shan't kill you—though it is somewhat curious they haven't already."

I'd thought the same thing a thousand times, if I'd thought it once. "Am I cursed, sir?"

"Only in the figurative sense, I'd wager." He returned to his workbench. "In the literal sense, doubtful. While I'm no expert in curses, neither is anyone else within a thousand miles of London —and what you describe would be a curse of a high order. Therefore, unlikely. Not that we oughtn't check, if only to eliminate the possibility. Step over here."

He returned to his bench and located a vial containing a powdery concoction, turning and motioning to the glamour on the floor at the far side of his bench. I stepped over and into the circle.

"I'm more worried that you're under the influence of a demon, in some fashion." He approached me, sprinkled a few shakes of the powder into his palm, and spoke a quick enchantment. "Close your eye."

I did so. He blew on the powder. When I opened my eye, a glowing gust of brilliant blue enveloped me, as if I'd stepped into a miniature blizzard of crushed sapphire. After a few moments, the color faded. Swaine motioned for me to brush the excess powder from my chest, my face, my hands. "Well, you're not under demonic possession, always cause for celebration. No stray demon is lurking near your person. Also good." He slid the cork back into the vial and rubbed his chin. "William Easterbrook."

I swept the last of the powder from my sleeves. "Sir?"

"Easterbrook. A most paranoid practitioner of the unseen arts. Spent his life worrying over a curse allegedly cast upon him by the wife of his great-uncle. He wouldn't lift a spoon if he hadn't tested it for curse magic. Sip from a glass. Step over a root. Clearly not a fellow to bring along if you were in a hurry. But he did leave behind the most comprehensive collection of curse detection in all of English magic—before he died, ironically, of syphilis. Wait here."

"In the glamour, sir?"

"In the glamour." With that, he strode out into the night, leaving me alone with eight corpses whose visages grew no less alarming as the minutes ticked by and the wavering lantern flames kept the shadows moving as though alive. I tried shutting my eye, but that only made me more aware of the trembling of my knees. Was it getting colder? Did something shift in the far corner? My mouth went dry. The bucket of water may have well been in London for all my willingness to step outside of the glamour and help myself to a sip. After what felt like half an hour, Swaine's footsteps crunched in the darkness beyond the door and he returned, a book tucked in the crook of his elbow.

"You look like you've been holding your breath," he said. "Nor do your ears require your shoulders to shield them. You're quite safe, as I said."

I tried to hide my exhalation.

"Now." Swaine put the book down on his bench, his finger already opening the pages where he'd marked it. He made a soft clicking sound with his tongue as he scanned the page. "Here's what I dislike about curse magic: repetition. Each strand of the curse seems to require a separate greeting. Hello, and who might you be? And who is this next to you? And this?" He traced a finger along several lines of text, reading. "Rather like weaving, if you enjoy that sort of thing. Which I don't." One page, then another. More clicking his tongue. A shake of his head. "I suspect two-thirds to be unnecessary. Redundant. If you're going to accentuate each separate order of *invisibili instinctu*—meaning, unseen impulse, roughly—you're forgetting that all the upper harmonics are contained within the base order." He glanced at me. "Like the ghost notes on a violin string."

I knew nothing of violins, other than that they sounded pretty when playing a waltz. Still, Swaine didn't appear to require any input from me.

"Fine," he said after a few more minutes, closing the book with a satisfying thump. "This should suffice. Unless you have syphilis."

"No, sir."

"Well done." He selected three glass bottles from the back of his workbench and set about mixing two dark powders with a pinch of an herb I couldn't identify. "At least Easterbrook stayed with the basics when it comes to instantiating the incantation. Of course, I would too if I felt compelled to examine every new piece of wardrobe, every new bottle of ink, every mirror I encountered for signs of being cursed. Maybe that was the curse, after all."

His last observation seemed to amuse him, but I couldn't muster a smile with the corpse of Silas Wilkes staring up at the shadows not ten paces away. Not to mention the talk of demons, curses, and magic. Once Swaine had the proper proportions mixed together, he took the small bowl in one hand, lifted a candle with the other, and turned to me. "You may step out of the glamour."

"Will it hurt, sir?"

"It's a spell, not a strapping. You shan't feel a thing." He motioned me to a spot away from the bench. "Now hold still. And be patient—the incantatory phrases are bountiful. And must be woven one strand at a time, God help us."

He approached me with the candle. Holding it a foot from my face, he whispered a long string of words I didn't understand. The flame stretched high from the wick. He tipped the mixture from the bowl into this tongue of fire, continuing to whisper. Snapping flares in the various shades of the prism danced in the air before me, combusting into thin embers, glowing filaments that drifted around my head, untouched by either wind or gravity. When all the mixture had burned so, a shining veil floated around my head, multi-hued and bright.

Swaine paced around me in a circle, speaking one line after another: "*Felafricgende feorran rehte. Hwilum hildedeor hearpan wynne. Gomenwudu grette. Hwilum gyd awræc*" and so on, the sonorous phrases seeming to turn in on themselves, snakes devouring their own tails; syllable after syllable, word after word, the flow transforming ever so slightly with each iteration, a different touch on the ear. The flecks of illumination spun around me, a thousand floating parasols of sun-touched dandelion seed. In places, my skin tingled as though brushed by a strip of silk. The thought occurred that I'd just allowed a self-professed practitioner of magic—illegal, infernal, and immoral, by all accounts—deliberately cast a spell on me as I stood obediently still. Would *he* curse me? Make me his eternal servant? Ravish me with no hope of defense? Enchant me to become a murderer, taking the role of the late Doyle and Flynn? Make me into a sprinting corpse?

A little too late to entertain such thoughts, I realized with a sinking resignation.

I closed my eye, hoping the entire year would vanish right along with the view in front of me.

The spell took another quarter of an hour. The next time I looked, the swarm of tiny lights had dwindled to faint lines of red, spreading farther and farther from me, some reaching the dark corners of the barn. As a last shiver ran along the backs of my legs, Swaine came to a stop, the last phrase rolling off his lips. Silence filled the barn, save for the wind knocking the doors on their rails and sighing over the roof. He snuffed the candle wick between his thumb and forefinger. A gray scribble of smoke rose.

"No curse on you, Miss Finch of London." He stared at me: a puzzle still. After a moment, he turned to put the candle back.

"The spell—it was beautiful, sir."

He took another step and stopped, his head turning in my direction. "Beautiful?"

"The magic. The light, sir."

"I beg your pardon? What light?"

"Around me. The light that shone. Hundreds of little—I don't know—flares. Spinning."

He turned fully. "There was no light."

"There—wasn't? But. Well. I saw it. All over."

"Are you talking about the candle?"

"No, sir. The other light. I thought it was the—the spell."

His gaze fixed on mine, his eyebrows lowering. A glow emanated from his hands, running up along his sleeves, brightening at his temples.

"There," I said. "More, around you. It's not the same. It's like mist, mist at sunrise. Catching a golden color. Don't you see it, sir?"

In an instant, the glow faded. Swaine tossed the candle over to his bench. He raised both hands, palms facing me. "Which one?"

The center of his right palm shone with a curious ripple of red, low huffing flames.

"Right," I said.

"And now?"

Neither of his hands glowed, but the candle on the bench shimmered. I pointed. "That, sir. Not your hands."

Swaine put a knuckle to his lips. "Stand back within the glamour, if you would." His voice lost the bemused rhythm of his earlier comments. I did as he bade. "Now, I want you to remove the pendant I gave you earlier, but remain within the glamour."

"Is that, well—safe, sir? After what you said?"

"You're quite safe. Within the glamour. And I'm here."

With some resistance from my unruly hair, I soon had the pendant in my hand.

Swaine nodded. "Now place it on the ground outside of the metal filings."

I did so. The flesh between my shoulder blades crawled.

"When I tell you—and *only* when I tell you—please step outside the glamour. Do you understand?"

"Yes. Yes, sir."

He covered his mouth with his hand. I couldn't catch the words he whispered, though the sound of them echoed queerly in the barn. The feeling between my shoulders grew uncomfortable, spreading around to my sternum. Within the chains of the strange pen in the corner, the enormous man with the crushed head sat upright, a horrid groan seeping from his throat. He stared at the far wall, motionless. Of all I'd seen that evening, nothing frightened me more than the sight of the hulking man going from prone corpse to animated in an instant.

"Exit the glamour now," Swaine said, keeping his eyes on the man. "And get ready to step back in the moment I say so."

It was suddenly the last thing on earth I wanted to do—but I realized that if Swaine had wanted me dead, he'd had ample opportunity already. With clenched fists, I stepped out, one foot, the other. The moment my back foot passed over the metal filings, the man snarled, turning his ruined head until his lone eye found me, glimmering with malice. With terrifying speed, he leapt to his feet, hurling himself at the chains. Bursts of blue-white lightning crawled across his bare chest and arms. His mouth filled with crackling blue flames. Overhead, two planks tore from the roof with a screech of pegs and a tearing of wood. Splinters showered the spot where I stood. A shadow flitted past the stars overhead, now visible in the opening.

"Back in!" Swaine motioned at me.

I didn't need any prodding. As soon as I landed within the glamour, the enormous man swung his head this way and that, searching, still crashing up against the magic. The shadow over the roof vanished, leaving only a small patch of stars in place of darkness. Swaine said *"Dæge hæfde ambyrne isen, Navallahdraegur"* and the man collapsed backward, hitting the ground with a bone-jarring thud. Not a limb moved. Not a finger. Nothing. Swaine watched the man for a few moments, then turned to me. He stepped to the glamour. He bent and retrieved the pendant, staring at me as he held it out for me to take.

I did so, not needing to be told to put it back over my head. "Can I—"

"Yes."

Gathering up my nerve, I stepped outside of the glamour again. The man didn't move. None of the corpses stirred. Swaine continued staring at me.

"Sir, I don't understand," I finally said.

"You don't?" Swaine said, as quietly as I'd heard him speak. "Not at all?"

I shook my head. My stomach twisted into a knot. What was he going to say? "No. No, sir."

He brushed a stray lock of hair from his forehead.

"I find that almost impossible to believe, Miss Finch," he said. "What haven't you told me?"

"I've—I've told you everything, sir. I've no reason to lie to you."

"Then you've no idea what you are?"

"What I am? What does that mean?"

"A witch. It means you're a witch." He crossed his arms in front of his chest. "Of which there have been none for nearly one hundred years. Not here. Not in Britain. Not anywhere across any ocean, north, south, east, or west. Nowhere."

Witch.

I reached out to steady myself, suddenly light in the head.

Witch?

5

HAUNTED AND FORBIDDEN TO TRESPASS

I sat on a stool beside Swaine's bench, staring ahead, not registering the barn, the bodies, the looks Swaine gave me as he performed one test after another. *Do you feel this spell?* Yes, like pinpricks on my scalp. *Can you move this copper ingot across the surface of the workbench with just your mind?* No, not at all. *Without the pendant on, standing within the glamour?* No, still no. *Do the glamours glow or shine to you?* Neither—but I notice them immediately. They stand out, somehow.

Pendant on, I could walk about outside the glamour with no hint of notice by any infernal presence. Pendant off, and it would be only moments before the ghost that had damaged the roof made itself known. Not a ghost, I corrected myself: a demon.

Swaine found it endlessly fascinating. I was terrified. The tests continued.

What did it mean? How had I never been told? Why? Who was I? Had all the death around me been my fault? Such questions filled my mind, splashing and clawing like rats heaving themselves from a sinking ship—the ship in this case being everything I thought I'd understood about myself before hearing the word *witch* applied to me.

Swaine lifted his gaze from yet another book he'd carried in from the manse, opening his mouth to instruct me on yet another test.

Before he could speak, I raised a hand. "Sir?"

He straightened. "Yes?"

"Might I take a break please? I feel rather weak."

"This shouldn't take long. And it's utterly the key to it all. You see, if the visual artifacts—beyond the realm of normal senses—of the spells we've tried are clear to you, the forces involved in wards must also register in some fashion. Very different from glamours. I've always sensed they organize energies in a fashion unique from anything else, and this might well prove just that. There's no record of it anywhere, but my guess is that you'll perceive—"

I must have looked a pitiful thing indeed, for he paused.

"No, of course," he said. "Are you thirsty?"

"Yes, sir."

"And when did you last eat?"

"Yesterday, sir. On the ship."

"Yesterday? Why didn't you say anything? This won't do." He stood. "Come. And don't suffer in silence, Finch. I've left my social graces well behind and would hardly demand more of you. Such conditions are suitable enough for my own needs, and I can work through the night with nary a pause—but I'm a poor host indeed, guilty as charged. Come."

He swept up the lantern. When I followed, he shouldered open the barn door and headed toward the manse again. The air had grown sharp and iron cold. As I shadowed him through the entryway, he said "Glamour," reminding me not to step on the lines of the circle. We passed the study and he led me to the kitchen. A large hearth glowed with the graying embers of an earlier fire. He clunked the lantern down on a sturdy table—yet another repository for books—and pulled a tin from a shelf. As with the other room, the section of the kitchen he used was clean and orderly, while the rest of it looked to bear a decade's, or several decades', worth of dust and disuse.

"You can stoke a fire and make tea, yes?" Swaine said.

"Yes, sir."

He handed me the tin. "Marvelous. I like it strong. Now, you'll find cornmeal about here, somewhere. Near it, molasses. What little milk I have has spoiled, I fear—but give it a sniff. You can make mush, I take it?"

My stomach growled so fiercely that I almost let that suffice in answer. I nodded.

"A large bowl for me. I like it thick, and don't be stingy with the molasses. You may help yourself, as well—now that you mention it, you do look on the brink of joining the others in the barn, and we can't have that, can we?"

"No, sir. Thank you, sir."

"Splendid. You'll find me back in the barn. You know by now what not to step on." He regarded a stack of books. "Now, where is my Fletcher?"

"Sir?"

"Fletcher. Archibald Fletcher. A book, Finch. And not a kind one, mind you. Yet one I think might shed some light on our . . . situation. Unfortunately, reading Fletcher is rather like being a farmer, turning a field loaded with stones that dull the plow and try the patience. Yet he has his moments of insight, nestled in among the more stubborn boulders. So a'plowing I shall go, should the book have the decency to stop hiding from me."

Not finding it among those on the table, he shook his head and left, calling back that the water for the tea should be boiling, not just hot. I stared after him for a moment and shook the tin. Tea. I set about to prepare it, throwing kindling on the fire, adding a pair of split logs from the rack. A sooty kettle needed refreshing. I filled it with water from a bucket in the corner and hung it in the hearth.

"A few rules to mark, Finch."

I startled, knocking my head on the mantlepiece. Swaine stood in the kitchen doorway, a thick book in hand. "Don't touch my books, or my papers. No venturing off alone—manse or surrounding property. There are dangers waiting for the wrong moment of curiosity, even beyond your particular situation—a staircase on the verge of crumbling, cistern holes left uncovered, transoms ready to collapse, doors that may well bind or lock behind you. More crucially, if you see—or think you see—anyone else, be exceedingly wary. Don't approach them. And, good Lord, whatever you do, don't speak with them. Really, do your best to ignore them. Clear?"

I worked through what he'd said, my worry deepening. "Yes, sir."

He looked around the kitchen as though taking a quick inventory. He nodded and left, his steps receding down the hallway and out the door. I wondered what he meant by not speaking with anyone else. The darkness that pressed in on the kitchen from the doorways and the two windows grew even more menacing as I thought about his warnings. Still, hunger has a way of forcing other concerns into the background—be they corpses, witches, or magic—so I busied myself in making the first decent meal I'd had in over six weeks, and one I still count among the finest of my life.

As I later crossed from the manse to the barn, balancing a steaming teapot and a tin bowl brimming with hot cornmeal mush drenched in molasses in one hand, a lantern in the other, the wind sent fingers prying beneath my collar, grasping at my ankles, tugging my hair into my eye. I lifted the lantern, the lone point of light in a sea of black.

Witch, the thought rang in my head. *A witch.*

Hail fell in the darkness, tapping the ground on the other side of the manse. The hemlock trees sighed beneath the stars. The night had all the trappings of a nightmare—yet I felt the wind in my hair, saw the blood stains by the wagon. If I crouched and touched them, I'd find them still wet, I knew. No, I was awake. Wilkes was dead. And I was alone. Again. And a witch. A *witch*. That thought alone propelled me out of the darkness and into the barn, where a spill of warm light pushed back against the night.

Swaine didn't appear to notice me as I entered the barn, busy as he was scratching notes into a bound journal, his quill moving with precision. Before him, several books sat open.

"Sir? Your tea," I whispered.

Swaine continued to write. "The edge of the bench."

I juggled the bowl, teapot, and a cup I'd found, setting them down with care. I dug a spoon from my pocket and put it beside the bowl. Swaine licked a finger and turned the page of one book at his elbow. "Why use two words when a score will suffice?" he sighed.

"Fletcher, sir?" I said.

"Fletcher, indeed. To say that the man was verbose is rather like saying that the Atlantic is wet. Why, listen to this patch of bramble that I just trudged through." He flipped the page back and read aloud, his voice taking on a nasal tone: *"'Tis when autumn eventide sets this feral forest a'smoulder as with the glow of Hell's infernal chambers that one begins to apprehend the discorporal touch of the darkness in this land, the soul and the nerves preyed upon by the blackest currents of Witchcraft and Sorceries of most insidious origin, whose reach extends from beyond the borders of midnight to reveal a Great Realm winding unseen, beyond sill and threshold, beneath Rivers."* He turned. "I might have simply written *Salem is unquiet, from a planar perspective.* Much more succinct, wouldn't you agree?"

I wasn't sure what even his simpler phrase meant, let alone the sentence he'd quoted.

"Salem, sir?" I said, instead.

"The said same *feral forest.*" He reached for the tea and poured it, appearing satisfied at the steam released and the tarnished copper color of the liquid itself.

Full or not, my stomach clenched. "The Salem—of the witches?"

"You are familiar with some other Salem of note?" He sipped his tea and nodded once in approval at the preparation.

"*This* is Salem? We're *in* Salem, sir?"

"At the edge, yes. Perhaps you appreciate why I find it ever so curious that you might suddenly arrive here. A witch."

Salem. Infamous throughout the empire, dreaded by even the most stout-hearted Englishman. Haunted and forbidden to trespass by order of the Crown. No wonder the darkness stretched without end. I'd heard the stories, as had every citizen of the Crown, no doubt: the seventeen families aboard the doomed ship *Westenshire Bell*, cast off along the unsettled coast. The town they carved out of the wilderness, and the pact with the Devil that they'd made. Spells and trickery used on the settlers of Boston. Black magic, curses, people flying through the twilight air like storm-tossed scarecrows. Dried up wells, wilted crops, and the unending night that had enveloped the town as the Lord had served his justice. Witches prowling graveyards, vanishing into marshes and woods.

"But I'm not a witch," I sputtered.

"The tests we performed beg to differ." He tapped the book before him with the spoon. "And the more I read, the more I'm convinced."

"But—I've never cast a spell. I've never made a curse. Or a hex. Or anything."

"Irrelevant. Being a witch isn't about what you *do*, but rather about what you *are*."

"I'm just me, sir. That's all. I've never been anything else. Not —special."

"Save for the demon stalking you. Which, if I were to guess, began at approximately the same time that you—well—began your womanhood. If you see what I'm getting at."

I felt my face flush and, after a moment, nodded. My first flow hadn't been but a fortnight before my father been slaughtered in his workshop. Before that, no hint of tragedy had shadowed my life, save for the death of my mother at the cruel hands of yellow fever some six years earlier, a common enough tragedy for London at the time. But after my father had died—with me fully into womanhood, as Swaine said—the relentless scythe of death had swung in every direction around me, driving me from one side of London to the other, and eventually across the Atlantic.

"There's precious little convincing literature on witches, I'm afraid," Swaine continued. "The usual blather about Satan's spawn or sinful women. Transparent, hateful nonsense. No, a witch is a human—but with more. More sensitivities to the unseen energies that permeate the visible world. Heightened awareness. Able to manipulate energy, instinctive ways of inter-acting with such forces. And, of course, a vulnerability to demons. Hence the demon—or demons—that I suspect became drawn to you, causing such havoc to all those nearby."

Everything he said, I hated. I wanted him to stop talking. None of it was true, surely. "Then why didn't it—or they—just kill me, then? If I was—what you say? Sir."

"They probably couldn't find you properly. Or couldn't harm you properly." Swaine stirred the mush with his spoon and took a mouthful. "I'd certainly be interested in testing both theories. The question is a fascinating one."

"It's not fascinating. They killed everyone in my life, sir."

"Well, of course." He'd glanced down at the book as I'd spoken. Tapped a finger on the page. "Tragic, yes. Now, I've read an account postulating that young witches, as children, possess a form of natural camouflage from demons. They have it, or they're trained to develop it. Unclear. In either case, it would make sense, and I'm sure there are analogues in nature. And of course there would be the efforts of the parents to protect them, using their own witch-nature, which would presumably be sufficiently advanced. Let's assume your father wasn't a witch—the traits favor females, ten-to-one, though there have been males referred to as warlocks, clearly a ridiculous designation. And let's further assume that if he were a witch, he'd have told you, and also likely not have been killed by the rise in demonic activity around you— then that points to your mother. Tell me about her. What was her name?"

The mere mention of my mother sent a familiar pang of grief into my heart. "Patricia, sir. Patricia Finch. Born Patricia Carey. She was lovely. And not a witch, sir."

"She died when you were how old?"

"Six."

"And she never cautioned you about anything unusual? Never demonstrated any curious behavior? Abilities?"

"No, nothing." I pictured her sitting in her sewing room in Mayfair, her skin pale as cream, her lovely hazel eyes not missing a detail, her auburn hair catching highlights like copper in the early morning sunshine of a London spring. Beautiful, clever, fragile, gentle—no witch. "She was lovely and kind, but got very nervous about things. She stayed home, mostly, save for her routine errands. And even then, my father always accompanied her. She didn't like crowds or noise, sir. She read a lot of books. She couldn't keep herself in books, she loved them so. She was— just a normal mother, sir."

"She never mentioned demons?"

"No. The thought would have terrified her, sir. She was quite superstitious."

"How so?"

"The usual. Cracking mirrors. The number thirteen. Spilling salt. Ghosts—"

"Ghosts?"

"Not like—like demons. Spirits, rather. She wouldn't go into the cellar alone. She'd always make one of my brothers or Father go with her. The attic, too. At night, the darkness frightened her."

"But did she ever *see* ghosts?"

"No. I think she was just afraid, sir."

"And no magic—nothing like that?"

Her smile was magic. The stories she told me. How she held me, her only daughter. It seemed like a different world.

"Not like—" I wiggled my fingers in the direction of the candle, "—that."

"And her parents?"

"She was an orphan, sir. A foundling. Her name was pinned to her dress. She remembered nothing of her family."

"Curious," Swaine said. "Still, she may have been a witch. Unless it can skip a generation. Possible."

"How could she have been a witch and not known she was a witch?"

"Remember—a witch is what you *are*, not what you *do*. You spotted my glamours, you saw magic, not thinking any better of it."

"I thought it remarkable, sir."

"But you didn't think *I* didn't see it. You assumed your sensory perceptions were normal. They aren't. Now, is it possible your mother went her entire life not understanding that her perceptions weren't normal? Were these fears of hers—the nerves, the superstitions—tied in somehow? A reaction to facets of the world she didn't understand? How old was she when she died?"

"Late twenties, sir."

"Maybe she resisted it. Fought against it. Ignored it," Swaine said. "It certainly doesn't sound like she utilized it."

"But no demons stalked us. Not then."

"Fair point. Could she have instinctively known how to hide herself? To hide her children? Those are just the first possibilities that occur to me. I suspect we'll never know—yet the fact remains: you're here, you're a witch, and you had to have gotten it from somewhere." He looked me over. "I'm rather jealous, I'll have you know. I've often wondered what the unseen arts would be like if they could be the *seen* arts. Yet for all the fuss, historically speaking, over witches—one might as well assign odious motives to being born with blue eyes, or to attaining six feet in height. Random luck."

"I'm—not sure it's lucky, sir."

"Note I didn't specify what kind of luck."

I stared at the flame in the lantern.

"Well, out with it," Swaine said. When I frowned, he leaned forward. "I can practically hear the questions clanging around in your head, Finch. So, out with it."

"Isn't Salem cursed, sir?" I said. "By the witches?"

"Hardly. Rumors carried from fisherman to fishwife to tavern, etcetera, veer ever so quickly away from reality. Still, such rumors serve to keep the deserted lanes leading here quite empty, for the most part. I see to the rest. And do note you're the first and only witch I've seen here."

He seemed to mean the last bit as a joke, but I found nothing funny in having just been told that virtually nothing of what I'd believed about my life was correct. I recalled Swaine's initial assessment of me: if I wasn't cursed in a technical sense, I was certainly cursed in the figurative sense.

Perhaps sensing my growing despair, Swaine continued, "Salem is certainly worthy of caution. That said, I've managed to live here quite reasonably since late spring, in spite of the alleged inadvisability of doing so. Not to mention the illegality. Strictly speaking. Not nearly as difficult to get around as one might imagine, given that the old gentleman whose primary concern is this unquiet countryside rattles about Boston looking for his teeth, most days."

"Old—gentleman?"

"Doctor Ephraim Rush, yes."

"The magician of Boston." I'd heard of Doctor Rush, of course

—famed on both sides of the Atlantic for protecting Mass-achusetts against a return of the infernal threat—*the witches*—that once sprang from Salem.

"The Royal Doctor of Magickal Sciences: let's give the man his due," Swaine said in a tone of voice that implied quite the oppo-site. "And in fact he once did impressive work, albeit five decades ago. I hear these days, the good Doctor confines his magic to the vanishing of delicacies and the conjuring of titters as he beguiles the city's matrons with his *bon mots* and clavichord recitals."

He reached out and rapped his knuckle on the cover of the book before him.

"Successor to Fletcher here, as a matter of fact. Fletcher was the first such Royal Doctor to be officially sanctioned by His Majesty—an earlier Majesty, to be clear—in the Massachusetts charter. Fletcher, then a man named Henrik Krauss, then our Doctor Rush, whose tenure has eclipsed that of both his prede-cessors by four decades. And all three making names for them-selves by dutifully standing watch against . . ." He raised his index finger and whirled in a circle as though to say *All of this ordinary barn in the midst of an ordinary countryside.*

"But he's supposed to make sure there are no more witches, isn't he?"

"As I said—there hasn't been a witch here in nearly a century."

"Until me."

"Until you. But fear not, Finch. I very much doubt you're about to terrorize the colony, and thus would be of no concern to our good Doctor Rush."

"But if he found out?"

"I'm not sure how he would—especially if you wear the pendant, which, in addition to shielding you from the attention of demons, ought to keep you undetected by any of Rush's witch-poles." He clearly saw the question on my face before I even opened my mouth. "Witch-poles. Glamoured lanterns set atop black hickory poles, placed throughout the colony, though most reside in and around Boston itself. Designed to detect witches— or so the claim has been maintained for half a century. I personally believe the Doctor has largely gone through the motions for decades. The witch-poles, along with his planar readings and various attempts at catalogue and cartography of any rumored disturbances in this part of the colony, have likely done more to soothe the worries of one Governor after another than anything remotely useful in terms of the infernal. Still, one can hardly blame the man for justifying his rather unusual position."

It didn't strike me as comforting in the slightest to realize I found myself in the only colony armed against witches by the only Royally-sanctioned magician in the empire.

"But everyone knows the stories, sir," I said.

"Of course they do. Because people are parrots. The vast bulk of what anyone says is merely a repetition of some other person's words, passed on like cheap currency, *ad infinitum*. Hoping for an *original* thought from someone is distressingly akin to shouting down a well and waiting for a reply."

Not knowing what parrots and wells had to do with witches, I carried on. "The witches *could* cast spells, though—couldn't they?"

"Of course they could. And so could you, with practice. So can I," he said. With a flick of his fingers and a whisper I didn't catch, all the books before him lifted inches into the air, and dropped again with a bang that made me jump back a step. "There. A spell. And I'm no witch."

I eyed the corpse of the enormous man behind the chains. "But what you did with him, sir."

He straightened up and sniffed. "Yes, well I'd like to see a witch try that."

"It's magic, though. Isn't it?"

"Magic? No."

"Witchcraft?"

That latter suggestion was met with a roll of the eye that made me wonder if I'd pushed too far with my questions. "Hardly. And since you seem determined to chase this point the way a wily barn cat might chase a furtive mouse, I will explain this to you. Once. Listen carefully." He paused until I met his gaze. "A witch is born a witch, no more, no less. Such an individual can see into a darkness that others can't, they can manipulate the currents of planar energy that courses between worlds by some form of instinct. By birth. Witches and *only* witches. I suppose a witch might learn any number of spells, as well. As a magician might."

"So you're not a magician, sir?" I said.

"Not when I can possibly avoid it. No, within the study of the unseen arts, for those of us not born witches, there are two paths one might take. One is that of magician—*Doctors of the Magickal Sciences* as they are known, and of course now mostly faded into obscurity, their heyday passed, no new such practitioners in the making thanks to the outlawing of English magic at the end of the last century. And in Europe before that by a good fifty years. No, not for me, treading the well-travelled paths of incantation-based thaumaturgy." He poked at the bowl. "The way that you made this, the gathering of ingredients, the following of basic directions: that is a magician. Part soup chef, part schoolboy memorization, and entirely beholden to what their circumlocutory predecessors deemed proper approaches to the unseen."

He crossed his arms and raised an eyebrow. "Then what am I? That's what you're getting at, I can feel the question gathering up behind your lips, my mysterious, half-strangled little Finch."

He walked over to the pair of bodies behind the chains. "There is a second path within the unseen arts—a less trod path. A shifting, difficult, and treacherous path." He lifted one hand. The corpses' limbs jerked. I stepped back. Both corpses opened their eyes, turning their heads to face Swaine. "That other path is the art—and I mean art in the highest sense—of *sorcery*. The summoning, binding, and manipulation of the denizens of the unseen worlds that collide with our own. Hunting, seeking out, and mastering. My will against theirs. My life risked against even darker perils. All for a glimpse behind the curtains that separate the limited reality that we see from the magnificent reality that is."

He waved his hand and the corpses fell still once again.

"Denizens, sir?" I said.

Swaine turned to me. "Demons, Finch. Demons. The very same infernal spirits that hunted the last known witches to extinction. Until you appeared, that is."

My mouth had gone dry again.

THE STUDY OF GENIUS

A nd so began my education in the study of genius.

Upon announcing that my fearful plight was fascinating, Swaine's full attention swung to the books before him. Half an hour went by. Another trip to his study to retrieve yet more books. An hour passed. Curiously, I appeared to be as forgotten as the wagon outside, or the daylight past, or the breakfast he'd presumably consumed that morning. I saw first-hand that whilst genius often burns with a tremendous glare, likely as not it will only focus its brilliance in one direction, as a bulls-eye lantern illuminating but one part of the surrounding darkness.

I waited off to the side, taking a seat on an empty wooden box. Swaine turned from one book to another, mumbling to himself as he did. He might pause and tap a finger thoughtfully on a page, or bark out a quick laugh as though he'd proven—or disproven— an argument. Now and then he stared at lantern flames, or at the corpses, or at me. At one point, he muttered "Such utter nonsense," closing and shoving aside the book he'd been reading as though it had personally offended him. He looked through another stack of books as yet untouched, shook his head, and grabbed up a lantern. He almost faltered when he spotted me. "Ah, still here, Finch. Of course you are. Well. No more pussy-footing around this magician's opinion or that. Let's try something."

He stepped over to the chained pen beyond which lay the old man and the huge man with the bashed-in head. "Our friends here might be able to help me make up my mind as to whether I believe half of what I've just read. Come."

The skin on my face tingled as I approached the chains, a prickling sensation as if I'd just walked face-first through a spider web, perhaps one crawling with spiderlings. "These chains are glamoured, sir?"

"You see it, or feel it—or both?"

"Feel it, more, sir. On my face."

He stepped beyond the chains and began tugging the breeches off the enormous man. "Quite a gift you have, Finch—if only most of the world wouldn't care to see you burned for it. Not to mention the demons and what they'd like to do with you. As for the chains, you are correct. The intention is bound within the iron, coiled and wrapped around each minute portion of the metal, packed in like the black powder behind the ball in a muzzle. Intention, indeed. I must say, I appreciate the phrasing of your late father." He turned. "Have you a guess why I should inset these layered glamours into the chains at this location?"

I turned my eye away from the disturbing sight of the enormous man's private parts. "To keep people out, sir?"

"No. Try again."

"To—" I stared at the two bodies, and I knew. "To keep these two in, sir?"

"Indeed. And what do you find noteworthy about these gentlemen?" He held the lantern out over the bodies and stared at me, saying no more. I looked from him to the corpses. The old man looked like little more than broomsticks wrapped in a stained night-shirt, although his face retained a snarl. A hint of soot and smoke rolled off him. I shifted my gaze to the huge man next to him. He looked even more terrifying with no clothes, arms akimbo, meaty fingers curled into claws, his gaping mouth wide and full of rotted teeth. I stared at the top of his head—stove-in, that much was clear.

No bashing. The words rang in my memory. I glanced across the barn to the bodies we'd dragged in, my gaze landing on Flynn. *You're bashing.*

I looked at Swaine. "They were dead, like the others," I whispered. "But they moved."

A smile touched the corner of Swaine's mouth. "Yes, they moved—yet they are as dead as dead could be, Finch. Dead as dead could be." After he finished disrobing the corpses, Swaine gathered an array of items from his workbench: fine pins that shone like silver, a stone bowl filled with dark filings, deep red shavings of what I took to be wax, thin bands of glinting metal.

"Then what are they—if you don't mind, sir?"

Swaine examined the metal bands and spoke in a hushed fashion. "*Draugr. Dreag. Lich. Dybbuk. Revenant.* They've gone by different names. Lazarus, perhaps—I've had my suspicions. The ancient pinnacle of sorcery, Finch. Life to the lifeless. Defiance to the tomb. That's what they are."

"Your sorcery brought them back to life, sir?" It struck me as horrifying. The idea of tampering with the greatest barrier of all —death—had the effect on me of bearing witness to the universe gone wrong, of time running queerly, of a flagrant offense to the ways of the Lord. Death was the end, and August Swaine claimed to have turned it into a perverted beginning.

Swaine pushed his hair from his eyes. "Yes, a bit much to wrap your mind around, I see—but this is how humanity pushes forward."

Push humanity forward? I wasn't sure if he meant that emptying the cemeteries was the future of mankind, or rendering the concept of a cemetery obsolete. Either way, I found it terrifying. Swaine held the pins, one after another, into the flame of a candle, then dipped them into the wax shavings until they were coated with melted wax.

"My technique is noteworthy, if you have an interest in these things," he said. "While bringing a simulation of life to a body could hardly be called a breakthrough—in some ways it's a classic effort of the art—I've done something unique. Each subject required half a dozen hours of careful incantations, primarily of my own devising. A clever start. I then pricked them in thirteen locations with a silver pin forged in the fire of wood from the heart of a peltogyne tree. Purpleheart. That wood was, of course, enchanted with a specific ward. Following a pattern of glyphs across their chests and backs, I activated a precise application of iron filings shaved from an ancient bell that I paid a fortune for. A bell of the dead. Wax seals to hold in place the thin bands of silver. My own creations, mind you."

He paused, staring at the revenants.

"From there, the purest expression of the art: a demon named, a demon summoned, a demon bound. A demon under my thrall as the summoner."

As I looked with an even deeper horror at the hulking man missing half his head, Swaine followed my gaze. "Our friend there is now the prison of the notorious *Blakkr Haugbui*— the *Dark Ghost*, a demon first summoned and documented by an Eleventh-Century Norwegian sorcerer named Ase Storstrand. Summoned the entity from a plane of existence known as the *myrkva dys*. Roughly translated, it means 'the growing dark beyond the grave.'"

He nodded toward the old man. "And within the elderly gentleman who smothered in a fire—or so Mr. Flynn assured me —I bound one of *the shadow men of Jalulu-d-din*, the *zalem sakhs*, inhuman spirits first noted in the Uruk period of ancient Sumeria."

The strangeness of the names lent an even darker air to all he'd said. "How did you—"

"Find them in the first?" Swaine said.

I nodded.

"Books, Finch. Scrolls. Vellum," he said. "Rumors. Legends. Travels, all across Europe. I've poked around in ruins. Haunted forests. Notorious sites of infernal unrest. Inhaled more dust than I care to think about, my nose pressed into ancient volumes found in libraries, private collections, countless book dealers. If one knows where to look, one might find record or sign of a demon—or better yet, the name of a demon. It all starts with the demon's true name."

"I—but—that sounds, I don't know—dangerous. Terribly. Sir."

He slung back the cold dregs of his tea. "The hazards involved have certainly left a well-documented trail of wreckage and grisly ends, so fair enough. But here's the thing—in all such cases, we're talking about the perils of but a single demon. What then of two, straining against my will? What then of seven others, unseen, yet keeping watch day and night on this very spot, keeping intruders —both living, and otherwise—at bay?"

"If someone wanted a full appreciation of my achievements, they might do worse than to start there," he continued. "Not only have I successfully summoned nine obscure and powerful malignant spirits, I've also managed to keep them all tethered, nearly effortlessly. The key is to leverage control over successive demons by harnessing some of the power of the demons themselves. Groundbreaking. Believe me, there's not a jot of it in any of the tomes. Not an intimation of such techniques in any of the discourses. This parallel binding spreads the load across so many individual demons that guiding them requires trivial effort on my part—none of which would be possible without the marvelous energies that course through this place, so foolishly regarded as haunted. Do you understand?"

Understand? No. What he said was ghastly—yet he made it sound reasonable. He was what Silas Wilkes had striven to be: a master at his craft, his ability plain to see, his confidence speaking to the depth of his skills. Still, I nodded.

"You see, each of the demons under my thrall makes it easier to pull the unseen strings of the next," he said. "Unheard of. A breakthrough the likes of which hasn't been seen in the art in, I don't know—centuries." He pulled a watch from the pocket of his waistcoat, letting it glint in the lantern light. "This watch alone— bound in planar sympathy with the rings our friends are wearing —took a full month of layering with interconnected bindings and wards, harnessing the deep planar forces thrumming through Salem."

Only then did I notice that each corpse wore a metal ring around their left index finger.

"The rings and this timepiece anchor a vast webbing of forces drawn from the hidden realms from which spring the dark art of sorcery, Finch. *The undiscover'd country*, if you will. Having imbued the mechanisms with my combination of spells, I can control the wills of all these demons using only a fraction of the effort that a single demonic binding formerly required. Quite brilliant, in fact. I should mark the date."

I looked back and forth from Swaine to the bodies, who had taken on an even darker guise now I knew each contained an actual demon. "But it's not—dangerous?"

Swaine sipped his tea and nodded. "Oh, it's terribly danger- ous. Objects hurled. Blades. Hammers. Chests. It's why I make prodigious use of powerful glamours and wards, as you've noticed. Further, demons lie, they deceive. It would do well to note that while a demon will kill you if they have to, what they truly desire is to possess you."

"Sir?"

"To own your will. To grind you into madness and then oblivion, taunted cruelly, a hostage within your own body. The fabric from which nightmares are woven, wouldn't you say?"

"That sounds horrid, sir."

"It's worse than it sounds. Run through with a bayonet on a battlefield? Death will come, mercifully. Torture ends. Starvation. Conflagration. Enslavement. None can match the terrible emotions beyond despair that a demon will engender, nor the malicious glee with which such a demise will be exacted." He lifted a pin and examined the tip. "Should one survive—whether through one's own titanic struggle to banish the demon through magical techniques that even I find daunting to contemplate, or to be saved by a fellow sorcerer powerful and accomplished enough to drive out the demon: so much for the life you'd known. Such wretched souls become no more than husks of their former selves, their spirits brittle and scorched, their minds forever teetering in the twilight between the present and the hours, days, or years they'd spent under the shadow of an inhuman entity. Some never speak again, while others speak of nothing else, in voices hoarse with fright, eyes shining and fixed on a place no one else can see.

"As if that weren't enough, most bear physical depredations because of their possession. Tremors. Blindness or acute pain in their eyes. Limbs that clench like stone, or burn with unseen flames. Inner clocks whose broken gears no longer allow for sleep, or wakefulness during the days. Senses of smell and taste forever distorted. A constant sound of nearby murmurs and whispers haunting quiet moments, strange shouts in their ears heard by no one in the vicinity."

He placed the pins in a line, apparently satisfied that all were correct.

"Most devastating, a flowering growth of doubt that spreads like ivy across all the pillars of one's life, hinting you'll never be free of the demon, that a presence still lurks in the deepest recesses of their minds, biding its time, waiting to snatch back broken bits of will and soul, at any moment." He picked up his tea cup again; finding it empty, he settled for gesturing with it. "Most such unfortunate souls take their own lives within a handful of years, at most."

He absently handed me the empty cup and approached the chains again. "And demons can be devastating to a witch—for the literature suggests demons bear a special killing instinct so powerful that possession isn't even considered. Perhaps it's not possible with a witch, it's unclear. Unsurprisingly, the witches left little record on the matter. Still, of what we know, tearing, rending, and flaying of a most savage nature is the most frequent interaction."

"I wasn't killed, sir."

"Not yet, anyway." He rubbed his beard. "Which is why I suspect there's more to the story. What puzzles me is why not? And, by extension, why then was Salem once home to at least seventeen families of witches who scraped by here for nearly two decades before vanishing, leaving behind nothing more than demon-swept ruins? What changed? Were there no demons here before they arrived—or did their defenses fail them? Did they attract more demons? Was something else at play?"

"I thought the colonists drove them out, sir?"

"Don't believe it for a moment. The government of the colony might have claimed all sorts of things, but I'd be surprised if they'd done anything more than quake in fear. What happened here has all the markings of a catastrophe with roots beyond this world. An eruption of demons. A collision of witchcraft and perilous, unknown forces. It's happened before." He pulled out his timepiece again and waved his hand above it before opening it. The hair on the back of my neck rippled. Both revenants sat up, their eyes rolling open. I dropped the teacup, which luckily didn't break. Swaine stepped forward, inspecting his creations.

The enormous man cocked his head like a dog hearing a distant cry. "In fact, I bound the demon residing in this one in another such village. Heggen, it was known as. In the depths of the Krokskogen Forest outside of Finneflaksetra in Norway. Likewise abandoned, although for more than two-hundred years. The country folk still tell of the shadows singing lullabies beneath the windows, announcing the coming of the Devil. They won't go anywhere near it to this day. I bought myself several permanent scars seeking this demon out amongst the fallen hovels there. Very nearly died. Harrowing ordeal."

He fell silent and raised his hand. Both revenants got to their feet, turning to face him. I shrank back into the shadows.

"Now," Swaine said, "of immediate concern is why my friends here disobeyed me when you arrived. Very naughty of them—I gave neither one permission to leave their spots, yet both did. Why is that? Well, we've determined they respond to your presence, true—further confirmation as to your being a witch. But note they didn't lunge or hurl themselves at you. I wonder, then, if their initial reaction was to the demon stalking you. Demons don't get along, as a rule. They rather lose their minds when the opportunity to devour each other arises, as we saw."

He left the revenants and went to the barn door. "Best if we do this outside. Come along."

With just a moment's hesitation, I hurried after him. We stepped out into the darkness. Swaine led me past the wagon.

"Perhaps you might unhitch these horses later," he said absently. When we'd gone thirty paces down the lane, he stopped me. "This should do. What I want is for you to stay here for a short time. The demon likely will show himself soon enough. Don't move. And whatever you do, don't run off."

Swaine started back toward the barn, leaving me shivering beneath the stars. "Alone, sir?" I called after him.

"You have the pendant I gave you?"

"Yes, but—"

"Then you'll be fine. I'll be nearby. I won't have a stray demon haunting my home, Finch—so it must be dealt with. I've enough to concern me as it is. It shouldn't take long, as I said."

With that, he slipped back into the barn and closed the door, giving night back its darkness. I crossed my arms. Chewed my lip. Turned in a circle, horrified.

Salem.

How had I ended up in Salem, outside a barn full of corpses, standing under the midnight heavens, alone? And all at the behest of a man I'd known for all of four hours? Swaine wasn't like anyone I'd met before, true—yet I'd allowed him to convince me to stand by myself at the edge of the most accursed town in the entire New World. Had I lost my mind?

A movement snapped me out of my thoughts: a shade, darker than the night, sliding along the side of the barn. I froze. My hand drifted up until it touched the smooth metal of the pendant, a reassurance. Or at least the barest thread of one. My heart flipped around in my chest and I fought to keep from running off in the other direction. A breeze pulled at my dress with the abruptness of an impatient tailor checking the fit. The door to the barn opened again, lantern light spilling onto the trampled ground. One then the other revenant stood in silhouette, their heads turning in my direction. They started toward me. Slowly, their hideous countenances blended with the night as they moved farther from the barn door.

The thought occurred that Swaine had tricked me: I'd witnessed his ghastly work, seen his face, heard his confession of illegally practicing the unseen arts, and could link him with a number of murders. He'd lied to me in order to get me outside, on my own, and would have his horrid servants kill me out of sight.

Perhaps I'd even become the next revenant in his collection.

I took a step back, and then another, as the revenants neared, my breath coming in quick gulps. Finally I could hold my ground no more. I ignored Swaine's directive and spun, sprinting off, my

arms flailing as I navigated the unfamiliar ground in the faint
moonlight. I'd never had a nightmare so stark. Corpses, witches,
demons—they all seemed to close in on me at once. A cry burst
from my throat. I went no more than ten yards when my heel
rolled sideways on a rock, sending me sprawling to the ground. A
frigid wind gusted over me, the starlight flickering. I curled into a
ball as the pounding footsteps of the revenants raced toward me.

"*Wis wordcwida! Wen ic talige!*"

Swaine's voice echoed out into the night. Overhead, great
lines of blue-white spun, brilliant webbing wrapping over and
under a dense shadow. Swaine left his spot near the side of the
barn, revealing himself the shadow I'd first noticed. His hands,
held aloft, shone with a blinding glare. The revenants stood on
either side of me, their arms spread, shielding me from the eruption of magic that filled the air above me. As Swaine neared, the
light from his hands connected with the blue lines, and he
shouted the words once more. A terrible shriek rose from the
shadow within the magic, the sound making me squeeze my eye
shut even as my skin rippled into gooseflesh. Chill bands of
energy crashed over me as the ground shook with tremors. An
instant later, a bright flash burst overhead, brighter than the
moon, before fading. After a moment, I pulled my hands back
from over my head.

"I said not to run," Swaine said. "You ran."

"I'm—I'm sorry. I panicked."

"Demons want you to panic. It's why you can never panic."

I thought *panic* was, by definition, a lapse of control—so how
could I control a loss of control? I sat up. Swaine approached me,
crossing into the overgrown patch of meadow that fronted the
manse grounds. The two revenants straightened and stood
motionless. Swaine's breath plumed in the chill air, as did mine;
not so the revenants, who might have been statues, their flesh in
the dim light little different from the rocks in the meadow, pale as
the birch intermingled with the pine and hemlock where the

meadow grew to the edge of the woods. As I stood and brushed the dirt from my hips, I noticed the trees to the east standing out against the eastern sky. Dawn neared, revealing hoarfrost thatching the ground in spots.

"I'm sorry, sir," I said.

"Well you can be thankful I've practiced the correct wards." He straightened the bottom of his waistcoat. "The demon shan't trouble you again, I'm fairly certain. Driven off—I felt the shift in the air as he fled. Usually a good sign."

"It was the one?"

"I believe so. The revenants reacted to it instantly—yet this time, they remained firmly under my control. My technique needed some minor adjusting, but it worked. Now to make it permanent, which will require some additional glamouring of these two. But I believe they'll afterwards be exquisitely tuned to the presence of any demon who might come sniffing around you. You're welcome, and I think it confirms again that my guesses about your nature are correct. Your natural protection appears sufficient, or has until now—but I think some reinforcement is called for."

He slid the watch from his pocket again.

"If you are in fact a witch—again, I believe we may answer that in the affirmative—there may be some value in your being here. I'm no believer in fate, mind you. But I am a believer in opportunity. We may have one, thrust upon us as it may be."

I wasn't sure what to say, for even then my pulse hadn't returned to normal. How he'd been able to think so quickly through all the ramifications of my circumstance, thinking four steps ahead through the implications it meant to his work, to my well-being, all of it—well, if that wasn't genius, I wasn't sure what else it might have been.

He turned. "So much work to do—but let me give you your first, and perhaps most important, lesson in sorcery: know when you're nearing a mistake. It's an instinct that takes years to hone, but there is no more crucial skill. Exhaustion has no place around such beings, and as eager as I am to see what we can do here, all it takes is a single mistake for it to turn fatal in an instant. Can't have that, can we, Finch?"

Remembering the people who'd met their ends at the hands of the demon now banished, I nodded in agreement.

He raised the pocket watch and whispered. Both of the revenants staggered to the barn door, slipping out of the fading shadows of night. Swaine slid the timepiece into his pocket and wiped his hands on his breeches. "And what say you now of sorcery, Finch?"

I wasn't sure what to say, aside from being overwhelmed. Overwhelmed at having just seen walking corpses. Overwhelmed at feeling magic crash over me. Overwhelmed at all I'd seen, heard, learned. I suspected that wasn't the answer Swaine was looking for, however. "It's impressive, sir. And—and genius," I said, grasping for something positive.

"Yes, well—once I have considerably more confidence in the disposition of my revenants, we can explore the proper adjectives. Until then, we'll make do."

Sunrise wasn't far off. No birds joined in a song to greet the day and the silence unnerved me. It all looked so desolate, hardly less frightful than when the night smothered it from my view. I wondered what my future held in store.

"Sir?"

"Pardon?" Swaine said, engaged with his watch. He didn't look up.

"If—well—about me, sir." I shifted.

"Yes?"

"What about me, sir?"

"You have somewhere pressing to be?"

"No, sir."

"And you have your pendant?"

"Yes, sir."

"Good. You must never remove it. Do you understand?"

"Yes."

"That is the correct answer. As for the rest, I shall give it some thought." My questioning of how my fate had become Swaine's decision to make must have shown on my face. "Now, now—no sour frowns here. Believe me when I tell you I already have enough to think about, thank you very much, and the question of a young witch's fate isn't among the additions to that list I was in any fashion keenly hoping for. And unfortunately, I can hardly allow you to stroll off, head full of a rather extensive sense of my work here, ready to reveal every last detail the next time you stumble into trouble, which seems to be your *forté*. No."

He turned back to his watch, winding a nub on the side of it.

"Listen, Finch—until I can think of a place for you, I'm afraid you're stuck right here. Make the best of it."

7

FIFTY-NINE MORE MINUTES

I wasn't about to remain in that horrifying situation, of course. The decision was mine. And so it was when Swaine —exhausted, curt, and complaining about every little thing by mid-morning—announced he needed to sleep, I saw my opportunity. First, however, I had to help him as though I'd been his personal servant for years. Bed-warmer, filled and inserted in his silken sheets (he claimed his skin was too sensitive to sleep within anything but) for precisely one quarter of an hour. Water drawn from the well, stationed at bedside table, one glass, one pitcher, one sprig of mint fetched from a tin in the kitchen. Curtains pulled, every shard of daylight hunted down and eliminated. No noises were to be tolerated. I was to rest in the kitchen until called for, and should further have a meal and tea ready for him within ten minutes of his awakening. As for when that would be—why he could hardly anticipate the hour he would wake until he'd slept. With a final reiteration that I wasn't to wander, he ordered me from his bed chamber, whereupon I padded downstairs to the kitchen. I waited to see if sleep would claim him, or if he'd stomp around, calling out for me for some final chore to ease him into slumber.

A glimpse into the actual price of dealing with a genius, I was learning.

I remained mouse-quiet, listening to the creak and sigh of the manse, wind and sunlight popping a board or window frame here, whispering with a draft there. Resting my eye for just a moment as I leaned back in the lone chair at the pine table—I fell asleep, exhausted.

No dreams troubled me until I snapped awake hours later, confused and startled, stiff in the neck and my tongue dry as old paper. Sitting up, I saw the sunlight had crawled across the floor-boards of the kitchen, the western-facing windows shining. I listened and heard no sounds from above.

Hurrying, cursing myself for having slept, I quickly scrounged a few days' worth of supplies—biscuits, a slice of honeycomb wrapped in a sheet of paper, two carrots and a handful of wrin-kling peas, still shelled—and put them into an old sack I found and shook free of cobwebs and dried crumbs. Each step I took and each item I gathered sounded cacophonous in the silent manse. I judged that I had at least a few hours of daylight with which I might put distance behind me. Not pausing, I tiptoed along the hallway, over the glamour, and out the door, quietly closing it behind me. With a glance at the barn and stable—and all the madness they contained—I followed the overgrown lane down the hillside, eventually breaking into a sprint and hurrying out of sight of the property.

The lane bent southward away from the ruins of Salem, the forest soon closing in. My footsteps accompanied the sigh of wind and branch, and the distant murmur of the ocean. Again, I heard no birds. No passage of squirrel, deer, fox, or whatever else might make its way through an afternoon. While I knew little besides London, the oppressive silence around me was queer. I wondered what potent magic had driven off everything that crawled, trod, or flew. And the witches: what of them? Had they been pummeled, strangled, dragged down into earthen graves?

Hunted down by ravenous demons? Been turned to stone or wood, never to move again?

I hurried, hoping to outrun such thoughts. After a while, the path crossed a river, half a dozen paces wide and slow. A plank bridge spanned it. The wind dragged brown leaves across the water. It was at that moment that the skin between my shoulder blades broke out in gooseflesh. Before I let myself grow any more frightened, I stepped onto the bridge, my weight making a loose board thump. A curling reflection of the sun rode the river's surface. At the far side I stopped, and the lane continued on, empty, edged with stretches of hobblebush and buckeye, fern and hazel.

That's when I smelled the ripe stink of decomposition, heavy in the air. A stir of wind brushed the back of my head and something moved in the shadows beneath the bridge. I stepped back, telling myself that my imagination had taken flight; of course it had, after all I'd seen and heard. But, no—scraps of darkness gathered, seeping out of the empty air and spinning like leaves caught in a whirlwind. The temperature plummeted as the inky darkness grew in height, assuming a ghastly shape of stooped shoulders from which limbs angled queerly, stretching to the ground, trailing into black tendrils. A long shape I took to be a head, sprouting pointed horns in twisting clumps, darkened in the center around five shining orbs of violet light, the sickly color of deep bruises.

The overwhelming sense of malice nailed my shoes to the ground, stunning me with its ferocity. Swaine's warnings replayed themselves in my head. The demon—for I had no doubt as to its nature—lifted from the surface of the river. As it moved closer, more shadows gathered around it as though its presence wrung the leftover midnight from the air. A deep throbbing vibrated in my chest, in the soles of my feet, with a pressure in my ears. A terrible fear crashed over me. The paralysis broke, and I turned and fled. I stumbled as I looked over my shoulder, just managing to not fall. The demon followed.

I ran faster than I'd ever run, and then faster still. So fast that I came upon a pair of riders before they even noticed me.

The older of the two men wore a gray shirt that strained at the girth of his belly, while his younger companion had a dark vest over a loose, stained shirt, a faded tricorn tipped back on his head.

I waved my arms. "Help! Please. Help me!" They reined their mounts to stop.

"What troubles you, lass?" the older one said. The other rider pulled a pistol from beneath the fold of his shirt.

"It's coming after me. Please, sirs—we need to leave," I huffed, winded from running. I kept glancing back, waiting for the sight of the phantasm to loom into view. A twitching along my neck told me the demon neared.

"Aye, we'll help thee," the one with the gun said. He swung off his horse. "Come on, then. Climb up here, and I'll deal with whatever this be. This road's not one to wander, miss."

I hurried over to his horse. The rider stepped in front of me, quicker than I'd expected, grabbing me by the collar of my dress. I yelped, startled. The barrel of his pistol kissed my temple.

"I bloody remember you," he said. "And you're not going anywhere."

I couldn't breathe. He pressed the gun to my head until I couldn't lean away any further from it. My insides turned to water.

"How's she alive?" the older one said, still on his horse said.

"Because Flynn and that bald friend of his are idiots," the one who held me said. He spat. "They've probably been searching all night for this one."

As he spoke, a jolt of recognition slammed through me—I'd heard that voice. Raining bodies today, lads, he'd called out from the ruined house where I'd nearly been murdered.

"Told you Flynn's useless," the mounted man said.

The skin on my arms rippled. Without warning, both horses spooked, the nearest rearing up in the air, the other trying to toss its rider.

"Jesus," the older man said. He rose in the saddle, yanking the reins, trying to calm his horse. The man pulled the gun from my temple, raising his arm to shield himself from the terrified horse next to us. He dragged me to the side of the lane—much as I tried, I couldn't tear myself from his grip. The horse kept trying to buck the older man off, while the other horse walked backward, swinging its head back and forth, snorting, eyes rolling back, nostrils flaring.

Without warning, the shadowy demon burst from the trees and into the older man, sending him flying from the saddle, one boot coming off in the stirrup. He landed with a bone-crunching crash on the lane. Both horses screamed and bolted, smashing into the underbrush that lined the way, disappearing into the trees.

My skin crawled, my bones and stomach, too.

The demon—dark as thunderheads—swooped onto the downed man. A horrified yell tore from the man as he dug his heels into the ground and shoved himself back. He didn't get far. As the shadows enveloped him, frost spread across his face, his chest, his fingers. His shrieks choked off as his head disappeared, smothered. A biting wind howled around branch and trunk. Frost spread across the lane, angling out from where his limbs thrashed.

The man with the pistol pulled my head back by the hair. "What is this—what have you bloody done?"

A voice filled the air, speaking strange words. August Swaine stood in the middle of the lane, his hair awry. He wore breeches and a night-shirt, and shoes with no stockings. He held a brilliant silver medallion in his hand. As he approached the demon, the shadows lifted off the heavy-set man and flew at Swaine—but

Swaine didn't slow, didn't pause, didn't change his tone of voice. The demon tried to entangle him, gore him, slice him, but couldn't reach him. The air between him and the demon wavered like water, bright with golden lines of magic. With a crackle, the lines turned bright red, shining like embers—and the demon hurtled through the trees, striking one trunk then another, cracking them both as it flew deeper into the forest.

The heavy-set man in the lane—now dead—steamed as the ice and frost across his skin warmed in the day's heat.

Swaine turned to the man in the hat who held me. "I would advise you to let her go."

The ruffian jammed the pistol against my head. "This is your devilry?"

"Coming from a man holding a gun to the temple of a young woman, I find your choice of words ironic."

The man pulled me into the trees. "You want her back—you'll pay me for her."

"You're in no position to demand much of anything. Release her. Now."

"Five crown. And she's yours."

Frost snapped and fractured its way across leaf, blade, and soil, coming from the direction the demon had gone. Reaching for us.

"He was one of them," I shouted, all too aware of the barrel of the gun digging into my face. "Where they killed Master Wilkes. Where they tried to kill me."

"Liar," the man said. "Sodding little liar."

Our breaths grew visible as the temperature plummeted. I ripped myself from the grip of the man as he stared at the ice crystals spreading across the forest floor.

"No you don't," he said. He swung the pistol to my face and pulled the trigger. The pistol barked and a tongue of flame and smoke jetted from the barrel, not a yard from me. I flinched, expecting to be shot. When the ball didn't smash into my skull, I opened my eye. The sphere of lead hung in the air, spinning an inch from my face. I watched as a skein of frost covered the ball, just before it dropped to the ground between my feet. The man who'd fired the shot stared at me, the hard look on his face sliding into one of surprise.

"Jesus bloody—"

That was as far as he got before the demon hit him from behind. As soon as the warping of the air touched his outstretched hand holding the pistol, the man grunted, jerking his arm back. The pistol—and the hand that held it—fell to the ground. His eyes widened as thin streams of blood spiraled around him as though flying off a potter's wheel. Shadows wrapped him like ivy, like thorns. He fell—in pieces. As the last slice slapped to the lane, I stared at the heap of shredded bone, organ, cloth, and blood before me, my stomach rising into my throat. The stink of bowels filled the air. The demon reared up.

Swaine stepped forward, thrusting me out of the way, shouting words that made the air tremble. Again, the demon shot backward, taking branch and bough with it. Swaine watched the destruction—ten yards, twenty, longer until it was out of sight. After a minute, he turned to me. The air was thick with the heavy tang of blood and the cloying stink of offal. I stared at the glistening meat, bone, teeth, and shredded clothes; even the pistol was reduced to slivers of wood and steel, fanned out at my feet.

"Finch," Swaine snapped. "Are there others?"

I lifted my gaze to Swaine. "Demons?"

"Men."

"But—"

"I will handle the demons. Are there more men?"

"No. I don't think so. That might have been all of them." I thought hard about the house where they'd killed Wilkes. I'd only seen a pair of horses, maybe only the ones I'd just seen bolt.

"Perhaps you believe me now about the dangers of demons," he said, pushing his loose hair back from his face. "But if you're going to make a habit of ignoring what I tell you—then you may as well leave, right now. I've hardly been waiting for a fourteen-year-old girl to appear to turn my carefully wrought order into chaos. Witch or not. Capable of brewing tea, or not." He crossed his arms and nodded. "I don't need the distraction. I only know so much about witches, in any case: there's little I can offer on that score, fascinating though it may be. So, go. Just leave. I will see that no infernal entity troubles you for the next hour. I suggest you don't dawdle."

He turned and started back toward the manse. I looked at the lead ball between my feet.

"You stopped the shot from his pistol," I called after him. "With magic."

"No, with sorcery." He didn't turn, he didn't slow. "By the way, the words you're looking for are 'thank' and 'you.'"

"Well I'm sixteen," I shouted. "Not fourteen."

"Bravo for you. Fifty-nine more minutes."

I watched him go.

"And not a word to anyone, Finch," Swaine called back over his shoulder, not stopping. "Or you'll wish your end will be as gentle as what you witnessed. My demons are familiar with your scent now, and they can find you anytime I wish them to. Don't think your witch nature can save you every time. Nor the pendant I gave you. Doubting me is a mistake. And while you're at it, best avoid good Doctor Rush's witch-poles—this colony doesn't have much stomach for witches. Adieu."

I watched as he disappeared around a bend in the path, hidden by the unruly boughs and trunks of the forest. My gaze drifted to the remains of the men. However terrifying Swaine's work and powers, he'd saved my life twice since I'd come into his presence. Moreover, he hadn't died: drowned, strangled, beheaded, crushed. None of those. He'd walked straight at a demon. Fearless.

Yet everything he'd said, done, and told me—particularly

about myself—terrified me beyond all measure. How could he not be mad? Crazy? Lying? I was no witch—I could think of nothing worse.

So I stood there in the breathless afternoon, alone, no guidance forthcoming from the forest shading the road around me. I raised my hands and looked at them: solid, blood flowing through them. Averting my eyes from the gruesome remains in front of me, I glanced at the lane as it bent south, away from Salem.

Tightening my jaw, I turned and ran back after Swaine.

8

A RADIANT SHIP ALIGHT ON A DARK SEA

Summer passed into Autumn. Chores became routine, and my studies all-consuming. Swaine had me reading and practicing basic magic twelve hours each day, sometimes sixteen. One night in late October, when the air held a crisp bite and the stars glimmered, I hurried from the barn to the manse with a tome tucked beneath my arm. Ahead of me, the manse shone with candle and lantern, a radiant ship alight on a dark sea. From my vantage it looked as though I'd stumbled across a ball in mid-soirée. Silhouettes passed back and forth by the windows, casting shadows out onto the overgrown gardens. Yet no carriages lined up in the drive. No melodies from strings plucking out a waltz reached my ears. Clink of glass, laughter? No, only silence. This was what my life had become: an eerie dreamscape. I hurried in through the kitchen door, only to be greeted with a loud thud from the front of the house, and Swaine calling for me.

"Coming!" I called out. I hurriedly stirred the pot of soup I'd hung in the hearth, then darted down the hallway to the entryway.

"He always trips on it," Swaine yelled from upstairs. "Help him. And you have the Girabaldi?"

"Yes, sir." The book was *Incantus Magesterium* by Antonio Girabaldi. Girabaldi was one of the few magicians from the Sixteenth Century Italian school of Magia Nera whom Swaine thought worthwhile—though he insisted that Girabaldi's later works were in fact written by the magician's scheming brother-in-law after his death, as evidenced by a marked downturn in quality, with many of the magical constructs being utter nonsense.

"Try not to take all night, then."

Swaine had only told me to fetch the book three minutes earlier—but time was an unpredictable quantity when he was deep in his work. Before I ran it up the stairs to him, I put the book on a low chest by the stairs and tended to the revenant struggling on the floor. It was Mr. Flynn, always troublesome. I locked my arms beneath the revenant's shoulder and heaved him upright. His legs kept walking, making the effort awkward. If it had been a ball, we'd have been the worst pair of dancers, by far. I got him to his feet, and he set off shuffling. I wiped my hands on the side of my skirt, detesting everything about his presence.

All seven revenants circled the manse, demons mastering the mechanics of the flesh. Every few hours, Swaine had them reverse direction, taking the circuit of stairs, turns, obstacles, and uneven surfaces from a different approach. It was my job to rearrange the obstacles every hour. One of my jobs.

"Name?" Swaine appeared at the top of the stairs. He wore a bandage around his brow, fashioned after an incident involving a demon who'd developed a fancy for hurling cutlery. Swaine had yet to apprehend the fiend, though he assured me he would catch it even more decisively than he'd caught the fork tines with his forehead. He'd assured me it was normal. For just as a blacksmith sometimes got burned, or a furniture maker sometimes found a splinter of wood driving into flesh or under nail, a sorcerer sometimes had trouble with a demon.

I thought for a moment, watching the revenant Flynn shuffle off. "*Attynbyrn*—that's the first part, sir."

"I didn't ask for the first part, Finch. The whole name is what I'm after. Remember your mnemonic."

The names of demons held the key to binding them, so the ability to commit them to memory was crucial. Demon names contained power. Harnessing that power required precision. And a finely honed memory, as Swaine had told me on a dozen different occasions. I thought carefully.

A gleaming dream of tomb and crypt.

"*Attynbyrnvescumintrypt*," I said.

"Good. And the chief danger of this demon is what?"

"I know it's not the one that strangles."

"No, it's not. That's not, however, what I asked."

My hand by my side, I tapped my forefinger and thumb together, a habit I'd developed in studying with Swaine. "*Attynbyrnvescumintrypt. Attynbyrnvescumintrypt.*" I wracked my mind —and then had it. "Stairs, sir. Stairs and ledges. He lures people."

"It."

I cringed. "Yes, sorry—it. It lures people." Demons are, strictly speaking, neither female nor male. They are, however, quite capable of mimicking either or both genders to suit their needs when interacting with humans. I found it impossible to separate what my eyes saw from what my mind knew, however. "Lures them and then shoves them."

"Which means what?"

"Which means that I must never let myself be near Mr. Flynn —er, *Attynbyrnvescumintrypt*—near the tops of the stairs, the well, or any of the upstairs windows if they're open."

"Probably best even if they're not. The demon once hurled the wife of a Hanoverian glassmaker through the window of the Town Hall overlooking the Schmiedestrasse. The window was closed by all accounts."

As if Flynn—demon or not, it was hard to think of him any other way—couldn't get more horrifying.

"And let's have no more confusion about these demons," Swaine said. "Their fatal predilections must be iron-firm in your mind at all times. Now, the book."

I grabbed the Girabaldi and hurried up the stairs, placing it in Swaine's outstretched hand.

"*Attento*," he said. He opened the book and flipped chunks of pages. He found the passage he sought within a quarter of a minute, no more.

Not lifting his gaze from the text, Swaine stepped aside as a young woman approached the stairs. I'd been trapped beneath her when I'd first arrived in Salem. Holding the hem of her dress a hand span above the creaking floorboards, she walked with a smooth grace that Swaine assured me she'd never achieved in life. As she passed me, I remembered that she was the corpse inhabited by the strangler demon with the long name I couldn't for the life of me master. The mnemonic had something to do with tracing rivers unheard shivers until the light of day delays the crying of the jays and something about a forest. At the stairs, the revenant glanced down and descended, not missing a step.

"The eyes look better, sir," I said. Swaine's earlier attempts with the eyes failed: the bound demons, allowed actual sight through the eyeballs, displayed their madness and malice plain to see, the violence driving the eyes, jittery and cruel, to circle and spin and twitch so much that even Swaine found the effect disquieting. Refining the process over the summer, he'd settled on a method that left the tracking of the eyes a bit slow, but altogether less frightful. Anyone farther than a yard away might think the revenant needed nothing more than a strong cup of tea.

"Still work to be done, but at least they're not tumbling headlong down the stairs every three minutes," he said, having found the page he sought.

I wrinkled my nose at the waft of decay that trailed the young woman.

Swaine noticed as well. "Wait." She stopped at the bottom. "Let's see if we can't find her a more beguiling perfume, shall we?"

Part of his technique had been designed to staunch the onset of decomposition. The results had been mixed. Swaine closed the book and set it aside. I followed him down the stairs. At the bottom, he held out his elbow for the young woman and said "Arm." She slid her arm around the crook of his and they walked thus, a man and wife, or a gentleman scholar and his young admirer. Myself, I hated to touch the revenants.

We passed through the entryway to his study. A fire in the hearth set shadows huddling in the corners. Swaine slid his arm out and commanded her to stay still. He shuffled through the papers on his writing desk.

"*Ignis*," he said. The candles before him sprang to flame. He lifted a sheet. "Here we are. I've had thoughts on a better mode of preservation."

"The others don't smell as bad, sir," I offered. While the other six revenants had a musty smell that reminded me of a damp basement, the woman before us was notably worse.

Swaine scanned the leather spines along one of his book-shelves. "I'm not surprised—nothing about the demon within her is normal. Quite a treacherous reputation, the demon: a *kelverring* spirit, known additionally as dream-poisoners or *taxique nocentes carnificem*. They've rarely been documented in the literature, as most attempts to bind and control them proved fatal to the sorcerer in question."

I frowned. The revenant stared at me. As a witch, I drew the demons' ire, even if their ability to act on it was circumscribed. My hand drifted up to the pendant around my neck: no demon could harm me as long as I bore it. Aside from being stared at by living corpses, being a witch had little to recommend it, I'm afraid

—yet by then, I'd grown weary of wondering how it had all become my lot in life. Swaine thought my nature allowed me faster progress in my studies of magic, but it all felt difficult to me.

"This is the one," Swaine said, pulling out a thick book. "A French translation, the best I've found. *Les Vie des Cadavres*. It means: *The Lives of Corpses*. The time of the plagues was an impressively fertile era for the art of necromancy, as you might imagine. This volume was one of a dozen locked away by the Catholic Church underneath piles of inhumed bones in the catacombs below Paris. It wasn't inexpensive."

He brought the book to his workbench, turning the fragile pages open to a silk marker. He read for a moment.

"Ah, yes," he said. "Four drops of *ahyddon*." He moved to his workbench and opened a drawer. He lifted out a small brass box and handed it to me. "Open, don't spill. Observe."

I slid the cover aside to expose a blackish, rust-smelling powder.

"*Ahyddon*, also known as sepulcher ink," he said. "Dried marrow, ox blood, and ground human teeth. Along with a particular spell, it's used in sealing crypts."

Consulting both his notes and the faded French text, he assembled the other articles: essence of violet, rainwater, a gray ash made from burned sage, and a curious silvery liquid that danced and shimmered. He weighed and checked each ingredient for impurities, explaining their origin and the role they would play in the spell as he went. Studies never stopped. When satisfied, he handed me a steel measuring knife.

"When I name the ingredient," he said, "repeat back to me where it comes from and what its role is. Then add it to the mortar."

I took the knife. As Swaine called out the materials, I recited what he'd taught me, and added them to the mixture. He explained the various ways in which the specific order could alter the effects of the spell. When I'd gotten through them all, grinding the resulting paste with a pestle, he nodded.

"Excellent." He pointed to a brass crucible. "Mix thoroughly and put it into that."

"It's safe, sir?"

"Well I wouldn't eat it."

I scraped the mixture into the crucible, and then, at Swaine's direction, held it over a flame until the concoction bubbled. "Set it there to cool," he said, pointing to a stained marble slab. He turned to the revenant. "Now we shall make her gentler on the nose. Clothes off."

The revenant began a rough approximation of disrobing that failed when she couldn't manipulate any of the ties along the front of her dress. When she yanked it over her head, the material at the shoulder tore.

"Stop," Swaine said, holding up a hand. She froze as she was. "Help her, Finch. We have miles to go with their fine motor skills —which reminds me: we need buttons, and lots of them. Sorting them will help."

I approached the revenant and undid the ties of her dress, helping her slide out of it and her under-clothing, until she wore nothing but the ring on her left hand. The glyphs drawn on her had faded. I guessed her age before death to have been only mid-twenties, and her body said they'd been hard years, leaving her with scars, broken ribs that had healed poorly, stretch marks along her belly, burn marks on her legs, and sagging breasts. With her clothing off, the reek of decomposition was profound, and I put my sleeve to my nose.

Swaine touched her distended belly. "Bloated with gasses. We'll deal with that later—and certainly not here in the study."

I put her clothes in a neat pile at the foot of the workbench.

"Once I refine the revenation technique," he continued, "the process of putrefaction will not only cease, but reverse, bringing fluids, organs, and veins back into a life-like stasis.

Unfortunately for her, we're too late. This is the best we can do."

He pointed me to a glamour of protection he'd created around his desk and bench. Charcoal formed the hex, outlining a precise shape on the floorboards, traced with copper filings shining with magic. Over the past two months, Swaine had increased the number of such stations around the manse and property, locations where demons had no power and couldn't penetrate, either to harm or to attempt possession. I stepped inside the markings.

Swaine spoke the incantation and repeated it three times. He appeared to shut all other considerations out of his mind—body still, eyes closed, breathing slowly. A warm wind rose from the brass crucible, fluttering the candle flames on the workbench as he finished the final septet of phrases. My eye widened as I saw the mixture's surface change from dark maroon to ice blue. A sharp pop sounded as the surrounding air changed. Swaine opened his eyes.

"There we are," he said. He lifted the crucible and examined it, then looked at me. "What do you think—should I touch it?"

"I wouldn't—no, sir."

He reached in and lifted out a smidgen. "Incorrect. As the incantor, I'm entirely immune to any effects of such a spell. It would be a different story with you, however—so stay well clear of any of this." He smeared a dab behind each ear of the corpse, moving her hair aside to do so. He then hand-painted markings in several spots: the collarbone indentation, beneath each breast, on her sides at the level of the third rib, three fingers below the navel, the sacrum, and one final swipe between the legs. He stood back. A quiet crackling sound rose from the revenant as a pale blue light limned her skin, tracing whorls and arcs. As quickly as it began, it ended.

"There," he said. "Come, observe."

With a tinge of unease, I stepped out from the glamour and

approached the woman. Ice crystals gathered in her eye lashes
and frosted her pubic hair.

"Touch her arm, and tell me what you feel," he said.

I reached out and rested the back sides of my fingers along
her arm—she was cold to the touch. I leaned in and sniffed. The
stink of the grave had vanished. In its place hung the scent of a
frozen lake: winter air, thick ice, a landscape buried in snow.

"Her eyes, sir," I said. Earlier a dull brown, her eyes were now
a shocking blue, the blue of a clear sky.

Swaine tilted her head. "Interesting. The patterns of her irises
have changed. I shall make a note of it. Put her clothes back on if
you will."

I gathered up her clothes. Swaine turned to his notes, dipping
a quill to document the detail. "I'm not surprised that such a key
feature might be unmentioned in the literature, given the inex-
cusable lack of precision that plagued the evolution of incantation-based thaumaturgy. And such practitioners have the
temerity to call themselves magicians—disgraceful."

He shook his head and wrote. The quill scratched across the
paper. As I settled the dress over her, I stopped—the air grew
rank with the repellent odor of decay. Swaine stopped writing.

"Into the protection, Finch—now."

I let go of the dress and darted back within the lines of filed
copper and charcoal. A rush of foul wind swept up out of
nowhere. Candle flames slanted then extinguished. The fire in
the hearth flared into brilliance, then huffed out, leaving the
study lit by the faint red glow of embers. Papers spun from the
writing desk and scattered across the floor.

Swaine joined me within the circle of protection. The blue
gaze of the revenant followed him. The stink in the air was nigh
unbearable. Silver cracks spread in the panes of the nearest
window, accompanied by a delicate tinkling sound as dozens of
wicked shards formed. The rotted wooden muntins between the
panes bent. I lifted my hands in front of my face.

"Hold still," Swaine whispered. The window burst into two score glass knives just as Swaine's right hand moved. Wind came from all directions and the shards of glass stopped six inches from us, hung in mid-air. Before I could exhale, the shards moved forward again. One hung less than an inch from my eye, another pointed at the middle of my throat, and the third pierced my clothing, the tip pressing against the pendant I wore.

Swaine reached over and grabbed the shard at my chest between his index finger and thumb and pulled it back. The glass gave, then slid back. My pulse thrummed in my ears.

Night air swept in through the missing window, rattling the paper strewn across the floor. A shadow slipped from the darkness of the corner by the window. The shard of glass slid the pendant up toward my throat.

"*Ignis*," Swaine commanded, motioning at the hearth. Flames blazed. In the sudden light, a woman stood before us—not tall, homespun skirts faded and tattered, her face on the fair side of plain. Her skin shimmered as though lit by moonlight falling through shifting trees.

"Sir," I whispered.

"Something's here," Swaine said. "A presence."

"A woman, sir. Right there." As I spoke, she lifted a hand and the shards in front of me swept sideways—I stepped back just in time to avoid being sliced. The glass flew around the room like a sextet of sparrows, glinting with the firelight, once, twice, then slamming into the revenant, piercing inches deep into her right cheek, her throat, her right breast, two into the side of her hip, and a final one into her thigh. The revenant's newly-blue eyes didn't register a thing, but after a moment, she crumpled to the floor. Swaine put both hands to his head, his face twisted in a blaze of pain.

The intruder stared at me. "*Ignis*," she whispered. The candles on the workbench and writing desk sprouted flames a foot high. Fire blossomed in the corners of the walls, on the papers on the floor, at the spines of his hundreds of books. Swaine's trousers caught fire. I heard the shattering of windows throughout the house, the creak of post and beam as the walls tilted, quaking of floorboards and timbers. Swaine hit his legs, slapping the flames out with his bare hands, dancing in a panic. I scanned my skirts and sleeves, but was spared the touch of fire.

The woman lifted her arms. Windings of light appeared to wrap her, silken and brilliant. In the flaring light, she approached me, reaching out. I backed off, careful to remain within the protection. When I could go no farther, I stopped—she stood before me. She put a pale hand to her throat.

"*Wæron æpelingas eft to leodum fuse to farenne!*" Swaine yelled. A wind whirled in a vortex in the middle of the study, then boomed out into a gale. Magic danced across the walls, the ceiling, everything in Swaine's study as the winds rose. In an instant, the woman disappeared. The fire on Swaine's breeches blew out. As the wind rose, the flames huffed and tore, sparks pulled straight into the air. Faster and faster it spun, taking every paper with it, pulling over candles, sending quills flying. I shielded my face with my arms. The door banged open. Then, the flames were out, snuffed.

Swaine staggered and whispered, "*Steppen.*"

The wind ceased. Papers kept twirling, gliding to the floor. Wisps of smoke circled. The room fell silent save for the settling of the building, boards and sills groaning and popping. The room reeked of soot. I took a few shaking steps and grabbed at the mantel above the hearth, my hands trembling.

"My God." Swaine put a hand to his forehead. His voice sounded unsteady. "That power—did you feel it?"

"Who was she, sir?"

"I saw nothing but a ripple of shadow—a demon, no doubt. But with strength beyond the manifestation of fire. The planes themselves trembled."

When I described the woman I'd seen, he shook his head.

"Don't pay too much attention to the guise. Perhaps your inces-
sant questions about the witches are being picked up on and
manipulated. We need to be careful."

"I didn't think she was a witch, sir." Or had I? I wasn't sure.

"Demons sometimes know more about our thoughts than we
might imagine." He knelt by the motionless revenant and closed
his eyes. Shook his head. "My demon is gone, the binding shorn.
Unheard of. I feel nothing, sense nothing." Even after he'd
removed his pocket-watch and manipulated the magic, nothing
changed. "I don't even know how it's possible."

"Gone?"

"Not a trace remains." With a sigh, he stood, massaging his
temples. Patches of his clothing hung loose, burned. "Concerning. Also, intriguing."

"Sir?"

"I believe we just witnessed an expression of the richest vein
of demonic activity known to sorcery," he said. "Untapped. Ready
to harness."

He ran a shaking hand through his hair. Possibility gleamed
in his eyes. No, it wasn't a set-back, as far as Swaine was
concerned—it was a glimpse of what might be. The future. His
next great breakthrough, drawing ever nearer. I didn't share his
enthusiasm. Every shadow seemed to hold a threat, as far as I was
concerned. A faint ember glowed in the hearth while darkness
pressed in from the silent woods.

9

WITHOUT THESE BOOKS

Daylight revealed the damage. After checking and re-checking every glamour on the grounds, unwilling to take further chances with this new power showing itself in Salem, Swaine bade me to catalog the harm the house bore while he set about salvaging the books in his study. The stinging odor of blackened wood and scorched paper hung in the air, and would in fact take weeks to fade. When I returned to the study, I found my master slouching in his chair by the hearth, hands over his face.

"Well?" he asked, not moving, his voice muffled.

I glanced at the list I carried. "Seventeen broken windows, sir. A number of bent hinges. Great chunks of fallen plaster in four of the upstairs rooms and the hallway. Four doors with loosened stile, mullion, or panel. Six of the runners are cracked on the stairs. The bannister looks—"

He raised one hand. I stopped.

"I don't care a whit about hinges," he said. "Or cracked runners."

I folded the paper I held. He mightn't care at the moment, I knew—but he would care eventually, when the moment came. I slid the paper into my pocket.

He took his hands from his face and sat up. "Does a mother value her children, Finch?"

"Sir?"

"Does a mother value her children?"

"A mother—loves her children, sir."

"Would you say I *value* my books?"

"You *love* them, sir?"

"With more ferocity and devotion than any mother ever has, Finch. Any mother." He swept his arm. "And look about. The ruin. The catastrophe. Each volume licked by the flames is a wound I bear in my heart."

Most of his collection had gone untouched. Many bore superficial wounds confined to their covers, perhaps with edges smudged with soot. Yet some looked beyond salvage, covers hanging by singed threads, blackened spines crumbling to ashes. As I stared at the books, damaged and otherwise, I found myself thinking not about Swaine, but about my own mother. She'd loved books every bit as much as Swaine, as well as I could remember: they were her solace, her sanctuary. When my father ran errands, she lost herself in books, re-reading the same one over and over if no other was available. She was thrilled to borrow one or two books during a season, and I could only surmise that a room shelved floor to ceiling with books would have been her idea of Heaven.

Yet would she have been pleased to see her only daughter surrounded by books if she also knew of the corpses, demons, and unseen arts that comprised my days? Such thoughts left me uneasy. Who had she really been, passing on her dark gift to me without a word? Had she been waiting until I was older? Had it all been a terrible miscalculation? Such thoughts soured in my mind the longer I examined them, the conclusion inescapable:

her silence had brought ruin to our family and kept me from ever having a normal life.

I approached one of the damaged books, Thomas Wexler's *Mediam Regionem*. I tried to line up the scorched portions of the volume.

Swaine rose, shaking his head. "I can't even bear the sight of such a magnificent book reduced to ash." He stormed from the room. I listened as he banged around the first floor and the kitchen for half an hour. I busied myself, trying to bring some order to the shambles of his study. When he at last returned, bearing a full kettle of tea, I worried he'd object to my handling of his books. Instead, he looked resigned.

"Each one, you see, is a locale I've visited. Dwelt in," he said. "Each acquisition a prize. Each author an old friend. An inspiration. A vexing instructor. A rambunctious fool, in some cases." He set the kettle down on his writing desk. "Here's the thing, Finch: read enough books, and eventually the larger contours of reality begin to reveal themselves—one thread crossing here, another leading there, yet another intersecting the first two, and soon the vast beauty and breadth of life stretches out from your vantage, connected by that sumptuous web of words and the minds who spun them. Without these books—I wouldn't be who I am."

"I'm—well, I'm so sorry, sir." I shifted, unsure what else to say. "I've put the worst ones over here, sir."

Swaine poured himself a cup and sighed. "I suppose I can't put it off forever. Let's have a look. Don't mind me if I weep." He came over to the table where I'd gathered the casualties.

He poked at the ruins of one thick book. "Well if I had to pick a book to go up in flames, Hoell wouldn't be the last on my list." Another sigh. "Sixteenth century, Welsh. Gwillim Hoell. Once devised a notorious spell alleged to turn a ram's horn into an instrument designed to peer into Hell and locate the souls of the more sinful among the English aristocracy. It did nothing of the kind, of course. It only served to help the charlatan peer beneath the skirts of wealthy widows."

Next to it sat another volume with half its pages charred to cinders.

"I could make out the name Barnave on the front-piece, sir," I offered.

"Yes. Jérome Barnave of Dauphiné." The recognition elicited no more than a deep frown. "Barnave's contribution to the arts was a technique for spying on individuals using entrained pairs of mirrors over great distances." He sipped his tea. It seemed as though speaking of the contents of the books was at least pulling him from the gloom. Or maybe it was simply the tea. "The chief danger with mirror magic being that opening such channels is a two-way proposition, and there is often no telling what sort of planar entities might gain an interest in the caster themselves. In fact, Barnave eventually disavowed his eponymous spell, and would under no circumstance tolerate the presence of any mirror or reflective object in his presence for the remainder of his life. A polished silver tea set would send him fleeing, by all accounts. Can you imagine?"

I was going to confirm that I couldn't, but he'd already grunted in frustration at the sight of the next book, a stout volume blackened on the outside, half the pages devoured, reduced to cinder.

"Blackwell," he said. "Lord Humble Blackwell. Damn it all."

I saw the cloud descending on his brow again. I hoped to stave off the darkest of his despair. "What did he study, sir?"

"Glamours and the planar implications of warded metals used in them. Only the most widely regarded authority on the subject, which I've consulted dozens of times since arriving here."

"And did he recant his work, sir?"

"Recant? Heavens, no. Not Blackwell. The man was the son of the 7th Baron Blackwell of Warwickshire. A promising young alchemist who turned to sorcery after marrying a local commoner. She was alleged to be a witch, interestingly enough. Said marriage, naturally, forced Blackwell to sever his ties to the Blackwell fortune. His family never gave up the conviction that he'd been spellbound, seeing signs of the Devil in all circumstances surrounding the affair. He never spoke to them again. His work is—was—lively, thorough, committed."

The morning sunlight fell in across the scorched books. "Are there any books by women, sir?"

"Of course." He looked over the collection. "Though, thankfully, none appear to be among the murdered here in this gruesome mortuary."

He pointed to a few spots along his shelves. "Right over there is Milread Laird. Also known as Sister Agnes of Deeside. She spent her life in the Abby of St. Hilda, in the Grampian Mountains of Scotland, creating that lovely, exhaustive encyclopedia of demons. She claimed they were shown to her in visions from God that spanned nearly her entire life. Let me add my voice to those who contend that Laird was herself, in fact, a sorceress. Striking accuracy and detail fill her work. Further, records of the Abby indicated that the sisters never suffered from the notable depredations, robberies, or malnourishment common to the sparse villages and towns in that notorious area of the Highlands, lending credence to the theory."

Stepping to a closer bookcase, he tapped the spine of a slender volume. "Emelie Du Marien, a French noble woman whose travels to Safavid Persia uncovered a strain of planar entities known by the Sufis as *shadow-asps*. Quite an inspiration. She lived a life free of convention, notably eschewing dresses for breeches. How shocking. Sadly, though perhaps unsurprisingly, she was shunned by most of the leading male practitioners of the art during her time. Pure foolishness. She disappeared while crossing the Southern Carpathians with her longtime companion Claire Claudel, herself something of an underrated practitioner of magic."

His voice held no scorn, no mockery, no condescension. I realized that Swaine's dedication to the art was so profound as to negate any such distinction as sex, nationality, or ethnicity. He cared for the work. The intellect. The art. He held his finger on the edge of Du Marien's book for a moment, then turned back to me. "Let's get through this grim accounting. What next?"

"This one is only damaged on the bottom corner, sir." The brown cover bore the title *Die Schimmernden Rand Mitternacht.*

"Ah, *The Glimmering Edge of Midnight,*" Swaine said. "Werner Schmeling's insights into the nature of those entities dwelling just below the surface of the visible world. I adore it. The muscular prose—it captures the exuberance of proper pursuit of the sorcery. Schmeling left Saxony as a young man, pursuing sorcery from Amsterdam to Vienna to Kalmar during his short life. The man was a genius. Died at the age of twenty-seven, decapitated by a mirror during a summoning gone awry. A bit how I feel seeing that rare book damaged."

"I wonder if we mightn't get this one back together, sir." I nudged the first one I'd touched, the one that had driven him from the room earlier. "It seems to have split down the middle, with only the center of the pages scorched. Maybe just a few pages are lost."

"Even a few pages of *Mediam Regionem* burnt is an appalling tragedy, Finch." Swaine looked over the broken spine. "Wexler was the first English magician to posit patterns of planar variation that follow a cycle that can be tracked. Oscillating in complex cycles of 4 and 11 years for the first, 9, 12, and 23 years for the second. The poor man only lived to see half his predictions confirmed. His apprentice Thomas Adams went on to chart the shifts of three more planes before disappearing during a carriage journey between Burton-on-Trent and Leek in the spring of 1672. According to testimony to the local constables, the driver of the carriage had arrived in Leek empty of his sole passenger, reporting nothing unusual, save for a thunderstorm with little rain that had been heralded by the appearance of a peculiar flock of ravens."

"Ravens?"

"Notably, there exists a long tradition of English raven magic, often used to murderous ends. Perhaps he'd made enemies. The matter was never satisfactorily resolved."

Swaine turned to the last two books on display. Pages devoured, spine and binding destroyed, remnants of paper blackened and fragile. He put his tea down and ran a hand over his brow.

"Those are the worst, sir," I said.

"The demon might as well have disemboweled me on the spot. These are the works of giants, Finch. Giants." He looked as stricken as if his innards were in fact spilled out across the floor. "Irreplaceable." He leaned over the first book—though it was more ash than book. "The Great Man."

I didn't dare speak.

Swaine shook his head. "The greatest German magician of them all: Gustav Koeffler. Pioneered the theories of planar behavior. Documented the existence of seventy-nine different planes. In fact, he came to believe there might in fact be an infinite array of them. Planes wrapped within planes in an unending process of bifurcation, a cosmic nesting, a staggering mosaic of realities."

"The same—planes mentioned by Wexler, sir? I've never really known what that means, sir. Not when you've mentioned it."

"You haven't? Good grief—don't let a mystery linger. You merely have to ask."

Easy for him to say—he'd never tried to interrupt himself mid-explanation. A fraught proposition, I could attest.

He continued, "Planes of existence beyond our own. Invisible realms. Some of pure energy, others of nothing but the absence of light, of life, of matter. Among these are planes that are home to beings and intelligences that are entirely inimical to what we see around us. These would include demons, and other malign entities."

"But where are they, sir?"

"They're all around us," Swaine said. "Koeffler memorably described it thusly: 'You hold within the palm of your hand universes: spiraled, knotted, nested, and alive, over and above, under and through. A vast web of glittering life and beauty, linking all that you see with all that truly is.'"

I looked at my hand and saw nothing but a streak of soot.

"Inside," Swaine continued. "Within. And yet, for the most part, out of reach, save for those locations or instances where one plane—or more than one—collides with another. In those locales, the veil between worlds becomes thin, allowing passage. Much of sorcery depends on these sort of intersections of the planes. They make summoning possible, you see."

I wasn't altogether sure I understood.

"Koeffler's methods of planar explorations and cataloguing his findings were exquisite. Such crucial work. Dangerous, as well —yet he lived to be seventy-nine. Towering intellect until the very end. On his death-bed, he retained his poise, his final words a remark of sterling poetry." Swaine paused as though swallowing down the emotion that had thickened his voice. He cradled the blackened husk of the book in his hands, his face pale. "'*So viele räume innerhalb des himmlischen villa, ich freue mich jeden zu erkunden.*' It means: 'So many rooms within the heavenly mansion, I look forward to exploring each one.' Koeffler's work changed the course of my life."

After setting it down with care, he turned to the last ruined tome. Every page had burned, the thick cover barely holding together. "I can't even touch it," he said. "A jewel in the art. That foul demon has robbed the world. This is the rarest of the rare: Myrgjöl Grímhildr's *Srávobhiśśravasíyas*. An original. From 1483, the classic work on magical wards. Printed, as a matter of fact, in the village of Heggen, before it met the misfortune I told you of.

Where I bound the demon now residing within our large, half-headed friend. So many connections to this work." He stared at the charred cinders. After a good minute, he sniffed and ran a hand across his forehead, leaving a black streak. "I take little comfort in the fact that my copy of Angus Hume's English translation escaped the flames. Serviceable rending of the text—but no poetry, shorn of its numinous mellifluence, its awe."

Swaine turned away from the pile of destroyed books, bringing his voice back to his normal—rather loud—timbre. "We shall leave this tragedy behind us, Finch. Such is the price of falling in love with books. Still, there are more in the world. On the morrow, we shall venture to Boston, where perhaps other volumes await us, ready to make our acquaintance. Along with other materials and sundry I've ordered. For now, let's give these priceless ashes the proper burial they deserve so that we might start afresh."

"I'll help, sir. Anything I can do."

"Well done." He drained the rest of his tea and straightened up. "Let me comfort myself by noting that it could have been worse. Why, do you know there was an infamous book of spells by a maniac named Derrik Hill that had the most unfortunate defect of occasionally bursting into flames? It took out dozens of fine collections across Britain before the remaining volumes were properly quarantined."

And with that, we set about righting the library back into something resembling order. By then, I was starting to see what my master meant about the larger contours of reality—book after book opening a new world. Yet I couldn't help but notice the glaring absence of even a single book by a witch.

10

A GOLDEN SPIDER

An autumn rain fell as we rode along a dank Boston street the next day. Streams of run-off hung like clear rope from the corners of roofs, sluicing to the cobbles of the street, while oil lanterns on posts and alongside doorways pushed back at the overcast morning. Although Swaine had found it suitable enough for me to drive the team for most of the trip, as the river had come into view, he'd taken the reins himself. Appearances, after all. The street rang with the sounds of hammer, saw, and mallet. Passing by workshops, I caught glimpses of bellows and fires in forge and kiln, my heart tightening recalling my father's shop, and of lanterns shining on workbench and jig. I listened to the calls of the artisans, barking instructions to their fleet-footed apprentices, trading jokes with one another across puddled lanes. Wondrous noise, after Salem's unending silence.

Swaine pointed out some of the city's witch-poles: set back from the roads and cordoned off by rusting chains, the black hickory poles reached a height of eighteen feet, topped with elaborate lanterns designed to reveal the presence of witches. "There are sixty-six of them, in total," Swaine said. "A clever device of

Doctor Rush's own design, based on the principles of transmorgative elemental energies. He had them erected in the 1690s."

"Will they light up if I pass underneath?"

"Not as long as you keep your pendant on, I shouldn't think. Shall we try?"

"No, sir. Thank you."

Swaine brought the wagon to a halt outside a shop where an engraved sign read "Winslow & Sons, Fine Merchants." He turned. "Seen, not heard."

I nodded, taking the reins from him as he climbed down. As soon as I hitched the team, I followed Swaine through the green-painted doorway of the shop. A fire warmed the front room. Candle holders, writing desks, walking sticks, mantel clocks, and wigs filled three-quarters of the room, while a collection of waistcoats, neck cloths, caps, and frock coats decorated the longest wall. Swaine walked past it all. One of the shop assistants greeted him and led us to a desk in a nook set off from the main room. A gentleman looked up from a ledger book.

"Mr. Swaine," the man said, rising. "A pleasure."

"Mr. Winslow."

The man placed his quill in the stand and came around the counters and shelves. He clasped Swaine's hand and inclined his head in a graceful bow. Of slender build, Winslow wore his graying hair pulled back from his forehead. A pair of half-height spectacles perched on his nose, and his attire was well-tailored and expensive, from the embossed buttons on his waistcoat, to the shining buckles on his shoes. He peered over his spectacles at me.

"Your servant," he said.

I curtseyed.

"Indeed," Swaine said.

Winslow looked me over as though determining what price he might put on the tag and then turned his attention back to my master. "Please. Let me get you a cup of tea to ward away the chill."

Winslow called for one of his assistants and led Swaine nearer to the fire. I remained off to the side.

"I'm relieved that I may at last tell you that your orders have arrived," Winslow said. "Delayed only a tiny bit by the recent spate of wagon searches led by the Governor's men."

"Searches?" Swaine said.

"They're looking for Rattlesnakes." When Swaine registered no familiarity, he continued. "Members of the so-called Rattlesnake Society, a poisonous thorn in the side of our good Governor. The tongues of Bostonians wag for little else these days. It began last year. Anonymous pamphlets lampooning the Governor and taking to task the wealthy businessmen of undisputed influence in and around Boston. Harmless pranks, I'd surmised. The Governor thought differently, yet with each new warning from him, a larger crop of still more pamphlets and posters sprouted, each more biting than the last. Last month, the mysterious Rattlesnakes dumped a barrel of manure on the steps of Boston's Town House. And just last week, an unflattering effigy of the Governor was hung from the gallows by the Haymarket, bearing a placard around its neck that read *Whitelocke's Time Is Over*. Since that midnight statement, it has been wagons searched, homes and businesses raided—and still no snakes' nest uncovered."

A young assistant carried a tray in and set it by the fire. He poured two cups and was dismissed. "A long way of saying that I apologize for the delay in your shipments," Winslow said.

Swaine reached for the tea. "Your facility with such acquisitions never fails to impress."

Winslow nodded. "I'm eager to provide such service and discretion as you desire."

Swaine had told me that Winslow offered what Swaine valued most: no questions, and no prying. He knew the value of pounds and of his own reputation, and treated both with respect. I could see that everything about Winslow's manner focused on pleasing my master. After a further minute of exchanging pleasantries, Mr. Winslow led us through to the warehouse that extended behind the establishment. Crates, trunks, and boxes occupied the large storage room, unpacked to varying degrees. A pair of servants, Irishmen by the sound of them, lifted a bronze statue of a gaudy angel from a crate. Winslow led us to a group of items set apart from the others.

"Here you are, sir," he said.

Swaine looked over the parcels and items. He lifted bottles from a small chest, holding them to the light of the windows. Two dozen bottles, each containing a teaspoon or two of powder, dark liquid, or other ingredients.

"They meet with your satisfaction, sir?" Winslow said. Swaine tilted the bottle he held. The small tails within shifted, stiff.

"Quite, Mr. Winslow."

"Difficult to procure, as you know."

"Doubtless."

He returned that bottle and lifted one half-filled with crushed yellow flowers. "Aconitum vulparia," he said, sparing me a glance. "Wolfsbane." He put it back. "And the silver instruments? From Mr. Thomas Pomeroy? Where are they?"

"Ah," Winslow said. "The one delay, I'm afraid. Flooding near Barnsley made Pomeroy Hall inaccessible. Rest easy that the procurement will arrive with as much haste as a flooded moor and an Atlantic crossing can allow."

A bell rang in the outer shop. Winslow ignored it, and continued to help Swaine inspect the shipment. The sound of footsteps approached, accompanied by voices.

"—momentarily, Madam."

"I'm in a hurry," a woman said.

"Madam, I must insist."

Laughter bloomed from the doorway to the establishment.

Winslow frowned. A young woman with shining dark hair pushed through the doorway. She wore a hip-length charcoal jacket with a hood and matching petticoat and waved a dismissive glove at the shop assistant who trailed her.

"I'm sorry, sir," the assistant said. His face was flushed.

"Not as sorry as Mr. Winslow will be for making me wait for my new gowns," the woman said. She flashed a charming smile at Winslow and then shifted her gaze to Swaine. "Don't tell me you're whispering to someone else that they're your most important client, Mr. Winslow."

"Madam Whitelocke," Winslow said, bowing from the waist. Even I sensed his discomfort.

The woman turned to Swaine. "Our good shop keep lays on the flattery with a trowel, wouldn't you say, sir?"

"I find Mr. Winslow well-mannered, in all cases, Madam," Swaine said.

Whitelocke pursed her lips. "Unlike those who barge into back rooms."

"To be fair, there are gowns at stake," Swaine said. I was impressed, having been on the receiving end of countless orders, complaints, and outbursts of temper, and witnessing him padding around the manse, hair wild, in a nightshirt and scuffed boots. He now appeared as polished and engaging as Mr. Winslow himself.

"I don't believe we've had the pleasure, sir." She lifted the hem of her petticoat and curtseyed. "Mary Whitelocke, at your service."

"Madam Whitelocke," Winslow said, squaring his shoulders and putting a cramped smile on his face. "I'm nearly concluded with my other client—"

Swaine leaned forward in a gentle bow. "August Swaine, at yours."

Whitelocke's gaze sharpened. "Am I to take it you are *the* August Swaine?"

"I didn't realize that the definite article could sound so grandiose."

She turned to Winslow and swatted a glove at him. "You never mentioned that you had such a renowned client, Mr. Winslow."

I thought Winslow looked like a man overdue for a bowel movement. After surveying the crates and boxes, Whitelocke turned back to Swaine. I wondered how she knew of him.

"Tools of your trade, then?" she said.

"Hardly a gown among them," Swaine said.

"Yet I detect a hint of obsession satisfied nonetheless."

"Perhaps you do, Madam."

"When I was in London," she said, "you were quite the talk at Court. Sending a phaeton throughout the streets of London, pulled by no horses—pulled by nothing. A chair with a Lord of somewhere or other, lifted one-hundred feet above the brown Thames."

"Such tales grow in the telling, Madam."

"Do they?"

"You may observe the two ordinary horses of my team outside."

"A darling of the capital's newspapers," she continued with a smile, giving him a direct look, "until our dearest Majesty appeared to grow a trifle jealous. Perhaps egged on by certain men of influence with their own agendas. My interpretation, sir."

"No, you've hit the center of the target in one shot," he said.

"Just after your infamous debate, wasn't it?"

"Which I won by a lap," Swaine said.

"Which left you hunted by the King's men, not to mention exiled from London's influential circles."

"Circles that teem with all the invective that disappointment, ignorance of facts, and malicious falsehoods are wont to make fertile," Swaine said. Perhaps the others in the room missed it, but I could see his feathers ruffle.

"That must have been dreadful," she said.

Swaine fiddled his thumb into the pocket where he kept his watch. "Only for the short time it took for me to realize that my detractors were in fact the precise definition of the smears they were ever so busily hurling at me. I was breaking uncharted ground—they were treading the same banal paths of unctuous, small-minded greed and aggrandizement that every forgotten do-nothing has ever trod."

"My. Don't hold back."

"Forgive me, Madam."

"Nonsense. Criticism is easy. And how many of their names do I recall? None, sir," she said. Swaine looked pleased at her comment. "Still, you left."

"My new work has beckoned me elsewhere."

"To Boston. How remarkable," she said, brightening her voice. "I should think you might like an introduction to our good Doctor Rush."

Swaine tilted his head. "I've retired from the unseen arts, Madam—and all the angels-on-head-of-pins arguments that arise when two such practitioners so much as note that the sun is shining."

She smoothed the front of her jacket, holding his gaze. "And here I am, interrogating you. Please forgive me. I shall let you conclude your business without further prying and distraction, sir."

"But a few minutes more, and good Mr. Winslow will be free to let you have at your gowns, Madam Whitelocke."

She returned his slight bow with a practiced curtsey. "I hope to have the pleasure again, sir."

"As do I, Madam."

With one more look into his eyes, she went to the door, waiting for Winslow's assistant to open it for her. She glanced at me for a moment as though I were one of the many items bound for delivery to one of Mr. Winslow's wealthy clients, only less interesting. The assistant led her out. Once they left, Winslow approached Swaine. "I beg your forgiveness," he said. "My policy is strict. My assistant shall be relieved before the clocks ring noon."

"Such measures are unnecessary."

"You have every right to be furious, Mr. Swaine."

I must confess surprise that my master appeared unperturbed by the interruption.

"With certainty—and yet I'm not, sir," Swaine said. "Inevitably, my presence shall become known."

"You're far too kind," Winslow said, frowning. "As they say, it's difficult to stop a Whitelocke in Boston."

Swaine glanced toward the door. "So I've heard." He adjusted the black ribbon that tied his hair back at the nape of his neck, then turned back to Winslow. "And the other matters we've discussed?"

"Ah, yes." Winslow's voice grew quiet, and he clasped his hands behind his back. "It may be more difficult."

"As is my work, Mr. Winslow."

"Without question, sir. Without question. General White-locke has gotten involved."

"Madam Whitelocke's brother?"

"The same, yes. Reports of grave robbing—largely ignored earlier—have become a significant concern."

Swaine looked unhappy. "Are there no other issues in the colony requiring his attention? I find it hard to fathom, sir, that it should be such a problem as to require that level of attention."

"As would I—save that the grave of a certain William Abbot appears to have been plundered over the summer, body and all the rest stolen. The Abbots are one of the Governor's largest benefactors. They own three merchant ships, and half of the city's market stalls are stacked with trade connected to them. Just last week, the silken coat he was buried in was found for sale among the rather suspect possessions of a man known for trafficking in stolen items. An investigation ensued, culminating in the discovery of the theft."

Swaine sniffed. Flynn's handiwork, I guessed. I thought of the revenants and realized the bearded man with the ill-fitted clothes, a co-passenger to my arrival in Salem, was very likely the missing corpse. They'd taken the burial clothes right off him, sold them, and dressed him in whatever tattered clothes they themselves could spare. I kept my face neutral.

"Then am I to be deprived of what I require?" Swaine said.

"I need to find a different source, someone who can keep a low profile while General Whitelocke is scouring the city for the grave robbers. There are already soldiers from the Governor's Own Regiment stationed at the cemeteries, I hear tell."

"I need those materials, Mr. Winslow."

Winslow nodded. "And you shall have them. All I ask of you is your patience, given the unfortunate circumstances."

Swaine sighed. "Very well." He patted the pockets of his coat, looking distracted. "Finch, fetch my billfold. I must have left it in my satchel."

"Yes, sir."

I hurried to the front. Madam Whitelocke sat by the fire, tea and biscuits set on the table next to her. I kept my head down, but out of the corner of my eye, I could see her following my progress.

"You there, girl," she called. "Come here."

Pausing, I looked at the door, then her. "My master, ma'am. He needs something."

"Yes, I'd say he needs a servant who doesn't look as though she crawled out of a chimney." She tapped the end of the umbrella by her side, waiting for me. With a glance back at the hallway to the warehouse, I approached her and curtseyed. She smiled at me in a way that told me she was used to getting what she wanted. Her eyes were the color of pale slate, and I found them striking. "How old are you, child?"

"Sixteen, ma'am."

"What's wrong with your eye?"

I fought to keep my hand from reaching up to touch the cloth over it. "Lost it as a child, ma'am."

"I see," she said. "Although silly me—poor choice of words."

My cheeks burned.

"Hold your arms out," she said.

I did. She pointed to one of Mr. Winslow's assistants. "Go stand next to that young man." I nodded, and stepped over to the assistant who looked like he'd rather see me outside in the rain. "Closer. Back to back."

She studied us, and then nodded, waving me along. "Your master will be glad for my expertise in such matters," she said.

I hesitated, then curtseyed, and hurried along to the front door. Outside, I was glad for the cool of the rain against the flush of my face—when it came to my eye, all I ever felt was shame. As my brothers had pointed out, I was a cyclops, and I could look forward only to marrying a man of equivalent deformity. Missing a leg, maybe. Or a nose. Possibly, if I were lucky, just a few fingers. While they'd just been boys enjoying the pleasure of teasing their lone sister, the message had taken root all the same, making me ever more conscious of my appearance. I forced the thoughts out of my head and climbed onto the wagon. Swaine's satchel sat beneath the bench. I shouldered it. The rains had lightened, filling the air with a fine mist. My nose filled with the wind coming off the harbor. As I went back into the shop, I hoped that Madam Whitelocke's amusements were over.

She scratched out a note by Mr. Winslow's desk, her back to me. I moved as quietly as possible, and fast. She cleared her throat. I paused, just outside the door to the warehouse, wincing. I turned around, but her throat-clearing had been directed at one of Winslow's assistants, who picked up yet another dress from a shelf and held it up for her review. She shook her head.

"What're you keeping him waiting for?"

I jumped. One of Winslow's assistants had come up behind me. I nodded, annoyed and frightened, and pushed my way through the doorway. The assistant followed me. Swaine took the satchel from me. The assistant shouldered me aside.

"A gift from Madam Mary Whitelocke, sir," the assistant said. He held out a bundle. A folded note sat atop it.

"What's this?" Swaine said. He took the note and read it aloud: "*My Good Sir—a gentleman of your renown ought to have a servant wearing apparel within a whisper of fashionable. These should fit your girl, the green with room to spare for growth. Also, please tell dear Winslow that I never forget a lovely item, no matter how little use it might appear to hold for me (the patch). Yours, etc. M.W.*" Swaine looked up at Winslow, and then over at the clothing. "Why, how lovely. You must thank Madam Whitelocke immediately for her generosity. I am much indebted."

He folded the note and slipped it into his pocket, then turned to the assistant. "You may put it with the rest. What is this about not forgetting?"

A smile touched Winslow's face, and he tilted his head. "I must give Madam Whitelocke credit—she never forgets a thing if it involves silk or brocade." He reached over and lifted a small velvet bag from the bundle the assistant held. He wiped dust from the top of it and reached inside. "The handiwork of Monsieur Alaine Dufres of Paris. Lovely workmanship. I recall showing this example of his craftsmanship to her—she thought it splendid. I'd forgotten about it, to be honest."

He pulled out an eyepatch. The patch itself was embroidered in a flowery pattern, maroons and gold against a dark blue. The ties were equally detailed. "Shall I?"

Swaine nodded. Winslow motioned me over to him and directed me to remove the cloth over my eye. The assistant stared at me. I met his gaze. He knew better than to say a word. Winslow slipped the patch over my eye and knotted the ties behind my head. It wasn't what I was used to: less cumbersome and my face felt bare. Winslow turned me around. "She has impeccable taste."

"I shall post her a formal thank you before the day is out," Swaine said. He spared my new eyepatch but a glance. A mirror in a gilded frame leaned up against the side of an armoire, so I snuck a peek at myself. The eyepatch was lovely—and only highlighted how ungainly the rest of me was. My dress was clean but faded and growing small, torn in places, and frayed along the hem. I was in need of more than one bath every fortnight, and my hair hung lank. And while Madam Whitelocke thought I looked like a chimneysweep, the face that looked back at me—freed from the tattered cloth, and wearing the colorful eyepatch—struck me as older than I'd remembered, matching how I felt inside. Did I see my mother in it? Was it truly the face of a witch?

Swaine looked over the rest of his shipment. His gaze landed on a flat package, wrapped in brown paper and twine. He pointed to it. "And that?"

"Ah, yes," Winslow said. "Rather curious. It didn't appear on your list, or in the inventory of your prior orders. You'll note, however, that it bears your name. Is it something you'd expected?"

Swaine hefted the package. It appeared to be a book. "I'd not specified anything such as this." He turned it over and paused. I saw the name Swaine written in dark ink on the back corner of the wrapping.

"I have no other orders of books unaccounted for, sir," Winslow said. "And since it appears to have your name, you may open it with my consent. I more than trust your confidence should it not be for you."

Swaine turned it over and pulled the twine off, then carefully unwrapped the paper. Inside was a book, slender and bound in old leather. The spine and the front cover were worn, the letters that adorned the front barely legible. It looked to have been mishandled and water-damaged and carried a moldy scent I noticed from six feet away. He cracked open the cover with care. The pages showed further water damage, but, curiously, no print. "The pages are blank," he said. He leafed through a few, a dozen —and the expression on his face changed. He inhaled.

"Is it yours?" Winslow said. "Perhaps an older order through a different merchant?"

"This came here how?"

Winslow folded his hands, shaking his head. "It was just inside the back door, after we'd brought in several items from the docks last week. I suspected that it'd been tucked away in with the other things—there were a number of trunks, it may have wedged among those. I take it you recognize it?"

Swaine didn't answer, his gaze drawn back to the book. He appeared both repulsed and entranced, startled and yet unwilling to fling it to the floor—as though it were a golden spider, a snake of jade and ruby. "I need this all loaded onto my coach, immediately, sir."

"Of course, sir."

"At the back of your establishment, if you please."

"Very good."

Winslow summoned assistants. Swaine folded the book underneath his arm, pale as the French linen that sat folded on a chest behind him, and strode to the back door. I followed as he stepped out into the lane that ran behind the row of shops. He closed his eyes and moved his lips. An instant later, I detected the uncanny presence of a demon with a prickling of my skin. A patch of the fine rain whirled in unnatural directions. Swaine looked along the lane, gazing at doorways, windows, and rooftops. Other than an apprentice to a shot-maker trimming lead and dropping the balls into a wooden bin two doors away, there was no one in sight.

"Sir?" I said.

He motioned with his hand. "We mustn't tarry. Get the wagon. Now."

Glad for a reason to step away from where the demon brooded, I ran around the corner and readied the team, pulling the wagon around to the back just minutes later. Winslow and the others stood inside a large wooden door they'd opened. When I pulled the team to a stop, Winslow directed his assistants to lift the crates and chests, securing them in the back of the wagon. Swaine's mouth had gone down to a tight line. He reached into his satchel and pulled out a leather billfold. Counting out a handful of bills of credit, he handed them to Winslow, not taking his gaze from the lane, clutching the book in his other arm. "You'll find this sufficient to cover your expenses above and beyond the bill of goods."

"'Tis a pleasure fulfilling your needs, Mr. Swaine."

With the last of the chests secured, Winslow mentioned future service and assurances that my master's next order would be handled with alacrity. A black dog slunk along the side of the building, tail down and eyes watchful. An unease grew—something tickled my senses, a pressure, a wave breaking before something large.

"Come, Finch," Swaine said quickly. "Our cue has come to leave."

He slipped the book into his satchel, tossed it up into the driver's bench, then leapt up after it, snatching the reins from me. He turned to Winslow.

"I shall check on my order within the fortnight," he said.

Winslow bowed. "Always my pleasure, Mr. Swaine, and rest assured that—"

Swaine shouted "Ha!" to the team, snapping the reins, and setting us off in a clomp of hooves and the grind of wagon wheels. I looked back, seeing Mr. Winslow staring after us before turning back into his shop. Swaine said nothing.

I learned later that had we lingered but a minute more before setting off for Salem, we would have seen the head of the shot-maker's apprentice relieved of its perch upon his neck, swept off in a surgical manner and hurled through a window across Pudding Lane with explosive force, glass shards littering the ground like January ice, the talk of which soon spread throughout Boston, in circles both high and low. While the constables searched for a suitable explanation for the apparent murder, none were ever offered to the public at large.

11

THE SEEDS OF MIDNIGHT

I n the weeks following our visit to Boston, the book consumed my master. Days and nights revolved around it. Meals. More tea than I'd ever known a person to drink. Ink, quills, candles, lantern oil, all shouted for in the depths of the night, whispered for in the gray before the dawn. He locked himself in his study, the various details of his sustenance and hygiene left to me. I brought him fresh washing bowls and emptied his close stool. Sometimes, I'd hear him muttering to himself when I knocked. Sometimes he'd let me in, if only for a moment or two, bearing a tray with a bowl of pottage or greens. Peaches I'd picked not far from the manse. An armload of fresh firewood for the iron caddy by the hearth. Other times, he'd ignore my knocks altogether, and I'd have to settle for leaving the tray at the threshold where it stood a chance of being snatched inside at a later time.

I couldn't guess what the tome was, or how it beguiled him so. Questions on my part were met with an upraised finger and a sharp tut.

So I did my best to manage affairs as I thought proper. I

carried on cataloging the damage from the demonic intrusion, seeing to it that Swaine's papers were sorted properly, that the books were divided into those requiring new bindings, those with only surface scorch marks, and those untouched. I spent time each day studying *The Magickal Properties of the Knowne Base Metals* by Edward Neile, written in 1643. Swaine felt it a reasonable introduction to magic theory, with the observation—and caution—that Neile never found a metal or alloy that didn't merit an extra page or three of guesswork beyond what was demonstrably known. My keenest interest—learning more about witches—had foundered once I'd exhausted the few sources within Swaine's collection. Mentions here and there, some accurate—and most not, according to Swaine. Any explorations of my own abilities were to be done strictly under his tutelage, given the profound risks involved in doing anything of the kind in an area riven with demons. No guidance was forthcoming with Swaine locked away with his strange book, so I kept to Neile.

Beyond that, I cooked, and cleaned. Dusted. Explored the various disused and unkempt rooms, sorting through pieces of furniture with cracked legs, dusty mantels, shelving that had slipped its rails.

As I investigated, I remained cautious, and always wore my necklace. I sometimes sensed the nearby presence of a demon, and learned to give them their space. When the sensation grew particularly malevolent, I retreated to one of the protective circles. One dreadful evening, at least half a dozen of the infernal entities surrounded me for the better part of four hours, hurling knives, racing chairs across the floors, trapping me within the glamoured markings. Swaine, in one of his rare stretches of sleep, didn't hear any of it. On another occasion, the peeled paint on the front of a small door that led to a storage eave assumed the guise of a horrid face, replete with horns, a forked tongue, and cruel eyes that followed my movements. I tacked a mildewed curtain over it.

One revenant in particular—poor Wilkes, I'm afraid—found ways to appear where I didn't expect him. Just inside the cellar stairs when I needed to fetch the broom that hung on a hook. In a closet. Gazing in through the kitchen window at night as I readied more tea for Swaine. Aside from the horrid startle, my neck always broke out in chills. Swaine told me the demon in question was known as *Softfoot Peter*, first documented and bound by the legendary Yorkshire sorcerer William Postgate. Troublesome from the start, the demon became infamous in the summer of 1610 for slipping his bindings to occupy the body of a recently deceased Pickering farrier named Peter Fox. After strangling the mourning family of ten to death, the demon-inhabited corpse prowled the North York moors for a fortnight thereafter, strangling any lone travelers he happened upon. The demon finally inhabited the body of a hound who'd been decapitated (perhaps the origin of the tales of headless hounds run amok on the moors) before Postgate cornered and rebound the fiend. For a time. Postgate was found dead not half a year later. Strangled, of course. I found that placing a sack over Wilkes' head spared me the worst of the crawling sensation on my throat. Swaine tolerated my solution with a shake of his head.

The demons found my cleaning an irresistible target for their mayhem. I'd often find a room I'd recently organized in terrible disarray, everything turned upside down, or strewn across the floor. One room had the floorboards pulled up and left with the rusting nails exposed, ready to be trod upon, while in another I found a broken sewing table pressed to the ceiling. Breaking window panes was yet another favorite. Frost, heat, or stench plagued dark corners for no obvious reason. And although I grew cross, I remained ever alert, with extra caution after sunset, at the tops of the stairs, and near those doors capable of slamming cruelly.

When the demons stayed quiet, I kept the horses in heather and hay and mucked their stalls unmolested, taking what

companionship I could from the time I spent with the animals. I
dedicated a few hours each day to organizing Swaine's workshop
in the barn, finding places for his latest deliveries, tidying up the
corners, facing the labels on every bottle and box the proper way.

I swept, scrubbed, and polished. With study, I worked out
how to replace broken panes of window glass with others I found
in a crate tucked off in the corner of the barn's loft. I cleared away
one of the smaller rooms on the second floor for my own, dragging in the least mouse-eaten mattress and blankets I found, after
beating them free of dust and washing them. I hung the four
dresses that Madam Whitelocke had purchased for me,
committed to keeping them clean. My hair and face received
several scrubbings each week, determined as I was that no one
should again think I crawled out of anywhere, let alone a
chimney (though when I did, in fact, crawl out of many of the
manse's chimneys after clearing them of old nests, thick draping
of cobwebs, and the bones of an ancient family of raccoons, I
made note of how filthy I'd become. It was far worse than what
Madam Whitelocke had suggested.) As viewed in the one mirror
I'd found in one of the slanted rooms on the third floor, I felt
pleased with my appearance, in a fresh blue dress and with my
new eyepatch.

The days grew short. One such late afternoon, with the
western sky glowing behind the trees outside, Swaine appeared
in the doorway of the kitchen as I rolled out dough for more
biscuits. The haunted look that had taken roost on his face since
our trip to Boston had broken, replaced by a serene expression
made all the more remarkable in the last rays of the day. I
straightened up, brushing off a streak of flour that had decorated
my apron.

"You've been a busy Finch, I see," he said. His tone wasn't one
of reprimand, or annoyance—rather, he sounded pleased.
And calm.

"I wasn't sure what else to do, sir. I hope you don't mind."

He stepped into the kitchen. "Mind? Nonsense. You've turned this house into something approaching its rightful state. Unlike my narrow, barely practical burrowing. Did the demons trouble you much?"

"Now and then, sir."

He nodded. "They've been antsy. Vigilant." He walked over to the table. I'd set out a platter of rolls to cool. "May I?"

"Of course, sir."

With a delicate grip, he lifted the still-hot roll and tore off the end, watching the steam rise. He sniffed it, then put the bite into his mouth. He nodded, looking at me. "Delightful. Who taught you to bake? Your mother?"

"Yes, sir. I followed her around the kitchen since I could stand, sir. Until she died."

"Well, she did a fine job."

"There's a berry preserve I made, sir." I pointed to a glass jar. "I found bushes of them growing wild, not far off. Mulberries and raspberries. I also found currants, chestnuts, and filberts. They seemed fine. I discovered a tin of old sugar, too—though more would be nice, sir."

Swaine opened the preserve, and used a wooden spoon to smear some onto the roll. He looked to have lost ten pounds since the book had come into his possession. "We'll see to it. Another trip to civilization is in order. You haven't grown too lonesome for living companionship, I take it?"

I shifted on my feet, then looked at him. "It never bothers you, sir?"

Pausing with the spoon in jar, he met my gaze. "It hadn't until I realized the pleasures of fresh rolls." It wasn't much of an answer, which he appeared to realize after a quiet few moments. "Look. This is rather new, having to worry about anyone else, having my work seen, half-seen, witnessed, guessed at." He looked to mull it over as he spread the preserves. "Not my natural inclination, if you want to the truth. Moreover, if I'd wanted a servant, I could have found one. Or made one."

I frowned. I wasn't altogether certain what answer I was looking for. On one hand, no one had been horribly murdered around me for the first time since my misfortunes began. What I'd done to the manse had been my idea, of my volition, and a source of unexpected pride. And while Swaine could be more than difficult in his own way, I'd discovered a growing fascination with him and his work. Yes, there were the demons, and corpses. The despondent gloom that night brought was sometimes so overwhelming that I huddled beneath my blankets, wishing to be anywhere else. But where else would I be safe—or anyone around me be safe—given the curse I'd been bequeathed? Salem would seem like the very last place for a witch to find safety, yet I had. Of a fashion.

"That said," he continued, "I haven't had to worry about the nonsense that pulls me from my calling since you've arrived. Food. Drink. Nature's interminable duties. That saved me. Not just time, but attention. And what I've seen, Finch—what I've seen has opened my eyes. These have been the most important weeks of my life." He paused. The color of sunset washed across the table where we stood.

"Is it that book, sir?"

He stared out the window. I imagined his mind drifting through the walls to his study where the book sat on his desk. "Do you know what it is, Finch?"

"A book—of sorcery?"

"Wrong," he said, drawing his attention back to the kitchen, and to me. "It is *the* book of sorcery: the *Occultatum Ostium*. The Hidden Doorway. A guide to the *impuri cuiusdam mundi*, the world sinister, the shadow world that mirrors the common world of life. And quite a history goes along with it. Lives lost, murders committed for it. Strange appearances and disappearances. There is but one copy—and now it's here."

"You didn't buy it?" I said.

"It is not a book that one can buy." He leaned forward, his hands on the oak table. "It finds its own way. From one sorcerer to another. True sorcerers, mind you. The greatest of their age."

"So someone sent it to you?"

"I doubt that very much. It's been over a century since any record of it has appeared."

I was still trying to work out how he'd gotten it, if no one had sent it to him: had it wrapped itself in paper and twine and floated across the ocean? Had it worked its way up from Hell, grinding through the floorboards of Winslow & Sons? Had a demon carried it unseen?

"The pages are blank, you see," Swaine said. "At first. Yet every time it's opened, it may reveal a new puzzle. New text. Diagrams. Some sharp, clear, piercing. Others obtuse. Grudging. There's nothing like it. A section may appear, full and rich—yet the longer it's read, the fainter the text gets. Some words burn like embers. Phrases ring in the mind long after they're read, the fading note of a giant bell. Days, in some cases. A week."

"But—who wrote it, sir?"

"Its origin is cloaked in rumor—though it's clearly the product of a sublime application of magic. I've heard it said to have been the masterwork of an eighth century German sorcerer whose name, upon the enchanting of the book, vanished from the world, from the minds of all who knew him, from even the tongues of his own kin. It's also rumored to have been brought out of the Far East as part of a trove of oddities carried by foreign traders. Still another tale speaks of an Anglo-Saxon liege with a dying son making a grim bargain with a sorceress of the forest—the man's soul was bound into the book in exchange for his son's life. No firm records exist. And while there are various accounts of it threading through the literature, no one's ever claimed to know who first came into possession of it. Or where. Or when. All that can be agreed upon is that a most powerful magic is bound to it. And that the book has a mind of its own."

It sounded frightful. And even more so for Swaine having locked himself up with it for so long.

"It is the keystone of the art," Swaine continued, his voice betraying a level of enthusiasm I'd never seen in him. "The code to unlocking the universe—and it has taken all that I thought I've known about sorcery and shattered it. All of it. Shattered. And all those pieces have been rearranged into the most beautiful mosaic I ever imagined." He went to the window. "Do you know what this place is, Finch?"

I was certain he wasn't looking to hear the words that first came into my mind: *cursed, lonesome, queer, frightful, unlawful to occupy.* "Full of demons?" I guessed instead.

"Rather too full—and you're on the right track. For you see the reason so many demons plague this stretch of coastline has to do with the planes."

I'd seen nothing but untended meadows, weathered buildings, and roads disappearing beneath bramble and fallen leaf.

He turned from the window. "Now, my research over the past few years has led me to believe that Salem is home to more than one plane. In fact, I'm now relatively sure that we stand in the shadow of a powerful planar confluence, greater than any to have been recorded in history. Multiple planes intersecting, a great spiraling of unseen worlds. A vast reserve of energy just waiting to be tapped—a raw resource that might allow me to bypass the heretofore assumed limitations of sorcery." He folded his arms, leaning against the cabinet beneath the window. "Binding demons without requiring their names. Accessing new types of magic. Opening different worlds. Now, I haven't yet worked out the precise manner in which to harness these energies—but the book has pointed the way as clearly as any beacon: temporal eddies and harmonic resonance. Not unknown theories in the arts, but ones that have languished for far too long. Think of them as energies leveraging existing energies, and not altogether different from the work I've been exploring with multiple, parallel bindings."

I didn't understand much of what he'd said, but I'd also never known him to be so relaxed and open about his work—he wasn't snapping questions at me, wasn't distracted, wasn't testing my attention. I wanted to enjoy the moment while it lasted. "The book said that, sir?"

"It—*intimated* it," he said. "Nothing with the *Occultatum Ostium* is ever overt. It speaks in riddles, in metaphors, through diagram and symbol. Yet it's given me the key I've been searching for. And that key, Finch, lies in the concept of densely packed glamours capable of opening up the so-called *seeds of midnight* that exist where the planes collide. By harnessing them properly—probably through carefully arranged harmonic shadow control—the energies enfolded within can blossom out, increasing the magic involved ten-fold. Or more. And at no cost to the original enchantments—the standard barrier that restricts the effects of spells, you see. I believe I can bypass such limitations, here, in this place."

"And it's not dangerous, sir?"

"If left without order, yes—but the key, I think, is sympathetic entrainment, a concept found in harmonic resonance work." He seemed to be talking primarily for his own benefit; and just as well, as I had no idea what *sympathetic entrainment* or *harmonic resonance* even was. "Linking these energies via a device capable of generating a winding movement at a consistent speed. That's where technology has traditionally failed. Mechanical technology at a small scale, done with precision, accuracy, reliability. For instance, a clock—"

He paused, brow furrowed. I was afraid to make a sound or movement for fear of distracting him. The sunlight faded from deep red to a dimming rust. After a few moments, he brushed the crumbs from the front of his vest and stared around the kitchen as though seeing it for the very first time. "So yes, Finch—it's dangerous. As has been nearly every step that advanced humanity. We've work ahead. Work the likes of which the world has never seen."

12

MY DEEPEST NIGHTMARES

A week later we ventured into the heart of old Salem for the first time. As afternoon stretched long over the hills, we stood before an abandoned bridge. The incantations that shielded us as we made our progress from the manse had taken Swaine most of the day. While he'd focused on safeguarding our passage, I'd lugged the small trunk of necessary ingredients and items, handing him whatever he called for: needles made from human bone; several slugs of copper; white powder that shone with a pale blue light; a sharp knife he used to draw forth a bead of his own blood, and mine as well; more. I carried food and water in a tattered pack, to keep us going. The efforts had taken all my concentration, and Swaine looked worn. Eight hours had brought us no farther than a mile, to the banks of the river.

My master looked at the rotted bridge, rubbing his brow. The town and the collapsed wharves on the far side stood silent on the edge of evenfall. Deepening sunlight slanted into missing windows and the gaps between weathered slat and joist. Empty hearths moaned with the wind off the harbor. Despite the abandoned appearance, a growing terror bloomed inside me, a reaction to the disquiet of a place gone bad. What had the witches found here? What remained? My pulse quickened.

Swaine registered my unease. "I feel it, too. The atmosphere is potent."

I adjusted the pack on my shoulders. "We're not wanted here, are we?"

"No, certainly not."

"It's horrid. Sir."

He stared at the town beyond the bridge. "I shall make no claim otherwise. Tales or not, there is a measurable danger here, as much as we might find anywhere under the King's Colors—it's wound in among the shadows, coiled in the unquiet night, burrowed through in a thousand spots across the town. Thus our precautions." He squinted against the chill wind that rattled the last curled leaves of autumn in the tall oaks nearby. "Which should also serve to hide our presence from any clever magic the renowned Doctor Rush might maintain nearby designed to alert him to any disturbances. I've not found any—but he's a wily old bird. Or at least he once was."

The thought hadn't occurred to me. "There aren't any witch-poles, are there?"

"You could take off your pendant for us to find out."

"Sir?"

"Now, now—just a jest. That would be the very last thing you would ever want to do this close to the heart of old Salem. And there are no witch-poles, per se. As for other, similar construc-tions, we must assume the answer is *yes*, in one form or another. Perhaps bringing a witch along with me isn't one of my brighter ideas—but who knows? Maybe you'll see what I miss, in which case the arguments *for* will outweigh the arguments *against*. You might prove useful after all, Finch."

"Thank you, sir."

"It seems to be a curse of mine: where others see ruin and threat, I see promise. Look around carefully. It looks bereft of anything but detritus, no? Yet unseen amongst the tumbled walls and rotted foundations of this place lies a treasury far richer than anything under guard for any of the world's monarchs, sultans, or lords."

Looking at the weathered remains before us, I struggled to believe it. Swaine gauged the fading daylight. From a pocket in his waistcoat, he pulled out a small device: wood and brass, it fit in the palm of his hand, and looked something like a small bearing compass. Instead of a sliver of magnet seeking true north, however, the device had a minor demon bound within the silver end of a one-inch needle. Swaine and I both watched as the needle quivered. The demon inside was drawn to the weakest stretches of the barriers between the planes, making the device an indicator of planar alignment. The frantic movements of the needle showed that planar fields around us had shifted even since our last measurements earlier in the afternoon. Swaine frowned.

He scanned the nearby landmarks, adjusting the compass, tracking its movements. "We can risk no further glamours of protection from here out. Such complexities of energy would render any incantations unpredictable, and risk exposing us to whatever prowls this spot." He tucked the compass back into his pocket.

That didn't sound promising. I looked back to the manse atop its promontory. I wanted nothing more than to return to its familiar safety. Twilight seeped out of the low spots around us, spreading and pooling as the sun slipped behind the hills.

"What do you think, Finch—can you cross this?" He nodded to the bridge.

I looked over the rotted planks. "I think so, sir."

"Brilliant. Go ahead, then."

Hefting the trunk, I stepped from board to board, avoiding the moldered and missing ones, listening to the sound of my crossing echoing among the pilings that rose from the silty water.

The wind gusted. I kept my head down, and when I reached the other side without incident, I waited for Swaine. As he began his cautious crossing, I looked at the deserted hint of road. The stillness was deceiving, for as the dusk deepened, I sensed demons.

Swaine approached. "We're edging into the most dangerous acres in the New World." The exhaustion that had set in after hours of incantations had fallen away—his eyes were clear, his gait sure, his cheeks holding a high color in the freezing air. He reached into the satchel he carried and unfolded a damaged map. Across the top was printed the title *The Infernal Town of Salem in New-England by Cap'n Philip Dawson, 1654.* I'd seen Swaine spend hours hunched over the map, studying every last tittle and hash. He spent minutes comparing the map to where we stood. I glanced back. The daylight dwindled.

With each step we took, a potent emotion gripped me: desolation. After just a few minutes, I stopped. Mournful, that's what it was. A dull soul-ache at the turning of the hours and days of that cheerless place.

"You sense it, don't you?" Swaine said. He waved me to follow him. "Remember this, Finch—it's not *you*. It's the energies here."

I shivered. "From the witches, sir?"

"Doubtful. More likely the residue from the infernal energies they were exposed to, still powerfully toxic after decades. You'd do best to ignore it, and any other strange emotions or thoughts that take hold here in the presence of potent magic and planar fields."

"What about demons?"

"They're here, too—and I'll wager they'll make themselves known soon enough. Demons are the vainest of entities."

He consulted the map again, pointing out shadowy Read's Hill and distant Leach's Hill. We walked a half-mile farther along the ghost of the road, moving through bishop's weed and thistle. He nodded toward a field to our left, beyond which stood a house. "I believe these were the old grazing fields of Thaddeus

Rivers. One of the lesser warlocks, and one of just six men among the first settlers carried aboard *The Westenshire Bell*. This should do. Come."

We stepped over a fallen rail fence, splintered gray and dotted with lichen. The strange emotion grew stronger, blooming into anguish. I did my best to ignore it. We followed the line of the fence, having to search now and then in the meadow grass grown brittle. We approached the remains of Rivers' house. Leaning walls had warped the sills, and the faded paint, once an earthy red, was nearly lost beneath stains and damage from the seasons. I looked beyond the overgrown fields as the sun disappeared behind the hills. A brilliant slice of the sunset caught the roof of the house and a shiver rolled down my back.

"I fear we started out too late," Swaine said.

He hurried to the house and stooped through the slanting doorway. I followed. Inside, I heard the roll of the nearby tide as a faint breath, while the wind split into a chorus of drafts through stone and board. Nothing prepared me for the deep sorrow that coursed through me. I froze, overwhelmed.

"Finch," Swaine said. I realized that I'd groaned. "What is it? What do you sense?"

I shook my head, as though to clear it. "The angles of the house, sir. They all feel wrong." As I looked about, I reacted with unease to the lines of the boards, the slant of the roof, the tilting windows. "It's as though there's more than one house here. One overlaid atop one another. More than one—world, all running through the house around us." I caught faint glimpses, impressions, of stairs going up one flight, two, ten, twenty, up into the stars. Dozens of rooms, hundreds, more. And down, cellars beneath cellars beneath cellars, leading to places ripped from my deepest nightmares.

"Then we'd best not tarry," Swaine said.

I tried to shake off the feeling of disorientation that wrapped me and followed him to the main room. The boards squealed underfoot and our steps kicked up fine dust that mingled with the scent of aged timber, hardened resin, and mildew. Beyond the doorway, a larger room opened. As we entered it, we passed through currents of freezing air. I felt the pressure of the air change against my face, my hands. A hearth build of field stones sang with the wind. Empty windows looked out on the growing twilight. Somewhere above us, a loose clapboard banged against a beam, *rat-tat-tat-tat-tat*.

"It's time," Swaine said. "Get the hexed nails in place."

I set down the trunk and opened it, concentrating entirely on my task, pushing aside the sensations that overwhelmed me. I took out a mallet and a tiny bag containing four thin nails that Swaine had layered with protective spells. Hurrying, I went to the doorway leading into the room, fumbling out the first nail. I raised it to about head-height, trying to keep it steady. "Here, sir?"

Swaine looked over and nodded. "Three taps, no more."

With more concentration than I thought I was capable of, I set the first of the nails into the splintered doorjamb: one, two, three hits with the mallet. I got the other three nails placed, finishing the final one just as Swaine reached into the trunk and pulled out a contraption of brass and wood. Nine inches long, six wide, six tall, it had two hinged, fitted openings on each of the long sides. The device had been built earlier in the year by Robert Twelves, a precocious apprentice to the noted Boston clockmaker George Graham. Swaine originally commissioned it for another purpose altogether, but had modified the internal mechanisms based on the ideas he developed out of reading the *Occultatum Ostium*.

"I dub this a *planar clock*," Swaine said. "With which I put my theories to the test—and begin the process of peering past the corner of the universe."

He placed the device on the floor. As he'd shown me the night before, it relied on a combination of sorcery and mechanical clockwork. The device held, imprisoned in the mechanism, one known, named fiend: the bait. When the incantations that hid the clock loosened to reveal its presence, the demon bound within would attract the attentions of a greater fiend; for while demons always found humans curious and behaved malevolently towards them, they were relentlessly vicious towards their own kind, and would attack on sight, unless restrained by sorcery. Should an unknown demon pass into the trap, another set of spells would descend, making it impossible for it to escape, the springs and escapement of the clock dancing in time with the spells laid within the gears.

"If this works," Swaine said, carefully readying the planar clock, "it will open up a confluence chamber, tapping into the harmonic resonance nodes—the *seeds of midnight*—just long enough for the capture of a demon. Such trapping of a fiend without relying on a name is unheard of in sorcery."

I leaned over, watching.

He wound a brass key set in the left of the interior of the mechanism. "Just like winding a clock, easy. And then we slide these open. Like so."

Opposite the escapement and miniature pendulum were three chambers—each large enough to fit a good sized egg—with hinged lids, each with a spring. Swaine opened them, clicking them into position against the tension. Steel fittings held them in place.

"And if this works," he said, "the possibility exists that we might one day clear Salem of all its demons in one shot, giving us unfettered access to the massive energies lying dormant here. With that amount of power at our disposal—an unimaginable resource—we can bend the course of the future, reach unattainable goals. This is how the arc of mankind turns."

The silver-plated interior of each chamber bore engravings across all six surfaces, and each harbored a different set of dormant magic symbols. A separate compartment near the escapement held a glass globe that Swaine removed. He put it aside. The pernicious ill feelings that swirled around us grew more intrusive, and I found it hard to pay attention. Swaine looked to the door. *Rat-tat-tat-tat* came the knocking from above us. "Yes, yes—we've come under scrutiny. Hurry. The candle."

I rooted through the trunk and found the short candle, faintly red. Swaine took it and placed it into a holder built into the device. Next, he asked for a tinderbox, unwilling to risk even the simplest fire incantation.

"Ingenious, this," he said as he struck the fire-steel against the flint, dropping sparks into the unrolled char cloth. As soon as he had a small fire going, he held the candle to it and brought the wick to life. He blew out the char cloth and folded it up again, holding it up for me to take. I did. "To my knowledge, there's never been a more powerful containment magic placed into such a small physical anchor as the scrap of paper within this candle."

He set the globe over the flame. The light did little to hold back the quickening dark. I noticed that his hands shook, ever so slightly. Fear? Excitement?

"The paper will burn away within the hour, releasing a powerful summoning—at which point we'd best be far off. In the meantime, the mechanisms of the planar clock will generate a subtle ripple in this plane, which will cloak it from the entities I seek to capture." He stood up and wiped his hands, motioning for me to gather the trunk. "A ring is melted into the candle's base. And when the demon I've bound into said ring appears, tethered to our device—why, there's no telling what we might catch with such tempting bait."

I thought of all he'd told me of the dangers of Salem and wondered how wise that was. As he latched shut the trunk, I returned to the slanted doorway and paused. The atmosphere changed.

"Sir," I whispered, peering out into the gloaming. The horizon shone with fading sunset while the fields and trees that lined the overgrown road darkened. A figure stood silhouetted in the orchard. "The demon, sir. From the library." The woman stood unmoving, the cold wind snapping the edges of her cloak sideways, strands of her hair whirling with it.

"The same appearance?"

"Yes, sir. A woman. Plain features, striking eyes, dark clothing." It was no wonder the demon had lifted such thoughts of witches from my mind—they occupied my mind all too frequently. If I could have forgotten all about it—or, better yet, never heard it in the first place, returning back in time to my old life—I'd have been all too glad. Yet there the demon stood, in the guise of a witch. She lifted a hand. I stepped back from the doorway.

Swaine left the trunk and looked out into the twilight. "Fear not. I have something here that it won't like."

He pulled from his jacket pocket a circle of hammered steel, which he'd earlier in the week infused with a potent ward. Demons would find it baleful, he'd explained—a blinding glare that crossed planes. *Or so we'd best hope*, he'd added. My hand reached up to my necklace, reassuring myself that it was still there.

"Fetch the trunk. We're leaving." Swaine stepped outside. The moment I followed him, the appearance of the house shifted, as though I'd stepped back into the real world. Before us, the figure didn't move. Her hand remained raised, her finger pointing at the house behind us. "We shall walk right past it, to the bridge. Beyond that, we'll be safe."

As my eyes adjusted to the deepening eve, I saw the woman's —the *demon's*, I corrected myself—face revealed as though by starlight: slender nose, high cheek bones, pale eyes that watched us. The skin of my neck, shoulders, and scalp rippled into gooseflesh. We started to the road, stepping into the overgrown grass, and made straight for the bridge. "That's right," Swaine said. "Not much farther. We follow the fence, to the lane, to the bridge, and it will be easy as—"

"*Ignis.*"

The strange voice whispered just behind us. I leapt sideways. Flames appeared on the sleeves of Swaine's coat. The woman stood next to me, her cloak and skirts the color of charcoal and ash in the dusk. She reached for me.

Swaine wasn't as unprepared as before, however.

"*In frigore flamma!*" he cried. The flames snuffed out in puffs of gray smoke. The apparition put a cool, pale hand to my forearm—it felt as weightless as if it were made of cobwebs. I recoiled. Swaine yanked the ward from his pocket. As the metal circle that contained the ward came into sight, the entity mouthed a silent shriek and flew backward, leaving a trail of embers across the meadow that fronted the house. Twenty feet, thirty, farther. The bits of fire crackled, the wind sweeping up the sparks.

Swaine backed away, holding the metal high. "Fast, now. We need to get across the bridge." He reached out and grabbed me with his free hand. I needed little encouragement. We sprinted along the fence line in the light of the emerging stars. The many tales of demonic wreckage and grisly ends Swaine had told me paced me, urging me on, faster, faster. We reached the lane without the demon coming closer. Another fifty yards, and we'd be at the bridge. The woman stood by the Rivers house, tracking our progress. A sudden wave of noxious energy rolled over us, lighting up the windings of sorcery nearby. My heartbeat hammered and Swaine paused.

"The planes are shifting," he whispered. "Leave what you're carrying and run."

A grinding sound reached us as we darted across the field to the bridge. Behind us, the chimney on the Rivers house keeled to the side, dropping with a ground-shaking boom. In the lane, a flurry of dust rose, spinning with bits of dry leaf and twig. I let the trunk thud to the ground and shrugged off the pack on my shoulder. The ward that Swaine held glowed red. With a cry, he dropped it to the ground, where it blazed white-hot. Patches of grass around it kindled into flame. The eddy in the lane grew larger, grabbing more dirt and branches. The mounting sense of dread tightened into a panic.

"Now, Finch! Now!" Swaine yelled. He needn't have worried—I outpaced him. Embers spun up as we ran across the field, flames springing to life around us.

I watched my steps, paying as much care as I could to whether my clothing or my master's was burning. At the bridge, I bounded across as though I'd done it a hundred times. Swaine took more care. I held out a steadying hand at the far side and guided him across the final planks. As we dashed back within the glamoured protections, Swaine turned. Water murmured below the bridge. Behind us, the figure of the witch faded into the gathering night. The fires smoldered, but didn't spread.

"We're safe here," Swaine said around deep breaths. "All that work. The glamours. We're safe. From here back to the house. Safe."

I scanned the darkness of Salem. Nothing followed us onto the long stretch of lane where we stood. My legs shook and my pulse trilled.

Swaine pushed his hair back from his eyes. "We may have done it. We may have."

"Will it be safe?" I said. "The clock?"

I couldn't imagine that what we'd placed on the creaking boards of the abandoned house of Thaddeus Rivers would remain untouched.

"It should still be hidden. That's the idea," he said. "And if it works, I will have opened an entire new discipline of sorcery. Can you imagine?"

I realized in that moment that August Swaine was a man who stood at the edge of a vast, unexplored plateau untrodden by any other practitioner of science or magic. He stared off into the dark-

ness over the old town, and I could see his panic turn into exhil-
aration.

"Come, Finch," he said, turning to me with a nod. "We've
earned ourselves a meal, I believe."

We turned, two lone figures following the glamours of protection back along the blue-black lane. The moon rose through the
silent woods, our only witness.

13

DEMONS FOR THE TAKING

M y master steepled his fingers against the bridge of his nose, staring at the work bench. Behind him, the planar clock sat on the floor. For seven days it had remained within the decrepit house of Thaddeus Rivers, in the quiet of old Salem. We'd retrieved it after a day's worth of careful preparations, and now it sat at the center of a tetragon formed of narrow lines of silver filings, the corners aligned to the cardinal directions. Candles sputtered around it, and threw crackling sparks as flecks of nitre, carbon, silver, and sulfur, embedded in the wax, ignited. Sixteen glyphs formed a compass rose extending one hundred feet from the spot of binding, layered with magic protections that had taken Swaine hours to cast. Three magical workings he'd spoken in English. Out of extra caution, he'd cast others in their native tongues: Latin, Old English, Arabic, Aramaic, Low Saxon, and even one excruciatingly long spell in the Faröese of the winter-dark regions of Scandinavia. The atmosphere in the barn grew charged.

I remained off to the side of the workbench, well within a glamour of protection.

Swaine ran a hand across his chin and straightened the many

piles of papers. He righted one of the quills. He'd spent several hours readying himself, alone in his study. I'd listened at the door and heard nothing: no turning of pages, no scratching of notes being made, no whispered mutterings to himself as he was often wont to engage in, no pacing. Risking a peek through the keyhole, I'd seen him sitting upright in the chair before the hearth, his eyes closed, and I knew he'd gotten himself into a state of concentration so focused as to be mistaken for stillness. I'd tiptoed off, careful not to disturb him, left with my own thoughts about what the planar clock might have caught.

Swaine opened his eyes again. "No point delaying further."

"It's all set, sir?"

"The incantations and adjunct summonings are correct—yet I sense subtle fluctuations in the energies. I assume it's related to the forces here in Salem, so there's little to be done about it other than to hope that it introduced no unpredictability that might allow for my castings to warp or redirect themselves."

"Is it from the demon, sir?"

"Doubtful. If the planar clock has done its job properly, whatever entity we've caught should have no influence beyond the containment spells." Swaine moved around the barn, reexamining the candles, the glyphs, the filings.

I looked at the device with trepidation. Having learned more than I'd ever cared to about demons, I appreciated the many reasons why—even with the multitude of protections employed —the practice of sorcery was almost uniformly derided as folly. From the Fifth Century observation of Hierius of Athens that summoning a demon was akin to inviting a hungry lion to inhabit every shadow for the remainder of the sorcerer's life ("*skiá liontári*"), to the magician Percy Brasher's conclusion that "*The question of possession in a sorcerer is simply a matter of when, not of if —for no matter how much care is taken, there is never care enough against such fiends,*" one could be forgiven for equating sorcery with madness. Brasher himself was profoundly influenced by the frightful end of his great uncle, Henry Brasher, a sorcerer who allegedly became possessed by the demon known as the Reaper's Sigh, and hung half the children of Pinner, England before impaling himself on an iron fence one terrible night in the winter of 1655.

Moreover, what Swaine was attempting was unheard of: binding a demon to his will with no knowledge of the demon's name. The names of demons, required by traditional methods of sorcery, must be won through perilous interlocutions—and book after book recounted that more than a fair share of sorcerers had died playing that chancy game of tricking a demon into revealing its true name. As for relying on the historical records of known entities, Swaine claimed the method flawed: in the first place, it left out a multitude more demons and other planar entities whose names could never be known; in the second place, the named demons knew this weakness and, being wary, were even more resistant to summoning. The revolutionary intent of Swaine's invention was to bind demons without the need for their names.

"It's time." He loosened his neck, this way, that. "We either redefine sorcery, or die trying."

"Die, sir?"

"If I've allowed even one incorrect element to slip in, it might cost me my sanity, or worse." He stepped over to a point between two candles. "Now let me concentrate."

I held my tongue. Swaine stayed outside the line of silver. The air surrounding the clock grew strange—it wavered, slender lines of shadow spindling out, mixing with faint glints of light, as though the whole arrangement sat at the bottom of a fast flowing river. I wondered if I ought to have accepted Swaine's offer to remain in the manse, after all.

Swaine reached into his pocket and retrieved a small brass key. "Amongst all the various spells I've layered here, I deliberately left one small passageway open—enough so I may do this."

He stepped over the lines of the glamour and knelt. With steady hand, he slid the key into the keyhole. *Click, click, click.* The key released the delicate tumblers. Swaine withdrew his hand. He sat back on his heels and lifted a thin sheet of tortoise-shell he'd place nearby for this moment. "And with this, I shall close the remaining gap. By the time the mechanisms release, the integrity of the containment magic will be unbreakable." He touched the sheet to his forehead, his lips, his chest, then raised it to speak the final spell. I held my breath, my pulse racing.

Swaine spoke: "*Naanaalankaara deeptam sphatika maninibham.*"

As he finished the final word, he broke the tortoise-shell in two. The air shifted. Swaine placed the two halves on the floor and stood up, brushing his hands along his breeches. The mechanism within the planar clock filled the barn with a sharp ticking as the series of pins slid from the springs. Inner clasps came free, and the lid swung open with a tension-released rattle. The pendulum spun, and the escapement ticked as it had during the earlier tests of the device.

"One," Swaine said.

The first chamber opened. I swallowed.

"Two."

The second chamber opened, the silver inside of the door catching the light of the nearest candle.

"Three."

All three chambers inside the device stood open. The ticking continued. Neither of us took our gaze from the clock. A minute passed, then another. Swaine didn't move.

"It can take time," he whispered.

One candle-flame fluttered, then resumed its steady burning. A faint light emanated from the leftmost chamber, as of delicate starlight through fog, brightening into moonlight on stone. The flames wavered as currents of energy rolled through the barn, sending flecks of old straw and leaf to cling to the wooden beams, sucking the feathers of quills on the workbench together, lifting the hairs on my head and sending the hems of my skirt to grasp at my legs.

The light from the clock grew so bright I saw the grain of the old wood of the hayloft. Curls and helices of light traced the contours of the barn. Swaine nodded. "The bindings are holding. So far." He lifted a quill—separating it from the others with a crackle—and dipped the end in an inkwell, his own shadow stretching crisp as printer's black across the bench. On the top sheet of paper, he scratched a few quick notes regarding the timing, consulting his pocket watch.

Swaine lifted the quill and turned. He glanced at me. "Do you see anything, Finch?"

"Light, sir. Above the device, weaving beams of light. Like the sun shining through deep waters."

In the corner of the barn, a shadow seeped through the wall. Another grew near the doorway. Soon, a dozen shadows hung in the air.

"Sir," I whispered. "Shadows."

He scratched out another note. "Likely refractions from another plane. Ignore them."

The temperature in the barn plunged, and the air grew foul, common precursors to an infernal presence, I'd learned.

"Something is happening in the middle of the floor, sir." A figure coalesced. The air shimmered in a web of fine cracks. In the far corners, the shadows I'd noted trembled. My palms grew sweaty, and I wiped them on my dress.

The barn doors rattled, and the ground shook, just once— and the demon stood before us.

"It's here," Swaine whispered. "The air is darkened."

"I see it, sir."

"Good. Describe it."

I wanted to turn away, not look more closely. Half again as tall as Swaine, the demon resembled a misshapen, bipedal pig, enormous and horrifying, covered in scorched and crackled skin the color of seared meat, hind legs bent backwards at the knees. Tendrils of acrid smoke lifted from it, moving as it swayed back and forth. The gasping of the demon filled the barn, deep, booming, and thick as the fiend coalesced. It stretched its grotesque limbs and twisted its head on the thick neck, filling the barn with the cracking sound of knuckles and tendons loosening. The sight of the fiend set my flesh to break out in chills, my knees to knocking. My voice trembled as I gave Swaine my impressions, barely aware of what I said.

After he'd written down my halting observations, he put the quill aside and took a handful of steps to where the demon brooded. The demon's glowing yellow eyes, points in the blackness of the face, pinched and focused on my master.

"You shan't get away, so I warn you not to try," Swaine said, his voice commanding and firm. Even so, I noticed beads of sweat at his temple.

The demon turned to me. The urge to flee was so strong I barely managed to hold myself in place. It stepped forward on horribly crooked legs—and it wept, a piteous babbling. One misshapen forelimb extended toward me.

"It's—weeping, sir. Holding out a—a paw."

"Ignore everything it does," Swaine said. "It's trickery."

I didn't move, keeping my ground. After a moment, the demon reared its head back and then leapt at me with a keening shriek. Its maw opened and steaming mucus hung in quivering strands. I raised my hands and turned my head. Swaine didn't flinch. All the bindings he'd layered into the space lit up, lines of glimmering flame, arranged in an intricate pattern between us and the demon. The light drove the demon back on its haunches.

"Behave yourself," Swaine warned.

The demon roared. It swung its head back, clawed, and filled the air with a wretched stench—but the protections held. The barn filled with thunderous air as the bindings strained. Papers flew, books flipped, tools crashed against the walls, and the air pressure grew so great that my ears popped. I struggled to keep my footing.

"I am your master!" Swaine bellowed. "Silence."

The bright webbings of flame closed in around the demon. It howled as the bindings shrunk into its flesh at head, limbs, and torso. Charring smoke and steam hissed where the thin lines of potent sorcery traced patterns and symbols onto its skin. The demon's eyes closed in agony and it stilled. Swaine reached into the pocket of his waistcoat and pulled out the twin to the key with which he'd opened the planar clock. He raised it to his forehead, then spoke.

"*Adraefan.*"

One simple word. The bright scrimshaw markings of the spells on the skin of the demon grew blinding—white, to gold, to orange, to a deep red—then faded to hints that shifted like cooling embers. The demon rose to full height, staring once again at Swaine. It made no move to attack him though its eyes shone with malice.

"Well?" Swaine said.

Smoke coiled from the fiend's mouth. It showed its foul teeth and spoke in a voice of charred flesh and stone that set my every nerve on edge. "Master."

"You're mine now," Swaine said, narrowing his eyes. "Best get used to it. I shall call you as needed."

He walked past the demon. The demon trembled, but made no feint or lunge at him. Swaine knelt and closed the chamber lids within the planar clock. They snapped shut with soft clicks and the demon vanished: bound. Swaine put the key back into his pocket and stood up. He turned. Lines of sweat ran down his face.

I went to speak, but my mouth had dried. Clearing my throat, I said, "It worked, sir?"

"Exactly as planned. Exactly." He reached one shaking hand

up to his face and wiped away the sweat drops—or were they tears?—that gathered in the corners of his eyes.

"And it can't—escape, sir?"

"No. It's under my will. Just as firmly as any of my other bound demons. Incredible." He shook his head in amazement. "We're in new territory now, Finch. On the brink of redefining the unseen arts. Demons for the taking. Incredible resources at our fingertips. Generations have quailed at the mere mention of this place—but no more. We have the chance to turn Salem into the birthplace of a new epoch of mankind. The cradle of a better civilization."

I was still too horrified by the way the demon had stared at me to share in Swaine's enthusiasm. Sleep seemed far off, birthing a new hope for mankind or not. Even stepping outside of the glamour of protection I'd watched the summoning from took more nerve than I'd admit. As Swaine warmed to the idea of reaching a new summit, I eyed the planar clock on the floor as one might an adder that hadn't quite stopped wriggling.

14

THE PURSUIT OF THE UNSEEN ARTS

L ater that evening, I walked around the long oak table in the manse's kitchen, past the racks of pots and ladles, knives and tongs, past the rows of drying herbs and flowers I'd strung up in front of the windows. I peered into the stone oven and saw it wasn't hot enough. I grabbed a poker and stirred the embers, adding more wood. My master had retreated to his room, exhausted, with firm orders to leave him undisturbed until his grinding headache subsided—offering me a brief glimpse into one of the prices of sorcery: *accersitus vomica*, 'the summoner's bane'; a well-documented by-product of demonic binding said to resemble the effects of a steel band around the head, tightened inexorably.

I took the opportunity to make us rolls and buns for the next few days. I pushed my thoughts away, and watched the fire grow, bringing the oven to the proper heat. Over and over I recalled the demon's leer with a shiver. I glanced out the windows toward the barn more than once. Swaine had assured me that the fiend was locked away within the planar clock, and behind the many glamours and glyphs that crisscrossed the barn. I hoped so.

I stepped into the pantry I'd organized and gathered flour,

sour milk, thick butter, and more. Soon, I had one hand on a wooden bowl as I mixed the dough in a rhythm as natural as drawing breath. The heat of the oven and the smell of the dough took me away into the familiar: kneading, pulling, tearing at the dough until I had a two dozen buns laid out. I loaded a tray into the oven, lingering in the warmth, staring into the shifting flames. Standing the peel on end, I watched as the buns rose. Behind me, the kitchen door boomed open and slammed shut, causing me to bound over to the glamoured circle of protection in the corner. The chill air gusted for a few moments. I'd grown annoyed with that demon, of late—he'd nearly taken my fingers off my right hand with a closet door on the second story as I'd been reaching for a dustpan. Swaine's contention that such an inconsequential demon—no more than a 'noisey-ghost' or *poltergeist*—was simply a nuisance that would have to be borne until more pressing threats could be attended to had done little to lessen my feelings on the matter.

"There's a clock waiting for you, you little cretin," I said to the closed door. "And you're lucky I don't know how to bind you. Yet."

I took the resulting silence as proof that I'd won the skirmish and continued with my baking. Within the half hour, I'd loaded a second tray into the oven while the first batch cooled on the long table, dusted with sugar I'd powdered. I wiped my forehead. As I turned to check on the oven, noises moved down the second-floor hallway overhead—a faint pounding at first, far off in a distant part of the house. I wondered if my master had stumbled on the way out to use the privy. The ruckus grew louder, with scraping and slamming, pounding on the walls, the ceiling, the floor, as though a troupe of acrobats and musicians and brawling thugs moved in voiceless unison. Plaster dust fell from the cracks overhead. A chill rolled from the ceiling, and I shuddered. I dropped the peel I held and ran to the circle of protection set up in the corner of the kitchen.

The racket passed overhead—and stopped. The silence after

the uproar alarmed me. I waited, hearing nothing but the snap of the fire in the oven.

"Master?" I called out. Nothing. I glanced out the nearest window, toward the barn, wondering if the demon had broken loose. Or had the other demons under Swaine's thrall taken exception to their new sibling? I raised my voice louder. "Master?"

No reply. I'd once dropped a ladle during an evening when he'd demanded to be left alone, and the string of his invectives had been instantaneous. Him not responding to my shout disturbed me more than the sounds themselves.

The noises started again, louder, by the servants' stairs that connected the second floor to the kitchen. I touched the necklace I wore, afraid to take a step beyond the enchanted circle drawn on the floorboards. The silence lasted for a dozen beats of my heart—I counted the thudding in my ears—and then the sounds resumed elsewhere, farther off than when they'd begun. It sounded as though the narrow attic was being attacked. I called for my master three or four more times, but again got no response.

After an agonizing internal debate, I dashed from the circle to the door to the servants' stairs, lifted the latch, pulled. The weighty door scraped along the boards of the floor as I tugged it. An unnatural shiver rolled over me, head to toe. I rushed up the stairs, sprinting to Swaine's room.

"Master? Master?" I pounded the door with my fist.

Nothing. I knelt and looked through the keyhole. The fire in his hearth had burned low. Straining to make out where he was, I saw a form under the blankets of his bed. I hit the door with my palm, twice.

"Master!" He didn't move. Odd shadows slanted on the walls and angled up from the corners.

As I looked more closely at the bed, I gasped. An object floated above it, and I took only seconds to see what it was: a ghastly face of skin, jagged around the edges, torn from a human head. Worse, I recognized it as the face of the red-bearded man who'd strangled me; the damage he'd sustained after being slaughtered by the demon had been so great that Swaine had declined to attempt to bind a demon within his corpse, and we'd disposed of him down by a purling brook on the far side of the meadow. I froze. A moving black stain floated behind the face, a distorted haze that rolled along the wall, the boards of the ceiling, keeping pace with the mangled scrap of skin. Tendrils of shadow stretched down to the books on Swaine's night-table. A peculiar terror gripped me, unlike any I'd felt before—no corpse, no demon had frightened me so. I lifted the latch, only to find that it didn't budge, not a hair's width. I hit it harder, the metal digging into my hand. It didn't give—a force had sealed the door shut. I kicked at it, calling for my master.

I pressed my eye back to the keyhole. The inky blackness and face descended over Swaine, a slow smothering. *Where were his demons?*

"He needs you!" I shouted. "Save him!"

Would they? Were they bound to? All that Swaine had told me had made it sound so, yet in their malice, it wasn't hard for me to imagine them holding back, darkly gleeful to see their master meet his end.

I ran back to the stairs, calling for the revenants—and there they were, gathered at the bottom, bunching up. Before them, a pair of carving knives from the kitchen slashed the air back and forth, floating, seemingly untouched. The blades sliced at the revenants, stabbing, driving them back, filling the stairwell with the sound of flesh ripping open. A blurring distortion in the air, like a patch of murky water illuminated with a sickly light, spread from where the knives swung. A demon.

There was no help to be had, I needed to open the door myself.

I kicked at it, I searched for something to smash it in with, but found nothing more suitable than a heavy candleholder that did little beyond denting the wood. My eye fixed on the hinges. Could I pry them off? I dropped the candleholder and ran my fingers over the iron of the hinges. They were bolted on tight, unyielding.

Iron desires to please, but can never be fully trusted.

The words came back from Edward Neile's *The Magickal Properties of the Knowne Base Metals.* I squeezed my eye shut. I'd been trying to memorize various passages of the book—particularly the spells that the author had transcribed. As I'd found with the mnemonics that Swaine taught me, I had a knack for such memorization.

I stepped back from the door and concentrated. When I had the proper phrasing in mind, I raised my hands—as I'd seen Swaine do—palms to the hinges. "*Ferrum audire, ferrum torquent, ferrum adspiret. Liberare ignem penetralibus.*" I tried to sound like Swaine, firm and commanding, though I'm afraid that it came out more like a frightened plea.

For a moment, nothing happened—and then my palms itched, growing hot. I held them out, facing the hinges. Orange light seeped from hands, tickling my skin like dancing nibs of quills. My eyes widened. Tiny sparks leapt into the air and my hands began to burn as though they were just above candle flames.

The spell wasn't working.

Worse, the pain in my hands crossed a threshold into agony. Panic set in. I knew enough even by then to realize that the spell couldn't simply be repeated—not without risking a magical backlash even more powerful. I waved my hands, desperate to stop the burning.

A witch is born a witch, no more, no less. Such an individual can see into a darkness that others can't, they can manipulate the currents of planar energy that courses between worlds by some form of instinct.

Fine. With no idea what I was doing, I imagined the center of a flame, the exact heart. As I did, I felt that I'd grabbed hold of a slender wire, a wire that connected to my hands. Raising them, the air before them shifted as though blown by a brisk wind.

Out, into the hinges. Into the iron. Inside.

A tremendous surge of energy ran up my spine and along my arms, shining with strange light, deepening into a glow so red and deep as to be liquid. For a moment, it felt altogether too powerful—as though my limbs were on the verge of sprouting flames, as though I'd be reduced to cinders while I stood there, a young pine tree engulfed in fire, throwing off embers. Steadying myself, I held my breath, trying to keep the crashing energy from sweeping me away. Cupping it in my hands as though it were water, I flung it at the door. It flew from my palms and caught and spread across the front of the door, onto the door frame, gathering on the hinges and the latch. Was it the spell—or something else within me? I had no idea, I only knew that energy poured out of me: stunning, potent. I gasped. The hinges of the door shone brighter and brighter, and a great explosion of color burst from them, a glimmering whirlwind of flame.

With a shattering of iron, the hinges and latch clanged to the floor, broken and glowing. And not only them, but the hinges on every door on the hallway, sending the doors all falling in, boom after boom. The power in my arms went from a geyser, to a trickle, to nothing. I staggered forward, dizzy. The door fell inward with a crash, slamming to the floor. Freezing air rolled out from Swaine's room. I took two unsteady steps in, treading on the fallen door.

"Master!"

The shape over Swaine's bed turned. Cheeks, flopping nose, scraggles of beard dangling beneath the rough mouth, empty eyelids, a grotesque slit of a mouth with lips that curled into a terrible grimace—the sight of the red-bearded man's face brought me right back to the horrors of my first night in the colony. The face and the stain behind it drifted, focused on me for the moment, the decomposed flesh stretched into a hideous simulacrum of curiosity and hunger.

"Master," I called out again. "Wake—" Before another syllable could pass my lips, a shadow slammed me to the floor, leaving me pressed down by what felt like a wagon-load of fieldstones. A doorway of sorts opened in the air above me, shrouded in black shadow. Within, spinning stars back-lit great arcing pillars of bone, a winding cathedral, snaking, twisting, diminishing to a distant point. Fangs appeared by the hundreds, encircling the opening. My lungs found no air. The foul veil expanded and a voice, a mind, touched my own, a more intimate touch than I'd ever imagined. The thoughts burrowed into my brain.

"You can stare at me like the sun on your last day, witch. Stare at me like the serpent hanging still in nothingness, stare at me until your very skull crumbles away in the burning sand. You will see me."

The words rang out in my head. If I'd had any air, I'd have screamed. I could only gasp. A brutal coldness ran up my arms as though I'd shoved them shoulder-deep through a hole in a frozen sea. The side of my face went numb. A power enveloped me with a stunning force.

Swaine's voice. He blasted out words as fast and loud as he could: *"Denne der man in pardîsu, pû kiuuinnit! Hûs in himile, dâr quimit imo hilfa kinuok, pidiu ist durft mihhil!"*

Light leapt across the room, over the roiling and swollen thunderhead that filled my sight, in a great blue-white flash. The room shook and items fell from shelves, from the writing desk in the corner. I shut my eye and covered my face. The bed, the floor itself shifted with a thud. Timbers throughout the manse shuddered. The air bent and I gasped. With a boom, the pressure righted itself. Small items rolled to a stop on the floor. Bits of ash from the hearth fell like gray snow.

Swaine stood near the foot of his bed in his long nightshirt, his hair gone wild, visage pale. Nothing else filled the space. He rushed over and knelt. "Are you hurt?"

I wasn't sure. I moved my arms, my legs, tried to sit up. He caught me by the elbow and helped me. Strange flashes of color danced around the room, the ghost colors left in one's vision from staring at candle flames. "I'm not sure. I think so, sir."

Swaine glanced at the room. He lifted me to my feet.

"By God, but your quick thinking may have saved us, Finch. It had me—it had me so far down that I wasn't even aware of it. Very nearly the end." His voice shook. Once he saw that I was steady, he righted several candles and lit them with an incantation. He looked shocked, and ran a shaking hand over his chin.

My arms tingled as I got to my feet. In the middle of the floor, a tiny wooden box sat on its side. The surrounding air trembled. "Is that—what is that?"

"Don't touch it," Swaine said, raising his voice. He approached it. "It's an older device of mine based on Koeffler's concepts of translocational manipulation. I never thought I'd need it—but now it seems like the bloody best four days I ever spent. Good Lord. I'll need a dozen more. At least. And you should best carry a few."

I stepped back from it. My shoe pressed onto something soft, and I recoiled as I saw that it was the corpse's face, lying on the floor like a discarded nightcap.

I shuddered. "What was it, sir?"

Swaine went to the night-table, running his hand over the aged cover of the *Occultatum Ostium* as if to assure himself it was intact. In truth, I found the sight of it loathsome—its curious dimensions, the scars of mildew across the cover resembling a vomit stain, the stray bits of binding hanging from the spine like the legs of a centipede. I stayed well away from it as a rule.

Swaine checked the corners of the room, the walls, moving his hands to and fro in concentration. "Enormous. And it swept right in. Not good. Not good at all. It was a planar umbra. An entity, a monstrosity in a nearby plane—one so powerful that its mere presence projected a shadowy darkness into this room.

Remarkable. I suspect it was attracted by the summoning with the planar clock, in some fashion. Quite concerning."

"I thought it worked properly, sir."

"It did. That still doesn't make it *safe*, apparently—not that much of our work is. No. I may have pushed further than I should have without better protections in place. If we're to effectively harness the powers here, the planes will need to be stabilized. They're clearly far too unpredictable."

I'd assumed demons to be the worst thing about Salem. Knowing more terrifying entities and dangers lurked just out of sight did little to slow my still-galloping heartbeat.

"I called for you," I said, glad to at least hear that I kept the tremor from my voice.

"Yes—I heard. But it had me in its thrall. I couldn't move. It— it wound in, somehow. While I slept. Past my demons. Past the glamours." Apparently satisfied that the integrity of the room was intact, he approached me. "It was only when you distracted the intruder that I was able to snap out of it."

He stared at me.

"You served me better than my demons, Finch," he said. "It would have devoured me."

"Devoured?"

"Soon enough. It needed to seep a hair further into my thoughts for me to relinquish the protections I keep about me as I sleep—but it was close."

Wiping his hands on his nightshirt, he lowered his head in concentration. After a minute, he looked up. "My demons return. I shall have them patrol every nook and inch of the house and barn. With luck, we'll know—"

The air in the open doorway warped with the presence of a demon, the one that always made my throat feel exposed. Bits of the iron latch and hinges rattled on the floor, and Swaine stared at them with a focused gaze. A frown appeared.

"I didn't mean to, sir," I said quickly. "I didn't know what else to do—it was shut. Sealed off. By that thing—the umbra. The planar umbra."

He snapped his gaze to me. "You did this?"

"Yes, sir."

"Magic." He sounded doubtful.

I paused. "Yes. Maybe. I don't actually know, sir."

He looked back at the rattling bits of metal. "Neile?"

"I tried a spell of *iron-breaking*, sir. From his book. But it didn't seem to work properly."

He motioned with his hand, and the demon moved along, stilling the broken metal. His hand ran across the beard on his cheek and he stared at me with dark eyes.

"But then I tried—" I faltered. "To simply *make* it work. From within. Manipulating the energy—like a witch might." As I spoke, my face grew red, and I found that I couldn't look at his eyes, only at the floor in front of me. I saw him cross his arms in front of his chest. "I'm not even sure how I did it, sir. It was just—well, it just happened. And I'm afraid I couldn't really control it. I think it may have ruined the other doors, as well."

When Swaine spoke, his voice was uncompromising. "This is a place of sorcery, Finch. *My* sorcery. A lifetime's worth of study and discipline. Do you think magic—or, heaven help us, *witch-craft*—is something you can just take on yourself? Like memorizing a poem? Like tidying up the pantry? Who exactly do you think you are? A vain, little upstart."

I swallowed. Met his gaze—he looked furious. "I'm sorry, sir. I realize I'm just a—"

"Just a what?"

"Just a servant, sir. A servant girl, sir."

The silence stretched out. All I could do was stare at the floor and wait for his fury.

"Is that right? Well then please listen carefully, servant girl: the world is more than happy to give you a ready-made identity, and all the dreary expectations that do or don't come with it. If that's all you're after, congratulations, you have got little struggle ahead of you. If, however, you wish to write your own description of yourself—you ought best relinquish the notion of *just* anything. *Just* this, *just* that."

I glanced up. He continued.

"All the best of us do. Do note, however, few people you'll meet will be pleased when they sense or decide that you've strayed outside your cage whilst they remain comfortably contained within their own. It's up to you to decide what matters for you—your own life, or the life that others would have of you. I think you might guess which shore I stand upon." He turned and went to fetch his clothing. "And another thing, Finch—you'd best learn to take a compliment better than that."

"But—what?"

"*I'm sorry, sir,*" he said, mimicking me. "Nonsense. Never apologize for the pursuit of the unseen arts. Bravo—bravo, bravo, bravo. I didn't think you had it in you, but you've surprised me yet again." He tugged on a pair of breeches beneath his nightshirt and motioned for his shoes. "But I urge you to be exceedingly cautious with witchcraft. I can give you no first-hand guidance, number one. The last witches to occupy this spot on the map didn't fare well, a rather resounding number two. I would suggest that you abstain from all such efforts—at least until you've come to understand the basic principles of both magic and sorcery. While they're not at all the same, I suspect you'll find insight. Discipline. Good habits. Understanding. Can you make me that promise?"

Thinking how close I'd come to seeing the energies I'd summoned spill out of control, I had little reason to refuse. "I promise, sir."

"Fate is a curious thing, wouldn't you say?"

"Fate, sir?"

He nodded. "Fate. Whatever fate brought you here, to this place. A witch—one whom demons want. One whom the colony would jail, or worse. One whose very presence could also land me in jail. Altogether the last person I'd ever choose." He shoved his feet into his shoes. "Perhaps you're the apprentice I need, after all."

I wasn't sure about *fate*. It was *death* that hounded me, nipping at my heels, all the way into Salem. It remained all around, in the corpses who walked the hallways, in the tales of mayhem, preserved like insects in amber, on the pages of the books in Swaine's library. And I'd almost seen it strike close to the center of the target once again, for if I hadn't managed to open the door, Swaine wouldn't have been able to talk about either fate or the apprentice he needs.

The shards of iron on the floor drew my eye. I'd done that. Witchcraft. My hands still tingled from the feel of it. How might I truthfully write my description of myself, as Swaine suggested? I wasn't sure. Could my mother have done something like that? How much of her daughter was I? A leaf on a branch on a tree, a line of women, strong women, witches going back generation by generation—was that my story? The thought made me dizzy. And yet of all the emotions that swirled through me, vivid and bright as the energy I'd drawn forth—pride, wonder, excitement, relief —one rose above the rest.

Terror.

15

ROARING HEART OF A FORGE

"Finch!"

The floorboards knocked as my master, in his study on the floor below, hit the ceiling with a broomstick, impatient. I opened my eye. A candle guttered on a small stand before me, beside Angus Hume's translation of Grimhildr's *Srávobhiśśravasíyas*. I was an hour deep into my daily practice of wards, a crucial and fundamental element of the art that Swaine insisted I learn after the incident with the planar umbra. Swaine himself knew two-hundred twenty-one wards against demons, and could do seventeen of them instantly. The best sorcerers in history knew no more than five, he claimed— and he assured me that five would be all I'd ever need, but that I'd best be an expert in those. My life and soul might depend on it.

The chime of a bell reached my ear and the floorboards banged again.

"If you think I have nothing better to do than ride out to listen to that man moan about his back for the better part of an hour— reconsider every assumption you've ever made, please." Swaine's muffled voice ended my concentration.

I leaned forward and blew out the candle. "I'll let him know —and meet him, sir," I called out. "Sorry!"

Hurrying out of my room, I straightened the front of my dress and headed to the main stairs. Several steps bore gouges from the trunk loaded with blankets, boots, and sundry that had careened down the hallway and onto the stairs a week earlier like a runaway carriage. It would certainly have killed anyone standing in its way. I still needed to fix the steps.

Swaine muttered some further displeasure as I jogged down the stairs, his voice floating out of the open door to his study, but I ignored him. He was in one of his moods. The entryway I passed through was clean: floors polished, plaster patched, a fresh coat of white paint on the walls and ceiling, all work I'd accomplished as autumn turned to winter. The rest of the manse was coming together, room by room, hall by hall, more so now that my master had allowed the revenants to be useful in carrying barrels of paint, sanding floors, and a dozen more tasks that could free up more of my time for studies.

I hurried to the kitchen. A brass bell, no larger than a sherry glass, hung in the air, swinging back and forth. Having decided he no longer cared for strangers bringing certain deliveries directly to Salem—too many complications, an observation I didn't take altogether personally—Swaine devised a system of companion bells to signal a delivery. When I rang the bell before me in return, both parties would know to rendezvous at a little-used bridge in the outskirts of the nearby town of Andover. It would take me two hours or so to make the trip. I grabbed the bell from the air. The ringing paused. I rang it three times: *Yes, meet me.*

Outside, I readied Swaine's wagon and headed off down the lane from the manse, sparing a glance at the snow-dusted remains of Salem that stood beyond the fields and across the river. Our explorations had grown more cautious, primarily restricted to mapping the edges and contours of the regions of planar activity while Swaine dedicated the bulk of his hours to developing what he believed to be a technique for neutralizing the greatest dangers. For myself, I wasn't sorry to stay away. My thoughts often returned to the brooding malice of the abandoned town. The silence at night, the stillness at dusk, even the look of the daytime shadows. The slant of the light over sagging roofs and frowning doorways. The slate-gray harbor beyond. It was impossible to put it entirely out of mind—though riding away from the place always lightened my mood.

And so my mood remained as I eventually neared the wooden bridge spanning the Shawsheen River, some ninety minutes later. At the sound of the straining of the hitches and the clop of my horse breaking the lonesome silence, the driver of another wagon raised a hand in greeting. Huddled in his coat, he slouched. I pulled the wagon to a halt on one side of the bridge, dismounted, and walked across the bridge.

"Mr. Preston," I said. "Lovely to see you."

He doffed his tricorn at me and gave me a smile comprised of the few stubborn teeth that remained, brown and crooked, in his gums. In his prime he'd clearly stood no taller than five feet, and his prime was well past. "Miss Finch."

"My master expected you earlier in the week. He's been rather cross about it."

"Aye, a terrible slow fortnight it's been, lass," Preston said. He ran a hand over his balding dome. "What with this trouble and that in the city."

I nodded. "I understand, Mr. Preston. Yet you know my master. Not a patient man, as I'm sure you appreciate."

"I do, I do. And I apologize if I kept him waiting, lass. I only mean to get him what he needs. Secret and unseen. As promised, and no mistaking."

"Then let's see what you have." I ignored his further stream of explanations and headed around to the back of the wagon, hoping the delivery would be sufficient to quell Swaine's foul mood. Peeking over the side, I cursed silently. Two corpses, that was it. "Mr. Preston—you're making it hard to keep my master happy."

The old man climbed from the driver's bench, grunting as he did. He hobbled around to where I stood, waving his hands as if casting a spell of his own that might dilute my master's coming annoyance. "Soldiers about, night after night. Searching for the lads who keep putting up those pamphlets. *Rattlesnakes*, they call themselves. Governor's not happy at all. Making him look foolish, and all."

"Still. My master is paying you for bodies, sir—a dozen bodies." Before us, the two corpses sprawled on the bed of the wagon, their features pale and sunken, lips pulled back, necks arched in the rictus of death. One wore a shabby dress, tight-laced up the front, with hair hitched up above a painted face. She looked young, a few years older than I was, which I found disturbing. I turned to the other, a gnarled man who didn't look to weigh much more than the frayed coat that fell loose round him. Dried soil gathered in the corners of the wagon, on the corpses' clothing, in their hair. From the stink, the corpses were more than a few days dead, their clothing and skin the worse for it.

"That's not all, though, Miss," Preston blurted, grabbing a sack tucked into the corner, sensing my displeasure. "With the pox and all, I also come across these. Snuck in through a window to get them." He held open the sack.

I looked inside and turned away quickly. "Mr. Preston, really."

"Wouldn't charge him the full price, course."

I looked away. A man willing to procure corpses had few lines he wouldn't cross—Swaine himself did, though. Preston worked his tongue over his lonesome teeth, saw the look on my face, and nodded.

"But—given the difficulties," he said. "You can just have 'em. Remember what your master said, now. That's right. Just trying to do my best to get him what he requires, lass." He held out the sack.

"They're infants," I said. I made no move to take the sack.

After an awkward few moments, Preston nodded, and placed the sack back into the wagon. He wiped his hands together. "To your wagon then, is it, lass?"

"Thank you, Mr. Preston."

He nodded and raised the gate on the wagon, then limped back around to the front. As he reached up to climb into the driver's seat, he grabbed his back and slipped from the wagon to the little-used lane.

"Are you all right, Mr. Preston?" I said, walking around the wagon.

"Sorry, Miss Finch," Preston grunted. "This'll pass. Sorry thing, this back of mine. Ideas of its own, I sometimes think."

He lifted an arm, hoping for help—but I ignored him. A strong wind swept through the thicket of hemlock that marched off along the lane, mist veiling the lowest boughs. Trunks, fern, and thorn receded into the woods. I felt a presence coming closer. Swaine and I both agreed that I'd become more visible to demons since I'd used my witchcraft to rescue him—perhaps the most compelling argument against attempting to use it further. In the shadows of dusk, alone in the morning sunlight, crossing from manse to barn in the evening, the feeling of being observed rarely left me. Still, it wasn't as though I had no defenses. I touched the glamoured pendant I wore and concentrated, readying the demonic ward I knew the best, nervous that I'd never *had* to use it.

The nearest trees burst apart. Trunks cracked lengthwise, raw wood blazing through the torn bark, while branches fluttered and shed their green shoots. Violent clacking and howling and snarling sounds filled the air, drowning out Preston's groans. I

ducked as a pine branch whacked my shoulder, leaving a streak
of pitch on my sleeve. An inky shadow whirled before me, crackling with veins of red light. A malign will assaulted me, wanting
to hurt me—to shred, tear, and strangle me. Fearsome claws on
the ends of whip-like tendrils emerged from the shadows,
rending the air.

I held out my hand and yelled: "*Sivrit wart enpfangen als im
daz wol gezam, mit vil grozen eren im was da niemen gram!*"

A great meeting of force, pressure, and collision built, and I
stepped back. A crack of thunder erupted before me, shaking the
ground, air whipping. The sounds ceased. The winds stilled, leaf,
bud, and cone whirling to the lane, dotting the wagon. For a few
moments, I sensed the demon moving to and fro, unseen, and
then it vanished. The surrounding air—the surrounding planes
—thrummed in its wake. Even at such an early point in my
sorcerous training, I'd become sensitive to such disturbances, and
there was no mistaking it. I lowered my hands, scanning the
woods before me. My pulse raced, but I'd done it: the ward had
worked. I didn't relax my guard, even so, for day by day, the
demons around me grew more brazen.

Within the quarter hour, I had Mr. Preston on his feet,
bending with no pain, his mouth running with a gratitude I
found a little much. A simple conjuring of heat, familiarity with
the anatomy of the spine and muscles—thanks to the many
corpses I'd dragged and prepared for my master—manipulating
the shoulders for nothing more than effect, and Preston prattled
on that decades had lifted from him. His wagon emptied and the
corpses hidden away in Swaine's beneath a sheet of canvas and
between pairs of empty crates, I handed him a small sack of coin.

"After what you've done for me back, lass—feels wrong to
even take this." He didn't have much trouble slipping the sack
into his coat pocket, I noticed.

"He's expecting more," I chided him. "You'll get me in trouble
if it continues this way."

"Course, course. With my back fixed so, shouldn't have no troubles. The fuss'll calm down soon enough. Always does."

"His work doesn't slow."

"Neither do people meeting their maker, so I'll have more for your master."

"More than a pair, I daresay," I said, giving him a smile.

His gaze drifted to the broken tree by the side of the lane, and he nodded. "Your good master's business is his own, lass—that much I'll say. But none of it'll be mucked up for lack of our quiet friends. I'll see to it."

Preston climbed back onto the emptied wagon and picked up the reins. I watched as he turned along the bend in the road and soon disappeared behind the curve lined with towering elm, winter bare. The sun shone off the slow-moving waters of the river. I drew my cloak close and turned my wagon back in the direction of Salem.

BY THE TIME the manse came into sight, the sun tilted toward the west. I worked away the chill carrying the two bodies to the barn. Once inside the shadowed interior, I sensed the residual magic in the air from Swaine's latest work. His workbench was neat—I kept the candles, notes, sulfurous tinctures, painstakingly collected herbs and dyes, the other major and minor phylacteries for his work ordered and at the ready. The newest revenants lined the barn walls, struck here and there by bright chinks of sunlight, standing motionless like a group of strangers waiting for something to begin. They all followed me with their gazes, drawn, as with the feral demons, to the witch in their midst. As revenants, though, they could do little more than stare. While the phenomenon still unnerved me, I'd learned to live with it. Stepping over to the nearest one, an older man with a belly big as an overturned wheelbarrow, hanging pasty from beneath a stained shirt, I ran through his mnemonics, recalling his name: *The vales of mist hold fowl and fauna, Ku-us-sa-ra Serśkana.* Even thinking the name wordlessly brought a groan from the revenant, though it remained otherwise still.

I turned to the smaller workbench that Swaine had given me for my work, opened a ledger book and wrote down the time and location of the latest demonic contact. My scrawling handwriting —my master likened it to the markings left by a wounded sparrow limping across a page after stepping in an inkwell— tracked every time a demon tried to attack me, and I rather took to the habit of notating such incidents. Writing them down gave me a tinge of control. Or at least the illusion of control, comforting nonetheless. Still, the pattern trended inarguably upward of late.

As Archibald Fletcher had discovered, Salem was home to a planar confluence of profound complexity. If one dug deeply, rare references to such areas of concentrated infernal activity existed. Even the natives who'd dwelt along the coast from the mists of time had kept away from this particular shore—too many evil spirits. I often wondered if it had just been bad luck, then, that the captain of the *Westenshire Bell* had chosen this particular harbor to abandon his passengers, not willing to carry them any further despite their having saved the vessel as it floundered at the height of a terrible storm—revealing themselves as witches fleeing the Old World in the process? How quickly had they realized the nature of their new settlement? Fletcher seemed to think it hadn't taken long at all—but as the rest of the colony shunned the eighteen families cast off the ship, they seemed to have made do as best they could. For a time.

I turned my attention to the two new bodies. Swaine wouldn't be pleased to find but a pair. He'd been eager to summon a particular quartet of demons he'd confirmed with the acquisition of a long-sought tome of notes of Emelie Du Marien.

He'd returned to the practice of utilizing only known demons for the process of revenation after a failed attempt to bind the spirit he'd trapped in the house of Thaddeus Rivers with the planar clock. The *pig-demon* (for that's how I thought of it) had made for a terrible revenant when Swaine had bound it into the body of a red-haired woman in her sixties: glaring eyes, cruel laughter, and a wattle of loose flesh beneath her chin swinging back and forth as the revenant proceeded to smash apart half the barn before Swaine subdued it. Each subsequent attempt to tame it had ended similarly, forcing Swaine to admit it wasn't safe to keep the revenant in any state at all. In the end, he'd bound the foul pig-demon into an antique amulet and locked it away.

The body was disposed of. A revenant shorn of its demonic bindings is of no further use to the sorcerer. The complex process of readying a corpse for revenation appears to preclude the repetition of such steps. Relatively little research had been done on the topic in the face of the towering amount of anecdotal evidence wherein subsequent attempts at revenation ended in grotesque mimicry of the desired outcome: bones shattering, heads twisting in the wrong direction, intestines projecting out from sundry openings, eyeballs hanging from optic nerves, all the while the revenant mewling and groaning, heaving itself to and fro. As the Reverend Geoffrey Hale of Horsforth, West Yorkshire, himself a former sorcerer, noted in his rather sanctimonious account of the art, *On Sorcery* (1655):

The eye of Nature and the Lord may be evayded in the first instance of such Black Tramplings into the realm of the tomb, yet the hubris of a second such Trespasse will with certainty drawe forth Their ire, with a clear visage of the punishment awaiting the incantor at the moment of his Own demise.

Swaine himself felt it due to subtle damages to the tissues combining with residual magic, enough to disrupt the proper start of any new bindings. Worse for me, even after I'd dragged the useless corpse down to a brook behind the barn, it'd reeked enough to be smelled from the barn. Swaine directed me to a bin of lye in the workshop. I still recall the horrid way that the revenant's face softened like a rotting pumpkin afterwards, and have long had nightmares about that unpleasant task.

After properly stowing the newest bodies, I examined the dead girl. Her eyelids were half-open, the eyes themselves like dull seashells, staring out at nothing. My master had told me to regard the sight of a corpse as a gift: *As strong a testament to the infinite stretches of darkness that bookend this brief sliver of existence you'll find.*

In his more expansive moods, he offered up any number of such pleasantries.

As I looked at the dead girl, I just thought it sad. I was to strip the bodies, remove any jewelry—which with these two, seemed unlikely—wash them, and ready the items for their revenation. I rolled up my sleeves. Learning to deal with the bodies had been horrible, at first, but repetition brought forth a certain balm. Still, I procrastinated, looking instead over the items on my master's bench. Every item had a purpose, each capable of unwinding the stitchings of the seen world to reveal the unseen. The siren song of it resonated in my heart, as unexpected as any other turn that Fate had dealt me.

I held my hand out. At a quick word, a low blue flame danced in my palm, fluttering.

Magic.

When Swaine had taught the spell to me, he'd explained that, in many ways, it differed little from setting a candle alight: the flame stood for the caster's will; the wick represented the strands of planar energy, the dormant sources of potential that wound unseen through this world and the planes adjacent; the wax, the substance of the visible world.

But if magic was the light of a candle, then sorcery was the roaring heart of a forge. Magic might illuminate a dark room of secret knowledge, but sorcery—well, sorcery could pry up the edges of the universe itself, revealing a vastness beyond both life and time.

I considered the fire in my palm.

Yes, anyone could cast a spell—so Swaine insisted. Given enough practice, dedication, guidance, yes. Attention. Retention. Intention. Much as I found it hard to fathom, that I was a witch was neither here nor there, save for the peril it brought me. But I'd decided that if I was to bear such a burden, then I would do all I could to challenge such a Fate. To immerse myself so deeply in magic and sorcery that no demon could touch me or anyone in my life, ever again. Fill my days and nights with study and practice. Take the tools afforded to me by Swaine and rise above the lot I'd been given. I'd come to wonder if my mother had known she was different. Would the word 'witch' have even occurred to her? Why would it?

Had her life been one of unexplained difference, of being terrified, of making do? Of clutching together a patchwork of fears, beliefs, superstitions, and coping methods in order to achieve even a semblance of normalcy? If she'd had the chance I had, could she have spared herself a life lived under constant worry, clinging to routine, relying on my father with such ferocity?

She couldn't—so I would.

August Swaine was willing to give me what my mother never had. Yes, he was temperamental. Fickle. Brilliant. Preoccupied. In all of his mercurial states, demanding. And to be sure, it was difficult to envision more harrowing circumstances. Danger permeated Salem, untapped energies that rumbled like a tremendous underground river. Yet Swaine offered me hope like no one else had. Or could. And as for the dangers, I'd grown certain that Swaine would be the one to harness them, to master Salem. His was a genius unmatched, capable of breaking the barriers that had confounded even the greatest practitioners of magic and sorcery.

And I was his apprentice.

The blue flame in my hand became orange, then yellow. It stretched long in my palm. The eyes of the dead shone with it. It wouldn't be long before Swaine called for me, impatient to begin, so I snapped my palm shut, extinguishing the fire. I had work to do.

16

TALK OF SPIRITS

While my master was without question a genius, after more than two months of study I'd developed a certain genius of my own at keeping everything in his orbit running smoothly. To his credit, he'd by then ceased to approach every last one of my utterances as though I were a hopeless dullard. While his initial instinct had been to over-explain even the simplest task lest I sod everything up, he might now merely gesture and bark my name. When I asked him a question, he no longer assumed that I'd already made a mistake. He often stopped what he was doing to detail out the answer, occasionally thrusting a book into my hands and telling me to take the question further and see what I found. Where his first inclination had been to live like a squatter in a dusty, cobwebbed, decaying house—well, I'd put an end to that. He'd hardly have admitted it within my earshot, but a well-run household suited him, and allowed him to keep his pace and his work without finding himself gnawing on moldy bread, or realizing that he'd not changed his clothes in four days. Having grown up with six brothers, I knew how to navigate the inherent tendency of the untamed male to devolve to a coarse, uncivilized state.

As part of managing the unceasing entropy that surrounded August Swaine, I undertook a weekly trip to pick up supplies. I'd woken to find a fresh dusting of snow on the ground. By the time I left the deep forest behind me, dawn lit the meadows that lined the road. I neared Andover again in the blue shadow of early morning. Swaine's first house in the colonies was nestled, unused, in a dale deep in the woods there, where we allegedly resided. As I passed the edges of town, smoke rose from chimneys, and a handful of roan cows clustered at the edge of a trampled field. I felt a surge of relief at the sight of life, so welcome after the sullen brooding of Salem.

The road wound between low stone walls, marking off fields sculpted under drifts of snow and orchards of bare trees. Day broke. The near edge of town held but a dozen small houses, across from a tavern. A cock crowed, and I heard a door bang closed somewhere out of sight. I pulled the wagon up in front of the tavern's stable, passing by the sign that read "Knox's Inn & Tavern," then climbed down and hitched the team. A red-haired lad of about my age, Bertram Nagle, carried a bucket from the well past the corner, nodding at me as I waved. I pushed open the tavern door, stepping into a warm, large room with white-washed walls and floorboards painted green. Wide sash windows let in the morning sunlight and a fire burned in a hearth, beside which stood two stools next to a pile of netting and twine. A woman of about twenty carried a pot to the hearth and smiled when I appeared. Her name was Iris, and she had lovely freckles and an earthy beauty that had kept half the lads of Andover drawn to her as the hound was to the hare—until she'd crushed all their dreams and married one Ethan Knox, proprietor of the inn. With one child already crawling about, she was heavy with a second. Seeing a healthy, living family always gave me a stab in the heart, thinking of what had happened to my own.

"Goodness, is it Friday already?" Iris said.

"That smells amazing."

She hung the pot. "You should try some before you leave. Pheasant, parsnips, carrots. We made it earlier this week, and there wasn't a smudge left in a single bowl."

Swaine had various packages and weekly supplies sent to Knox's, by way of a merchant associate of Nathan Winslow. Having goods make several stops before they ended up in the quiet tavern at the lonesome edge of a wooded town assured that my master's presence and work drew as little attention as possible. "Did the delivery arrive?"

"Late yesterday. But it's here." Iris put the cloth she'd held the pot handle with over her shoulder. "The driver was stopped twice, can you believe it? Searched both times."

"Stopped?"

"Aye. By the Governor's men. Driver wasn't happy about it."

Nor would Swaine be happy to hear it, but I ran through the list of what should've been in this lot. Nothing remarkable in any fashion: food stuffs, new linens, doorknobs, buttons, a new coat for my master that had taken six weeks of hounding for him to submit to visiting a tailor on King Street in Boston for fitting. The Governor's soldiers would find more of the same in any dray or wagon they stopped within thirty miles of Boston itself.

"Quite a week we've had," Iris said. "Do you know we were visited by Doctor Rush? Tuesday," Iris said. "Asking all kinds of questions—though he complimented me on the stew."

Doctor Rush? Swaine had just that week spent an hour reading me passages from Rush's most-lauded work—*On the Principles of Planar Cartography* from 1704—powering his way through three scones and as many cups of strong tea as he underscored the myriad errata and false assertions made by the good Doctor when he'd been in his prime. I tried not to show too much surprise on my face.

"How exciting," I said. "What kind of questions did he ask?"

"The kind to keep me up half the night." Iris wiped a tabletop with the cloth. "Had I heard any talk of spirits. Any word of hauntings. Strange figures seen on—or off—the roads. Any graves disturbed. Can you imagine?"

Yes I could. I furrowed my brow. "Now I won't sleep. Thank you Iris."

She laughed.

"Can I see the delivery?" I said. Swaine would want to hear of Rush's visit straight away.

"Course you can." Iris led me through the public room and out into a pantry beyond the stairway. Crocks, casks, flour bins, and cordwood stood along one wall. I glanced out the window and saw a flock of grackles lift up from the ground and speed into the trees, their shadows roiling across the snow. In the corner, I examined the supplies. One decent-sized wooden crate I couldn't at first account for, but as I looked over the side of it, I saw the markings and perked up: the clockmaker Robert Twelves' latest device. Built to Swaine's specifications, it was a more powerful version of the planar clock, designed to clear vast stretches of planar fields in one go: a *resonance clock*.

"Brilliant," I said.

"How's your master doing?"

"Well enough. As long as he has his books, he's fine."

"He's lucky to have you, that's what I think."

"He might be," I said.

Swaine, according to our cover story, was a retired bookbinder turned collector of rare books, teaching me the craft of book repair. I was, not a stretch of the imagination, his orphan apprentice, brought over from London. Unfortunately, Iris and her husband were so kind and encouraging—an earnest young lass running errands for her reclusive master—that I felt shameful. They often threw in ears of corn, or a loaf of fresh bread, or a gallon of beer for me to take home. Iris pointed to a parcel wrapped in a cloth. "Two loaves of pumpkin bread. The spices are lovely. For you and your master."

"You're too kind," I said.

She convinced me to stay for a bite before loading the wagon and setting off for my master. She buzzed around the public room readying it for the day as I sat by the hearth eating pheasant stew. Delightful. The stew, and the company.

I spent all my time with Swaine, and precisely *none* was spent chit-chatting about the affections of young men. Iris had a kind nature, and a sharp eye for discerning the scruples—or lack thereof—of the young lads in the town, and those nearby. She ticked off such charms as they had, and weighed them fairly against their deficits. I added my own observations, based on the few I'd passed any words with in the time I'd been coming to Andover. Of late, she'd nudged me to consider the affections of the red-headed Bertram, her younger brother who cared for their invalid grandfather in a small cabin two miles from the inn.

I must admit I thought Bertram daft.

Gangly, freckled, unruly hair the color of copper—and always ready with an inscrutable joke he found riotous, and which I found bizarre. Any attempts at conversation he made with me quickly veered off into baffling territory: his theory that holding apple seeds in one's cheeks would decrease the need for sleep; his study of an alleged Hindoo practice for slowing aging, involving drinking the air; the development of a style of poetry that could be used as coded military communication; the like.

It was absurd—I saw nothing in common with him, my identity was a lie, and all of my brothers' teasing about my eye had rendered me incapable of believing that any lad might show the slightest interest in me, in any event. Still, entertaining such gossip with Iris was a break from corpses and demons.

"He asked about you again." Iris stacked tin mugs near a cask. "Bertram. Just the other day."

I lifted the spoon to my mouth and left it there. "He what?"

"I told you."

"Me?"

"You."

Ridiculous. "What did he ask?"

"He thinks you handle a wagon well."

"I do—but that's not a question."

Iris smiled. "His *real* question was whether your master would point a musket at a suitor, or not."

I put the spoon down. "He did not say that."

"Well that's what he was getting at."

"Iris."

She straightened the bonnet she wore. "I knew you fancied him."

"Would you just tell me what he said? And I don't fancy him." At least, I didn't think I did up until that point—at the very least, I hadn't until the idea *he* might fancy *me* had come up, my introduction to the fact of nature that there's nothing so enticing as believing one is desired.

"He asked whether I thought you wore such nice dresses on purpose," Iris said.

"How would I wear them by accident?"

"Meaning, for his sake, I believe."

"I don't—they're what I have."

The dresses. It transpired that my master had taken up a regular correspondence with Mary Whitelocke since their introduction at Winslow & Sons. Nothing scandalous, mind you. He more often than not read them aloud to me, relying on my feminine judgement—such as it was—to warn him off from any shoals or breakers he might drift toward. To interpret Madam Whitelocke's true intentions. At first, I surmised that he was just part of her collection of interesting men on whose renown she traded. I later came to believe her interest in my master went deeper than that.

I will say she had a sharp wit, and I will also say money appeared to flow away from her at a remarkable volume. When I once suggested that the Governor—her father—ought to raise a tax on the colony's dressmakers to recoup his expenses,

Swaine had told me to behave, although I'd heard him chuckling well after I'd left his study. I bore a letter from him, or back from her, every so often amongst my managing of the coming and going of the household, said correspondence moving through Mr. Winslow. Whitelocke's letters often bore a scent of perfume, while I tried my best to make sure that Swaine's bore no trace of decomposition, sulfur, or any other sorcerous residue.

As for the dresses that my would-be suitor Bertram had asked after, I'd apparently become something of a charity for Mary Whitelocke. Besides quality attire befitting a quality servant, I'd found myself in possession of half a dozen fine dresses of silk, lace, and velvet. Hats, gloves, sleeve ruffles, capes, shoes, cloaks, and gowns were sent my way at regular intervals. And eye-patches—by then, I had a collection of a dozen of them, many of them commissioned by Mary herself to complement or match the other outfits. At Swaine's urging, I wrote a proper thank-you note for each one, searching for a fresh variant of *thank you for the unexpected but lovely gift, how thoughtful of you* to reply with. What use I had for a room (for I'd had to convert a full room in the manse into a wardrobe for storing them) full of fancy attire in the demon-infested, lonesome reaches of Salem, wasn't clear, although I will confess that occasionally having something other than books, magic, and my studies in my life had become a guilty pleasure.

And I will further confess that in choosing what I might wear as I rode to Andover, I sometimes erred on the side of pretty. Mary Whitelocke would certainly have approved.

"Nor was I surprised to see my brother finding an excuse to help around the tavern this morning," Iris said. "Knowing it's Friday."

I looked at the outfit I wore—a pale brick colored riding habit that had been included in our monthly shipment from Winslow's not a fortnight earlier—and put one hand to the patch on my eye, of beige silk with a delicate herringbone stitching around the edges.

Iris walked by me and put a light hand on my shoulder. "You look lovely."

Before I could protest that I hadn't even given a thought to how I looked, thank you, the door opened. A young man came inside, followed by another man and a woman, the same age. They wore cloaks and the clothes of laborers, faded, a patch here and there.

"Francis," Iris said.

I glanced up at the mention of his name. Iris had told me more than one story of her husband's brother. Trouble followed him more closely than his own shadow, apparently—one of the reasons for the recent feud that had erupted between the two brothers. I saw the resemblance in the color of the skin, the shape of the nose, the eyes. He was an even more handsome version of Ethan. I found him striking.

"Is he here?"

"No, and you're lucky he's not."

"Perfect. Just need a little food for the road."

Iris wasn't pleased. "He'll be back in an hour."

"We'll be gone in a quarter that." Francis went back through to the pantry. I heard him rummaging about.

"And what am I supposed to tell him? That you barged in and started pilfering?"

"You can tell him exactly that," came his voice from the pantry. "You can tell him that a few loaves and a wheel of cheese and a few of these sausages are small change compared to the years I hauled firkins up from the cellar for him. You can tell him anything you'd like."

The other two looked about. The young woman wore her pale brown hair tied back, without a bonnet. She had a sharp nose and pale eyes. When she noticed me looking, she stared back at me, scrutinizing my patch. After a moment, I looked away, concentrating on finishing my stew and on not blushing. Iris hurried off into the pantry, and I listened to the two of them quarrel. Something smashed on the floor and broke, causing Iris to raise her voice. After a minute, Francis strode out from the back, balancing a load of goods in his arms: two wheels of cheese in pale rinds; a string of linked smoked sausages; a sack with what smelled to be dried apples; a jar of honey; four hard-crusted loaves of bread; another sack that looked like it held potatoes; dried meat rolled in an apron. Iris followed him.

"Ethan will be furious," she said.

"That's what he does. Also, whose wagon is that out front?"

"What does that matter?"

"We need a wagon. Cold work trudging through the snow."

"You got here on foot," Iris said. "You should leave that way."

"We only need a ride."

"Why don't you go?"

Francis handed the goods to his companions and turned to me. "Is that your father's wagon?"

I blinked. "My master's."

He walked over and smiled. "We're in a bind, you see. We need to get back to Boston. Our ride didn't work out, and now we're stranded." He pulled coin from his breech's pocket. "We can pay."

His eyes put a flutter in my stomach. I entertained the thought. Swaine might not even notice if I were gone for the day. I suspected that staring into Francis' brown eyes for a few hours mightn't be altogether bad—but, no. I had work to do, and the package was something that my master had been waiting for. "I'm sorry, but I can't."

He knelt next to where I sat, and I discovered that I didn't have a ward or glamour on me that worked against his charm. "Maybe I could ask your master."

"She's alone, Francis—and that's the way you ought to leave her. Alone. Just leave."

He ignored Iris. "So you could, then." He didn't let go of my gaze. "You might like it. I could tell you all about my sister-in-law —she's not always so rude, for instance. You could see Boston. You'd fit right in."

"I wish—that I—but—" Where had my words gone? My sense seemed to have been drawn into his eyes and trapped as a demon caught in a planar clock. My cheeks warmed. His lips looked so soft. Before I babbled further, I reminded myself how vile lads could be, thinking of my own late brothers—although Francis struck me as being of an entirely different species altogether. Still, no. "I'm sorry. My master needs me back. I should go now. Actually." I stood. He kept kneeling before me. "But thank you. Again, sorry."

Iris put a comforting hand on my arm. "See you soon," she whispered. She turned and snapped the dish towel draped over her shoulder at her brother-in-law, forcing him up from his knee. "You'd best leave some of that coin for Ethan. You still owe him nearly four pounds."

Francis raised his hand, warding off the whip of the towel. Their arguing continued as I brought the goods out to the wagon and busied myself with securing the small crate in the back. Soon, Francis and the other two stepped out from the tavern. They left me in peace, heading off down the small lane, toward Boston. Once they were out of sight, I wondered if Bertram had admired my dress from somewhere near. I didn't spot him, and decided that it was just as well—I'd surely realize how much more handsome Iris' brother-in-law was, which wouldn't be fair.

A few far-off homes marked the edge of Andover. The rest of the land fell away to woodland that wore fresh winter ornaments of snow and ice. A red-tailed hawk circled high up. The wagon's chains and posts rattled as the wheels clambered across frozen tracks in the lane. For my amusement, I played out in my mind what Swaine would do if I asked him for romantic advice. Would he do as he did when any mention of my womanly cycle came up, and claim the urgent need to find a particular book, feigning preoccupation? Or would he offer references for any number of amorous glamours I might use to guarantee the desired result, and challenge me to learn five of them by week's end? Of course, he might very well suggest a demon ought to accompany me while in the presence of a suitor, just to keep his own peace of mind.

I sighed—for I was certain I knew *exactly* what he would say, which would be: *Why on earth would you concern yourself with such nonsense when we're on the verge of ushering in the greatest age in the annals of sorcery? Have you lost your mind, Finch?*

One couldn't help but notice that August Swaine lived the life of a bachelor well past the point when a suitable marriage would be expected. I was unaware of him expressing more than a curiosity whether Mary Whitelocke, for instance, had suitors of her own. Heart-struck with romance? Easier to imagine him doing hand-stands while singing. No, my master was cut of a different cloth. While romance might not wield much—or any— sway over him, his views toward the fairer sex were as enlightened as anyone I'd ever met. He didn't treat me as though I were by nature subservient. For instance, *Is this your father's wagon?*

With my attention so consumed, I didn't notice the quartet of figures by a bend in the road. After my first surprise, I recognized them: Francis and the other two from the tavern, along with another young man, plump with a wispy beard. Within my general shock at seeing them was both a dose of caution—for it seemed odd, even then—and a hint of excitement, for there was something about Francis that made me wobbly. Francis himself stepped out into the road before the wagon and raised his hand in greeting. I slowed the wagon to a stop.

He bowed. "I should apologize for my behavior back there. Too many ghosts in that place, and they get my dander up. Families." He said the last word as though it explained it. The word just made me think of graves. The others watched me.

"It's fine," I said, shifting on the driver's bench. "Ethan is lovely, and I'm sure that you're—lovely, too."

Francis smiled. "Why, thank you." He came around to the side of the wagon. "Here's the thing, we're in a spot. If it were just a matter of time and sore feet, walking back to Boston would be fine. There's more at stake. We need that ride. Desperately."

I wasn't sure how *a* ride had suddenly turned into *that* ride, but he made it hard to keep my thoughts altogether straight. "I'm sorry—I do have somewhere—I mean, I can't. I don't have time. Or permission."

"We're wasting time," the woman called. Francis silenced her with a look.

He turned back to me. "Ignore her. What's your name?"

"Kate." The word popped out before I even had time to consider whether it were wise or not.

"Kate," Francis said. He made it sound older, more sophisticated. "We will need the wagon."

From the corner of my eye, I glimpsed the two lads approaching. I looked from them, to the woman—who stared at me with overt hostility—back to Francis. "Sorry?"

He lifted his hands as though everything were obvious. "It's simple—you won't get in any trouble. *We'll* be the ones in trouble, if it comes to that. You were just waylaid by horse-thieves. You couldn't help it, there were four of them. Or five. Or six, whatever you wish."

I was still confused, my common sense lagging well behind what was happening around me. "But I know you—who you are."

"Ah, but you didn't know who *robbed* you." Francis lifted a kerchief tied around his throat, lifting the edge up over his nose and covering half his face. The others did likewise, even the woman. "Because they were masked. Because these old roads near the signs aren't well protected by the Governor's men anymore. Too good to protect the citizens around here."

One of the other others put his hands on the wagon.

"But I know who you are," I repeated. "And you'll be jailed. Or worse. As horse-thieves."

"But you won't tell anyone." Francis lifted himself up on the running board by my side of the wagon. "If it helps, think of us as horse-borrowers. We're simply relieving you of the wagon for the day. You'll find it at the edge of Cambridge, by the river. I promise." His eyes drew me forward, made me want to believe it—but then I thought of my master and how long he'd waited for the resonance clock from Robert Twelves to arrive. They weren't going to steal it from me.

"Get down," I said, raising my voice.

"You're not keeping it—just get out," the woman said. She stepped up to the horses and reached for their tack. I snapped the reins hard, and the horses heaved forward. The woman cursed and leaned back. Francis and the other lad nearly fell, but grabbed at the sides of the wagon well enough to hold on.

"It's easier if you don't," Francis said. He leaned forward and got a grip on the reins, pulling them back. The team faltered.

I reached below the hems of my skirts and pulled out the knife I kept beneath the seat, a dagger with a five-inch blade. I'd spent my life around all manner of blades and guns—my family were renowned weapon-smiths, if you recall—and had more than a facility with them. Swaine had been reluctant to allow me to acquire and carry such a blade—a practitioner of the arts was a cut above needing such things, he insisted—but had relented once I'd demonstrated that I could handle a blade far better than he could. I pushed Francis away with my hand that held the reins. "Back off, right now."

He leaned back, out of my reach. "The butterfly has a stinger," he said. I swung the blade around and thrust the tip at him. He leaned back farther.

"Kate, you could make this easier for all of us," Francis said. He kept out of reach. I spun and flashed the steel at the one closest. Another climbed into the back of the wagon. They were on three sides of me, so I stood up and sliced the blade through the air in a wide arc. One of them laughed—which infuriated me.

"Put it down, one-eyed butterfly." I glanced over to the woman and saw her pointing a pistol at me. "Pistol wins."

I stood still. The woman came closer, the pistol trained on my head, the black opening of the barrel fixing me with its terrible stare.

"I'd do as she says," Francis said. With a grunt of frustration, I flung the blade into the back of the wagon where it stuck in, blade-first, vibrating. Francis smiled. "There we are—was that so difficult?"

The closest lad peeled the reins from my hand, and I had to let him. Francis motioned for me to climb down. "You were terrified, but you put up a good fight. The robbers overpowered you. Gruff men. Indifferent to your pleas. You barely escaped."

He stepped aside, even offering me a hand down. I ignored it. The woman came closer, still aiming the pistol at me.

"And just in case you think it might be wise to reveal what you know," Francis said, "don't. We know where you live. We'll come for you, and your master. That's a promise."

"I don't like it," the woman said.

"Kate here is smart. Feisty. She'll know what to do, and what not to do. Because all she's going to have to do is go to the river in Cambridge tomorrow morning—and she'll have her wagon back. Everything untouched. Nothing could be simpler."

Nothing could have been worse. Even if they were willing to abandon the wagon, I had little faith that all the goods in the back—the crate from Robert Twelves' shop, in particular—would still be there come dawn. Worse, there would be nothing simple about walking back to Salem and telling Swaine that his shipment had been stolen, and I'd let it happen. No, it wasn't simple.

"We should tie her up," the woman said. "Or, better yet, shoot her."

That was all I needed to hear. Without waiting, I turned and shoved my hands in her face. I whispered a spell of translocational manipulation. The words set in motion a pendulum back in my room at the manse, the entrained planar forces of which connected with the small ingot of iron in my pocket. A focused ripple of energy ought to have knocked the gun from her hands. Instead, a blinding glare erupted, wavering like sunlight through icy water. Magic spilled from my outstretched hands—much stronger than I'd anticipated, much stronger than I could control. My entire body vibrated with the force of the energy.

She cried out and flew backward a dozen feet as though a cannonball had slammed into her. She grunted as she hit the ground, snow plowing up behind her. The pistol slid beneath a patch of chokeberry bushes. She tried to get to her feet, but with the barest of thoughts, I lifted her into the air, then bashed her to the ground again. Her limbs splayed as she struggled.

I fell to one knee with a powerful wave of vertigo, nausea filling my throat and setting my skin to crawling. For a moment, my bones burned like red embers. The air around me vibrated, the ground stirred. Still crouching, I stared at the light spilling from my palms: it danced around the woman. Her eyes were wide and her mouth worked, but no words came out. Her limbs shook. I felt like I could crush her with just a thought. The spell seemed to whirl further out of my control, knocking snow off of the hemlocks that rose over her, swaying the branches, cracking some of them.

"Jesus Christ," one lad in the wagon said.

I inhaled, trying to properly end the spell, turning to Francis and the others. "Go. Now."

Francis made the mistake of reaching for me, apparently still seeing nothing but a girl.

"*Ignis in florem et ramos choro,*" I said. With an arcing wave of my hand, licks of flame appeared on the clothing of Francis and the two other lads, sprouting in strips. Before they could even react, the flames grew, bright petals unfolding along their limbs

—much more fire than I'd intended. As I knew from my own studies, nothing quite grips one's attention like the sight and heat of fire blossoming upon your clothes, and in an instant the three of them were dancing, staggering, and beating wildly at themselves. I stood up, buffeted by waves of energy. Turning to the two lads still in the wagon, I redirected the spell I'd used on the woman.

They careened over the walls, landing hard on the road. I didn't waste a moment, leaping into the driver's bench and sending the team off with a yell and a crack of the reins. I didn't glance back until the horses were at full speed. My head spun from the force of the spells. I had to steady myself as I craned back over my shoulder. Francis stood in the midst of the lane, staring after me, his coat and breeches smoldering. Smoke wrapped the scene. The other two lay on the ground, having extinguished the flames by rolling about in the snow. The woman was prone, likely stunned and sore.

For all the practicing I'd done under Swaine's supervision, I'd never used that much magic with no preparation before. My hands trembled and my chest hitched as I worked to calm myself. The surrounding energy lingered, flashes of light trailing from my hands, streaks of it stretching out behind me like tatters of silk. The figures in the road shrunk and then disappeared from sight as I rounded a curve. I glanced at the dagger, still embedded in the back of the wagon, vibrating with the roll of the wheels. My master was right—a practitioner of the arts needed no other weapon.

I thought of what the woman had said as she'd pointed the pistol at me. She'd been wrong.

"Magic wins," I whispered.

17

NO UNNECESSARY MAGIC

Yes, I shouldn't have done it in the first place.

That realization sunk guiltily into my bones from the moment I lost sight of Francis and the others. Magic was forbidden and I'd just given a wild demonstration of it to four people, exactly none of whom had my best interests in mind. What a fool I was. But it didn't stop there, for I kept it from Swaine.

Relentless remorse, shame, and worry haunted me from that day forward.

Swaine had been so exuberant at the arrival of the long-awaited crate from the clockmaker that he didn't notice either the guilt in my eye, or the residue of magic that clung to me. I was too frightened to tell him. After a long and fitful night of fretting while hard rains lashed the windows, I'd risen with the dawn, determined to come clean to him with the entire story—only to find him in a thunderous mood, having discovered that one of the mechanisms within the device from Twelves had been damaged in transit. I balked, sensing he'd not only be livid at what I'd done, but trebly so since I'd spent the afternoon and evening of the day before feigning that all was normal.

Every time I passed by a window in the manse, my gaze turned to the distant lane, half-expecting to see a quartet of figures approaching. Or a company of scarlet-coated regulars from the Governor's Own Regiment, sent to investigate the rumors of magic near—or in—the vicinity of old Salem. All the while, I ran through the unpleasant possibilities over and over, as though committing them to memory.

Concentration? Out of the question.

While Swaine moaned and growled as he struggled with the new device, I retreated to my room, hoping to lose myself in my studies. It didn't work. As I sat at the small table in the corner, staring at the *spirit-tablet* before me, all I saw was Francis and the others, clothing scorched, bringing the entire story to a local constable. Or a Regimental officer in Boston. Or to Doctor Rush himself.

I wondered if Swaine noticed how much I was using the privy.

Still, I had to put it out of my head. I double-checked that I sat within the proper glamour and tried—again—to attend to the spirit-tablet. I dipped the nib of the small quill into the enchanted ink and set it into the planchette. Closing my eye, I whispered the proper phrases and detected a disturbance of energy above the tablet. Engaging in such automatic-writing was to be a first step in my mastering summoning proper, channeling into the unseen world while surrounded by protections: the expectation was that I would familiarize myself with the guile of demons.

I placed my fingertips lightly on the edge of the sheet of paper tacked to the tablet. Ripples of magic ran up my fingers. As Swaine had instructed, I closed my eye and focused my attention on the energy. When my mind wandered (and oh how it wandered), I tugged it back. For ten grueling minutes, I herded my restless thoughts back to the energy, over and over, a busy shepherd with a headstrong flock. Nothing happened. I didn't hear the quill scratching the paper. The planchette remained still. Of course, the harder I tried to concentrate, the more my mind squirrelled off in some other direction. Images from the day before elbowed their way to the forefront of my thoughts: the dark within the barrel of the pistol as the woman raised it to me; the charming smile on Francis' lips, white teeth and the stubble on his chin; the flames erupting over their clothes as magic coursed from my hands; the desperate sinking feeling in my stomach as their intentions became—

The flames. Why had they been so intense?

My thoughts snapped back to the spell I'd cast. I opened my eye. The paper on the spirit-tablet was free of a single mark of ink, the planchette exactly where I'd placed it. So much for that. I pulled my hands back and folded my arms, chewing at the corner of my lip. The spell I'd used—*Fire, Bloom and Dance*—should have traced burning embers across their clothing, sprouting a few flames here and there, no greater than burning candle wicks. Among the fire-based incantations, it was as tame as could be, designed to frighten, not immolate. Had I confused the spell with its more dangerous version, *Fire, Seek and Destroy*? I'd studied both—and was certain I'd mastered the difference.

Getting up from my table, I searched through the books on the small shelf I'd set up until I found Arthur Fish's *Principles of Elemental Manipulation*, from which I'd learned the spell. (Fish's work had sparked the great renaissance of English magic at the turn of the 17th Century, a flourishing that lasted half a century before the hidden arts were declared illegal by Oliver Cromwell and his supporters, a condition that continued even after restoration of Charles II to the throne in 1660.) I flipped open the book and worked my way through the various ribbons I'd used as place-markers until I found the two variants of the spell. As I re-read the incantation for *Fire, Bloom and Dance*, I was certain that I'd cast it correctly: *Ignis in florem et ramos choro*. No mistaking it; if I'd cast it once, I'd cast it dozens of times.

The more powerful version of the spell was entirely different, requiring a complex incantatory stanza that began with the phrase *Ignis quaerunt et sic repente praecipitas* and continued on through a jaw-cracking range of syllables that I'd struggled to scale properly even under the best of circumstances, let alone in the midst of an ambush with a gun pointed at my head. No, I hadn't accidently blurted the wrong spell—I was certain of it.

I leaned back from Fish's book, frowning. It didn't make any sense. I turned back to the spirit-tablet and froze.

NO PENDANT

The letters flowed out from the tip of the nib, a spidery stream of ink wound through the fibers of the paper, apparently having seeped out with no sound as I'd flipped back and forth through the two spells in the book. I blinked. *No pendant?* I reached up and felt the solid comfort of the pendant hanging between my collarbones: my protection against demons. I approached the spirit-tablet.

"You'd like that, wouldn't you?" I said, with no intention of listening to a demon's suggestion.

The planchette moved, spinning as the quill traced out one small letter after the next in a jittering line of ink.

BEHOLD

I sat back at the table and placed my fingertips onto the proper spots, glancing about the room. Bed, books, lantern, wardrobe, window, all as they should be. No signs of a demon, no signs of any disturbance whatsoever. By that point in my studies, I knew well enough the aggrandizing self-regard of demons— each, apparently, with a magnificent or terrible or devastating beauty to go along with their ferocity and might—to dismiss any such claims without undue worry.

"I don't see much, demon," I said. I steeled myself for the planchette to whip across the page or scrawl jagged lines or rip the paper itself as the demon lashed out the only way it could, as I'd witnessed in earlier sessions. Instead, it remained still. "And I'm not taking off my pendant, thank you very much."

No movement. Curious.

"Tell me your name," I said, getting right to the heart of the matter. The names of demons: more rare than gems, the key to sorcery. And the last thing a demon would reveal. But as the spirit-tablet was designed to safely—for the most part—observe the behavior of demons, it was among the questions Swaine expected me to explore.

As the seconds ticked by, I wondered if I'd lost the connection through poor concentration. The planchette remained motionless.

"Hello?" I said.

It moved and as it did, strong little tides of energy lapped at my fingers. The ink trailed the quill and I watched the letters form: *GIN*.

A knock at my door startled me.

"Finch," Swaine said, pushing open the door not half a second after knocking, as was his habit. (I'd learned to dress with my back to the door after one unfortunate such entrance months earlier; an event that mortified Swaine far more than me, to be clear. Still, he was quite incapable of taming his impatience when he had something on his mind.) "There you are."

I kept my fingertips on the spirit-tablet. The planchette stopped. "Practicing, sir."

"Yes, you may continue that later. We've work to do." He looked down at the paper. "A demon with a taste for gin. Can't say I've ever tried it, a decision reinforced in stark relief by the besotted wretches I've met who claimed it magnificent. Sagging faces, blood-shot eyes, grimacing mouths and all."

I closed off the incantation with a hurried whisper and stood. "Perhaps the demon is curious anyways, sir."

"Careful. The point of this exercise it to learn *not* to ascribe reflexive motives to demons, Finch. Observe. Note. Learn. Never forget that the unspoken—yet truest—story of sorcery is the story of sorcerers being killed by the demons they tried to best. It's why there have never been many sorcerers."

He often graced my lessons with such motivational statements.

Swaine continued, "From the most tentative novice being torn apart by a suddenly unbound demon, to a wily practitioner such as the great Wilhelm Schwarzhgut, rightly considered the greatest practitioner of the art in the last century, falling prey to the subtle entreaties of a demon he'd had bound to his will for nearly four decades, there is really no compelling argument to make for a person desirous of a long life to pursue sorcery. And if you think the danger ends there, it doesn't. Some planar entities have proven themselves so spiteful that even after their summoner has been flayed, tortured, and obliterated, they've continued to wreak their horror on the region wherein they'd been bound. The bleak haunting of the Bábolna Forest in the Kingdom of Hungary in the late Fifteenth Century. The infamous disappearance of an entire village near the townland of Lusmagh in King's County in Ireland a century later, attributed to the Devil of the Three Rivers. There are other noteworthy examples, but I trust you get the point."

The words *tentative novice* struck me more deeply than talk of places I'd never heard of, doomed by sorcery or not, but if Swaine registered my guilt in any fashion, he didn't spare it a second thought. "Yes, sir," I said.

"I understand well the early days of learning: the joy, and the freedom, and the intoxicating possibilities. You're gaining confidence—driven more by enthusiasm than talent, believe me—and beginning to think of yourself as a *sorcerer*." He crossed his arms in front of his chest and watched me, making me wonder exactly what he knew, or suspected. "But note well that the unseen arts are exceedingly hard to do well. There is your perception of your talents, and there is what is true, and unless you keep those both firmly aligned, you will make no progress worth discussing.

Splashing in the shallows while calling yourself a genuine practitioner of the arts is as trivial as pointless. No, the real merits are found when you abandon illusions, delusions, and confusions. All that is required is hard work, and sacrifice."

He turned and bade me to follow him.

"Sacrifice, sir?" I said, with one final look at the spirit-tablet as I hurried after him.

"Sacrifice. You can enjoy a life of simple pleasures and little accomplishment, or pursue the art. If you choose the latter, you must sacrifice the former. Trust me on that, Finch." He didn't slow at top of the stairs, nor at the bottom, heading through the entryway and out the front door. "Poring over crumbling books and burning your fingers while seemingly everyone else in the world is enjoying dinner or sleeping soundly is but a portion of the price we pay. And for our efforts, the art will then reveal itself to be harder still. You will realize that what the greatest sorcerers accomplished is so rare that you will question if it's even possible for you to be one-tenth as good as they were, let alone ever stand shoulder to shoulder with them."

He had to have known what I'd done—I was sure of it. Why else would he offer such a lesson? "That makes it sound so—well, futile, doesn't it, sir?"

"Only to the unambitious. Embrace the true challenge and you'll come to appreciate the art for what it is. Sometimes confounding, often impossible. Mistake, after mistake, after mistake. False starts and dead ends enough to make you question your talent, your judgement, your commitment. Listen closely: mistakes are your best teachers. Unless they kill you."

I swallowed. Was he expecting a confession? One burbled up behind my lips.

Swaine pushed open the door to the barn and paused. "Sorcery will break your heart, Finch—yet in the midst of that heartbreak, it may just give you enough glimpses of the numinous to allow you to bear it. Now if I haven't frightened you off, we have

work to do. I haven't given up on the device from the exception-
ally talented Mr. Twelves. Come."

Frightened me off? Was it just another discouragement-in-
the-name-of-encouragement lecture? After all, he'd mentioned
nothing of spells, fire, errands, lying, hiding, deceiving. His mood
was light again. No, he didn't know. I swallowed back down my
confession and followed him into the barn.

The resonance clock sat lengthwise on the workbench,
polished pine shaped like a two foot tall longcase clock, two
keyholes on the front, and an inside containing gears, springs, a
pendulum, and silvered chambers. Ingenious combinations of
magic and sorcery imbued the internal pins of silver and steel
with the power to create immense planar manipulations capable
of clearing a vast stretch of planar fields in one go. Swaine
approached it and put a knuckle to his chin.

"It should work now," he said.

"You fixed it."

"I'm not sure Mr. Twelves would approve of my handiwork.
His touch with a mechanism such as this is sublime, while mine
could best be described as crude and ungainly, but it ought to do.
What say we test it?"

Relief lightened my shoulders—this had been on his mind
the whole time. "Of course, sir. In the village?"

Swaine shook his head. "Good Lord, what are you thinking?
This is a test, Finch. A proof of concept—although if you'd care to
haul it into the old town and set it off, I'd be keen to hear how it
goes, should I ever see you again. Which I wouldn't."

I nodded.

"No, the orchard will do. The far side of it," he said. He
shrugged on his coat—the tattered one I'd convinced him to
dedicate to the barn—and threw back half a cup of tea, another
splash into the great ocean of tea he consumed throughout the
days. He pulled a heavy steel skeleton key from his pocket and
handed it to me. "Fetch the almshouse bunch."

The *almshouse bunch* was Swaine's shorthand for the group of revenants who had showed themselves to be useless, the result of unsuccessful attempts at refining his techniques. Unlike the more recent revenants capable of such feats as balancing on a peaked roof—there was one young lad on the barn roof even then, a planar weathervane sensitive to any incursions of demons from the nearby environment, turning every quarter of an hour, night and day—or of setting a table with service for a multi-course meal with nary a chipped glass or the clank of silverware, appearing as normal (if a little wan) household servants to any but the most discerning eye, the almshouse bunch was confined to the dark corner of the stable, seated on the floor, shoulder to shoulder, in silence.

Rather than sever the demons from the corpses, Swaine held onto those revenants for the sake of research. I hated being around them whenever my duties brought me out to the stable— I found them distressing, for various reasons—but when I'd asked if they could be moved, Swaine had pointed out that leaving them exposed to the weather would wear out their clothing and force us to see even more of them. He also expressed concerns over how their presence might draw further entities in, and he decided that they were safer in the stable, obscured behind several glamours.

While Swaine readied the resonance clock, I entered the stable and stopped short of the lines of protection that ran across the floor, keeping the revenants in their place. I'd assisted my master in those incantations, my work having imbued the mixture of ash and iron filings with the proper energies to contain the revenants. The technique was from a branch of magical science known as *harmonic shadow control*, which involves the manipulation of the many subtle orders of energy that matter generates; by focusing and filtering the various echoes and harmonics of these energies, materials can be manipulated to great effect. As the incantor, I had a particular sensitivity to it, and the lines of energy shone like delicate weavings that underpinned the lines of filings.

I stopped just on the other side and wrapped my fingers around the skeleton key warded with sorceries that would allow me to give commands to his revenants when I activated it. It could only be used by me. If any other individual were to come across it, it was simply a steel key with no matching lock.

I passed one hand over it and muttered *"Wigcræftigne wordum."*

The almshouse bunch, all six of them, turned their heads from the shadows of the stable corner. I stepped back.

"Get up. Outside."

They rose and shuffled out of the corner. First came the body of a thin, toothless man whose revenation (which had proceeded without note, at the time) left the body with a pronounced tremor of the limbs: his head nodded non-stop, as though he were desperately agreeing to whatever were taking place. Behind him came a middle-aged woman in a velvet burial dress (she collapsed on cycles of seven and thirty-one hours, the demon requiring up to two hours to manipulate the corpse again). Then a young man who, after being made a revenant, had burned his hands down to the bones in the kitchen hearth (I'd been the one to discover him, extinguishing him before the rest of his clothing caught fire). A pox-scarred young man with yellowed skin who moved with an uneven gait and couldn't cross any threshold that had been glamoured (Swaine had tried several solutions, none of which worked and he'd eventually given up, claiming he'd made a mess of the various wards, glyphs, and incantations). Next came a young woman whose presence caused any glass near her to shatter, for reasons that baffled Swaine. (Again, the revenation had appeared normal, and in fact Swaine had remained convinced for some time that the demon bound within was simply carrying on. Still, no matter how many variations of commanding it to cease he gave it, the shattering continued.

Given the delicacy of our work—not to mention the cost of new glassware and window panes—the revenant remained with the others.)

Lastly came a brown dog we'd found on a rainy November wagon ride back from Boston. The unfortunate creature had been run down by a horse, and had been dying in the lane when we came upon it, its back broken. I'd made the mistake of pitying it and asking Swaine if we might do something for it. He'd helped me to lift the wounded animal into the back of the wagon, and rode with it back to Salem. It had died before we reached the manse—but my master's curiosity had been piqued. He spent that night attempting to revenate the dog. While I'd feared that the dog's broken back would render the revenant useless, it had loped about in a loose and frightful manner, staring at Swaine with its tongue lolling from its mouth. Unfortunately, the revenant dog had frequently wandered onto the furniture of the manse, on tables, on beds, often tumbling down the stairs. It had taken to scraping and padding its way, at night, to a spot right outside the door of my room, and remaining there, its presence invariably waking me up and filling me with a nameless fear. Swaine agreed that it was unacceptable. (He felt it was because the dog couldn't wear a glamoured ring, and instead wore it on a collar around its neck.) He'd finally given up on it and banished it to the stable.

I led this frightful parade out from the stable and around to the snow-dusted orchards that extended out along the back of the property. We passed through an opening in an ivy-covered stone wall, the rotted remains of old trellises still reaching up on both sides. The morning had warmed, lending the air a partic-ular softness, notable because the weather around the manse grounds had been deep within the grip of early winter, with two large storms in the past week alone. Swaine had charged me with making a detailed record of the unpredictable weather fluctua-tions around Salem, which I kept in a large book of blank tables, making note of wind and other conditions, using a mercury thermometer and barometer that my master had had shipped from Amsterdam. While the autumn's worth of record-keeping had revealed no discernable pattern to the variations—which included a fourteen-inch snowfall overnight in early October, and an evening of humid thunderstorms with screaming winds in the first week of December—both Swaine and I were certain that there was, in fact, a pattern within the chaos that would reveal itself, eventually.

Swaine carried the resonance clock out ahead of the revenants and me, placing the device on the ground in an open spot beyond the last row of crooked apple trees. He motioned. "Line them up. Intervals of twenty paces or so. They'll be drawn to the resonance well, and this should give us some information from which to calculate the effect of distance."

I directed the revenants to form a rough line leading away from the instrument, positioning them one by one across rows of the old orchard. Once I returned, Swaine crouched in front of the device, holding it open to reveal a keyhole in the center. To either side, open chambers held gears, most delicate, but two of stout design, amongst the weights, pendulum and anchor, and escapement gears that mirrored each other. Set into one end of the device was a compass. Swaine double-checked that the device was aligned North to South. He pulled a smaller compass out of his coat pocket and confirmed the alignment. In the spaces beyond the double gearing were two chambers—larger versions of the containment chambers in his earlier experiments with the planar clocks, sealed with thin layers of metals that went beyond the simple lead or silver of the smaller devices: copper, bronze, tin, lead, silver, and gold in mathematically unequivocal arrangements, again mirrored, one set in each chamber.

He closed both doors. They clicked shut with the mechanical elegance that was Twelves' hallmark.

"There we are," Swaine said. "Nearly ready."

In each corner, a cylindrical chamber extended through the depth of the device, walled in polished silver and containing a narrow candle poured around wicks subjected to days' worth of incantations. Twelves had designed hinged covers for them, punched through with enough holes to allow proper airflow to feed the flames.

"I'd say it's time," Swaine said. He slid the key into the keyhole and turned it. I could see that the springs engaged. The movement was smooth, measured. Once, twice, each wind gaining more resistance, storing more energy. "A dozen will do us."

He continued on until he hit the final wind. He placed his hand on the front of the device and lifted out the key. "This little catch will release it." He pointed to a cone-like button that protruded from the metal next to the keyhole. "Once the flames are lit, we shall have a quarter of an hour."

He waved his hands over the resonance clock and said "*Ignis.*" The four candles sprung to flame, each a different hue as fitting the harmonic bindings imbued within: pale yellow, greenish blue, red, and the deep orange of sunset. He leaned over and closed each of the covers, *click click click click.* Straightening, he checked his pocket watch and looked at the device. Gears turned in a refined, mechanical orchestration. "We shall observe from a safer spot."

We made our way to a small promontory past the edges of the orchard and hunkered within a circle of protection that Swaine had put there months earlier, after one too many incursions by unexpected entities—one of half a dozen safe spots across the property. The line of revenants stretched away from the device, the furthest one well over one hundred yards from our vantage point. Nearest the device, the toothless man looked as though he was listening to a music box, nodding along.

"What will we see, sir?"

"I would expect the nearest revenants to be drawn to the clock, without question. Perhaps all of them. The demons should find the resonance well irresistible. Fascinating. Compelling. Needless to say, if we can safely lure some numbers of demons to one location, we may have a way to begin clearing the infestation of demons. A welcome turn of events." He consulted his watch. "Of course, it's possible that nothing at all will happen. Or the power involved may bring forth a quantity of unknown complications. For in sorcery, as with most endeavors, eliminating one set of problems often only serves to clear the decks for a new set. That's why we're back this far."

"And what if the resonance well touches the planar currents, sir?"

Swaine smiled. "Spoken like a budding planar cartographer. Fear not. The limits of the incantations remain well below such a threshold for just that reason."

"But the planar deviations can vary."

"They can. We should still be well within the prudent range, however."

"And if it peaks past that?"

"Fair question," he said, checking his watch. "Powerful planar magic inevitably risks side effects. Something along the lines of a flaring of *Flamme Zum Schießpulver*, or 'flame to gunpowder,' a potentially disastrous amplification of any and all spells. The unstable magic could expand in a massive wave. Quite fatal, in theory."

I closed my mouth.

Swaine nodded. "Now you see why we're doing it here and not in the heart of Salem."

"Is any of that likely?"

"We'll know in—" He looked at his watch. "Less than a minute." We both followed the sweep of the second hand. "And we begin in ten . . . five . . . one." He snapped the watch shut. After a moment, I sensed a change in the planes, and my attention heightened. A light tingle brushed my forehead, my nose, my shoulder blades. The air pressure changed. My ears popped as the air grew heavy, thick as if the storms of the night before had reappeared. The twisted branches of the trees knocked and bent.

"Displacement," Swaine said. "The air itself is reacting to the coiling of the planes."

As the energy grew, the forces coursing through the planes shocked me, powerful even from a distance. The muscles in my arms twitched and my stomach clenched. All across my face, a sensation of pinpricks. My hair whirled, getting in my eye, my mouth. Swaine scanned the scene before us.

"Yes. There." He pointed, and I followed his finger. In the air above the resonance clock, a swirling darkness bled out of nothing. The wind rose, and the shadow turned, growing larger. "Take a good look, Finch. What we're seeing is the controlled intersection of this world with several others. A resonance well, the winding in, winding down, and braiding of channels of planar force."

I gaped at it. Even as I stared, a thin line of darkness, like a handful of strings wound more and more tightly together, extended up into the sky. Twenty feet, fifty, one hundred, higher. It looked as though a portion of the sky tore. Swaine appeared thrilled, but the sight and sensation weighed me down with a primal terror.

"By setting up the proper resonance, we're coiling all the currents in this spot, linking them together for the duration of the running of the clock," Swaine said.

Several faint streaks of light appeared in the black above the clock, shining with the strange colors of the will-o'-the-wisp: grave-mold green, coffin-rot gray, death blue. The revenants shuddered. Trees swayed, and stray leaves spun like sparrows on the wind. Long tendrils of light stretched out from the opening, quickly extending hundreds of feet in length, rising up and up and up. The strange beauty of it held my gaze. All around the orchard, wind rose.

Next to the resonance clock, the toothless man shuddered, his head swaying side to side. Swaine pointed. "Do you see? The demon can't resist the draw of the planar currents."

"The next one is coming over, sir." The woman who collapsed too often shuffled in the direction of the device, her neck craned up to take in the shadows and light overhead. As the winds strengthened, the air crackled. A flash of lightning burst from the funnel of dark energy rotating over the orchard. A knot of fear tightened in my stomach. "How soon until it closes, sir?"

The clock held delicate brass hammers, each with a precise load of force, each poised to shatter a thin glass rod. The rods held incantatory charms, the proper combination of which would counter the initial spells, diffusing the surge of power that wound the planes. In theory, the other planes would return to their more common state. My master looked at his watch, then at the revenants nearest the device.

"Another seven minutes." Even as far back as we were, trees moved, dropping their dustings of snow, filling the air with whirling streaks of powder. The snow on the ground came alive, fine plumes racing over the contours of dell and rise.

"Should it be this windy, sir?" I raised my voice over the hisses and shrieks.

"Possibly." Swaine squinted at the far-off device, a note of uncertainty in his voice. "As the pressures equalize, the—"

As he spoke, the toothless man and the collapsing woman flew into the air, sucked into the shadows of the resonance well like scarecrows into a whirlwind. Further along the rows of the orchard, among the snapping branches of the leafless apple trees, the other revenants tumbled, slid, hurtled toward the device, cart-wheeling, crashing into gnarled trunks and being yanked free by the most violent winds I'd ever witnessed. None were spared. From all corners flew broken branches, dervishes of snow, old leaves. Stones and old fence rails careened into the center. One tree after another broke apart with the crack of muskets.

Above us, the twining shadows and light reared ever higher,

widening. My every nerve clanged with alarm as the forces crashed over me in wave after wave. Numbness, tingling, vertigo, nausea fought for dominance—yet I couldn't look away. Beyond the colors, I caught glimpses of depth, of structures, slate rooftops at dusk, stone passages, iron staircases. A world beyond.

"No—this is all wrong," Swaine said.

"But look inside it, sir."

"Look away, Finch."

"Stairs, a rooftop—"

"Finch!"

I turned to him. The panic on his face had the effect of a bucket of icy water splashing over me—I'd never seen him look frightened, not like that. He got up from his crouch, his hair whipping into his face, the edges of his jacket thumping like a flag in a gale. "I have to stop it before it destroys the clock!"

"But it's going to shut itself off, isn't it?"

"Not if it's smashed." He stepped out of the glamoured circle, struggling to stay upright against the winds that roared down into the orchard. Below, the brown dog spun up into the breach in the sky, disappearing into darkness. I couldn't see any of the other revenants—they were all gone. Beneath the towering darkness, the resonance clock spun back and forth, lifted off the ground by the strange energies and winds.

Swaine broke into a sprint, each step sending up a spindrift of snow racing along beside him. He tripped and spilled forward, then scrambled to his feet again, staggering down the hillside. Not knowing what to do, I ran after him. He shouted something, but in the maelstrom, I couldn't catch it. The entire landscape screamed with wind and snow, making it difficult to see, to find my footing. I ran as fast as I dared, my dress acting like a sail in hurricane, sending me headlong after my master.

A pair of trees near the resonance clock tore from the earth, root and branch, flying up into the breach. As I followed Swaine's already-fading footsteps through the snow, I struggled to keep

track of him. Patches of his worn-jacket flashed through the gusts
of flying snow ahead of me. I was hit on the back of my head by a
branch as thick around as my wrist, sending me sprawling. Grabbing my head, I resumed the chase.

By the time I reached Swaine, the disturbance spun overhead,
filling my ears with a deafening rumble. Magic snapped across
my skin, my clothing, the remaining tatters of trees. Swaine had
his arms wrapped around the resonance clock—which continued
to rise into the air, taking him along with it. I reached up and
grabbed the hem of his coat, holding him to the ground as best
I could.

"Drop," Swaine grunted. "Shatter. Now. Come on."

A deafening peal of thunder ripped across the sky, directly
above us, powerful enough to rumble the ground. As the noise
ended, the echoes of it fading out over the harbor, we crashed to
the ground in a heap, Swaine atop me, the resonance clock atop
him. The collapse drove the air from my lungs. After a moment's
struggle, Swaine rolled off me, panting as he set the device on its
side. Keeping his hands on it, he hung his head.

"It released, thank God," he whispered. All around us, the
orchard filled with the soft patter of twig and branch falling back
to earth, muffled in the snow. "I couldn't have held on for more
than a few more moments."

The towering darkness had vanished. The winds rippled out
from us, dying down.

"It's gone, sir?"

He nodded, gulping in air, exhausted. "Resonance well
released. Planes separating, retreating. Back to prime locations."

I stood up and helped him to his feet, dusting the snow from
my skirts, from his shoulders. "Where did they go? The
revenants?"

"I've no idea—but they're gone." He eyed the resonance clock
warily. "I'd call it an unalloyed success if we hadn't very nearly

torn a hole in the world capable of taking us, along with half of Salem, into it. Disastrous."

I shuddered—it was all too easy to imagine the worst, having been so close to not reaching him in time. "Do you know what went wrong, sir?"

"Something between anything and everything. The device. My fix to the device. The incantations I chose. The location I selected. The alignment of the planes. All of it. None of it." He shook his head. "So much for my little victory speech."

Knowing he wasn't going to rest until he'd at least narrowed down the causes of the failure, I said, "I'll get you food, sir. And tea—the strong kind. If there's anything I can help you with, I'll do that, too."

He reached up and rested a hand on my shoulder. "You reacted quickly, Finch. If you hadn't been holding me down—I can't bear to think what might have happened."

As we gathered up the resonance clock, Swaine waved his hands across the front of the device, adding a quick seal to protect it as he carried it back to the workshop. It was then I glanced to the sky and noticed something strange. Where there ought to have been nothing, there were three long lines, forty or fifty feet above us—they looked like imperfections in glass, smooth crystalline fractures that stretched up for hundreds of feet. As I moved my head, viewing them from different angles, I saw that they caught the fading sunlight strangely.

"Master." I pointed to the sky. "What are those?"

He craned his neck, shading his eyes. "What am I looking for?"

"Those lines, sir."

"Where?"

"Just above us."

He narrowed his eyes. "All I see are the bloody spots in my vision. Are you talking about that blur?"

"No—they're—some kind of magic. Or energy." The longer I

looked, the stranger it appeared. Thin strands stretched out in several directions, thin as gossamer, as though some portion of the sky had cracked. A curious light-headedness gripped me and I had to take a step to keep my balance.

Swaine scanned the sky for a few moments, not looking pleased. With a glance at his watch, and a few quick incantations, he was still no closer to figuring it out. He leaned back, his hands on his waist. He shook his head.

"I don't like it, not one bit," he said. "We must be extra-cautious until we have a better sense of what's going on here. The planar energies are far more complex than I'd anticipated—dangerously so. So from now on, no unnecessary magic. No more summoning. Nothing. Not until we know better what we're dealing with. We might not be able to snuff out the next fuse in time."

He hefted the resonance clock and started back to the manse. I took another nervous look at the peculiar deformation in the sky, and hurried after him, my worries over my mistake the day before glowing white hot again.

No unnecessary magic.

18

LIES OF A MOST MANIPULATIVE NATURE

Well I'd of course done more unnecessary magic than my master could imagine, the knowledge of which haunted me without respite. I jumped at every shadow. Corpses, demons, the strange defect that hung in the sky over old Salem—those barely registered. Would I return to the site of my mistake to find a smoldering hole in the sky? Ghostly fires that couldn't be smothered? Constables? Whitelocke regulars? Swaine himself, furious at discovering my lie?

Making matters worse, my master wanted me to ride to Andover in the morning, hoping for the arrival of another shipment from Mr. Winslow containing items pertinent to his efforts at identifying what had gone wrong with the resonance clock. I would have no choice but to go.

As dusk approached, a little voice inside treated me to an unhelpful commentary: *This is the final dinner before you're apprehended*, it said as I rushed through a bowl of soup and a crust of bread for dinner; *This is the last time you'll sleep outside of a jail*, it whispered as I lay in bed, quite unable to sleep.

It was a long night.

In the hour before the dawn, I crawled out of bed, dressed, and went to the stable. As I readied the horse and wagon, my fingers seemed dullards, slipping on the tack, refusing to buckle the bridle properly. My nerves did no better once I'd followed the lane through the forest. Three times in the growing twilight, I stopped the horse, ready to turn around and throw myself at Swaine's mercy. It was only when I decided that his anger and disappointment, in any imaginable proportion, would be worse than being placed under arrest that I resigned myself to my fate.

So on I rode, feeling weaker with each mile. My heart filled my mouth as I led the horse into Andover, each clap of his hooves, each creak of the wheels, each jingle of the harnesses seeming to break the early morning silence like the tolling of a bell. Each window stared out at me, the shadows inferring furious townsfolk watching my guilty progress. The lanes were obviously empty because the Governor's Own had ordered it so in order to apprehend me. The ring of a hammer ceased because someone had spotted me: *There she is, the one with the spells.* It was almost as though I were observing myself from half a dozen paces away, the hapless heroine in a puppet show, riding into folly.

I pulled the wagon to a halt. No citizens stepped from the doorways, muskets raised. No scarlet-clad regulars thundered down the lane on their stallions, shouting for me to freeze. Only a goat bleated from the field behind the stable of Knox's Inn & Tavern.

No point waiting: my mistake would either catch me, or it wouldn't. A fresh fall of snow made muffled crunches beneath my boots as I went to the door. I paused. *This is your last moment before they catch you.* I ignored the voice and pulled open the door. Warmth rolled out over me from the fire crackling in the hearth.

Iris knelt before the fire, settling logs with an iron poker. The public room was otherwise empty. She looked at me, startled— then she relaxed.

"Every time the door opens, I'm terrified," she said.

You look terrified because you used magic was what I heard. Then I realized what she'd really said. "Terrified?"

She leaned the poker against the side of the hearth. "Soldiers. The Governor's Own. They were just here an hour ago. They almost took Ethan away—thanks to his brother." She wiped her palm on her apron as though dirtied by the mention of her brother-in-law.

"Ethan?"

"Yes, Ethan. To jail. In Boston." She shook her head. "For being a Rattlesnake and plotting against the Governor."

"But he's not—is he?"

"No, of course he's not. He has a family. It's Francis. Who doesn't. Which is why he never gives a thought for family. Never listens, and now it's caught up with him. He's been arrested. Him and his friends. I knew it. I warned him. Ethan warned him. But all he ever has is more words. A well that never runs dry. And now he could hang for it. Ethan is beside himself."

Iris didn't look quite as bothered by the prospect.

"When did they arrest Francis?" I said.

"Yesterday. In Boston. And because they believe the poison spreads, they had to come up here and question Ethan for two hours. Rousted us out of bed. Babe squalling. They all had muskets. I was so frightened."

Nowhere near as frightened as I suddenly was: the four people who'd seen me do magic were now all in the custody of the Whitelocke government. I nearly retched. "That sounds terrible."

She shook her head. "It might turn out that way. Maybe it won't—maybe Francis will put his golden tongue to good use and talk his way out of it. Or the Governor will show mercy. Time in the stocks. A touch of public shame. Make a fool look a fool."

"Is he really a fool?" I said. He seemed quite the opposite of a fool to me.

"The worst kind: a smart fool. He could be a lawyer. A scholar. He could find a way to influence all the wrongs he frets over, if he was willing to lift a finger to reach his potential. Instead, he works at a printer's, setting type. Gives speeches in taverns. Skewers anyone who offends him. Thinks he has the right side of every argument—but he's a boy, inside. No responsibilities. No sense of family. No commitment." She straightened out chairs at the nearest tables. "And do you know where Ethan is—the complacent one, according to Francis? The frightful one? The wool-headed   dullard,   the   one   who   doesn't   care about *community* according to Francis? He's helping the pastor gather back his sheep after they got out. And after that he's going to help him rebuild his fence. That's what really matters. That's where a man's character shows."

Ethan was in all ways a decent man, yes. Francis was clearly the ne'er-do-well, again yes. But my mind was too busy doing math to hang on Iris' every word on the matter: if the Governor's Own had questioned the Rattlesnakes over the course of a night and gotten enough information to send men up to Andover looking for accomplices, then how soon until they heard—or pried out—the story of the fire spell? And how long would it then be before they sent riders to search the backroads of Andover? Or further afield? Would the name of Salem occur to any of them? To Doctor Rush, should he hear of it? Which he certainly would, as soon as a hint of magic was drawn from the Rattlesnakes' mouths.

My several days' worth of vague terror had gone from three minutes of blessed relief into a much more imaginable, detailed scenario leading to my imprisonment. I confess to not paying much attention to the rest of Iris' simmering anger at her brother-in-law as she showed me the latest shipment from Boston. The supplies Swaine wanted were among the goods, thankfully. I also found another letter from Mary Whitelocke.

Still, little of it made much impression on me as I practically heard the clang of iron bars in my future.

I was so lost in my worries that I missed the surprise—or was it?—appearance of Iris' brother Bertram as I carried the shipment to the wagon. Iris bade me farewell, claiming something or other needing tending on the second floor. Bertram watched from the doorway as I struggled with a wooden crate big enough to hold a pair of muskets (in fact, it contained six lengths of copper rods to be used in the modification of the resonance clock). After a moment, he lurched forward as though pushed by the memory of something Iris likely told him: *Give her a hand. Be helpful. Don't talk too much.*

"Here," he said. "Let me. You shouldn't carry that on your own."

"I can manage. It's not heavy."

"No—but it's awkward." He took one end of the crate, nearly managing to rip it from my hands. "I have quite an eye for awkward." His cheeks grew scarlet. "I didn't mean—I mean I can spot awkward. Poor choice of word."

"Because I only have one eye, Bertram?"

I didn't need a fire spell on him—he nearly combusted. Words escaped him, leaving him gaping like a fish pulled from a pond. Yet another distinction between him and Francis. Still, I didn't leave him dangling for too long. I wasn't cruel.

"It's fine. I only have one eye. I've only had one for fourteen years. I'm not ashamed."

He stumbled against the door. "No, of course not. Why should you be? I'm the fool. An eye for embarrassment. Both eyes, in my case."

I laughed in spite of myself. "You can just help me carry my things."

At the wagon, he slid the crate into the back. "Refreshing. No shame. Only pity for *my* shame. Here I am thinking you'd be mortified, but only because I'd be mortified. Only because I usually am mortified. One thing or another. It's my curse."

"There are worse curses to have."

"The eye?"

"Well."

"But you carry yourself with such—confidence."

"Hardly."

"Every time I've seen you. Confident. Capable. Like you've more than made up for only having one eye by seeing exactly what you're after. No hesitation."

"I suppose I don't think anyone's ever looking at me. The confidence of being invisible."

"Oh, you're not invisible. You make an impression. A good one."

"The only one-eyed lass around."

"It's not that. Though the patches are lovely. Exotic." The flush returned to his face, creeping up from his collar. "You just seem focused. Never confused. Or embarrassed. Or—talking far too much. Like I am."

He followed me back into the tavern as I retrieved the remaining packages: two sacks of dry goods, a wooden box packed with hay and metal gears, the letter from Mary White-locke. He carried the sacks for me.

"You never seem boring. Like me," he offered, setting them into the wagon. "Elected by my family to live with my grandfather and watch after him. He can't hear a thing. Which is fine, because I talk too much. But you—you're out and about, places to go."

"Chores to do," I said. "Errands to run. Not very different." Except for the demons. The tear in the sky. Witchcraft spilling from my hands. A fire spell that I shall rue. Wagonloads of dead bodies. And my impending jailing. All my secrets.

"Well you still manage it all far better than my uncoordinated stammering. We can be honest about that. No shame, remember."

I reached out and touched his arm. "You're kind to say so."

The surprise on his face at my hand resting on his arm lightened my mood. Sometimes a small pinch of gratitude was a potent ingredient, the key material in a powerful spell. I could have sent him to the ground with a kiss to his cheek, no doubt—but I resisted investigating the premise. Swaine would expect me back soon enough. I also still faced the possibility of being arrested *en route*. Tempting as it was to listen to Bertram's compliments—he appeared capable of more—I needed to face whatever lay in store.

"I hope I'll see you next time I'm in town," I said.

"Yes." The surprise hadn't lowered his eyebrows yet. I wondered if his words had all collided behind his lips. After a moment, he shook his head as though snapping himself out of a reverie. "Yes. I hope that as well. And if I can do anything to help you, such as carry things for you while embarrassing myself with one ill-chosen phrase after another, please don't hesitate to ask after me."

"An eye for embarrassing yourself."

"So they say, yes."

Bertram helped me up into the wagon and waved after me as I drove off from the tavern, wondering if I'd ever see him again.

BY THE TIME I reached Salem, the afternoon had turned bone cold beneath the blue sky. My cheeks ached from the wind. My eye watered. I hauled the supplies into the barn, glad to leave the wind outside. Seeing no sign of Swaine, I warmed myself with a kettle of tea and some rolls, then returned to my studies. In the corner of the barn stood a table holding an aqueometing device: a mechanism of brass, unstained oak, and curiously shaped blown-glass chambers. A quartet of arms extended from gearing in the center, driven by a pinion. Each arm ended in one of the glass chambers, and as the arms turned, each chamber passed beneath a glass quill that deposited a drop of water into it. It ticked at each turn of the clockwork, rotating the arms. The water dripped into the glass as the nearest chamber lined up beneath the glass quill. I approached it, halfway defeated already.

Through manipulating the device, I was learning the basic techniques of elemental energy control—the various uses of fire, air, metals, and liquids in transmorgative processes known as *transferent adaption*, which covered both simple alchemy and the more interesting use of recombinant elemental energies. In this instance, the energies extending out from the drops of water were supposed to be transferred to a larger scale, to fall from a glyph I'd scribed on the ceiling by the stables, resulting in a downpour of rain to be caught in a copper tub stationed there. The rain would *allegedly* be drawn from the source of the water I'd linked to the aqueometing device, which, in this case, was the well on the property. For all the attempts I'd made over several weeks, I'd yet to hear the patter of rain hitting thin metal.

"*Reiþ goþr Grana gvllmiþlandi, þars fostri minn fletiom styrþi; einn þotti hann þar ollom betri,*" I said. As with my earlier attempts, I struggled with the incantation itself, my concentration strained between the intent and the enunciation—resulting in a poor effort at both. The challenge was to be both relaxed and focused. Too tense, and my will choked. Too relaxed, and I bungled the words. I'd yet to find the proper balance.

There's no trick—only practice, Swaine had told me on more than one occasion.

Watching him do magic had the effect of witnessing a trick. I still searched for the *one thing* that would make it fall into place for me. I closed my eyes and circled my hand above the glass chamber, groping for that elusive point between effort and relaxed flow.

Again: nothing happened.

I lifted my hand away and frowned, shaking my head. The air

held the scent of smoke and flint, and acrid residues from my earlier study of elements. I reread my notes, held down on another worktable by a lead plumb. Next to it sat steel scribes, small glasses, and an inkwell. Across my small workbench lay books, some open, others in stacks, with places marked by corners of paper or old quills. I picked up Henry R.R. Gardener's *Transformative Processes of the Elemental Energies*, and scanned the list of incantations for transferent adaption, my finger tracing the musty page.

Water must be led, with nary a touch of forcing, the faded text read. *A firm sense of pull, and of gravity, are crucial—the conjurer must have these in abundance for the will to precede the flow.*

Swaine had taught me how to have a *sense of energy* that would lead the forces where I desired them to go. With fire, with iron, with stones, with breezes—I did well. Somehow those, I understood. I pictured in my mind a useful analogue of how to manipulate them. Fire and metal were the easiest. It had only taken me a week to learn how to light a wick, and after six more, I could bring a fully stocked candelabra to flame with a wave of my fingers and a whisper. Of course, as I'd shown with Francis and the others, I was capable of more than just that.

Metals each had a character I found intuitive, tactile—even silver, the most temperamental of them all. I showed what even Swaine admitted was impressive progress. A stone was, for me, a beautiful latticework, and the old stone walls that rode the edge of the property's ridge had sacrificed many fieldstones to my practice, the broken halves littering the ground in colors of iron, lead, and chalk, each one having sundered with a delicious *crack* that could often be as loud as a pistol shot.

But, water.

Water was my bane. Swaine insisted that while my hard-headed nature made me remarkably well-suited to cracking boulders, I'd need a good deal more humility and grace before water would register my bidding. As a consequence, he had me focusing on water four days out of each seven.

I hated it. The slosh of it. The idiotic splash. The way it sat there, testifying to my graceless nature, mocking me.

I put down Gardener, yet again. Before turning back to the aqueometing device, I gazed out the window. In the mid-afternoon sunlight, the deformation over the orchard rose like a cracked spire of ice, or an enormous lick of water that had become suspended and rigid.

Everything looked like water.

I whispered a curse. Swaine didn't care for demonstrations of frustration (those that weren't his own, leastwise). Frustration was to success in magic and sorcery as, well, water to a flame. His expectation was as clear as it was impossible: no matter how long I must practice, no matter how many times I'd need to run headlong into a wall, I must not complain. Complaints weren't reality —they were a rejection of reality and thus had no place in the pursuit of the unseen arts.

I placed my finger on the glass pane before me. The glass looked like a liquid. Like ice. But, it wasn't. I spoke a word from my stone studies, and delicate cracks unfolded like spider-legs around my fingertip. I pulled my finger back. It was as easy as water was impossible.

A shiver ran up between my shoulder blades. A demon lurked nearby. I instinctively touched the pendant I wore and looked about the room. A powerful set of glamours traced the edges of the floor and the corners of the walls, so I knew I was safe.

Annoyed, however. I looked unhappily at the door.

Not again.

I crossed the barn and swung the door open. A revenant stood so close that I suspected its nose had been touching the wood on the other side. It was the young woman whom Mr. Preston had brought up the week before, the one close to my age. It was the fourth time in as many days I'd found her nearby, staring and silent. This kind of nonsense had gotten worse since the work with the resonance clock; in fact, all the demons in the manse had grown agitated. Swaine had dismissed my concerns—after double-checking her bindings and my pendant—with the unamusing suggestion that she simply wanted to be my friend.

The demon was still in the phase of practicing her dexterity, walking the traditional routes around the manse while yet another revenant dealt with changing the obstacles. What she was doing standing in front of the door to the barn, I did not understand. Her hair was lank, the color of old wood, and her skin had the waxy pallor of death that never left the revenants. Her eyes were tarnished copper and she'd had a pretty face, with elegant cheekbones and a finely carved chin. In life, she might have been lovely; in death, she looked severe. Her infernal gaze met my eye. Was that a frown on her face? As I stared at her, I swore that I saw the hint of a tremor on her bottom lip.

"What are you looking at?" I motioned with my hands. "Go. Walk. Tumble. I don't care. Just go."

She ignored me. I didn't have Swaine's key. She—*it*—had no obligation to obey my command.

"Fine," I said. I turned and closed the door. "Stare at that all you wish."

Returning to the aqueometing device, I tried to focus my mind, but some part of me listened for the sound of the revenant leaving. She didn't. I tried to regain the proper state of mind. All I felt was my growing annoyance at the demon. So much for magic. I stomped back to the door and yanked it open.

"I said go—go. Right now, or I'll fetch your master," I said. Her dull stare disarmed me. I took a pair of steps toward her and put a hand to her breastbone. I shoved. It was always difficult to tell what a fresh revenant could tolerate, and it turned out she couldn't tolerate much. She tumbled backward, cracking the back of her head against the ground. Her limbs wriggled like serpents. She wasn't able to right herself.

"Please help me—I'm still alive," she croaked. Her voice was weak, and hoarse. She lifted a hand as if pleading. "Somehow. In here. With *it*."

"I rather doubt that," I said.

Her face collapsed in a mask of pure despair. Tears welled in the corners of her eyes. "I don't deserve this," she moaned, her chest hitching with sobs. "I was a good Christian. All I ever did was help my mother. How have I so offended the Lord?"

Never engage, Swaine had taught me, regarding the speech of demons. *You may rest assured that you'll find nothing but lies of a most manipulative nature. Even knowing full well such intent, the doubt they sow in your mind can be as difficult to remove as pine-pitch from your fingers.*

"You have a new lord now." I crossed out into the yard before the barn and hitched my wrists beneath her armpits and heaved her to her feet. Her bosom quivered with anguish.

"I'm in Hell." Her voice cracked. "Please, please—kill me. End this."

"Too late."

I steadied her and then moved her along by the shoulders until she was walking.

"You're the only one who will listen—please. Believe me," she whispered.

"Run along."

A cry of sorrow burst from her chest, but at least she kept walking.

I ignored what she's said and what she'd looked like saying it. The pity I felt was due to an illusion. I'd seen her corpse. Dead. It was deceit, those words of hers. Of *it*. As she shuffled off, a fall of powdered snow dusted me, sprinkling my hair and arm. I stepped away, irritated. Whirling snow spun from the barn roof. I shook my head at the irony of a demon having better luck at making something sprinkle down from overhead than I was having.

Back inside, I lost the better part of another hour failing, still, at water-based transferent adaption. I only broke my focus when I noticed something out of the corner of my eye, a movement outside the barn window. When I turned my head, I cursed. The female revenant stood outside the window, staring in at me. That was it. With my aggravation brimming over, I readied a ward to cast—I couldn't work like that. The demon would pay for its insolence. Just as I neared the window, I paused. The revenant lifted a hand to me.

But it wasn't her hand.

The pale shape of an arm and hand rose next to the revenant, and that's when I saw another figure superimposed atop—within —the dead lass. Faint, misty, unstable as a reflection seen on a slow moving river, a woman occupied the same space as the revenant. I stepped back, shocked: it was the same woman from Salem, the same one who'd appeared in Swaine's library, setting it alight.

She motioned. A thin voice floated in from the other side of the glass: "Take off your pendant. See."

As I looked, I grew dizzy, disoriented at seeing first the revenant and then a moment later the strange figure. Regardless, I certainly wasn't going to remove my pendant. Behind me, the door opened and Swaine walked in, wearing his dressing gown and boots, hair rumpled. He walked straight to the resonance clock, not even sparing me a glance, lifting up one of the openings to an inner chamber and shaking his head.

"Master—it's the apparition, sir."

Swaine ignored me. The woman beyond the panes motioned to her own throat, mimicking the gesture I'd make if I removed my pendant.

"Sir, she's—" I looked back at Swaine, but he was gone. The door was closed again. "Sir?"

With a glance at the figures outside the window, I stepped over to Swaine's workbench. For a moment, I thought the resonance clock had sprung a leak of some sort. Even knowing it contained no liquids didn't dissuade me of the impression. A dark spill seeped from the corner. Had my spell-work somehow have drawn well-water into it? That and other far-fetched possibilities—spilt tea, animal urine—crumpled as absurd as I stared at it. It was only then that I noticed the spill wasn't a liquid at all, but rather a distortion in the air itself, winding out from the corner of the clock. Warped and clear like an icicle, it grew longer as I watched, the thin end stretching and stretching.

From overhead came a series of thuds and the sound of objects sliding down the roof. I heard a trio of heavy thumps on the ground outside. I rushed to the barn door and shouldered it open. A head sat in the snow, eyes open and lifeless. Next to it, an arm. Further along the side of the barn, a leg. All from the revenant Swaine had made into a planar weathervane, sliced apart and tumbled from the peak of the barn. I stared at the body parts, open-mouthed.

Just then, the door to the manse banged open and Swaine hurried out, dressed now in breeches, a coat appropriate for the season, boots. "Into a protected circle—quickly!"

"The revenant, it fell from—"

"Finch!" He spoke the word like the bark of a musket, snapping me from my shock. I darted back into the barn, taking up a position between two column-beams, inside a glamoured circle. Swaine burst in after me. "Half my demons are trying to tear themselves free. The other half are baying."

"The clock, sir—something's happening to it."

Swaine pulled himself short, seeing the same curious windings of the space around the device. In the time I'd been outside, they'd grown, snaking out from each corner, the longest now nearly six feet in length, branching like tree roots.

"When did this begin?" Swaine said.

"Just after you left it."

"Left it?" He turned to me.

"A minute ago."

"I've been in my study all afternoon."

I looked from him to the door to the device. "But you were here. You walked in."

"I did no such thing."

"You did, sir."

"Finch?"

"I saw you—you were in your dressing gown. And boots."

He frowned. "What did you see—exactly? What happened?"

"You walked right there, opened the clock, looked inside. Shook your head."

"That was early this morning. After you'd left."

"I don't understand, sir."

"Stay where you are." He stepped back from the device and raised his hands. One long phrase after another passed his lips in a whisper. Flecks of deep red surrounded the distortions in the air, whirling about it like fireflies. Potent waves of energy passed through the barn. My skin tingled. My ears popped. The female revenant remained outside the window—but I saw no ghostly figure superimposed over her form. Swaine lowered his hands. The spell he'd cast dissipated, having made no discernible impact on the strange twists of shadow and light emanating from the resonance clock.

"It's no good," he said. "It requires modifications beyond any I can execute. It's changed on the inside—retaining some channel into another plane. No wonder my demons are panicking."

"If you put it inside a glamour, sir?"

"No, no—not unless you'd care to see every protection and glamour I've put in place neutralized in an instant." He paced as he spoke. "Such planar displacement—and would that I'd dug more deeply into the potential side-effects before our ill-fated experiment—desynchronizes the elements of such protections, rendering them useless in a wide diameter. A mile or better, as we saw. No, what this requires is a complex redesign. The *Occultatum*

Ostium has suggested a technique powerful enough to do what we need. No more fiddling about, either—this requires full attention. The hands of a professional. I don't think it can be put off. For now, however, we'll have to—"

He fell silent, looking past me. I turned and a small gasp escaped my mouth. Swaine and I appeared to walk in through the barn door, conversing. I immediately recognized it as having happened the afternoon before when he'd come to check over the calibration of the aqueometing device; the dress I'd worn, the teacup in his hand, the look of irritation on my face. While I couldn't quite hear our voices, a faint echo of our conversation seemed to zip around the workshop, flutters and trills barely audible. The image skipped around: at the door one moment, near the device in the corner, back in the middle of the floor, often breaking into two or more overlapping strands of motion.

"Sir?"

A pulsing crackle of energy surged through the barn, rattling bottles and tins on the workbenches, causing the arms of the aqueometing device to bounce up and down. The beams overhead groaned. Swaine cursed—one of the few times I'd seen him do so.

"What's happening?" I said.

"A temporal displacement." He turned to his workbench and started gathering up items, sweeping them into a satchel he kept off to the side. "Time is bending in on itself. We need to leave— this is growing far too dangerous. Help me. Everything on the first two shelves."

I stepped out from the glamour, still captivated by the sight of myself standing in the corner watching as Swaine adjusted the device.

"Finch, now."

Tearing my gaze away, I rushed over to the benches. "The resonance clock itself, sir?"

"No. It stays. Everything will need to be readied before

attempting to fix it. Days, at minimum. With luck, the displacement won't expand too far in the interim. Leave it as is. Bare necessities—that's what we need." He worked quickly, his words clipped and precise. "Ingredients. Tools. Books. As much as we can. I want us to be on the road within the hour, Finch."

19

GRAVE RAVEN

The house in Andover was dark, cold, and musty from disuse. A film of fine ash covered most surfaces, blown from the chill hearths over the course of two unoccupied seasons. I banged open the shutters and lit fires. Swaine hunched over a trunk of books, placing them carefully on one of the shelves in a small room off of the kitchen. I sneezed.

"The third trunk of books, when you have a moment," he called out.

"Yes, sir." I stepped back outside. A thin and miserly snow swept in from the west as we'd finally reached the spare house, smudging out the last colors of sunset, dampening the wagonload of hastily gathered books, writing paraphernalia, clothing, Swaine's traveling kit of ingredients for summoning and conjuring, several instruments he needed, and more books. I kept my hood up as I hurried to the wagon. Tall maples, barren of leaves, swayed on the wind. Behind them, thick woods of pine and hemlock stretched into the darkness, sighing as the snow gusted. I lugged the final trunk of books back inside, grunting as I struggled to keep my footing. With a wipe of my sleeve, I removed as much snow as I could before dragging the trunk to the small room.

"Are you sure you needed so many books, sir?"

"Books are my food." He knelt in his shirtsleeves, staring at the shelf before him. You might have thought him preparing to disarm a steel trap, so intent was his expression. "Should I starve?"

"No danger of that, sir."

He slid one volume out by the spine, then frowned and slid it back into place. "Here's the thing, Finch. You might look at my preference for books and solitude, and think *oh, how lonesome that must be.* Let me disabuse you of that notion." He placed some others nearby. "Would you like to know when I'm loneliest? It's when there are people all around me—talking about this and that, none of it rising above the mundane. Talk of rum, talk of dog races, talk of the Governor this or the Governor that, talk of the price of land. Talk of a new child, talk of a visit to Long Island, talk of a great auntie. No, please. Not interested. It's when I have to stand and smile, to listen to people pontificate on narrow nonsense, that I'm *most* lonesome." He pulled another suitable candidate from the trunk and cracked it open, flipping through the pages. "So, no—when I've a book in my hand, when I'm deep in my work, I'm never lonely. And do you know why? It's because I'm having a conversation. A dialogue. An argument. Not with myself, mind you—but with Blackwell, and Laird, and Schmeling. Those and their ilk are my companions. Souls of my temperament. Individuals of my sensitivities and inclinations. Those rare souls who saw life as I've come to."

He motioned to the book in the trunk before him. "That we don't share the same years in the sunlight nor the same spot on the globe makes little difference. And just knowing people such as that once lived, or in some cases live now, does more to ease my loneliness than any *hail-fellow-well-met* ever could. At my core,

I am deep in communion with life, and those who strode forth with the courage to see it with their own eyes. Do you understand?"

Having lost hours to my studies, knowing what it was to engage so fully with the thoughts and words of another that I'd forget to eat, to drink, surprised to see that morning had turned to late afternoon, I thought I did. My father, my brothers—they'd been happy using their arms, their eyes, on their feet, making, creating, hammering, sharpening. Yet since coming into Swaine's service, I'd come to think more often of my mother, devouring one book after another, quiet and still, but with as much light in her eyes as anyone I'd ever known.

"Will we need to return to Salem to fetch others, sir?"

"Don't get carried away, Finch—we're temporarily relocating to Andover, not sailing to India." He lifted out another pair of books. "At the very least, this ought to be sufficient to maintain our ruse of being bookbinders, should any inquiries draw too near."

As I opened the final trunk, I found the letter I'd brought back from the tavern. "There's this, sir."

Swaine took the letter and pried it open, unfolding it. "Oh, lovely. An invitation to a ball at the Governor's mansion. At the behest of Mary Whitelocke." He handed it back to me. "Post a polite declination, if you would. Absurd."

"Are you sure, sir?"

"More than."

The fire snapped in the hearth. I frowned, taking more books from the trunk and setting them on a narrow table. Swaine watched me.

"Well," he said. "Out with it. I sense an implied criticism."

"It's just that—well, Mary I'm sure expects you to go."

"She may expect all she wants. I'm not sure her expectations are my concern."

"She is a woman, sir."

"Meaning?"

"Meaning that she expects her expectations to be, at least, taken into consideration."

"And so I'm to fetch when told to fetch? Come when told to come? I'm a sorcerer, Finch—not a puppy."

"From a woman's perspective, sir," I said, treading delicately, "it's not about—obedience. It's about acknowledging her feelings."

"I return her correspondence, don't I?"

"Yes, you do, sir." I knew it well, as I was the one to smooth his otherwise clumsy replies before he set quill to paper. "But she'd like to go beyond correspondence, clearly. And it mightn't be a bad idea for other reasons."

"I remind you there is a temporal displacement in Salem. A rather harrowing situation to prioritize above others."

"Of course, sir. It's just that it might be a good idea *politically* to demonstrate—"

"Politics are for the snivelers and snakes, thank you."

"But with the incidents of rebellion—the Rattlesnake Society —and the vigor with which the Governor has his men scouring the countryside and city for any hints of disloyalty—well, it might be best for your work, wouldn't it, if there was a way you could demonstrate, publically, that your motives aren't in question? Sir." My words tumbled out. "They've been searching wagons. Arresting people. Questioning people. What if someone saw something, or heard something, about Salem? You'd be able to find that out. Forewarned and forearmed, sir."

"Who would have heard something?"

"I don't know, sir. But with the searching and the hiding, who knows? And more than that, the opportunity to be seen as you are by the right people in the colony—you're very impressive, sir. Nothing like the superstitions. It just might be an opportunity. As you've said, if you're ever to help move society forward to accepting what we do—the ball could be a chance. To do several things at once. All beneficial." Swaine stared at me. I didn't look away. "And it's only one evening, sir."

"Is this all because you wish to attend a ball, Finch?"

No, it was because I was desperate to find out whether a quartet of Rattlesnakes, now in the custody of Governor White-locke, had made mention of a one-eyed woman setting their clothing on fire. "The invitation is just for you, sir."

He turned back to his books. "I'll say this much: if I *am* to go —and I'm not agreeing to anything, mind you, though your reasoning has a certain strength to it—I shall drag you along as a human shield. Punishment for your impertinent logic."

I was about to suggest it would be best if I *didn't* go when a muffled clanging sounded from one of the trunks in the kitchen. A moment of confusion dissipated quickly.

"Mr. Preston, sir," I said. In the kitchen, I opened the trunk only to see the small brass bell lift into the air, ringing.

"The one time I don't need corpses," Swaine sighed. "Of course."

After a minute, the bell ceased its ringing, remaining hovering. "What should I tell him, sir?"

Swaine rubbed his forehead. "Fixing Salem will require the construction of a Koeffler Tap, a complex endeavor. There's that. The resonance clock needs significant modifications—even though the principles are correct. There's that. I need to enlist the help of Boston's rogue clockmaker if I'm to have even the faintest hope. So there's also that. Why not add more bodies to the mix?" He looked at his watch. "Fine. Tell him yes. At least it's close. Ready the wagon. We'll leave before nine."

I plucked the bell out of the air and rang it, once, twice, thrice.

By the time we reached the bridge in the far stretches of town, the night sky had cleared, leaving the tops of trees to glint with ice crystals in the moonlight. My fingers ached from the cold.

Bough and branch hung low over the lane, lending their shadows to the faint blue contours of snow. Ahead, I made out the shape of Mr. Preston atop his wagon. As we neared, I pulled the horse to a stop. The sound of the river filled the quiet. Preston climbed down from his perch. He tipped his hat at me.

"Good evening, Mr. Preston." I climbed down, followed by my master. While the two men exchanged greetings, I went around to the back of Preston's wagon and untied the ropes holding the canvas over the bed. Pulling the cover aside, I saw dank clothing over stiff limbs. For a moment, I didn't understand what I was seeing. Musket shots bloodied a linen shirt. A coat bore scorch marks. Bayonet stabs had sliced deep into the corpses' legs. Leaning over to inspect them more carefully, I gasped. The face I found was of one of the lads who'd been with Francis when he'd tried to steal my wagon. Reaching in, I found the other lad next, the one who'd climbed onto the wagon. Next to them was a third lad whom I didn't recognize. The bodies had been ruined by musket and bayonet, with wounds through a cheek, an eye, maroon blood stains across their clothing. And the burn marks from my magic were clear to see.

He's been arrested. Him and his friends.

I looked for any others—Francis, the woman—but Preston's delivery was limited to those three. My pulse hammered. As horrible as the sight was, a tremendous relief bloomed in my chest. Should I have felt pity? Sadness? Remorse, anger, outrage? Of course. I was human, after all. Injustice never failed to move me. Yet what I felt, I'm ashamed to confess, was relief: pure, unalloyed relief. The guilt would no doubt come later, but for the moment it seemed as though my indiscretion with magic may have well gone to the grave—if you will—with the corpses before me.

Swaine soon leaned over the bodies, inspecting them. "What is this?" He turned to Preston, crossing his arms before his chest. "Mr. Preston—I hardly know what to say."

Preston stood next to him. He rubbed a hand over his cheek. "Three of them, sir. Fair number."

"I can count, yes. All the way to three." My master reached down and pressed aside the collar of one of the bodies. "Shot. Stabbed. Beaten. Hanged—and that's just this one. Tell me, Mr. Preston, you couldn't also find one who'd been pressed to death? Beheaded?"

"Bodies is what you ask for, sir. I bring what I can get for you. But a day old, these."

Swaine examined the rope burn on the neck of one body. He pushed aside the legs of one lad. Around the neck of another hung a noose. He took the end of the rope in his hand and turned to Preston. The man flushed the color of a radish, clear even in the midnight darkness.

"Have I not insisted on discretion?" Swaine said.

"Not a soul did notice, sir."

"No? You merely climbed the gallows and cut them down, one at a time, and no one noticed?"

"Bit of excitement in the city last night. Whitelocke's men had their hands full."

"And it didn't occur to you that someone might soon note that their gallows are empty, hands full or no?"

"Took a winding route, sir. I wasn't followed if that's what you're getting at."

"What I'm getting at, Mr. Preston, is that I demand that our arrangement not involve soldiers, night watch, or constables. Nor anything else that might attract undo notice—such as cutting bodies down from the public gallows, words which I can barely force past my lips without sputtering."

Preston fiddled with his hat. "In and out, I was. Quick as you'd like. No one saw me."

Swaine stepped away from the wagon and shook his head. He looked at the bodies, exhaling a billowing cloud in the frigid air.

I turned to Preston. "Was that all of them? At the gallows, I mean."

Both men turned to me. "You were hoping for more?" Swaine said.

"No. But if they weren't *all* missing . . ."

"Yes?"

"Well, if they weren't all missing, then it mightn't have been noticed quite the same way."

"Are you suggesting that perhaps there were several score bodies on display, and a few missing around the edges wouldn't be noticed?"

"I just—I'm trying to picture it."

Preston's red face scrunched up. "No, no. Was just these three lads, Miss Finch."

"I see. Thank you, Mr. Preston." My mind raced faster than the water that burbled beneath the narrow bridge. Had Francis escaped? The woman? Was my secret still among the living?

"To your wagon, then, sir?" Preston said.

Swaine straightened and took out his billfold. "Fine. Yes."

Once the corpses were stowed and covered, Preston bade us good night, his figure fading into the darkness as he rode off in the opposite direction.

"Should I gather up the ingredients for the revenations for the morning, sir?" I said.

"I've no time for revenations at the moment. We shall store the bodies."

"At the house, sir?"

"With all your talk of politics and searching, keeping a trio of corpses at our temporary residence would seem to be more than a little risky."

The horse's passage was muffled by the fresh snow. "Back in Salem, sir?"

"God, no. Far too dangerous. You are familiar with the pond beyond the eastern woods in Andover?"

"Yes, sir."

"We shall bring them there, to the marshy end that abuts the larger pond. You will set them in a state of preservation, using de Burgh's Grave Raven."

"Me, sir?"

"Yes, you. You've enough experience now with Summerfield's second-order harmonic plangent. De Burgh's spell should be within your reach. I've brought the book along. And the ingredients. The Grave Raven requires the hour of midnight."

"You're sure, sir?"

He wrapped his cloak closer about his face. "Best not dawdle."

The Grave Raven was the earliest documented spell for the preservation of a corpse, staving off decay indefinitely. First recorded by the English magician William Langton, the spell was used to preserve the body of a young knight in the service of King John who died in the siege of Rochester Castle in 1215. The body remained lifelike ('as though the young man were but asleep' being the most common observation) for 300 years, until King Henry VIII decided it was an 'affront to the Eye of God.' Henry charged his Lord Chancellor Archbishop Thomas Wolsey with seeing that the spell was undone. Wolsey clandestinely sought the services of Alban de Burgh, a magician from York, who not only reversed the spell, but documented and streamlined the technique for casting it in the first place, thus leading to the distinction of *de Burgh's* Grave Raven. Wolsey recorded that when offered a chance to glimpse the faded bones of the knight to set his mind at ease that the spell had been broken, King Henry demurred, demonstrating his peculiar unease with dead bodies— noteworthy given the ease with which Henry saw to it that many of those closest to him achieved the state throughout his reign.

The ride back through Andover passed without my notice as I prepared for the spell, recalling all I could of Summerfield, de

Burgh, Gardener. With Swaine's guidance, I rehearsed the gestures and the words. I committed the list of ingredients to mind. This was a spell that demanded more of me than any I'd attempted: a base of harmonic shadow control, the transmorgative processes of elemental energies, a dash of transferent adaption, and—with the pattern of glamours bound to the corpses—a hint of sorcery.

In the time it took us to reach the spot Swaine had in mind, my confidence in my ability went from shaky, to sure. Then from committed, to doubtful. And from there to wait-and-see. The final leg of the journey found us carrying the corpses, one by one, from the back of the wagon and down a snowy slope beneath tall pine, all the while our steps compressing the snow, our labored breathing swept away on the freezing breeze carrying out over the marsh and open water beyond. The ghostly hoot of a great-horned owl echoed off across the pond. We soon had all three bodies by the black water. I looked them over. Mouths open, necks broken, eyes glazed.

Did I feel any guilt? While the answer ought to have been a firm 'no'—after all, I'd neither forced them to join the Rattlesnake Society nor had a witting hand in seeing them captured by the Whitelockes—unease tugged at my conscience. I reminded myself that I hadn't been the one who'd killed them. I'd barely even hurt them—and I could have. Perhaps it was my friendship with Iris. Francis could very well have been among the corpses before me. Would I have told her? Would it have been a betrayal if I hadn't? And who was I to do the same with these three unlucky Rattlesnakes?

Swaine knelt and lit a lantern. "Are you ready?"

Was I? Well, I knew one thing: I wanted to prove I could do it. Most of the world I'd met had ignored me at best, stared at my disfigurement at worse, and to a one had dismissed me as no more than a young woman who might, if she's lucky, find her true, small place somewhere within the world that men had made for her.

"I am, sir."

Turning away from the corpses, I took up the lantern. I opened the book to the pages I'd marked and gathered the ingredients out of the satchel Swaine had brought with us. Quartz dust, copper filings, one iron ingot for each corpse. A vial of *sepulchrum essentia*, a mixture of blood and oil. A small tin of sanctified earth. Six fire-hardened needles. Three shards of bone that had been taken from the skull of a man murdered under a full moon. A stone bowl. I arranged them all, just so, and measured out the precise amounts needed, checking and double-checking as I went, so deep in concentration I didn't register that Swaine had pulled out a small notebook and quill until I'd finished.

"Ingredients?"

"All set, sir."

"Precautions?"

"Everything looks fine, sir."

"Looks—or is?"

"Is, sir."

He went over to a boulder near the water and took a seat. "Marvelous. I shall take notes."

Notes? I suspected him of doing it to put further pressure on my performance, although I was tense enough it might not have made any difference. "Yes, sir."

He put his free hand on his knee and nodded. "You may begin."

I took in a deep breath, and tapped each ingredient before me, the final check they were each set for their cue. Although I was tempted to reread de Burgh's incantation one final time, I knew if I hadn't committed it to memory well enough by then, one more nervous reading of it under Swaine's gaze would hardly help. I took several long moments, still and relaxed, clearing my mind for the intense focus, my attention on naught but my breathing. When I reached the proper state of mind, I approached the bodies. I spoke the opening incantation, turning my palms upward.

"*Gebindan Þyder hē cwæð þæt isen ne mihte geseglian on ānum mōnðe, gyf isen on niht wīcode, ælce dæge hæfde ambyrne isen.*"

A charge ran across my palm and up my arm—warmth, shivers of vibrant ripples that washed across my torso, my neck and scalp. Before me, the harmonic shadows of the bodies made their presence known, multifaceted etchings of fine black lines appearing above and beneath them, strange contours that echoed the curves of the bodies. I returned to the lantern and mixed the ingredients, reciting the inner verses of the spell. As I completed the final lines, the mixture flared, sending thin filaments of pale white drifting off from my hands toward the corpses, reminding me of wind-blown snow. Swaine said nothing.

Approaching the bodies, I dipped my finger into the soft paste and drew a small circle on the forehead of each corpse. Their skin was cold. As my hand neared the filaments of shadow, the various strands of harmonic energy moved in different patterns, bending, the darkness deepening. I intuited the way I might control it: I might bend it this way or that; I might braid it; I might send ripples out around me. The strength of the connection surprised me.

"*Signantes litteras porta,*" I said. *Seal the gate.* I whispered the phrase with each circle I drew. Once the circles were complete, I ran a line of copper filings down the center of each corpse's torso. Moving in the opposite direction, I traced that line of copper with a line of quartz dust, the smooth material falling easily from my fingertips. Each pass I made I spoke de Burgh's transmorgification spell, which he'd (considerately) used English for.

"Raven of death, alight not on this fading breast. Wind carry thee elsewhere. For time doth no longer carry these remains in its stream. Years, decades, centuries shall pass as mere dream."

As the end of the line of quartz dust connected with the

beginning of the line of copper filings, a wash of midnight blue lit my arm and the first corpse below, emanating from the copper and quartz. I made a gesture, pushing farther into the shadows, turning my hand with thumb pressed against the bent knuckle of my index finger. The patterns twisted, and I sensed then the life of the magic itself—like reaching out and catching a gust of strong wind in my sleeve, on my hand. It sensed me and responded. As I moved my hand back and forth, it flowed grace-fully. Colors changed. The pressure of the magic shifted this way and that, responding to my energy. Was my nature as a witch helping, bringing me closer to the magic, creating a stronger connection? I entertained the possibility, albeit briefly—I already had too much to concentrate on.

I repeated the process with the other corpses until the edge of the marsh shone with the strange light of the elemental energies I'd tapped. As I retrieved the *sepulchrum essentia*, I glanced at Swaine. He nodded. I forced myself to concentrate, to not wonder what he was thinking. I picked up the vial and the tin of sancti-fied earth, putting the tin into my pocket. In the reeds, pale lines of light sprouted, here and there shining off the water. Swaine didn't look concerned, so I carried on.

I drew the symbols prescribed by de Burgh with the *sepul-chrum essentia*, on the eyelids, on the throat, on the palms. With each symbol, I spoke the phrase "Bound, encircled, the last light of day; the fingers of tombs, I cast thee away." I knew one of Swaine's difficulties with de Burgh involved what he viewed as melodrama within the incantations—melodramatic or not, I found it easier to commit to memory than the Latin and Old English sections of the spells.

Swaine remained silent throughout although I heard a few scratches of his quill as he made a note here or there. My knees had gone stiff with the kneeling, and I stretched them as I stood. The most difficult part of the spell lay just ahead of me: harnessing the harmonic shadow vibrations. The timing of a tongue-twisting incantation needed to match both gestures and the application of the final ingredients.

"Take your time," Swaine said. He knew how difficult the next section was. "The sorcerous mind has but one point of focus."

I nodded. Taking up the bone and ingots, I paused before the first corpse, the magic snapping the air above it. I found my breath, which led me to my center, to that feeling of being suspended from above, of being connected to the air and wood and ground around me, of having a wellspring deep inside.

The words of the conjuring flowed out as easily as the magic from my hands. *"On sefan sende—ne hyrde ic snotorlicor. On swa geongum—feore guman þingian."* As I started the first of six gestures, my magic connected to the energy before me, lifting my consciousness and awareness. The light of the magic brightened and morphed, the strands creating an intricate pattern woven of the iridescent yellow of spring blossoms, the ruddy orange of autumn maple leaves, windings of silver that glinted like ripples on a brook, and a bloody gold. Shivers ran along my flesh from scalp to heel.

I turned my hands, continuing into the next gestures, letting more magic flow out and connect with the brilliance in front of me. Warmth and cool currents rose and passed through the air. I exhaled slowly. As I passed through the next gestures, I slipped my hand into my pocket and took out a skull shard and iron ingot. Motioning with my left hand, I crouched over the first body and spoke. *"Geata dryhten, folces hyrde, wile wordum ond weorcum."*

While the words came out, I slid the iron ingot into the open mouth, pushing up on the stiff jaw to shut it inside. I ran two fingers on the lips, across the nose, over the eyes. *"Mægenes fultum wigcræftigne, nales wordum searwum, gearwe wigend wæron."*

I placed the shard of bone within the circle I'd drawn on the forehead. At that moment, the materials of my dress and my hair snapped with fine sparks, and the air above the corpse glinted with flickering light. The limbs of the corpse shook and a shadow spread out from underneath it, rising. It did, in fact, resemble a raven made of surplus midnight. It passed through the shimmering light, and as it did, a wave of icy air rolled out from the flesh, lifting the snow from the ground as it passed.

I sat back on my heels, watching as the sparks coalesced into intricate lines of gold light. The lines sunk onto the skin of the corpse, wrapping it in a fine skein, glowing briefly, and then fading. Even after the marks faded, I could see faint golden accents in the corners of the eyes, at the temples, along the crescents of the fingernails, at the hipbones.

I'd done it: de Burgh's Grave Raven. My pulse raced, the thrill of the accomplishment filling my chest with pride. I turned to Swaine. He inclined his head. "Well done. Now the others."

By the time I finished with the other two bodies, the look of death had left them. Their color had returned, and the bruises and minor wounds had faded, while the larger injuries didn't look so terrible. They might have been asleep.

"Where should we keep them, sir?" I said.

Swaine stood from the boulder, wiped his breeches, and put his quill and inkwell away. "In the water. No one will find them here—and they shan't decompose. We may retrieve them when we have the opportunity."

I grabbed the first corpse by his ankles and slid him to the water. My legs recoiled at the icy grasp of the marsh, but I dragged the corpse until he lay under two feet of brackish water.

Swaine helped with the second and third bodies. "I never felt alive until I first attempted serious magic," he said. "And then, in an instant, I knew: this is what my mind and heart were meant to do. I could do it all day, every day, and never, ever tire of it. My work revealed my place in the world—I saw how it all worked, how it all fit together."

"And now, sir?"

"Now, it's my sanity. It's there for me when all else is bother and strife. I cherish it more than ever." He slid the final body in next to the others. "You did well."

"Thank you, sir." I brushed a stray lock of hair from my face. "I felt—in control, for the most part. And it's hard to properly explain, but I think my senses—the witch senses—helped. I could feel my way forward. If I needed to. Sorry. I'm not explaining it very well, sir."

"Stick with the proper techniques, for your own sake," he said. "I can't teach you anything practical about witchcraft. Not yet, anyways. And until such time as we both acquire a confidence now lacking, it's far too dangerous for you to go exploring on your own. Especially in connection with traditional magic or sorcery. I can see dozens of ways for it to go horribly wrong."

Like a fire spell spiraling out of control, for instance. "The last one was difficult, sir—my timing was off, and the balance of the transference wasn't as even as with the others."

"You feel that it sufficed, however?"

Pale hints of their faces showed at the bottom of the marsh, where they leaned against one another like sleeping children. "Sufficed? Yes. It could have been better, though, sir."

"Yes, I saw that." He straightened up and wiped his hands on his coat. "But the fact that you were attuned enough to notice is commendable. One of the easiest to explain yet hardest to master elements of sorcery is that it requires a ruthless commitment to being aware of one's shortcomings, for it only takes one such failure to end in catastrophe."

"Yes, sir." My fingers were numb. I warmed them in my armpits.

"As such, an objective view of one's own talents must be maintained to the best of your ability, at all times—and we know how difficult that is. For in the magical arts, how easy is it to adopt the trappings, the attitudes, the expressions that satisfy the *impressions* of what it takes."

"Impressions?"

Swaine stepped from the water, shaking his boots and sending off drips into the snow. "Cast a spell, and one is a practitioner of the arts. How easy to imagine that taking that first step will lead, inevitably, to the next, and the next, and, soon enough: mastery. Well most make their biggest mistake between the first and second step—for the second step is to ask yourself: do I know what I did? Do I understand all the elements? Do I realize that all that I think I know is likely wrong, and that real progress will only come by tearing all my expectations down and approaching it all as I really am, which is to say as a rank amateur with years and years of such steps—one forward, a dozen sideways—before me before even the claim to the title of journeyman—or journey-woman—practitioner applies?"

As cold as I was, I wanted to remain next to the bodies, looking over what I'd done. To take it all in.

"Sadly, most fail right there," Swaine said. "It's easier to smile and think oneself a magician, a sorcerer, already halfway to greatness. Gather books. Set up a workbench with ingredients. Tell your friends and family you can't be disturbed—until supper is ready, of course—as you're working on your spells. The delusion starts then and dooms the whole enterprise. No, one must embrace the truth, and admit that if you call yourself a sorcerer, you're likely no sorcerer. Real sorcerers are too busy struggling with the art for such labels."

"How encouraging, sir."

"Looking for pats on the back, are we, Finch?"

"Hardly expecting them after hearing that, sir."

He smiled. "Yes, well. I'm giving you something better than a cheap little ornament of cheer. I'm giving you the truth. Now if you would step out of there before you catch your death, we may head home to warmth and rest."

I did, trying not to show the pride that swelled within my chest, another little secret. Swaine bade me to collect our materials and the lantern. He stood by the water and cast a spell that filled the air with a crackle as ice formed across the water, spreading out from the shore, covering the bodies, hiding them further. We left the winter nocturne soon after. If anything disturbed the unquiet waters of the marsh in the silence and darkness that followed, we weren't there to see it.

20

THE STONY SHORES OF TIME

A week or so later, Swaine and I set out on the road to
Boston at first light. A wind from the north sent
ringlets and curls of fine snow from the trees. Bird calls
echoed through the frozen woods—jays, crows, catbirds in the
shrubs near the lane. I said nothing of the dread of being discovered that had lodged itself in my core like the grippe.

As we rode toward Boston, Swaine kept his thoughts to
himself, leaving me to grow tense each time we neared a town or
village, looking for roadblocks, looking for soldiers on the watch
for a one-eyed young woman driving a wagon. First one and then
another town, and no one raised hue or cry. A farmer touched the
brim of his hat as we passed the pasture where he tended his
cows, just as the chimney smoke from Boston itself came into
view. Steeples shone in the late morning light, and I spotted the
masts in the harbor.

When I went to hand the reins to Swaine, he demurred. "If
anyone feels that a perfectly capable young woman ought only to
cower under the wing of the nearest available gentleman at all
times, that's their problem, and not ours."

I pulled the wagon up behind two others on the main road,

Orange Street, that ran through Boston's neck and led to the town gate for carriages, not far from the second gate, for travelers on foot. Regulars at the gate questioned those coming in, which I'd never seen before. I shifted, feeling my throat tighten.

"Oh, lovely. We get to chat with thick-necked soldiers." Swaine took out his pocket watch and sighed.

While he was content to dismiss the delay with another volley in his long war against the primacy of brawn in the world, I entertained thoughts of leaping off the wagon and sprinting off into the tidal flats that extended away from the strip of land that connected the peninsula of Boston proper with the mainland. By the time I'd worked myself into a state of panic, the soldiers waved us forward. Four of them blocked the lane, one an officer. Their scarlet uniforms shone bright, white facings on their coats, muskets with steel bayonets at the ready. From the insignia on the soldier's sleeve, I realized that they were from the Governor's Own Regiment, famous throughout the colony for their fighting prowess. One muscled regular held back a pair of hounds on leather leashes. Both dogs barked. The officer, a captain, raised his hand, motioning for me to stop. As I pulled the reins, I forced a smile onto my face. They looked Swaine and me over.

"Where to, sir?" the officer said. The other soldiers looked over the wagon, coming up alongside, looking both in it and underneath it. The dogs strained on their leashes, one of them lifting himself onto his hind legs, staring at me. I tried to hide how fast my heart beat.

"The Town House and various merchants," Swaine said.

"Just the two of you?" he said.

"Indeed."

"And where are you coming from?"

"Andover."

Having found nothing, the other soldiers milled about, watching us. Their eyes were hard, intent on their business and not on my discomfort. "Just for the day?"

"Would you like an hourly itinerary, Captain?"

The officer went still. All the soldiers watched my master. "Just for the day, sir?"

Swaine waved his hand, then crossed his arms. "Fine, yes. Just for the day. Then we shall exit this gate and presumably relay all our commercial adventures in as much detail as required. Yes. May we be on our way now, Captain?"

The officer didn't look pleased, but he waved us on. The dogs continued to stare at me as I reined the team forward. Regulars owned the twisting streets, stationed on street corners in groups of four or six, in pairs on their enormous horses. Everywhere I looked, slow flares of deep red with musket and bayonet watched over the rest of the street traffic. I navigated amongst the other wagons and carriages that filled the cobbled streets, past people on foot who dodged the horse-traffic. The air carried the cries of gulls, sailing on the wintry breezes above the harbor, bright in the sunlight. Laughter and snippets of talk floated between tradesmen and draymen.

None of the muskets at the gate had ended up pointed at me.

I realized in that instant that if my worst fears had materialized, then we wouldn't have gotten through. No, whatever they were looking for, it hadn't come from Francis and his doomed companions. The surrounding city looked brighter, more colorful, and I let out a slow breath.

"Can you imagine all this," Swaine said, motioning around, "this bustle, this commerce, this industry—in Salem?"

"I can imagine people fleeing for their lives. While screaming in terror, sir."

"Now, now, Finch. Let's not dig our heels in at what *is*, but consider what *might* be. I'm speaking of what shall happen after we've stabilized the planar disposition and then taken care of our little friends. After."

"Our little *fiends*, sir?"

"Ah, I imagine you've been saving that one up. Precocious. I'm

talking about a vision, Finch. You see a demon-swept collection
of ruins, while I see a town to rival Boston. You see weathered
decay and the bones of a failed effort, while I see elegant buildings, sided in browns and blacks, shingled in oak, with graceful
gables and tall windows. I see streets cobbled and true. I see well-
ordered activity, all centered on a magnificent *sorcerium*—from
whence shall spring a renaissance of the unseen arts, ready to
propel humanity into a new age."

"Humanity, is it, sir?"

He straightened his hat. "Why do you think I'm doing all of
this? If it were riches I were after, I would already dwell in a
palace filled with the greatest works of art, the finest library of
books, and the best wines and cooks. Somewhere warm.
Romance? If that was driving me, I could have one countess or
baroness after another, each as beautiful as Venus, propped fash-
ionably upon each elbow. Adulation and fame? Think what I
might do for kings or generals. Conquests, battles, intrigue. The
stuff of poems and song. Really, is that all you think of me?"

"The countesses and baronesses will be disappointed to hear
it, sir."

"Lovely of you to say. There's a reason the *Occultatum Ostium*
—that incredible book—found its way to me."

The *Occultatum Ostium* had been the first book Swaine
grabbed upon departing Salem for Andover. In the days since,
he'd maintained his obsession with the book: refining his
thinking about how to clear Salem of its demons. A day didn't go
by without him tucking his nose into it, running his fingers along
the strange pages as though it were the cheek of his beloved. I
believed if he'd had his way, he'd do nothing more than fill up
with strong tea and pore over the book for the rest of his days, his
evenings, and all the midnights that followed. But fair enough—
his explorations of the text had opened his mind to possibilities
he'd never considered, he claimed. Alluring links between
dissimilar fields of study he'd pursued, grand designs fitting for

his plans to turn Salem into the heart of a new sorcery, one that embraced both the richness of the history of the art and the latest in mechanical technology.

Let no one claim my master possessed small dreams.

We soon reached Boston's Town House, two and a half stories of brick topped by a three-tiered cupola and a gilded weather-vane. I hitched the wagon while Swaine waited, and then we crossed around to the front. Carved figures guarded the entryway: a lion (for His Majesty) on one side and the Whitelocke stallion on the other. The crowded Merchant's Exchange filled the first floor of the building. I followed Swaine between stalls of wools and linens; spice and shot in wooden boxes; pipes, tobacco, and wine; hose and hats; the powders and balms of grocers and apothecaries; stacks of plates and tins. All that brought Boston its fame, and the Whitelockes their wealth. It also no doubt brought them their troubles with the Rattlesnake Society, and the other political enemies which they'd acquired in their decades of colonial influence.

Through the pipe-smoke haze, bricklayer and stationer gossiped with toolmaker and cheese-monger, while iron-monger and blacksmith, hosier and shoemaker struck deals, filling the hall with talk, with greetings. Swaine made a path down the center, a prow breaking the rough seas, with me sweeping along behind them, until we reached a narrow alcove that opened opposite a dealer behind a stall piled high with bolts of wool in tan, heather, and white. The alcove held a pair of wooden benches, where waited one Robert Twelves, clockmaker. In his late twenties, he wore his hair unfashionably short, his pleasant face ending in a scraggly beard.

He rose in greeting. "Mr. Swaine, a pleasure, sir." He stood a foot taller than Swaine, which put him well over six feet.

"Mr. Twelves. How good of you to meet me." Swaine slid in across from Twelves and motioned for me to join him. "My assistant, Miss Finch."

Twelves looked me over and nodded. "Delighted, Miss."

"And business is good?" Swaine asked Twelves as he took a seat.

"It used to be, sir. Used to be."

"Did I just hear the past tense, sir?"

Twelves glanced at the nearby merchants. "Boston is a funny place. Close-knit. Or maybe suffocating."

"Suffocating? Oh, dear."

"Master Graham is the finest clockmaker in New England. A Godly man. A man who knows where every minute goes, every pound. Knows men across the colony. Not just clockmakers, but artisans of all kind. Suppliers. Patrons. Dealers. He's not without his pride, either." Twelves shook his head, a hint of despair wrinkling his eyes. "He feels I wronged him. After eleven years."

"In what manner?"

Twelves laced his fingers on the worn table before him, slender, steady. *The touch of an angel when it comes to clockwork*—so had Swaine described Twelves' talent to me.

"By working on the device of yours, sir. When he first found the plans I'd put together, he'd been intrigued. For half a minute. I'm not sure if he gleaned the intent or took offense at violating the principles of design he so passionately hews to, but he insisted I stop such work. His name and reputation were reflected in his assistant, he said."

He glanced at me. I forced myself not to look down at the table in shame.

"That might have ended it," Twelves continued. "But I kept working on it, sir. Working on my own. In my room. In the shop after Master Graham had left for the evening. Quite careful about not leaving as much as a single shaving of brass. A dull scraper. Wood dust. None of it. But—well, I believe word reached him, somehow, of your name, sir."

"I'm not sure how that should make any difference," Swaine

said. "I've never met the gentleman. Nor am I at all aware of how he might have learned about our arrangement."

"Boston is a funny place, as I said," Twelves said. "Connections matter. Information can be as valuable as coin. Some rumors from London reached his ear. About you. Not that it matters to me, obviously. But to my master, it did."

"How disappointing." Nothing could upset my master like gossip from London concerning him. I gave him credit for not stiffening like a ram-rod and launching into a critique of half of the King's court.

"Worse than disappointing, sir. He relieved me of my services. At a meeting of the guild at Cromwell's Head tavern. In front of most of the city's influential artisans, sir." His fingers remained folded. "And since that time, it's as though I don't even exist. I can't find a bench with any other clockmaker. Or cabinetmaker. Even finding a room to let has been hard. The merchants will have nothing to do with me, sir. A wall's come down between me and my career, sir. Boston might be through with me. After eleven years of apprenticing. Six years of indentured service before that."

I thought of Silas Wilkes with a pang. Another decent man only looking to make a mark in the field he'd chosen but for one stroke of ill-luck sweeping it all away. I had an unreasonable urge to reach over and put my hand on his, telling him all will work out—that Fortune would welcome him, if only one pence at a time. As my master's assistant, however, I could only give him a sympathetic smile.

"Your plight bothers me, Mr. Twelves," Swaine said, leaning forward. "Your craftsmanship is of the highest caliber. Your talent is unquestionable. And as one who has more than once ran into difficulties with his peers, I understand well the dismay you're experiencing."

"Thank you, sir."

"But I offer more than empathy. I offer something much

better: an opportunity to take your craft beyond the bounds of your peers. Or your former master. Steady employment. A workshop of your own. Unrestricted resources, materials, tools. I can offer you a patronage unlike any you might find in Boston."

I watched Twelves exhale, his shoulders slumping, relief smoothing his brow as he hung his head for a moment.

"There are, of course, conditions," Swaine continued. "Secrecy foremost among them. And I would require that you relocate to the site of my endeavors. You would work exclusively for me."

"In Andover?"

"For a start, yes."

Twelves stared at my master. Did he have an inkling where else Swaine had in mind? Was there a hint of conflict in his eyes? I thought so, but he nodded anyways, grasping at the lifeline my master tossed into the storm-tossed swells that threatened to swamp his career.

"Well done, Mr. Twelves." Swaine turned to me. "While Mr. Twelves and I discuss the specifics of the arrangement, please purchase the supplies we discussed earlier."

"Yes, sir." I took the list from my pocket and slid out from the bench. As I made a circuit of the various merchants within the Town House, filling a sack I'd brought, I found myself relaxing. No one gave me much notice, certainly not the soldiers. For a time, I lost myself in the jostling, the voices all around, the hum of civilization. As I handed over enough coin for three pairs of wool socks, the sound of the hall changed.

My gaze went up to the wide stairs to the second floor, where the council chamber of the Royal Governor occupied the east side, opposite the General Court chambers on the west side. A pair of regulars came down the stairs, followed by a stout man wearing dark-colored finery, a powdered wig, and a plum coat. He frowned, talking with a tall man in a decorated uniform, white breeches, black boots, wearing a saber at his side, and a silver gorget at his neck. From the manner in which I saw those throughout the wide hall turn and watch, I realized that I was looking at Hamilton Whitelocke, the Royal Governor of the Colony of Massachusetts. He looked straight ahead as he passed by where I stood, even as I curtseyed. From the insignia and gilt trappings of the man with him, I guessed him to be General John Whitelocke, the Governor's eldest son and Mary Whitelocke's brother, the man in charge of the colony's military. The crowd gave way before them, hats tipped in greeting, the Governor raising his hand in acknowledgement even as he remained deep in conversation with the General.

Swaine had gleaned from his correspondence with Mary that the Whitelockes divided the world, always, into two categories: those who were personally loyal to them, and those who'd betrayed them. Their sensitivity to this division was the key to how they approached their days, for nothing stirred their hearts to flame more than any reminder of that division, particularly as it pertained to the betrayers.

Thinking of the state of the executed Rattlesnakes, I didn't doubt it.

I continued working on the list after purchasing several pairs of wool socks for my master. I paused, finding a small square of paper among the socks. Thinking it something accidentally caught up in my purchases, I pulled it out. Nothing was written on the outside, so I opened it. As my gaze swept over the neat handwriting, my chest went cold.

We could use someone with your talents. Find the old well ten minutes north of the top of Ward Hill—be there at 4 o'clock tomorrow afternoon. Tell no one. If we don't see you, word will reach the wrong ears about you—and your master. Don't be late.

I stood there, reading and rereading the words. Scores of people stood within twenty yards of me, three times that again filled the building. Someone among them had slipped the note into my bag and was even then watching me. A Rattlesnake.

I scanned one face after another, mostly men, some women. Some caught my eye, others didn't. Francis and the others may have been caught and some of them executed, but not before they'd told at least some of their co-conspirators about what I'd done: the magic I'd used. I was terrified—so much so that I yelped as a light hand touched my shoulder.

"I knew that would fit you."

Mary Whitelocke stood behind me in a swell of dark satin and scarlet silk edged with lace, voluminous skirts brushing up against me. The loose curls of her hair were tied back with scarlet ribbons, matched by the choker on her pale throat. A tall regular stood by her side.

I folded the note into my sweating palm. "Madam White-locke." I curtseyed.

She reached over and ran a finger along the collar of my dress, where it poked out from beneath my cape, checking the fit. "I shall have to steal you away from your master for a proper fitting, one of these days—my eye is good, but I think that getting a proper dressmaker's touch on you would be far better." She put a finger to her pursed lips. "Perhaps before the ball."

Dressmakers and balls? I couldn't quite make the leap from Rattlesnakes. I'm sure I stood there looking like a fool for a long moment before I was able to shove a few sensible words from my mouth. "My master is very much looking forward to attending."

"Of course he is. Otherwise I'd feel quite snubbed."

I slipped the note back into my sack, keeping a smile on my face, forcing myself not to swing my head around every which direction looking to spot the Rattlesnake who'd given me the note.

"Snubbed—how unsurprising."

I turned at the voice. A young man of my age stood behind Madam Whitelocke, yawning. His jacket matched that worn by the Governor in cut and color, and his light-colored hair was tied back over a crooked collar.

"Don't slouch," Madam Whitelocke said.

"These interminable duties wear me out." he said.

"Ignore my brother." Madam Whitelocke spotted my master as he finished up with Mr. Twelves. She patted me on the arm and passed me by so she might speak with him.

Her brother looked me over. "You wouldn't perchance have any snuff you might spare me?"

"I seem to have left my snuffbox at home," I said.

"Near your eyepatches?"

"Excuse me?"

"You're the one." He tapped at one of his eyes. "She's bought those for you—prompting one of my father's more memorable complaints: *Am I to purchase every silken eyepatch from here to New York?* Letting him at the ledgers is always a mistake. Especially if you're my sister."

"Which would explain why you cast about for your vices from perfect strangers, then." I looked past him, searching for signs of the writer of the note. Was it the young man in the green vest? The gentleman looking up from a book by the stairs? One of the lads hauling crates of goods?

"Don't let my sister hear you call her appalling weakness for apparel a vice. No more pricey eyepatches for you." He looked at my eyepatch. "I will say it gives you something of a villainous air."

For a half a moment, I considered using my *talents* to set his sleeves on fire. I restrained myself. "Do your father's ledgers account for the funding of manners, perhaps?"

"They do. The return on investment is poor, however. You need only ask any of my many defeated governesses how mannered I turned out."

A lad with a black ribbon tying back his hair glanced at me from a table stacked with tiles twenty yards from where I stood. He looked away.

"And you have nowhere to be right now?"

"Sadly, I always have somewhere to be—though you may

trust that if I could disappear, like the good Doctor of Magickal Sciences can, if you believe the rumors, I would avoid all such interminable lectures outlining the duties I signed over my life to when born a Whitelocke."

"I won't say a word if you slip off."

"Don't tempt me," he said. "Too many prying guards, each one ready to drag me to the regimental dinner where I won't be allowed to slouch, tipple, or do anything other than pray for the clocks to speed up as I watch my brother pin new ranks on the collars of his best boot-lickers. My father will grumble about the slowness with which people eat. My sister will gaze at the various officers the way that a wolf sizes up a flock of sheep, and decide that, at the very least and to absolutely no one's surprise, a few new dresses ought to be in order. And Doctor Rush will nod off into his prunes." He made no move to leave. He glanced at Swaine as Mary spoke with him. "That's your father?"

"My master."

"You're a slave?"

"I'm an apprentice."

"An apprentice at what?"

"At the restoration of old books. He's a book-binder."

"How boring."

I wondered if he'd ever dragged a corpse by its ankles. "And you do what?"

"I wait to be fitted with an officer's uniform, even though I keep insisting to everyone I meet it's a terrible idea. And, by the way, making me an officer would be a terrible idea."

"How insistent."

"Told you."

Swaine and Madam Whitelocke approached. "Is my brother behaving?" she said.

"He says he's going to be an officer soon, Madam," I said.

"Ignore his petulance, dear," she said.

Her brother put a hand to his ear. "Sorry—my *what*ulence?

Flatulence? Why, I think you've mistaken me for someone else." He smiled, and turned. "Ah, Doctor Rush. We were just speaking of you."

Behind him appeared an older gentleman, one hand holding tight to his cane. Wisps of his hair had taken sail around his uncovered head. His stained teeth clenched a sputtering pipe while his other hand closed a timepiece and slid it into a pocket of his expensive-looking waistcoat. "Not overly fondly, I hope."

I tried to not show the crushing fear that enveloped me: here was the man, unique in all the empire, charged with keeping the colony of Massachusetts free, at all costs, of witches.

And I was a witch.

Swaine had just the week before spent an hour reading me passages from Rush's *On Planar Cartography*, powering his way through three scones and as many cups of strong tea as he underscored the myriad errata and false assertions made by the good Doctor when he'd been in his prime. I'd only thought of the witch-poles.

When I'd expressed my worries, Swaine maintained—courtesy of letters full of gossip from Madam Whitelocke—that Rush hadn't done a lick of interesting magic in at least two decades, having given in to a taste in Parisian tailors, fine brandy, and the attentions of Boston's leading women of society (and their mothers). Oh, there were the occasional demonstrations of cheap parlor magic—making wine glasses sing long musical tones untouched, lighting magic lanterns with silver-tinted flames on Twelfth Night, the pages of sheet-music on his music stand turning by themselves as he played the clavichord in his famed salons. And the good Doctor toured the colony each spring, making a great show of inspecting the graveyards and cemeteries of the colony's northerly towns and villages, of charting the positions of the planes, of remaining resolute in the face of the infernal, all of which—Swaine asserted—offered no discernable purpose other than to justify his own appointment.

"Now, now, my good Doctor," Madam Whitelocke said. "Trawling for a compliment is beneath your dignity."

"You've found me out." Rush looked at me, wrinkles folding along his temples as a warm smile appeared on his face and he fixed me with a keen gaze. He didn't appear to take me for anything other than a servant, perhaps one with a slightly unusual story of losing an eye.

Madam Whitelocke stepped forward. "Might I introduce you to August Swaine?"

Swaine stepped forward and bowed. "An honor, sir. Your work has long fascinated me, in fact. Particularly the Koeffler-inspired channeling you innovated back in the 1690s. A landmark in the magical sciences."

"Nearly as disregarded as I am," Rush met my master's gaze with clear interest. "A fading branch of magical science championed by a lone, provincial explorer of the arts. I'm rather surprised that such a dusty piece of magical history would ever have caught the eye of a modern London practitioner, Mr. Swaine."

He knew who my master was, which gave me a small shiver of pride. Madam Whitelocke's brother looked back and forth between the two men, and then at me again. I wondered what the Rattlesnake watching me thought—or perhaps they'd already fled at the appearance of the Governor and his men.

Swaine inclined his head. "As you would no doubt understand, I had years and years of anonymous hard work, unsung and unappreciated, well before I became the *bête noire* of the season at the King's Court. Why, in my youth, as I sought any scrap of tales of research in our field—well, your work was something I savored. To a young lad growing up in Lincoln, the tales of your work in the untamed New World were thrilling, I can assure you."

"How kind of you," Rush said. "And how long are you visiting for?"

"I've relocated altogether. The politics of London became altogether too stifling for my tastes. I've given it all up and traded it for the quiet life of reading, writing, and reflection. Having acquired quite a collection of books on various topics, I've been restoring them, making notes for a book of my own."

"A noteworthy endeavor."

"Perhaps I might bend your ear with some of my thoughts. We might compare the eternally missing entries in our libraries."

"The larger they grow, the more they reveal their shortcomings, don't they?"

Swaine nodded. "Well said, sir."

A regular approached through the crowd. "The Governor is waiting, sir and madam."

"And Grayson," Madam Whitelocke's brother added.

Rush moved his pipe from one side of his mouth to the other. "He can wait a few moments more for my old bones to shuffle the fifty-seven paces from here to the carriage. Off with you." He turned back to my master. "How fortunate that I find myself in the company of a man as learned as yourself, sir. Even now, as I trundled my way down the stairs, I was puzzling over a strange incident—perhaps your impressions might be just the thing I need to illuminate the situation, if you have a moment?"

A sudden dagger of fear slipped between my ribs. *Had there been reports of magic being used? Of flames and a young woman in Andover?* I tried not to appear stricken.

"I'm at your service, Doctor Rush," Swaine said.

"Excellent. We can walk. Lessen the damage to the Governor's teeth as he grinds them impatiently outside."

Rush started off through the length of the Town House, Swaine at his side. I tagged along just behind them, between the Whitelocke siblings, trailed by two regulars. The note stayed in my sack. No one made a move to mark me that I could see.

"In Andover, during an afternoon three days back," Rush said, "two young girls drowned in a pond. The oldest was only nine."

My attention snapped back to Rush. In a pond in Andover? I tried to get closer so as not to miss a word.

"How terrible," Swaine said.

Grayson Whitelocke leaned in to me as we followed. "The good Doctor is a reliable fountain of such cheerful stories."

I ignored him. Rush continued. "Tragic indeed. The girls' bodies were laid out to prepare for burial. A pair of coffins was made, and there they rested, in the main room of the family's home. Sometime late in the night, they spoke. Both girls. Their distraught father and mother, the other children, all woke to the sound of it, and then witnessed the movements of the corpses."

I kept myself from glancing at my master, or stumbling. *Which pond did this happen in?* I suddenly wondered.

"Both girls sat up in their coffins," Rush said. "Eyes open, but rolled up into their heads. They spoke in a tongue that none recognized, not even the local pastor, whom the oldest son fetched. While none understood what the girls said, all agreed that the words were terrible. Unholy and foul. It continued for hours. Nothing could stop the ceaseless abomination. They couldn't be pushed back into their coffins, their bodies stiff as granite, their skin still as cold as when they'd been plucked from the brackish waters of the pond."

Grayson glanced over at a choking sound from me, one I hadn't intended to make. I cleared my throat, begged his pardon, while the doctor continued.

"All but the father had left by then, unable to bear the sight and sound of it. He and his brothers and some of the other local men struggled with what to do. They considered dragging them, coffins and all, out into the night—perhaps of a mind to bury them for want of any other solution—when the girls ceased their speaking. They climbed from their coffins, eyes still rolled back, and walked out of the house, hand in hand. Dawn was a short while off. The men followed them with lanterns and torches. The pastor shouted the Lord's Prayer at them, to no effect. They

passed through a meadow and an orchard, across lanes, not stopping, not slowing."

We passed by a baker's stall lined with fresh tarts. Grayson
reached over and took one when the baker wasn't looking. When
I raised an eyebrow at him, he held the pastry up, offering it. I
shook my head, desperate to hear what Rush was saying.

"They returned to the pond they'd drowned in," Rush continued. "Walked straight in. Hair and funeral dresses rising as the
depth increased. And then they slipped beneath the surface, past
the well-known drop-off. They haven't risen or been seen since.
The men of town searched the pond in rowboats, while the father
spent hours and hours diving in the water, along with his brothers. They found nothing. They've kept watch since, yet there's
been no reappearance of either girl."

Swaine shook his head, running a hand along his short beard.
His mind surely went straight to the marshy edges of the pond
where we'd stowed the preserved bodies. "Quite concerning,"
he said.

"And so much for sleeping tonight," Grayson said, around a
mouthful of tart.

We neared the entrance to the Town House. The soldiers
cleared the way, and we stepped out into the daylight. A four-
horse carriage stood at the edge of the plaza in front of the building. Half a dozen mounted regulars waited nearby. The Governor
sat in the carriage, scowling. Next to the carriage, General Whitelocke conferred with an officer. Rush paused, lifting his walking
stick, and turning to Swaine.

Rush peered over the tops of his spectacles at my master.
"Knowing only that much—which is all that I'm aware of—what
would your immediate thoughts be, Mr. Swaine?"

"You trust the accuracy of the tale?"

"I believe I must."

Swaine nodded. "Then I would consider the infernal. A
malignant entity. A demon."

Rush nodded. "Indeed."

"You suspect something?" Swaine said.

"On the contrary," Rush said, "I can find no immediate explanation why the safeguards throughout the colony that maintain the delicate boundaries between the countryside and the planar regions might have been disturbed."

I could. I found myself chewing the corner of my thumbnail and lowered my hand with as little guilt as possible.

"Such planes are hardly static." Swaine said it lightly, the answer to an academic hypothetical.

"Wexler's theory of the Regionem Shift. I'm well aware. My tracking of the nearest planes is precise—I take such shifts into account."

"Why, of course."

General Whitelocke and the officer with him approached us. The General adjusted the fingers of his gloves. "The Governor has grown terse, and requests to know why the final twelve paces to the carriage have proven insurmountable."

"Doctor Rush has just been thrilling us with a seasonal tale of children," Grayson said, wiping the crumbs from the front of his coat. "Now I don't know about anyone else, but I could use a strong ale. Or three."

"We are running late," his brother said.

"Heaven forfend we should disappoint the clocks that rule our lives."

"Now."

Rush turned to Swaine. "I would enjoy it very much if you might call on me soon, sir—with such thoughts as you might have on what I've told you. 'Tis a stroke of unexpected fortune to make the acquaintance of a man of your reputation, and I would value your counsel."

"Likewise, Doctor Rush. I shall find the time."

With that, we parted company from the Whitelockes and Doctor Rush. Madam Whitelocke made Swaine reiterate his vow to attend the ball, while Grayson Whitelocke parted with a wink for me that paused for a moment too long for me to dismiss that he'd been mocking my missing eye. We watched as they entered the carriage and as the procession of soldiers and horses rumbled off into the streets. Swaine stared after the dwindling carriage.

"He's quite canny." Swaine turned and swept back into the Town House. I hurried after him. "He knew precisely what he was doing."

"Sir?"

"Really, Finch—you surprise me." Back inside, the din had grown now that the Governor and his entourage had left. Swaine hurried, and I had to work to keep up. "One of Mr. Winslow's lads, or perhaps a merchant, has jabbered like a jay. I've no doubt that the Governor's men have ears and eyes on most avenues of gossip. And of trade. My presence has been well known to him, I'd guess for some time now."

"So he was lying, sir? Trying to judge your reaction?"

"No, the story is likely true, which is concerning. He was sending me a clear message. He knows my history. He suspects a connection."

Swaine said no more, focusing on our business, but I could tell that he was ruminating on every word he had passed with Doctor Rush. I trailed along after him, carrying the goods he needed, paying the merchants, buying the items he'd forgotten that he would need until I was loaded down, a mule on two legs. At one point or another, I suspected nearly every merchant or patron of being the mysterious Rattlesnake, though no one appeared to spare me anything more than a cursory glance. Maybe that was the problem with Rattlesnakes, I realized: as the Whitelockes knew all too well, until they rattle, they're very hard to spot.

Back at our wagon, Swaine climbed onto the bench and waited while I secured our purchases and refastened the gate. I unhitched the team. A brisk wind from the harbor snapped the flag that flew above the Town House. I pulled the team out into the street. A pair of mounted regulars sauntered by.

"Does he know about Salem, sir?" I said.

"Would that I might dismiss the possibility entirely. Traces of my work are well-cloaked at the boundaries. Of course, any use of the arts done anywhere beyond those boundaries would only send a glaring cannonball soaring into the sky for him to see, as clear a signal as could be; thus my insistence that no magic take place outside of said protections. Now, potential disturbances to the planar balance within Salem—those are more difficult to account for. He may have detected something. Around the manse itself, were he to venture that close, my glamours and wards would be impossible to hide, but I doubt the old gentleman would go that far. No, the work is likely still hidden."

All I saw were flames climbing across shirts and breeches and skirts. *As clear a signal as could be.*

"Could he put some sort of spell on you, or us, to learn more?" I said.

"He wouldn't dare attempt any such spell in my presence." Swaine stared off to the side, his gaze seeming to register neither alleyway nor building, pedestrian nor soldier. "No. He's only guessed at *what* I'm doing. *Where* I'm doing it would never occur to him, for all his wards, his witch-poles, his planar readings. But all this talk of demons was directed at me—he knows my work, and he's most displeased. And he was telling me just that."

He looked at me. Fearful that my guilt shone like a glaring cannonball soaring into the sky, I spoke. "He—he didn't seem doddering, sir."

"You're right. The sharp mind that once sliced through the thorny problems of this colony is still well-honed, that much is clear. He may believe dull and pointless ideas, but he's no dullard himself. Not even close."

"And the demon he told you of, sir? Is it"—I almost said *ours* —"yours, sir?"

"That's what most concerns me. If the planar boundaries in Salem have indeed begun folding in on themselves, there's no telling what might be coming through." He said the last phrase nearly to himself, the cue I should leave him with his thoughts. I retreated into the silence.

Back at the town gate, we waited as a drover led his unsold sheep back out, and were then waved unmolested through ourselves, with just a quick look in the back of the wagon from the regulars. Swaine took to his thoughts, and I to mine, stark as they were. The note—*We could use someone with your talents*—seemed to whisper at me from the back of the wagon.

If only there'd been a spell to drag the hands of the clock back by days, a week—but even the unseen arts crashed fruitlessly against the stony shores of time.

21

BURN, OR HANG

I spied the abandoned well the next afternoon. Nothing moved near it. The rays of late afternoon stretched long through the trees, lending the snow and bare trunks an appearance of warmth belied by the chill temperature. I crouched by a wide chestnut tree, looking for signs of Rattlesnakes. Beyond the old well stood the ruins of a cabin, reduced to weathered logs and a stone foundation peeking out from drifts of snow. My approach hadn't crossed any fresh footprints or hoofprints. I didn't smell anything but winter: hints of pine pitch, tufted bark, fallen leaves, cold stone and soil draped in snow.

Minutes passed, silent but for the wind coaxing a murmured chorus of creaks, knocks, and dry whispers of stubborn leaves from the trees. Shadows lengthened.

There.

From beyond the fallen cabin, a figure emerged in a faded coat and tricorn. Francis. Behind him, remaining at the edge of the trees, the cloaked figure of the woman who'd pointed the pistol at me. Francis walked past the cabin, coming to a stop next to the well.

"You don't need to hide any longer," he called out. "It's cold. We're here. No sense spying on each other from a distance while we're all slowly freezing."

I looked around but didn't see anyone else. He put his bare hands between elbow and ribs, keeping them warm.

"All we want is to talk, Miss Finch," he said.

I got up from my crouch, pushing myself up on the trunk. "Your note wasn't quite so unassuming." My voice carried through the trees and across the distance.

He turned his head to my direction. "I'm never sure the promise of my company is enough to convince."

"You threatened me." I stayed where I was.

"Difficult times can require difficult measures."

"Your difficulties aren't mine."

He raised his hands. "This jacket is colder than the one *you* burned. So some of my difficulties are your handiwork."

"I meant your other difficulties."

"You're sure those aren't also yours? Not even a little?" He motioned for the woman, who came forward. "The Whitelockes' pet magician, Doctor Rush—he's not one of your difficulties? The laws against magic—quite strict, I believe—they aren't yours? The Governor's troops, ready to enforce them? Not yours, again? We have more in common than you think."

"What do you want?"

"What I want is for everyone in this colony to live in peace."

"You haven't left *me* in peace."

"We have a way to go. Maybe we could start with simply *living* —something my friends have been denied."

I recalled the sight of pale corpses in murky water. I said nothing.

He stepped closer to the well. "Does that make me wrong? Three of my friends are dead because we spoke up against the criminals who run the colony. More are in danger. Maybe polite requests aren't good enough."

"I didn't kill them. My master didn't kill them," I said. "We had nothing to do with what happened."

"We'll get word to the Whitelockes. Your magic," she said. "Everything. They'll drag the both of you off."

I stepped forward. "You remember what I did to you?"

"Try it again," she said. "See what happens the moment you lift your hands."

They obviously had others in the woods, probably aiming muskets at me. Could I have taken them all on, hidden and not-hidden alike? Probably—but with Swaine's warnings about magic being noticed by Doctor Rush, I didn't dare risk any more. Still, I wasn't in the mood for more threats.

"You sound awfully confident," I said.

Francis raised his hands. "This is what the Whitelockes want. Squabbling. Arguing. Fighting amongst ourselves."

"I told you this was a waste of time," the woman said.

"Enough, Clara," Francis said. "None of us can do this on our own."

Clara shook her head. "She's not going to help us. She was talking with the Whitelockes. Why would you even think of trusting someone like—that?"

"Because I'll do whatever it takes to make sure that William, Alfie, and Samuel didn't die for nothing." He came closer to me. "And Miss Finch won't betray us."

"Why wouldn't I?"

"Because if you do, you'll see your master clapped in chains. And it's not just the two of us who have the information. If anything happens to us, the message will be delivered before the sun sets." Francis paused, near enough now that I could see the color of his eyes. "You'll be there with him, as well. Questioned by Doctor Rush and the others. Your secrets laid bare. Your freedom nothing but a memory. There's a steep price to be paid here for using magic—but I think you know that already, don't you?"

"What do you want?" I repeated. Did I believe he'd arranged

for information to be fed to the authorities in the event I did something drastic to him? He could well have been lying, but even the smallest possibility terrified me. It would mean the end of everything Swaine had worked for, everything he'd trusted me with. Worse, I couldn't think of any way Doctor Rush wouldn't, under such circumstances, discover I was a witch—and all that would entail. Massachusetts hadn't been kind to witches: the only question was whether I'd burn, or hang.

"Access," Francis said. "To the Whitelockes. In their manse, at their ball. That's all I want."

"You don't need me for that. Nothing's stopping you from sneaking in on your own."

"Except guards, the Governor's Own, their dogs, pistols, muskets, barricades. People like us can't get within a quarter mile of their ball. Especially now. Trust me."

"I can't change a thing about any of that."

"Use magic. Get us inside."

I shook my head. "It's not that easy."

"You'll figure something out."

Were there ways? Of course. Could I think of any in the moment? Of course not. "No, it's not possible. Not—not with Doctor Rush there."

Clara shook her head. "I told you. She can't help."

"I think she can," Francis said. He turned back to me. "No one will be expecting it. You're not stupid, either—that much is obvious. You look like you've already thought of something."

"I haven't."

"But you will. You can."

A crow called out from the edge of the forest. Others answered it, their caws echoing out over the hillside.

"Don't you want them gone?" Francis said.

"I don't care about them."

"You like liars?"

"The world is full of liars."

"Killers?"

"Those, too."

"The cruel? Those who prey on the weak? Those who take everything they can for themselves? Break every rule when it suits them? Forbid magic? Strangle the will out of the people for their own ends—and blame the victims for their own misery? Because that's what we're talking about here. It's not a lark. We're trying to wake people up. To make them see that what they've grown used to as normal is nothing of the kind. That it's criminal." He came closer. "It's wrong—and I think you agree."

"You really don't know anything about me."

"I know more than most. Better still, I'm willing to use it against you. And if that has to be why you help me—I'll settle for it."

I didn't want him to see how rattled I was, so I stepped forward until we stood an arms-width apart. "And what's stopping me from turning you in to the Whitelockes myself?"

"The guaranteed promise of them learning about your magic."

"That doesn't have to stop me."

"It should," he said. "They've already caught Rattlesnakes. A few more won't make much difference. But if they put a stop to magic, the dark arts, the infernal? They'd leap at the chance, wouldn't they? Protectors of the populace. Guardians against the unseen. It would shake away all the doubts we've put into people's minds. They would love to have a rogue magician—or two—to dangle in front of the people. To dangle in front of the King's men. To dangle from the gallows on the Commons."

The nearby crow flapped from the high branches behind me and flew toward the west, leaving a curlicue of snow to fall in its wake.

"If I get you into the ball," I said, hating the words even as they left my tongue, "then what?"

"You don't need to worry about that part," Francis said. "The less you know, the better."

"Until I'm arrested for conspiring against the Governor."

"You won't be arrested. We'll keep each other's secrets. We'll both feel safer that way."

"That won't make me feel safer."

"These are difficult times."

We stared at each other. I didn't like the threat. I didn't like how he made me feel. I didn't like that I didn't see any way around it.

"You agree?" he said.

"I'm not joining your cause."

"No one asked you to," Clara said.

"We need your help, not your loyalty," Francis said. "A favor for a favor."

"It's not a favor. It's extortion," I said.

"You can think that way now. I understand. Maybe you'll think differently later on. Defiance might suit you better than you know."

"Just tell me when. Where."

"Night of the ball. Seven o'clock. The alleyway behind the Painter's Arms. Come alone. If you're not there within a quarter hour of that time, our message will be delivered." He tipped his hat, which I guessed to be a signal to the other Rattlesnakes watching from the trees. "You've made the right choice, Miss Finch. You won't regret it."

"You'd both better hope I don't." I gave them each a look, then turned and headed back into the woods as the sun set the tops of the trees ablaze against the winter sky. My threat felt as empty as the bare maple branches overhead.

22

YET ANOTHER GRIM TALE

Riven with paranoia, dread coiled like a serpent in my guts, I rode back through the early dusk. I hunted for a solution to my predicament that didn't involve yet more magic, yet more lies. A few lights burned in the windows of the Andover house. As I stabled the horse, I hoped Swaine hadn't even noticed me gone. The less I had to talk right then, the better.

I let myself in the kitchen door, listening. No sounds of Swaine reached me. If he heard me enter, he didn't feel the need to call for me. Just as well. I busied myself in the kitchen, stoking the fire, readying a supper of butter, bread, and squash soup. Full dark settled beyond the windows. When the food was ready, I went in search of my master. At the door to his study, I listened for a moment, heard nothing, and rapped my knuckles softly on the door.

"Master, can I get you some soup and bread?"

No answer.

"Master?" I repeated, more loudly.

I turned the knob and opened the door. With Swaine, such a move could be a mistake—if he were deep in thought. Yet the reverse—and subsequent tongue-lashing for being too timid to get a simple answer—was also true. I'd learned to err on the side of bold. "Master?"

His study was empty. Books in various stages of unpacking occupied most surfaces. A fire burned low in the hearth. At his writing desk, a teapot stood next to a half-finished cup of tea. I turned from his study and went to the stairs, fetching a candle. Draughts snapped the flame to and fro. In the narrow hallway, I searched the rooms, but didn't find Swaine.

There was no telling where he'd gone off to. Inspiration might take him on an errand, off to hunt for some forgotten item, or to attempt a conjuring out of doors. It was just as well. The longer I had to work through Francis' threat without weaving another hasty lie gave me more time to consider my options.

And so I did, staring into the fire in the kitchen while I consumed two fat pieces of bread smeared with fresh butter and a bowl of soup, lost in my thoughts.

Everything was difficult.

How was I even to get to the ball to get Francis inside? Swaine —given the situation in Salem—had decided against attending the Whitelocke ball, whatever social benefits might accrue. Did I dare ask him if I might go in his stead?

With a household in unbridled disarray, I'd have to expect a firm 'no.' A scornful 'no,' more likely.

Then, another deception. The thought made me queasy. *Sorry, sir—I forget that flour I'd ordered. I'll be back in six hours.* No, that wouldn't do. Each plausible excuse I came up with skittered away under scrutiny like mice fleeing candlelight in the night.

The thought of leaving it all up to chance left me cold. Would Swaine become so occupied that he mightn't notice my disappearance a second time? And for even longer? Counting on it would be foolish. Sneak away, knowing full well I'd face his wrath later? It seemed like the only route. Could I look him in the eye later and lie about it? Tell him I'd broken his trust for the sake of some foolishness or another? For a man?

I withered just thinking about it.

But there was no alternative, if it came to it. I couldn't confess all I'd done. Not then, after so much time. And even if he could forgive my transgression and the subsequent lying—which he wouldn't—there was no conceivable scenario in which he would agree to help the Rattlesnakes.

I stared at the fire, unhappiness perched heavily on my shoulders.

Swaine might well make the situation worse, I realized. He wasn't one to be boxed in. Or, God help us all, threatened. Some catastrophe or other would ensue, ending in one or more dead Rattlesnakes, the Whitelockes on the prowl, or someone in jail. Between Francis and my master, I didn't see calmer heads prevailing.

No, if I told him, he'd ignore Francis' threat, convinced he could talk his way out of any misunderstanding. That he could reason with Doctor Rush. That he could rely on the (unrequited) interest of Mary Whitelocke. And then the story of my fire magic would come out. His trust in me would be incinerated.

We'd both end up in jail.

Around and around my thoughts spun, searching for a scenario in which everything might work out for the best.

I found none.

By the time the fire burned low enough to chill the air yet again, the hour struck eight o'clock. I snapped out of my worry and looked about.

Still no Swaine. I threw another log on the fire and went to the door. I stepped halfway outside. Trees leaned over the house and stable beneath clear stars. The early winter cold gave the air a clarity, silent and sharp. No voices, no footsteps, no signs of my master. I walked out to the stable, doubting myself. When I'd put the horse away, the other horse had been there—I'd surely have noticed otherwise. Looking in on the horses, I saw I was right. Swaine hadn't taken a horse.

My concern growing, I walked the front of the property, looking out into the trees, into the moonlit road, the snow turning the scene ghostly. The house was dark, save for where the fires burned. The worry grew that Francis had already betrayed me—or Clara, more likely. She hadn't cared for me or the promise I'd made. Had she convinced Francis that they'd be better served with me and my master in jail? Had she tipped off the Whitelockes?

It seemed unlikely, not leastwise because no one had waited around to arrest me. The doors had been latched, no signs of a struggle. Furthermore, Francis needed me, or why would he have bothered in the first place? So, no—no arrest.

Just as I'd grown certain, the sound of hooves came to me from up the lane, along with the creak of a wagon. I froze. A moment later, the shape of a driver coalesced, slipping through shadows of the evergreens in the moonlight. My mind raced from one possibility to the next: Swaine, soldiers from the Governor's Own, Mr. Preston loaded with more bodies. It was only as the wagon drew nearer that I relaxed. Bertram lifted a hand and brought his wagon to a halt in front of me.

"Miss Finch," he said.

"Katie," I said.

His voice caught in his throat for moment, and he managed to get out "Katie" on the second try. "I thought, what with the cold snap, you might like some extra firewood. All afternoon quartering my arms down to jiggling strings with an axe in my hand, and I looked up and noticed I'd split a ridiculous amount of wood. All for just me and my grandfather. He shakes all the time. Not from the cold. From being old." He batted his gloved hands together. "So I thought I'd be more neighborly than I have been and see if I could give some of the excess to you. For you and your master. Spare his arms a bit of chopping."

I smiled. Swaine didn't chop the wood—I did, especially after we'd both agreed that the sight of a revenant with an axe in its hands gave neither of us any comfort. The only one of the revenants possessing enough dexterity to do it properly had a murderous air about him to begin with, so the chore fell to me. I'd developed respectable calluses and arm strength, on the positive side.

"He'll be very thankful," I said. "You're too kind."

Even in the dark, I saw him blush.

"He's here?" Bertram said.

"Resting."

He looked around. "I'll say it's a bit of a fright, riding out this way. Did you hear of the Harrow sisters?"

"The ones who drowned?"

"The ones who drowned and then walked their way back to the pond." He nodded his head to the east. "It's just over that way. Horrible. Horrible."

"Did you see them?"

"No, and I thank Heaven. But I know enough of the men who did to know it wasn't a fable. It was enough to bring Doctor Rush up from Boston, so that's something. Horrible." He shivered. "Can't imagine ever setting foot near that water again. Good bass there, too. Not that it isn't a hundred times worse for the parents. It is. Just, it's a terrifying thing. Do you know Andover used to be part of Salem?"

He nearly whispered the word *Salem*.

"I had no idea." Not quite true. Still, I didn't like where the conversation was going.

"I've a cousin down in Charlestown. Always tells me, 'Bertram, I've no idea why you'd keep living up in that stretch of land, so close to a town of such damnation.' I tell him it's not usually a worry. Tale of a spirit here or there can make for a pleasant shiver come nightfall. Used to gather them up, as a lad. Peering down into witch-wells. Running through burial yards. All a bit of frightening fun, I thought. Until a tale like this. Then, I wonder if he isn't more than half-right."

"I'm sure Salem must be worse."

"Do they have dead sisters walking about, I wonder?"

"They have no one walking about. Think about that."

"You know—you might be right, Miss—er, Katie. Still, I'd be happy not having to think about anyone walking where they shouldn't be. If you follow. Or bridges grown impassable. It's all a bit much for the likes of me."

"Bridges?"

"Oh, aye. A few days back, drayman with a cart full of pumpkins and squash was returning from day's market in Reading. Not much daylight left, from what I was told. Sun already down. As he neared a bridge that spans the Shawseen River, he saw a figure standing beside it. Tall and strange. Wide shoulders, thin elsewhere. Gnarled, like. He thought it no more than a tall scarecrow, stood up in jest. But as he rode closer, he spotted shadows gathered around the figure, whirling slowly."

I didn't like the sound of that, not at all. "The bridge on the old Alderbrook Lane?"

"You know it?"

"I do." It was where I met with Mr. Preston, the exact spot.

"See, my cousin might be righter than he knew."

"What happened?"

"Well, the drayman claimed the shadows hid most of this fellow's features, but he caught sight of skin. Pale skin. Pale as a maggot, he described it later. Eyes that glimmered. Arms that moved. The driver went to turn his cart around when the figure raised his hands and whispered something, then turned and crept underneath the bridge. The driver took a look, with his musket in hand. No sign of the figure. Nothing."

"Maybe the drayman had been selling his gourds with one mug too many of strong cider?" I offered. Still, the tale didn't sit well.

"Thought the same," Bertram said. "But the man couldn't get his horse to cross the bridge. Nor could the men he'd returned with after taking the long way home. No animal has crossed the bridge since. None. Two horses hurled themselves into the river, mad with fear, rather than set foot on the wood of the bridge. And not just horses. Any dog brought near the spot lowers its ears and tail, growling and trembling—scrambling to get away if dragged, even turning on its master. The road's useless—but no one's been able to find anything, no one, underneath it. And if that isn't bad enough, there's tales being passed about of a gaunt figure peering in through windows just around the time of sunset. Children crying out. Animals behaving strangely."

None of that sounded good. "Where?"

"Down by byway at the river. But here I am making myself frightened. You, too. Only meant to do a favor."

Had Swaine caught wind of such stories and gone to have a look? It was the first explanation for his absence that felt plausible. I reached up and touched Bertram on the arm. "No, you're sweet. And I'm not frightened of tales. Thank you—my master will be grateful."

For a moment, I thought he might tumble off the wagon. Instead, he blushed again and swung down. "Where's your woodpile then?"

"By the back door. I can help."

"No, no. A favor is a favor. And being forced to lug armfuls of wood is no one's idea of a favor. I'll do it."

I didn't want to bruise Bertram's pride, so I let him carry the wood. As he did, words tumbled from his mouth in a nervous stream: his grandfather's blankets, fixing a chimney, his sister's wrath at Francis.

"Is he really one of those Rattlesnakes?" I said.

"Knowing Francis—if he wasn't the very first, he was the one who *convinced* the first one. Full of ideas, he is. Always was. Got me to steal a bushel of apples for him once. I was only nine, but he made it seem a fine idea. Until I got hided for it. And he got the bushel of apples." He plunked down the last armload of quartered logs and exhaled, wiping his gloves free of splinters and bark flecks. "Apples are one thing. The Governor's reputation is quite another, is what I think. A golden tongue can do a lot for a fellow, but it can also let him dodge common sense, if he's got too much of a gift. Maybe it'll all be enough to scare some wits back into him."

"I hope so," I said. "For Iris' sake."

"Well, for his own sake. Some of his mates have already made unwelcome acquaintance with the noose. For a lark. He should be careful."

If Bertram only knew. I hoped the moonlight hid the guilt on my face.

"But there I go again, turning a pleasant firewood delivery into yet another grim tale." He shook his head. "I'm sorry. And I'll let you get back to your business. Please give my regards to your master."

"I only wish everyone was as thoughtful as you," I said. "There'd be no need for grim tales."

After an awkward moment, he nodded. "Well, enjoy. The wood, I mean. And I'd better get back to my granddad. Do you know we have the same conversation every evening? Sometimes more than once—but someone's got to watch over him. And I half-enjoy his talk, most of the time."

I walked with him back to the wagon and bade him goodnight. As he drove off into the night, I found myself sorry to see him go. He could stumble over his own tongue, true—but it seemed better than confronting the silence and worry filling the empty house behind me. I turned back and went inside, closing the door against the cold, guessing that if a demon or two had followed us down from Salem, Swaine might have detected it and gone off to investigate.

Except he would surely have left a note.

I took one final pass through the house. No note. Swaine's cloak hung on the peg near the front door, though that wasn't unusual—keeping my master properly attired against the weather was a constant challenge. Up in his bedchamber, I found the *Occultatum Ostium* where he usually kept it, which encouraged me; the flipside to his obsession with the book was that he wouldn't have departed for any significant amount of time without it.

So I used the time to research ways I might sneak Francis into the Whitelocke ball, regardless of how I might accomplish getting there. There were spells. I brought several books up to my room and read until I caught myself nodding my head, moving my eye across the words while no longer registering them. Deciding that none of my efforts would offer up an answer within the next several hours, I blew out the candle and climbed into my bed, exhausted from troubles, of my own making and otherwise.

23

SWALLOWED UP BY SILENCE

My dreams were ungenerous, determined to deny me a night's rest. Fragments of imagery tumbled through my head, one after another, in sequences untethered to logic, but united by a deep sense of unease. Noises troubled me: muffled cries, the thud of feet hurrying along echoing stairwells, banging on walls. The last was so vivid that I snapped awake, convinced it had been real. I strained my ears, but heard nothing. Or did I hear the trailing reverberation of a bang? I sat up, heavy-headed.

After a moment, I swung my feet to the floor. Had Swaine arrived home at last? Crediting my strange dreams, at least in part, to the mystery of his absence, I stepped to my door and listened. Nothing. Now, of all the things my master was, one thing he *wasn't* was quiet. Every door, slammed. Every tread on the stairs, emphatic. Even trundling around his bedchamber before finally going to sleep was a percussive sonata of drawers banging shut, books thumped to tables, shoes tossed in varying directions, followed by ten minutes of groaning boards as he settled into his bed, muttering the whole while.

While it was possible I'd slept through all of it in the adjacent room—perhaps explaining the discord of my dreams—I knew I wouldn't rest easily until I knew for sure. I opened my door and walked down the chill hallway. From the sliver of moonlight huddling beneath the window at the far end, I judged it well past midnight. I paused outside Swaine's door, yet again. No sound. Worse, I noted no essence of Swaine. No hint of the oil he wore in his hair. No aroma of tea or note of whatever tincturous smoke he'd generated with his research.

Risking an exhausted bellow of annoyance, I knocked on his door. "Master?"

When I heard only silence, I opened the door. No, it was all as I'd last seen it. He wasn't there.

Still convinced I'd heard something, I made another circuit of the house, padding softly in my bare feet. Everything appeared as I'd left it earlier. Fire burned down to embers in the kitchen. Swaine's study sketched in pewter and charcoal. Scraps of moonlight fell past the curtains in the room I'd practiced my elemental energy work in. As I approached the window, I stepped on a quill. I reached down to pick it up, and paused: it was only half a quill. I lifted it between finger and thumb, only to reel sideways under a crashing wave of vertigo, feeling as though I'd just done an unexpected somersault. I steadied myself on the window sill and noticed the quill in my hand.

The full quill. I stared at it. It had only looked like half a quill when I'd grabbed it. Examining it more closely, I didn't find a crease or crack or any manner in which it folded. I reached out with the quill and pressed it against the wall—only to be rocked with dizzying nausea a second time as the quill passed *into* the wall. I gasped, and pulled the quill back. It slid through the wall —or, what appeared to be the wall. Back and forth I moved it, gritting my teeth against the disorienting sensation that buffeted me as I did so.

I leaned back before tossing the quill at the wall. It disappeared.

Not good.

I lit a lantern and examined the wall more carefully. All looked sound—the baseboards, the wainscoting, the window sill, all solid, no different from any other portion of the wall. Yet the nearer I stood to it, the more my stomach turned. I detected no demon, but checked that I wore my pendant just the same. Still there. Looking over the table, I saw the pair of quills I'd used earlier—I remembered them well, for one was white and the other a brindled pattern.

So it wasn't my quill on the floor. Could it have been an old one? I doubted it, for one of the first things I'd done after we'd decamped to the house had been to give each room a much-needed sweep.

The idea hit me solidly in the chest: it was one of Swaine's quills. I turned to the door. Had it been open or closed when I'd returned from my meeting with Francis? Had Swaine's door been open? Could he have come through—perhaps led, perhaps investigating some noise or phenomenon, perhaps tracking some bit of his own magic gone awry?

And what? I wondered. *Disappeared through the wall?*

Curious, I grabbed a fire-poker from the hearth. Bringing it to the wall, I repeated my exercise with the quill, only to feel the iron grow cruelly cold in my hand the moment it penetrated the illusion of wall. So cold I dropped it. The resulting clang echoed queerly, as though through a space much larger than the small room in Andover.

I stepped back, staring at the fire-poker, now halfway disappeared into the wall. Approaching the window, I glanced at the wall once more, then opened the window, leaning out into the cold midnight air. The outside of the house looked normal: lashed by seasons, faded by sunlight, but solid. I snatched up the fire-poker and gripped it, slipping it outside the window and reaching until I could hit it against the side of the house opposite the curious illusion on the interior. *Bang, bang.* Solid as it looked.

Pulling myself back inside the room, I leaned the fire-poker against the wall beneath the window. I crouched before the wall where the quill had disappeared. This close, I noticed a slight feeling of motion beneath my feet, reminiscent of my journey across the Atlantic. As I brought my face closer to the wall, the feeling increased. I reached my hand out. With a disorienting sensation, my hand passed straight through, embraced by chill air. Unlike the air outside the window, this was a deeper cold, one that spoke of stone, of depth, of a place untouched by the light of the sun or warmth of the day.

Uneasy, I pulled my hand back. It appeared normal. Fingers flexed, skin warming.

"Master?" I called. Again, the sound carried onward in strange fashion. I sat back on my heels. Dare I look inside? Mindful of Swaine's many cautions surrounding demons and magic, I suspected a longer period of investigation might be in order—but by then I'd lost all patience. With his mysterious disappearance. With the strands of worry and strain knotted through my days. With the frustrations of the unseen arts.

So I ducked my head and stuck it, seemingly, through the wall. Not an artful decision. Nor a much-considered one, I'm afraid.

Once inside, I glanced around quickly, like a person thrusting their head underneath the surface of a dark pond. What I saw confounded me: a stone wall where the wooden wall should have been, a dim chamber open on three sides, hints of a floor some five feet beneath my vantage, a balcony to the right, lined with what looked to be an ornate iron railing, another wall to the left with what appeared to be a window opening out into a walkway lined by a marble balustrade, and in front of me, an even wider vista that spoke of space and depth. More curious, sprays of moonlight reached out here and there, implying window or doorway or rail—yet in more than one direction, as though lit by different moons. My face prickled with the cold.

Panicked, I slid back, furrowing my brow at the dislocation that crashed over me on finding myself sitting on the floor of my work room, staring at the wall. For a moment, I considered that I was still in the midst of a particularly convincing dream. But, no —my cheeks held the cold, my toes strained beneath my hips, my fingers felt the grain of the floorboards.

With a pinch more caution, I lifted the lantern and approached the wall. Lantern first, then my head again, this second glimpse afforded an even more detailed view of what I'd seen before. Rough-hewn stone was clear in the shifting flame, as was the pocked surface of the railing. The light revealed no colors beyond those of slate, bone, dusk. Not only couldn't I guess *where* I was looking, but even *what* I was looking at couldn't quite fit into my mind. The work of the world's maddest architect couldn't compare. With more light, I made out further passages, what looked like cobbled lanes, archways, blank windows, all in a dizzying profusion leading away from my strange perch. Leaning, I examined where I looked from: faded gray clapboards framed a narrow window with a metal frame and no glass. In the corners, strange bits of ironwork joined the framing.

I looked out, some wordless sense of familiarity dawning on me. Stairs, passages, archways. Then I had it: the otherworldly glimpses I'd seen in the heart of the resonance well above Salem when Swaine had activated the clock. While I couldn't match any specific features to what I'd seen before, the jumbled profusion was, in itself, testament enough.

Had Swaine found this? Had he made his way into it? I looked down and spotted the quill I'd tossed in, directly below. The floor appeared solid enough. I sat back into the room and picked up the fire-poker, then leaned in again and dropped it. It clanged onto the floor next to the quill, setting off a cascade of echoes out into the jumble of passages, stairs, windows, soon swallowed up by silence.

The floor seemed sturdy enough. I told myself I wouldn't go

far. Placing the lantern down next to me, I scooted onto my right hip and slid forward, until my feet hung down. I ignored the fact that it looked as though I were lying on the floor, cut in half. After a moment of anxious dangling, my toes touched the floor. I stood, able to grasp the lantern and bring it in with me. From inside, the window I'd come through appeared dimly lit, as though covered by a scrim of heavy wool. After a spike of panic, I realized I could reach back through it and, standing up on the balls of my feet, reassured myself I could clamber back into the room without trouble. That established, I turned around, holding the lantern aloft.

No breeze fluttered the lantern flame. The air had a dead quality to it, as though it hadn't been disturbed in a century. I crouched and examined the floor. Quill, fire-poker, velvety dust— in which I spotted faint footprints, leading forward.

Swaine's. I recognized the cut of his boot heel.

I'd been right, he'd found the same entrance. I took a few tentative steps forward, lantern held aloft. Stillness overwhelmed me. Looking more closely at the wall of the passageway, I found it to be without blemish, plaster the color of ivory. My fingers ran across the smooth surface. Who had made it? Despite the solidity beneath my fingers, I felt the answer to be: no one. None of the stonework around me held the breath of life, but rather felt as though they'd sprung from the backdrop of a dream, somehow willed into being.

Perhaps in response, my senses felt more finely tuned than I'd ever known them to be, the lifeless surroundings wringing more life out of my perceptions. The softness of the dust beneath my bare feet, pillowed silk. Stone beneath, immeasurably weighty, plunging deep into the earth. The air itself, unbreathed, scentless. All of it exuded a quality which I couldn't define, one which whispered of purpose, of a subtler order than was apparent in the jumble of construction.

And: danger.

While nothing stirred, a voice in my head began a low chorus of warning, the most base of instincts sounding the alarm: *flee*.

I ignored the voice, for the moment. Swaine had obviously come this way. The light from the lantern drew inky shadows around the tiny ridges of his footsteps. I followed them forward ten paces until the corridor ended, opening out into a cobbled lane that bent off in both directions, rising slightly to the left, descending to the right. Across the lane, a stone railing marked the edge. The view past it drew a dizzied gasp from my throat. Forward and down, elaborate staircases led from darkened archways and doors, stone buttresses rode from column to column, a spiraling lane described a wide ellipse plunging into dark depths, dozens of intersecting structures looming over it. A vast opening continued above, likewise surrounded by the expanse of stone and iron, wall and window, glimmers and falls of moonlight in dozens of angles.

I steadied myself on the stone railing, closing my eye to shut out the overwhelming vertigo and sense of scale. After a moment, I turned back to the cobbled lane and searched for signs of Swaine. The dust of the corridor was uneven on the cobbles, making it impossible for me to find disturbances. Even my own steps left virtually no impression.

To the left, the lane rose, slipping between tall walls on either side, blank windows staring out over its shadowy curve. To the right, a wide archway marked what looked to be the start of a tunnel cut into a rough-hewn edge of stone. And in either direction, who knew what followed?

"Master?" I called out.

Master. Master. Master. Master...

The longer my voice echoed out into the depths surrounding me, the more I regretted yelling so loud. Whatever this was, it wasn't a place for shouting, for the silence had changed, as though my call still ran on, a faint hiss, joined by a simmering resentment brought out of its long slumber.

Left or right? Up, down? As much as I wanted to run off searching, calling for Swaine, I knew I was overmatched. Unprepared. The very real possibility that Swaine had gotten *himself* lost wasn't hard to imagine. What chance would I stand? No, I needed to be more thoughtful. Or maybe I was too frightened, in that moment. Whichever truth moved me, I placed the lantern down, between the rails, clear to see from any number of directions. Oil enough to burn for a few hours. Maybe that would give Swaine the sign he needed, if he were indeed lost.

I backed away, uneasy at leaving the circle of lantern light. A small thing it looked, indeed. A lone glowing point in the weighty dark. In the corridor, I hurried back to the window I'd climbed in from, half expecting it to be closed, locking me in this strange world.

But my hands and arms found the floor of the house in Andover. I sighed with relief. Taking a last glance over my shoulder, I climbed back into my work room, wondering how on earth I might find Swaine.

24

A THOUSAND DREAM-FILLED NIGHTS

I paced. Peered back beyond the illusory wall. Leafed through books, looking for some—any—explanation for the sudden appearance of a world beyond the wall. I searched for Dr. Rush's *On Planar Cartography* before realizing it hadn't made the trip with us from Salem, not having crossed Swaine's threshold of irreplaceable.

It was only when I recalled a conversation I'd had with my master (regarding the possibility of needing to travel to New York or Philadelphia to find an alternative clockmaker had Mr. Robert Twelves refused Swaine's offer) wherein I'd suggested, naively, there might be a spell to allow him to make such journeys in a single step, that I found a thread to the mystery.

Traversing the planes is fraught with peril, Swaine had insisted. He told me of Lord Bartholemew Hunt of Buckinghamshire, an original member of Alfred Summerfield's Secret Doorway Guild. Hunt, who served for decades in England's House of Lords, had long studied magic at his estate in High Wycombe during the years when London magic flourished under Summerfield. After Summerfield's disappearance and the subsequent disbanding of the Guild, Hunt continued on in secret, teaching the arts to his four sons.

In 1687, after more than eight years of investigations, Hunt attempted to chart a course from his estate to his brother's home in Stratford-upon-Avon, traversing the hidden planar region that he had christened the 'Demonmere.' He neither arrived at his brother's nor returned through the enchanted doorway that he'd constructed at his estate. Tragically, his sons refused to accept his demise, and over the next three years, one after another, they rushed their studies and set out after their father. Thaddeus, Rex, William, and finally young Alfred each journeyed into the Demonmere, never to be seen or heard from again. It was when Hunt's only daughter Anne was studying the notes of her father and brothers in her later adolescence that the senior Hunt himself reappeared, staggering out from the enchanted doorway that the family had so long obsessed over, during a morning in September of 1710. Anne recorded that her father had aged preternaturally, appearing to be at least one-hundred years of age (his calendar years would have put him at sixty-four), and more than half-mad. Of his journey and experiences, he would speak no word, always close to tears. He often spent his days staring at the portraits of his sons. Anne reported that he would have "spelles and periods of great catatonia" where a sound like "distant and terrible winds" would escape his slack mouth, one of any number of strange phenomena that plagued the estate thereafter, which also included the appearance of bitter water seeping from corners of the ceiling, the inability for any mirror within the manor to remain uncracked, and the frequent movement of furniture at night. Both Anne and Lord Hunt perished when the estate burned down to timbers in the depths of the following winter.

Perilous, indeed.

Knowing we'd brought Hunt's most famous work, *Theories of the Hidden Planes*, from Salem, I located it among the unpacked books and scoured it, wondering if the thread I grasped at would prove to be no more than a cobweb. I scoured the book, flipping through chapter after chapter, until I found Hunt's first description of the Demonmere, the plane he'd identified while studying under Summerfield. The section occupied but a few short pages at the end of his book. As I read the words, my heartbeat sped up.

"My investigations revealed a complex accretion of Physical Space, primarily in the forme of exaggerated or warped corridors, rooms, and stairways, all barren of life. My belief is that said Physical Space in some manners springs from the dreams of Practitioners to occupy a region of interstitial space adjacent to our Worlde."

I reread it. . . . *warped corridors, rooms, and stairways, all lifeless.*

The essay continued:

"Created by and of the said same forces that drive Magick, I suspect the Demonmere trails the Practicing Magician like a wake follows a ship, connecting his work, one expulsion at a time, with Realms Unseen, Realms inhabited by shadows, by demons, by subtle malevolencies in search of entrance into this Blessed Plane. Is this the inescapable price of Magick? An ever-shifting Realm of enchanted detritus ready to spring forth the Infernal? Or might it be harnessed, highway and passage able to defeat the tyranny of Time and of Distance?"

Unfortunately, Hunt himself soon answered the question in disastrous fashion, going so far upon his unexpected return as to attempt to locate and burn any surviving copies of his book he could find, claiming the desire to never have *been born* in the first place inasmuch as his life led to the discovery of the Demonmere.

Yet at the time of his writing of *Theories of the Hidden Planes*, he'd barely explored this new plane, apparently planning on writing a full volume exclusively dedicated to it. He never did, however, leaving posterity—and me, alone in a house in Andover —with little more than a few guesses punctuated by his familial tragedy.

So where did that leave me? Was I doomed to wait years for Swaine to reappear? And if he succumbed to the fate of the Hunt sons rather than the father, never returning at all? The thought horrified me. I attempted to reassure myself: Swaine wasn't an ordinary magician, he wasn't barely trained; a sorcerer of uncommon ability, he possessed a mastery of most magic. No, it wasn't the same thing. Not at all.

Or so I told myself.

I read more, and found nothing. Hunt tantalized. Summerfield was silent on the matter. Koeffler, likewise. I recalled nothing of similar description in Doctor Rush's work. Book after book offered worlds of rare knowledge—yet not a lone sentence about the mysterious realm of dead passageways, empty lanes, and shadowed arches into which Swaine had disappeared.

Significantly more concerned than I'd been earlier, I fought back a surging panic. I approached the wall again. Did I dare venture farther into the empty world, perhaps with a rope or string trailing behind me in case I took a turn too many to easily recall my way?

No, no, no an insistent voice whispered. Was I simply treading the same path of logic the doomed Hunt sons had confronted? I stared hard at the stretch of wall. Yes, they were trained in the unseen arts—but so was I. And wasn't it true that I had more than they did, access to another source of power? Nothing about the account I'd heard or the material I'd just read suggested even a drop of witch-blood running through the Hunt line.

So they weren't witches. I was. Surely that might count for something.

Fine, another quick look. No farther than I'd gone before. Not an inch. I crouched at the wall and slid my legs through it. When I sat at the edge, I knocked the side of my head against the wall, cursing. Tracing the opening with my hands, I paused: it had changed.

I leaned inward. The same passageway below, quill and fire-poker still as I'd left them, my footprints now merged with Swaine's. I slid in, landing lightly, steadying myself. The lantern burned steadily where I'd left it. In the dim light, I examined the window from which I'd slid.

"No," I whispered. "No, no."

Instead of the wide window of earlier, I found an entirely different opening, one framed in dark wood of medieval design. It had to have been at least a foot narrower, half that shorter. In fact, the entire face of the wall appeared unfamiliar, made of thick slabs of dark board. Running a hand across revealed strange grain and streaks of pitch. Even more curious, the sensation of lifelessness hadn't disappeared entirely, but no longer distracted me. I could have been staring at any wall in Boston, or London.

The reason for the change eluded me, but the implication didn't. Turning, I made my way carefully to the lantern, the hiss of the flame the lone sound to reach me. The ten paces of earlier felt closer to twelve this time, a fact confirmed when I lowered down and found no footprints near the lantern itself.

Puzzled, I realized the layout and structure had changed in the time I'd been back in the house. I searched the darkness beyond the railing, scanning the middle and far distance for any signs of Swaine. With such a jumble of arch, runner, cornice, passage, window, and more, I had no confidence that what I saw was exactly what I'd seen on my earlier visit. Quite the opposite.

"Master?" I said, keeping my voice well below a shout. Even then, the word leapt about, here, there, further afield, a bat looking to escape my presence. The silence soon devoured it. As I stood there, bending my head forward, listening, the unaccountable desire to sprint off, to the left or to the right, gushed up inside me. Run, drag a hand along the multitude of surfaces, find a stairwell, run through a door, turn left, turn right, higher, lower, look in doorways, crawl through windows, scamper over rail and curb, hang down, drop out of sight, find a new level, a new passage, a new vista. Find one moon, then another, then who knew what strange night sky might open overhead. A thousand dream-filled nights beckoned, each corner promising a further descent into a reality unseen by mortal eyes.

I snapped myself out of such thoughts, shaking my head, noticing how my limbs trembled, eager to carry me away.

Backing away from the lantern, I focused solely on my steps, one after another until I reached the wall with the smaller window I'd climbed in from. Finally turning away, I scrambled back up through the curious window, breathing in the familiar air of the Andover house as though casting myself ashore after nearly drowning.

25

THE MAGIC OF UNKINDNESS

Time was the enemy.

The opening had shrunk, and shrunk yet again. Each time I checked, it narrowed—until I worried that the very act of checking it was hastening the process. When it was just wide enough to squeeze my head and one arm through, I found that the backside of the wall was carved granite, the opening that of a narrow window in a castle wall.

It grew smaller still in the hour before the dawn. So small that I could fit only my face into the opening. Horrified, I pressed and pushed, feeling about on the inside, running my hand across what felt like strips of reinforced iron framing a tiny window, that of a door in a dungeon, perhaps. Inside the room in the house, the rest of the wall had regained its substance. Worse, as I watched, the flame in the lantern I'd set out on the other side guttered. Maybe it would last another hour. Maybe not.

Desperate, I spent a quarter of an hour calling for Swaine, confronted only by the hopeless echoing of my voice fading to nothing with each shout. What would happen when the opening sealed off completely?

I wasted an hour looking through Swaine's books for a spell

capable of stopping the shrinking of the passage. Window spells, doorway spells—yes, I found a few, but none that accounted for an unexplained, changing entrance into another plane. A spell to project a false image through a night-time window (useful for trysts, alibis, or crimes, I supposed)? Yes. A curse to lay on a doorway designed to give anyone who passes the threshold a pure taste of their own demise? Yes, Giribaldi, true to the Italian school of Magia Nera, outlined one of those.

But nothing else held any promise. Of course, nearly half of Swaine's books were in the original German, Latin, French, or Spanish, doing me no good, as I had no fluency. Flipping through book after book only served to reveal my own inadequacy. What did I think I could accomplish?

A cruel chill had swept in during the night and I found myself shaking. Tending the fire in the hearth, a flash of insight came over me: I was thinking about it the wrong way. Stopping the entrance from closing, while dire in itself, was only part of what I really needed to do.

Find Swaine. That's what mattered. I knew there had to be spells capable of locating an individual. And moreover, if Hunt was correct about the source of the Demonmere's expansion, then it was more than possible that other openings into the plane existed—after all, if it was in part triggered by magic, Swaine (and I) had done plenty of magic in and around the Andover house, and much more in Salem. Could I locate another opening? Could I then use magic to find Swaine?

It felt a tall order. And where to start? I looked over the dozens of books strewn about the room. The thought of starting another random search brought the panic back. I could spend all day—and the next, and the next—looking for the proper spell, one that was within my grasp.

No, that wasn't it. There wasn't time. Without the proper guidance, I didn't see how I might—

I paused. My gaze went to the ceiling. Did I dare? More to the point: did I have any other hope? Without answers, no. Yet was there some other way I might find the answers?

Maybe.

I rushed out of the room and hurried up the stairs to the second floor. Sunlight brightened the frame of the window at the end of the hallway. Pushing the door to Swaine's bedchamber open, I crossed the room and looked down at the book on the small table next to my master's bed: the *Occultatum Ostium*. If Swaine knew I was thinking of so much as touching it, he'd have been furious. Yet—if he was desperately lost in the Demonmere, would that change his thinking?

My intuition failed me.

So did my patience.

With a grimace, I picked up the book, finding it heavier than expected. I brought it back to the room downstairs, carrying it out in front of me as though it were a venomous creature, ready to twist and snap at me. It had a strange heft to it, at one moment lighter, at another heavier. I set it on the nearest table, and hurried to the wall, running my fingers across the surface, looking for the opening. For a moment, I panicked, thinking it gone. Then I found it, no larger than my palm.

Turning back to the *Occultatum Ostium*, I put my hand on it, pulling over my chair. I sat, closing my eye. The feel of the book repulsed me. Even as I reminded myself that a book was a book, this particular book brought to mind corpses, things unseen that wriggled out of view of the sun, trailing lengths of cold scaly skin.

"I need to find my master," I said. "How can I find him?"

I opened my eye, then opened the slender book. It held no more than two dozen pages. The first page was blank. As were the second and third. The fourth and fifth. Expanses of yellowed paper, thick, worn—and empty. Starting to panic, I flipped ahead. There. Halfway through the book, I found a page with an illustration in faded black ink, with flecks of dull red and gold scribed around the edges of the drawing, appearing to be remnants of centuries-old illumination. The drawing depicted a standing mirror cleaved with a thousand cracks. From the broken reflection peered a dozen ravens, onyx-eyed, charcoal-feathered. Scribed beneath the drawing was a phrase: *Grenfense Hex.*

Hex?

I stared at the page, hunting for some other clue. To my horror, the illustration started to fade, beginning at the corners, working toward the middle as though consumed by unseen flames.

"No, please!" I put my fingers on the drawing to halt the process, but the fading ink rippled beneath my touch as if I'd splashed ink riding on the surface of water, and then disappeared. "Wait. Show me that again. Please."

The book ignored my pleading. I searched the adjacent pages. Blank. Every page in the book was blank again. I tried closing it and repeating my request. Nothing. I tried to calm myself, to reach the same state of concentration I'd achieved earlier. Still nothing.

"Grenfense Hex," I whispered. "Grenfense Hex."

I had no idea what the Grenfense Hex was. Again, I confronted stacks of books, any of which might—or might not—hold a reference to or description of that particular hex. And if it did, what was it supposed to do? I grimaced at the *Occultatum Ostium* for a few moments. After giving me that much, I wondered if it would elaborate.

The answer, after a concerted hour of trying to prod it into generating as much as a single word, was no.

Fine.

Grenfense meant nothing to me. I'd never heard of any magician or sorcerer with that surname. It might be a place (I'd never heard of), a technique (unfamiliar to me), a descriptor (in a language I didn't know). A nickname? A title?

No way of knowing, so I had little confidence of finding the proper haystack to pair with the strange needle I found in my possession. There had to be a different way. I thought of the image: the cracked mirror, the ravens. Those meant something. Mirror magic was a broad discipline. As was raven magic, a particular specialty of English magicians from two centuries prior. But which was it? The more I thought it through, I leaned toward raven magic—such specific imagery hadn't appeared for no reason whatsoever. And the mirror, I suspected, might be a reference to the Demonmere, a broken reflection of the world of the magicians who'd brought it into being.

Raven magic, then.

I tossed about Swaine's books, searching for the one book of raven magic he possessed, Richard Woolridge's *Beholde the Magic of Unkindness: Spelles of Corvus*. I found the book and started skimming it, knowing precious little about even the basic theory beyond the generally agreed upon observation that raven magic is tricky business. Spy on a person for a week? Relatively simple. Reveal a murderer? Significantly more difficult, for reasons unknown. The French magician Dominique Bretonneau—sadly, as with altogether too many female practitioners of magic throughout history, later hanged as a witch—once charmed her husband's mistress so that she couldn't as much as set foot in the entire eastern half of Saint-Georges-sur-Cher without Bretonneau hearing of it within minutes from the local ravens. There were spells to bind ravens with secrets. There were variants on spells for seeking lost items. A lost person? I found nothing, at first glance.

But there had to be something.

I tapped my finger on the page open before me, glancing back at the *Occultatum Ostium*. I put Woolridge down and reached instead for the heavy volume that was Gerard Boutham's *Astrum Occultatum*, a majestic encyclopedia of magical terminology, the masterwork of a lifetime of study. I opened it and scanned the epigraph: "Within the flame lies a spark infinitely deep. Beyond the zenith of the heavens stretch rivers of untold time. Betwixt dusk and night abides a united, supernal realm. Behold."

And beyond the shrinking opening in the wall remained my master, I reminded myself, flipping through the pages hoping to find a clue as to what a Grenfense Hex was. While under normal circumstances one of Boutham's particular gifts was to draw the imagination down unforeseen twists and forks with phrases such as "the mellifluous pattering of Helmholtz's Penetrating Fingers holds an alluring ratamacue, yet caution is paramount" or "another curious artifact is the so called 'shadow-room,' visible thereafter within a looking glass at any stroke of midnight," I didn't have the luxury. I turned thick hunks of pages, slowing as I moved through the Es and the Fs and into the Gs.

Greely's Crypt. Greige Conjuring. Greisen Dust. Grenfell's Glamour. Greuze Effect.

Nothing.

"Damn it." I straightened up, stared at the wall for a moment. *Grenfell.* It wasn't much different from *Grenfense*, and I'd noticed in my studies that older spellings often varied profoundly, given the obscure origins of various strands of magic.

And the difference between a glamour and a hex? When I'd asked Swaine, he'd told me that asking ten different practitioners would yield a dozen different answers, but he preferred the working distinction of a glamour being more active, requiring an instigating event, while a hex could be instantiated to constant activity in multiple locations. I turned back to the book and read Boutham's description: "*The Grenfell Glamour brings to raven magic the beguiling effects of rechanneling energies wrapped without and beyond the place in time occupied by the missing subject, a power subtle enough to bypass the flow of said time and locate the individual. A touch of avian artistry perfected by Richard Wooldridge.*"

That was it. Putting the book aside, I went back to Wooldridge, paging through the book with focus. And there it was: the *Grenfell Glamour*. I read the entry. As Boutham indicated, it was a spell for locating a missing person, involving the conjuring of a dozen shadow ravens. As for the ingredients, I needed wolfsbane (we had some from the same shipment at Winslow & Sons when the *Occultatum Ostium* had arrived), the feather of a raven (I knew Swaine had several in his trunk), an hourglass (Swaine had several), rainwater (we always kept some), a personal item from the subject (I had only to take his coat down from near the door), a piece of broken slate (we had lesson slates), spider-web (easy enough, the high corners of the house were draped in them), ink (of course), pure beeswax (yes), a map (possible), and soil (yes). The incantation was in Latin and didn't appear too difficult. I read and reread the entry, tapping a fingernail on the desk.

I believed it feasible—but was it? On one hand, I saw nothing beyond my capabilities. I'd done variants on all the steps in the course of my studies. Was I certain it would work? Not at all. Did I still possess anywhere near the self-confidence I'd tried to make Francis believe I had? No, I didn't.

But I had no better choice.

I gathered the pertinent ingredients. A map proved nearly impossible to find, wasting precious time. Swaine's papers held none, which had been my hope. I recalled seeing one—but back in Salem. Riding out to retrieve it was out of the question. I considered riding to Iris' tavern and asking her who might have one. I also considered making my own, from memory, fearing that a sketch containing no more than a rough approximation of three towns and several roads mightn't work for the spell. Just as I was about to try it, I remembered Archibald Fletcher's account of his time as the colony's first Doctor of Magickal Sciences. By the time I found the book, still nestled in the trunk we'd carried it from Salem in, mid-morning approached.

I brought the book to the room, paging through it as I hurried, finding the map I'd recalled near the front. Drawn in Fletcher's own hand, the map showed the eastern half of the colony, from the arm of Cape Cod up to the burly shoulder of Cape Anne and the towns along the shore. An inset box featured a closer scale view of Salem, harbor, rivers, and hills all notated. I pressed down hard on the binding, laying the book open on the table.

By the time I had everything ready to go, the morning was gone and the opening into the Demonmere had shrunk to smaller than my two thumbs pressed side to side. In the far corner of the room, I created the required glamour in a circle on the floor. Once done, I sprinkled the floor within with the mixture of rainwater, soil, and spider-web that I'd spoken the proper incantations over, making sure that it was evenly distributed. A faint glow appeared in the air, which was encouraging. Next, I gestured over the beeswax and spoke another phrase, kneading it in my palm until it was pliable.

"*Alveo sigillum,*" I said. The wax shone with a dull orange glow. I focused on it, slipping into the proper state of mind. Dividing it in two, I pressed one and then the other onto the north and south points of the glamour. At the table near the hearth, I picked up the hourglass, removed the piece of quartz that I'd enchanted, flipped the hourglass over and placed the quartz on the new top side. I paced around the glamour counterclockwise while holding a candle, speaking the incantation as I repeatedly lit the wolfsbane and blew it out, sending the fragrant smoke over the glamour. When I'd finished a complete circuit, I let the rest of the wolfsbane burn to fine cinders and fall into the glamour, then snuffed the candlewick with my fingers, speaking the proper word as I pressed the nib of the raven feather into the soft wax at the top of the candle.

Lines of faint light rose around the glamour, wavering like silken threads underwater, casting a queer glow. It fit with Woolridge's description. I nodded, pleased, and began the larger spell —where things got tricky. A major spell typically requires an intimate familiarity with the incantatory phrases, a familiarity which requires memorization over time, enough time that the words themselves become cues to the energy being harnessed and not the sole focus. I didn't have that time, so I cheated, reading the incantation from a copy of the phrasing that I'd made myself on a piece of paper. I'd read through the spell several times as I'd prepared the ingredients, committing the contours of the words to memory, a mental map.

A spell isn't just a magical password that opens the unseen energies, something that anyone could speak and achieve the result. No, a proper incantation takes place at the difficult-to-balance point where mind meets body meets energy, and being centered is crucial. No distractions, the mind focused—yet calm. Straining dissipates the effort, tension binds it. The magic is led, like water. It gathers by achieving a curious buoyancy of spirit, a raising of consciousness that reaches beyond the immediate surroundings.

Did I hit that delicate equilibrium as I attempted to conjure a dozen shadow ravens in my first ever attempt at raven magic? The channels of energy shifted, I will say that much. There were a few points where I struggled, my tongue tripped up somewhere between my eyes reading from the page and my mouth moving. Three of the four repetitions were without major flaw. On the fourth I accidentally skipped two lines as I repositioned myself and had to cut myself off mid-line and return to the lines I'd missed.

Before repeating the phrases, I paused. A chilling of my skin rose from my heels, along the back of my legs, up through my shoulder-blades. Hints of shadow seemed to flee from my gaze as I looked about: through the walls, through the plaster of the ceiling, scurrying away. Fear took hold of me, tightening my throat, twisting my stomach. I closed my eye for a moment, shaking my head. I had to keep going.

I hurried through the lines I'd skipped, completing the incantation.

As the forces within the glamour snapped into the proper order at the conclusion of the final repetition, power surged throughout the room. A strange light danced around the edges of the glamour. The air crackled and snapped, bright sparks of violet cascading over the floor, bouncing and colliding. I focused on completing the sealing gesture, speaking the spell's coda. The wax and twine on the floor glowed for a moment, then faded. The air pressure shifted and my ears popped. The room darkened around me. Whatever I'd reacted to during the casting of the spell had receded—I saw no more strange shadows, felt no more gripping terror. I watched the circle of the glamour.

Wooldridge had written of the shadow ravens' appearance: "The conspiracy will erupt like flames of darkness, ready for bidding."

Nothing happened. The light of the spell dimmed and faded, leaving me staring at the circle of metal filings and the ingredients I'd scattered inside it. While I sensed a lingering magic, no flames—of darkness or otherwise—appeared. Looking over the description of the spell again, skimming the words of the incantation again, I couldn't find a problem. All the ingredients were correct, and I'd used them in the right order. The mistake I'd made in the incantation had to be the problem.

The idea of trying the spell a second time gave me pause. *Something* had happened, and might have been enough to prevent me from succeeding on a second attempt. Spells, adding to their complexity, aren't a recipe that can be made as many times in a row as desired; the potency of each subsequent casting diminishes rapidly, following a curve known as Fish's Law, named for the great sixteenth-century English magician Arthur Fish, who charted the dissipation effects of multiple castings. Why it is so remained a matter of debate, theories ranging from the inevitable strains on the incantor's concentration, to the depletion of the hidden energies tapped by the spells.

Making my situation more fraught, if a spell was repeated

atop a first attempt that hadn't been fully realized, it was a near-certainty that the second attempt would misbehave, in some cases spectacularly.

All of which was why Swaine preached *precision*.

Furious at myself, I turned back to the glamoured circle and gasped.

Ravens.

Smoky things, they gazed about the room with obsidian eyes. Curls of darkness lifted from their backs, their wings, their tufted throats as though smoldering. Hints of deep red shone from between their feathers as they shifted on black claws. They turned their gazes to me, silent. As I scanned them, I counted, realizing with some alarm there were *thirteen* of them, not twelve. That wasn't right, but no matter—I was glad they'd arrived at all.

My heartbeat galloped. I'd done it.

I lifted Swaine's coat from the table. "Augustus Swaine," I said, using Swaine's full first name. "I bid you: find him, now."

One of the ravens croaked, startling me. As directed, I tossed the coat into the glamour. As it passed into the magic, it shredded, leaving no loop or warp of the fabric whole, landing fiber and string amongst the ravens. With a ruffle of wings and chorus of husky caws, the ravens took flight, filling the room with a whirling mass of black shapes. I staggered back, protecting my head with my arms. They spun counterclockwise, battering the walls, toppling candles, brushing over papers and quills. Two of them clung to the wall at the mysterious opening, claws scrabbling on the wood, pecking at the wood. Finding no way in, they joined the others. Before I knew what was happening, they found their way out of the room, spilling into the hallway.

I ducked my head and ran to the front door. According to Woolridge, they would fly off in a group, bound to locate Swaine —revealing his location on the map. Throwing open the door, the ravens swept past me, trailing strands of black smoke, sending me staggering out onto the snowy ground. Their shadows, blue against the white snow, sped across the yard in a shifting pattern. Bracing myself, I watched the conspiracy lift higher into the air. One after another, the ravens broke from the rest, flapping out in what appeared to be random directions: one through the trees to the north, another back towards the pond, another into the woods across the way.

As I stood gaping, I watched individual ravens flying off.

"No!" That wasn't right. One raven perched on the high limbs of a bare maple, staring at me. The rest flew out of sight. Not even a pair had come together.

I looked at the raven in the tree. "Where is he?" I shouted.

With what appeared to be an annoyed croak, the bird took to wing and headed south, leaving me standing in the snow, alone. After another minute of scanning the sky and spotting no birds save for a lone hawk in the distance, I hurried back into the house, slamming the door behind me. Back in the room, I knelt before the wall. Scratches from the ravens' claws marked the wood. I ran my hands across the boards and found nothing. No entrance. No disturbance in the wood. Not a dimple. Nothing. The opening into the Demonmere, gone. I slammed my hand against the wall.

At the table, I looked over Fletcher's book, set open to the map I'd enchanted at the beginning of the spell. Pushing back on the worry—*you failed*—whispering in the back of my mind, I continued on to the next step of the spell. Dipping the raven feather in ink, I held it over the map. The drops of ink would trace a path that would lead me to Swaine.

I flicked the feather. Tiny spatters of ink landed on the table, missing the map entirely. Cursing, I dipped the feather again and snapped it with my wrist, just over the map. Again, no ink dotted the paper. Some landed on the opposite page, more on the table, some tattooed the front of my dress. Again and again, I sent showers of ink over the book, but not the smallest fleck punctuated the map. Leaning in more closely, I watched as the ink slipped sideways over the map, flying through the air to decorate the table in an ever-growing mess of black dots.

According to the spell: my master was nowhere. I told myself the ravens had just left—*not as they should have, because you did it wrong*—and it might take more time. In fact, it almost certainly would. With a glance at the clock ticking on the mantle, I wondered how long it would take. Being half-past two o'clock, I suspected it might take as long as—

Half-past two o'clock.

The Whitelocke ball. I needed to meet Francis in Boston in less than three hours, and it would take me that long to simply ride there. I flung down the raven feather with a groan. How could I hope to help Swaine if I was in jail? Worse, even if I did manage to rescue him, it wouldn't do us much good if we were both then arrested by the Governor's men.

Trailing rage, frustration, and desperation behind me as the ravens had trailed their smoky darkness, I flew from the room, gathering what I needed. I hurried to the barn. The day had turned bitter, and a snowfall left an icy crust that glinted on the fallow meadows and between the bare trees that striped the snow with meager shadows. I saddled the horse who would bring me to Boston.

26

THE SUM OF MY SECRETS

I rode into Boston as a soft snow fell, muting the sounds of the city as the rooflines and streets merged with the dusk. Lanterns made halos. I hitched my exhausted horse on the corner of Queen Street and made my way toward the Painter's Arms, a stuffed haversack cast over my shoulder, my heart racing. The green door of the tavern opened as a pair of gentlemen entered, shaking their hats free of snow as they slipped inside. I searched for the alleyway, finding its narrow opening up against a cobbler's shop. No more than arms-width wide, it went back a good thirty paces before reaching a larger space at the backs of several establishments. Empty. I turned in a circle, went a few paces in one direction, then in another.

"You're late." Francis stepped from a darkened doorway. Clara appeared over his shoulder. Farther down, another pair of young men revealed themselves. "I was about to send my friends off with the message about you and your master."

"I said I'd be here." I was glad for the darkness: it hid my chagrin at having been surprised by them. I should've been more careful. "I need a place to get ready."

"This way," Francis said. Clara turned back into the doorway.

The other men watched us, but remained outside. Once I stepped in, Francis closed the door behind me. The air held a blend of biting scents, sharp and metallic. I stepped away from the door and into the larger space of a dye-house, where a lantern burned on a table. A row of giant vats stood along one side, while smaller casks, cut in half, lined the opposite wall. Discolored poles, topped with hooks, and a jumble of half a dozen buckets stood against the vats, the floorboards showing the stains of ten thousand drips. A narrow staircase rose along the back wall, leading to a catwalk that encircled the open area at second-story level, the windows frosted with snow. I dropped the haversack I carried to the floor and knelt beside it, prying open the hook and eyelets. I pulled out a silk dress of pale green, embroidered with a spray of white blossoms.

"What's this?" Francis said.

"This is how I'm getting into the ball." Mary Whitelocke would expect that I arrive wearing an ensemble she'd purchased for me.

"Don't you mean getting *us* into the ball?"

"One thing at a time." I shrugged off my cloak and stripped down to my shift, putting the dress into Clara's hands. "Help me with this."

She didn't appear pleased by the prospect, but she lent a hand, helping to hitch the back of the dress.

"So how are you getting us in?" Francis said.

"We're walking straight through the front door."

Once the dress was straightened, I had Clara help me with the rest of my outfit: a frilled riding cloak in a warm cream shade; a choker; my hair in a bowed braid; gloves; a pair of shoes covered in cream satin and brocaded ribbon.

"Unless you brought us all dresses, I don't see how that's possible," Francis said.

"You wanted magic. I have magic."

"Or she's leading us into a trap," Clara said, frowning. "And we'll walk up with her like fools."

"If I'd wanted you caught, I wouldn't have bothered with the dress—I could've led Whitelocke men right here."

They exchanged a glance.

"Then how's it going to work?" Francis said.

I appreciated that he gave me the credit of thinking it *would* work. I wasn't so sure. My plan was to use a cloaking spell. I'd found two that sounded promising. The first was Chester Trembley's *Undesired Countenance*, which cloaked the identity of an individual by leveraging the strongest inclinations drawn from the minds of the observers, convincing them that what they found most uncomfortable to witness amongst the sprawl of humanity was seen in place of the subject. Depending on the observer, the spell might create the impression of a thug, a diseased child, a priest, a wounded individual—whatever the observer would most readily turn their gaze from out of discomfort, fear, or loathing. It might work well in a crowded market or on a busy street, but I worried that at a prestigious ball, the effect might raise too many questions.

Instead, I'd chosen the seventeenth-century London magician Bellamy Howell's *Deflected Guise*, a spell that drew randomly on features of nearby individuals to obscure the identity of the subject—creating an illusion of altered appearance by replicating the hair or a hat from one passerby, nose from another, gait from another, cheeks and jaw from yet another. An unknowing observer was unlikely to realize that the features seen were no more than an amalgam of the features of the nearest people in the vicinity. The more dense the crowd, the more effective the outcome—though, of course, the opposite was true, if the location were sparsely populated. It felt more appropriate for a ball.

If it worked.

Rummaging through the haversack, I pulled out a wooden

box of ingredients and the copy of Howell's *Spells of Practical Enchantment*, bookmarked with a silk ribbon.

"A book?" Clara said.

"It needs to be done right—or you'll be walking straight into their Governor's hands."

"You didn't need a book before."

"I need it now."

"And if it doesn't work?"

"It will work if you let me concentrate." I carried the book and box over to the table where the lantern burned. A gust of wind rattled the windows. I opened the book and read through the incantation once more. When I felt as confident as I was going to be (shy of a month or more of practice and study), I pulled the ingredients out of the box, placing them on the table. Four glass beads. Two silver coins. A tin of charcoal. A vial containing a tincture made from hawthorn berries, wine, and ground teeth. Two short candles with glyphs scribed into their sides.

I lit the candles off of the lantern's flame and set them down. "Don't interrupt me," I cautioned. Francis and Clara said nothing. He looked both curious and tense; she impatient. Before each candle, I placed a pair of glass beads atop one of the coins. Holding my palms out over the candles, I recited the stanza of the spell:

Lo hide the one, whose Guise will turn to maske,
As hid 'neath shade, as fox amid the weeds,
Am now mirror'd in sparse unsparing taske,
For strangers stolen shift shadowed in the reeds,
And spare the Eyes and Senses gentle pleads;
Whose borrowed features now belong,
To Thee, to Thine, the profane Hand leads
To scribe well curves of the gathered throng:
Whose winsome glimpses and spare glances shall not linger long.

As I spoke, lines of fine gold appeared over the beads, swirling. Opening the tin of charcoal, I blew a pinch across the set of beads and coin, whispering "Shadowy canvas, cloaked to eyes." I concentrated and recited the incantation a second time. As the spell's potency flared, I felt the tendrils of energy spring from the beads, connected on slender filaments to my own will. The flames of the candles spit off sparks, rising in twists into the darkness of the catwalk overhead. Clara gasped.

I turned and waved Francis to step closer, taking up the tincture. "Be careful not to wipe any of this off or it will stop working." Opening the vial, I tilted it and poured a dab onto my fingertip, then traced figures onto his face: crescents beneath his eyes, four dots on his chin, a line along each side of the jaw and the nose, a circle in the middle of his forehead.

"It's cold," he whispered.

I stayed focused, ignoring how warm his skin felt and how intricate his irises were when seen so closely.

"Just don't touch it," I whispered. Once I'd finished with the symbols, I took up the set of beads and coin and handed them to him. "Put those in your pockets. Separate, if you have them."

I lifted the candle before his face, then said, "Beholde the borrowed guise."

With a gentle puff, I blew out the flame. The figures on his face shone gold for a moment, then faded.

"Oh," Clara said, putting a hand over her mouth.

"I feel a tingling," Francis said.

I nodded. "It will stay that way until the spell ends. Remember, don't touch your face." As the incantor, I couldn't see any change, but from the way Clara looked at him—eyes wide, mouth slack—I could tell that *she* did.

Francis looked at her. "What do you see?"

"You—it's not you." She furrowed her brow. "Your chin—and your skin—it's so strange."

"He's probably reflecting some combination of you and I," I said.

She looked at me, then back at Francis. "That's it."

"Yes, that's how the spell works. Now, your turn."

"Does it work on clothing?" Francis said.

"It draws the eye to the features of the face. The clothing is a more subtle reflection. It should be fine." I waved Clara over, noticing her wince. Her hands trembled. "Come. I'm not pointing a pistol at you. No need to be nervous."

I repeated the process with her. She flinched each time I touched the tincture to her face. When I finally blew out the candle with the closing phrase, Francis said, "Amazing."

"Yes," I said. "And what aren't either of you to do?"

"Touch our faces."

"Exactly." I put the remaining tincture and candles back into the box, then put that and the book back into my haversack. "Now, let's go to the ball, shall we?"

As we neared the Governor's manse, my skin prickled from the enchantment of the *Deflected Guise* as though I were being pelted by a fine storm of ground glass. Francis squinted into the falling snow, while Clara stayed close by his side. They looked just the same to me, save for a faint blue light that danced over their skin and clothes, a refracted glow from an unseen source—but to others, they wouldn't have been identifiable as their true selves.

At the crossing to Marlborough Street, the roads choked to a standstill with traffic, on foot and by horse. A line of wooden barricades stretched across one side of the small square, manned by a dozen armed regulars. They moved one length of wood aside to allow a luxurious two-horse carriage to pass through.

Francis leaned in to me. "This feels mad."

"It was your idea."

"My ideas don't always pan out. We just walk right past them?"

"You're with me. Don't say anything."

I approached the barricade, biting the inside of my cheek. A dozen different scenarios ran through my mind—and each one began the same way: with a Whitelocke regular staring at Francis, gaze slipping into recognition (*Rattlesnake*), recognition slipping into swift action. I wanted to turn around and flee. Instead, I approached an officer at the gate, the ranking soldier. Francis and Clara followed. He motioned for us to stop. If I hadn't been wearing the fine clothes from Mary, I suspected we'd have been waved off.

"Might I see your invitation?" he said.

I dug the invitation from my pocket and handed it to him. He glanced up at me, then over to Francis and Clara. His gaze didn't linger on them. The relief spread through my limbs as he handed the invitation back to me.

"This is for two: Swaine and Finch. There's three of you."

"Madam Whitelocke told me I could bring my cousin Helen, as well. A third guest."

From his expression, it didn't seem an unfamiliar problem for the evening. Social event of the season, and all.

"You'll have to check in with Mr. Hartley." He moved the barricade aside. "Follow the walk up the hill. He's at the front door. Have a lovely evening, Miss Finch."

"Thank you kindly, Captain."

We pass through the barricade and stayed to the side of the street. One of the largest carriages I had ever seen rolled past, behind a team of six. I looked into the windows, but the occupants rode behind pulled curtains of scarlet velvet. We soon came to another line at the entrance in a wrought iron fence, beyond which stood the Royal Governor's manse. Smoke rose from half a dozen chimneys and the windows shone with festive light. Liveried servants along with plain-dressed assistants tended to lanterns and kept carpets clear of snow. Boughs of holly hung on the doors and gates. Nearby stood another clutch of soldiers, the elite Governor's Own Regiment. We passed them by and joined a small crowd of people at the gate. A footman approached, one eyebrow raised in a helpful arch.

"Madam?" he said.

I waved my invitation and said, "Yes, I was told to check in with Mr. Hartley."

And older man in tailored velvet breeches and a vest over a silken shirt looked over at me, clearly at the sound of his own name. He stepped over.

"I'm Mr. Hartley." He gave me a thorough look. His eyes were a pale gray, and didn't appear to miss a loose thread or an unkempt strand of hair.

I nodded, with a curtsey. "I believe there's been some confusion, sir. I was left with the impression from Mary Whitelocke that I might also bring my cousin along with me. I hope I haven't inconvenienced anyone?" I showed him the invitation.

"Ah, Miss Finch," he said after a moment's glance at the paper. "I'm sure it's no more than a miscommunication, easily mended, a small *frisson* that shall only serve to make the evening all the more splendid. Madam Whitelocke was, in fact, asking after you no more than an hour ago. Come, come—you've eased my duties immeasurably in appearing with such purpose."

With that, he spun on his heel and led us into the manse, pausing only to let two serving boys haul a large cask in the door ahead of us. "The hive alights this evening, Miss Finch."

Francis and Clara stayed at my elbows, drawing no more attention from soldier or servant than any other guest. The entryway opened into a crowded foyer across from a wide set of stairs. The sound of jigs and minuets floated out of the nearby ballroom. Candles burned brightly in candelabra. Servants, vests buttoned, jackets flawless, moved smoothly. A line of guests extended out the door, dressed in finery. The Governor, wearing a splendid dress suit of mulberry silk embroidered with a golden floral pattern along the wide cuffs and lapels over silken breeches buckled below the knees, his wig powdered and impressive, greeted each of them, bowing, passing a quick word with the men, smiling at the women. A group of officers conferred nearby, and my pulse resumed its earlier gallop.

Mr. Hartley led us around the back of the crowd and paused. He addressed Francis and Clara. "Please enjoy all the hospitality we have to offer, and do find a moment or two to greet the Governor—he's committed to the pleasure of everyone in attendance this evening. If you will excuse us, Madam Whitelocke requested a private word with Miss Finch."

"Of course," Francis said, with a slight bow of his head. Clara had the presence of mind to curtsey.

Mr. Hartley led me from the foyer, his presence eliciting questions and clarifications from all quarters. His instructions leapt from one incident and decision to the next with nary a pause, and no hint of hesitation, a flick of his fingers enough to spring the staff into action. I saw that he was the true north to the internal compass of the household. Even if it was just a shift in their stance or a quick look over a shoulder, they watched him, tracking his location and trajectory, adjusting their work.

We passed by the kitchen, where cooks called out, kitchen boys stoked the hearth and carried buckets of water, girls and young women peeled, husked, and chopped at cutting boards piled high with sliced parsnips, carrots, turnips, and onions. Butlers carried out rounds of cheese on trays, cooling plum cakes. Casks of beer and hard cider lined the brick wall opposite the hearth, drawn forth into mugs lined up like infantry, marched by servers into battle.

Mr. Hartley led me up a carpeted set of stairs and to a doorway. He rapped quietly on the jamb. "Miss Finch, Madam."

"Ah, there you are." Mary Whitelocke emerged from the sitting room. "I trust Mr. Hartley hasn't put you to work, all hands on deck and all that?"

"A guest here shall only lift a finger to enjoy more food or drink, Madam." Hartley inclined his head at me and departed.

"If only the colony ran was well as Hartley runs the manse," Mary said. She took me by the elbow and, in a ruffle of dark satin and scarlet silk edged with lace, drew me deeper into the sitting room. Scarlet ribbons tied back the loose curls of her hair, matching the choker around her pale throat. "He tames chaos, whilst the men of my family seem only to have a knack for kindling it." She paused and looked at me. "I'd just been thinking of you. Why, it's almost as though I'd conjured you with my innate magical talents."

"My master would grow jealous," I said. "He believes that only he possesses that skill when it comes to my presence."

We stepped into a wide dressing room. A window seat and the many panes before it overlooked the lantern-lit manse grounds that stretched off from the width of Marlborough Street to the detailed lawns that backed against several other fine houses. Two couches of royal blue satin on carved mahogany legs intersected just past the window seat, a low table before them. On the table sat a tray with a tea service, the steam rising, and a pair of bowls filled with blueberries drenched in cream. The silver spoons gleamed with the light of the fireplace.

"I trust August wasn't concerned I requested a word from you alone?" Mary said. "Leaving him adrift in a sea of hopeless social confection, which he clearly loathes."

"My master sends his regrets, Madam," I stood with my fingers clasped. "His work has—"

"Not here, is he?" She waved her fingers at me. "One must make allowances when it comes to genius, yes. I'm surprised he agreed to spare you for the evening—it's clear he relies on you."

"That's kind of you to say."

"Not just kind. True. Sit, sit." She motioned to the couch, closing the door. As I sat, she joined me, sitting on the couch to my right. "Perhaps it's for the best."

I leaned forward to pour her tea. She put her fingers on the back of my hand just as it reached the teapot. "Let me." She

poured the tea for me, and then for herself. "No expenses spared
—an unnatural state of affairs for my father. But where his mind
recoils at the prospect of spending more crowns, his political
acumen, as always, trumps all else. Boston's event of the season is
an important ritual. Prepare to witness a display of flattery unpar-
alleled, and a parade of strutting that would shame the vainest
peacock."

"Thank you." I took the tea she offered.

"You've done well for yourself." She reached over and
straightened the frills on my cloak. "The ensemble works. That's
it—I can't bear to wait. I absolutely must see you in a gown."

"Gown?"

"Why, yes—it's a ball. I've selected three options for you. I
have a very strong opinion which the clear choice is, but let's see
if you can impress me further by confirming my instincts. Tea
down, come."

She led me through a set of tucking doors and into a separate
dressing chamber. Three gowns hung on pegs, with their various
accessories along a settee before them. Through another set of
doors, I spied as magnificent a collection of clothing, shoes, hats,
and sundry as I'd observed in any of Boston's finest tailor shops.
"Goodness," I said.

"I'm sure we can all be thankful I'm not a murderer or arson-
ist, given my unquenchable obsessiveness. Now, down to business, Miss Finch." Mary stopped in front of the three gowns and
put a finger to her pursed lips. "No, I have not wavered. The
proper gown might as well have a glow to it. I trust that you
see it."

I turned to the three gowns. Lovely waterfalls of silk, their
modest bodices fitted over corsets, their sleeves billowing and
ruffled. The hooped skirts flowed out to the sides, two of them
featuring open fronts over patterned petticoats that presented a
gorgeous counterpoint to the outer gown. The first was of a deep
ruby, embroidered with a black lace that ran up along the sides

in a flowered pattern; white ruffles lined the collar and the sides of the skirt, with a deep black petticoat. The next was of a lovely pewter shade that hinted at pale blue, more slender than the first, with five layers of exquisite draping below the bodice, and a large ribbon at the top. The final gown was of silk and satin, pale peach skirts with ruffled edges, and cream sleeves and bodice. As I looked at the upper details, I admired the delicate patterning of the lace and the ties over the front. Although it was more low-cut than the others, it reminded me of the delicate colors of dawn.

"They're all too nice for me." I wasn't being humble—it was true. I cut firewood, hauled corpses, singed my hair with spells. I'd just summoned thirteen shadow ravens, to no avail. Smuggled two Rattlesnakes into the ball. It was absurd that I should stand in Mary Whitelocke's dressing room, choosing between three of the most breathtaking gowns I'd ever seen in my life.

"We'll knock that sad humility out of your head," Mary said. She swatted me with her fingers. "One is *perfect*. Come along. You can do it."

I reached over and tapped the peach gown.

"Was there even a choice?" Mary said, pleased. "It's you, as a gown: a subtle first impression, graceful, and with more to it the closer one gets." She lifted it from the hook and held it up against my shoulder, studying me as a butcher might eye a cow. "I'll just come out and say I'm a genius, with a gift. It brings the color out of your skin and turns your eyes into honey. You are the muse that Mr. Faber didn't even know he had when he brought this wonder into existence."

"It's lovely." Spells. Soldiers. Secrets. With so much weighing me down, I found little else to say.

"Yes, well we'll see what this does to the young men—and the old men, keep your eye on them, they take more license with their hands the older they get, apparently—at the ball. You're in for quite an evening."

"Why do I feel as the fox must at the sound of trumpets and hounds?"

"It's delicious. You'll see." She sorted through several accessories, laying them across the material. "Aha, this." She pulled a cream-colored eyepatch from a small drawer. "Perfection."

"But—forgive me, Mary. I'm not sure I understand why you're going to such lengths—"

"For a servant?" She eyed me.

"Well. Yes."

"You're not an ordinary servant, are you?"

"But I am."

"Really? I'd say there's nothing ordinary about you. August Swaine's assistant could hardly be anything of the kind."

I looked at the eyepatch. Impeccable craftsmanship. "I've seen to it he's received all your letters, Madam—but I'm not sure what else I can do."

"Mary. And you may trust in my lack of surprise that your master hasn't made a move to respond to any of my overtures. My life is full of male relations with all the personal warmth of statues, men infinitely more consumed with cannons, regiments, rivalries than anything the fairer sex might offer. I recognize said same drive in August. No, I'm interested in *you*, Miss Finch—and what you might teach me."

"Teach you?"

"Yes. We must band together. Pretty little things, expected to engage in combat fought with delicate fans, batted eyes, and powdered bosoms—all for the sake of pushing our way past our competitors, be they Cabot, Adams, Geary, to land the affections of men who would prefer to huddle in small groups and discuss artillery. Isn't that how it's supposed to work?" She raised an eyebrow. "Well, what if it doesn't? What if we're capable of more than decorating the lives of blinkered men?"

"I'm not sure I understand."

"What if we could help each other achieve more? Sharing our

expertise. Encouraging each other. Claiming our own share of influence."

"I don't see how I might help you with any of that."

"You don't? There's nothing you might teach me?"

"Teach?"

"That's exactly what I mean: let's stop being so humble. You can do things unimaginable to most of the people at the ball tonight. Boston's finest—yet you rise above them all, despite your quiet demeanor." She swept her hand at the gowns. "I'll share what I have with you. You teach me magic."

Magic. The word hit me like a hammer to the stomach. I shook my head. "I'm not sure what put that idea into your head, Madam—but—"

She smiled. "Must we? Couldn't you rather give me credit for having a generous dose of intelligence, capable of combining observations to reach material conclusions? This is what I'm talking about, always selling each other short."

I sputtered out some further excuses, but she raised a delicate hand.

"Number one," she said. "You are August Swaine's assistant. Number two, word has reached me—quietly, as well-guarded word as is possible in this colony—that a confession was extracted from some poor printers' apprentices anointing themselves *Rattlesnakes* detailing the casting of a spell of fire by a one-eyed lass in the vicinity of Andover." She must have seen the color drain from my face, for she reached a comforting hand to mine. "Don't worry, they won't be spreading the tale."

"It—wasn't me."

"Of course not, dear. It was some other one-eyed lass apprenticed to some other renowned practitioner of magic. In Andover."

I stared at her. She didn't look away.

"Who else knows?" I asked softly.

She clapped her hands together. "See how much more fun it is when we stop lying to one another? To answer your question, not many others. You might imagine a tasty rumor like that would have a way of soiling my father's reputation as an effective governor of Massachusetts."

"But he knows," I said.

"He knows. My brother knows—John, not Grayson."

"Doctor Rush?"

"Now *that* is a good question." She lifted the chosen gown and motioned for me to shed my outfit. As it wasn't the first time that afternoon I'd disrobed in front of an unlikely stranger, I barely hesitated. "One would think *yes*, with him being the Royal Doctor of Magickal Sciences, given the rather precise charge of keeping the colony free of unbecoming displays of the infernal." She gave me a sidelong look. "But I somehow think *no*, from how my brother behaved. According to John, our good Doctor has been more excitable than usual on such topics, of late—to the point of exhausting my father's already limited patience for reminders that the very position of a Royal Doctor of Magickal Sciences under his command has made him simultaneously an outcast amongst the leaders of our sister colonies, and an irritant—or a joke, depending on who tells the tale—to His Majesty, who seems to always be one ill-timed report away from relieving my father of his appointment and installing one of his slavering London courtiers in his place. So I would assume such knowledge is currently held by my brother and my father, alone."

"And you."

"Why, yes."

I couldn't get in more than a shallow breath, suddenly. "So they know all about me. I can't be here."

She helped slip me into the gown. "Relax. John won't even be here this evening. He loathes anything splendid or fun. As for my father—if he even spares you a glance—will register your gender and station only long enough to dismiss you from his concerns, I'm sorry to say. Neither of them will expect anything those

Rattlesnakes said might intrude into their inner circle, so you needn't worry about tonight. It can be our little secret."

She steered me by the shoulders to stand before the full-length mirror and began the rib-cracking process of tightening, tying, and layering me into the gown.

"I only want you to teach me a little magic," she said. "Exhale."

As I breathed out, she pulled the gown tighter.

"There," she said. "Nothing dangerous, of course. A few things I might use to dazzle, should I choose to."

"But magic is forbidden."

"Forbidden merely means that people do it out of sight, doesn't it?" She gazed at me in the mirror, pursing her own lips. "We young women deserve a few more tools in our arsenal. Why should we spend so much time smiling prettily so we might make the men in our orbits feel pleased with themselves in the hopes of basking in the glow of *their* renown or influence—when we could make some of our own? Treachery, I know."

"I'm not sure what I can teach you," I said.

"Your master has clearly taught you. Do what he did."

"He knows nothing about what I've done."

"Really? A man of such accomplishment, retiring to the valley woodlands of Andover to bind old books. I've never believed it."

"But it's true. I got it all from the books. Without his knowing."

"Such loyalty suits you. Even it if doesn't particularly suit me."

Satisfied with the gown, she set about tying ribbons and a few strands of pearls into my hair. Powdered and rouged my face. Scented my wrists with perfume. As I looked at myself in the mirror, my thoughts went to my master—not Mary purring on about magic. And as for Francis and Clara, I believed I'd run out of room to keep all my problems in my head simultaneously. Seeing my own reflection gazing back at me, a laugh bubbled up in my throat. I only just stifled it.

Mary applied the finishing touches to her attire, and looked ravishing. She was as fully in her element as Swaine was with his glamours and summoning. She sidled up until we shared the looking glass. I may have looked lovely, but she seemed to have rode a lightning bolt down from Mount Olympus.

"Think about the mark we might make, you and I," she said. She adjusted the front of my bodice and smiled as though she already knew the sum of my secrets. "We of the fairer sex must be there for one another in this curious colony. It is us against them. Always, darling."

27

MASQUERADE

I followed Mary from the dressing suite and down the stairs, struggling to land my feet on the runners with so much skirt draped around me. Mary bypassed the line of guests greeting the Governor and led me into the ballroom. The high-ceiling shone with hundreds of candles glimmering on chandeliers. Dried flowers hung from the doorways, along with decorative wreaths of twined autumn branches. Tables lined one wall, stacked high with rounds of cheese and plum cakes; platters of roasted pig, boiled leg of lamb, beef, peas, pudding, tarts; desert cups of apples, peaches, and berries with milk and sugar; punch-bowls brimming with cordial, hard cider, and rum, filling the room with a heady perfume.

The dance floor was a magnificent pattern of light and dark wood in an elaborate parquet. In one corner, four string players plucked out a waltz. Before I'd been thrust into learning real magic, such a scene had formed the entirety of my idea of magic: my mother had told me dozens of times of the ball she'd once attended with my father, back when he'd been in the good graces of His Majesty. For a woman who'd grown fearful of varying her routine even a little, she'd painted such a picture of delight that even as a young child I glimpsed the joy she kept so well guarded, a hint of the vivacious young woman she'd once been. The thought wrung a splash of grief from my heart: what would she have wanted for me, her only daughter? A life filled with lovely balls in proper society? A life of books? Certainly not troubles of the sort I bore, alone, an ocean away from whatever promise London had once held for me. Shaking such thoughts from my mind, I followed Mary through the crowd, trying to emulate how she walked. Her leonine grace, which drew every eye to her, eluded me.

"Don't force it, darling," she said as we cut through the throng. "Simply be graceful. Feminine. You're not hiking through brambles. You're a woman."

After months of Swaine insisting that I ignore the low expectations a young woman might be held to, I wondered if I'd somehow adopted his gait as well. The idea flustered me. Mary introduced me to one person after another with the sobriquet of *assistant to the renowned August Swaine*. I suspect that had most of the people come across such a description in *The Boston News-Letter*, their eyes would have passed straight over it with no further interest, yet hearing it from the beet-colored lips of Mary Whitelocke, their eyes widened in delight, and they fell over themselves bowing or curtseying. It couldn't have felt more strange. Throughout all the greetings, I scanned the ballroom for Francis and Clara, eventually spotting them off in one corner. To me, they looked entirely out of place—commoners among royalty, even the servants were better dressed—but the magic held and no one appeared to give them a second thought.

With a tipple of Madeira here, a sip of strong punch there, I soon found myself part of a collection of young women mingling with young men, an arrangement conducted by Mary. I confess that part of me simply wanted to lose myself in the colorful ado of the ball, and before long I was in the midst of the dance floor, led by a young gentleman whose name I'd already forgotten, the son of a cloth merchant being all that I could remember. I held onto his arm, attempting to look more nimble than I was, struggling to anticipate the steps. One musician called out, and the circle split in two, men in one, ladies in the other, moving in opposition.

Around it went, until the reel ended—and I came to a stop in front of Doctor Ephraim Rush, whom I'd not even noticed amongst the dancers earlier. His dove-colored jacket and waistcoat shone with bright brass buttons, and while he wore no wig, his white hair was held back with a black bow. He smiled at me, regarding me over the tops of his spectacles. "Ah, Miss Finch, if I'm not mistaken."

"Doctor Rush." The dizzying warmth of the moment vanished, and I glanced about, half-expecting to see armed regulars pushing through the crowd to detain me. I saw only gentry dancing, drinking, laughing.

He extended one arm as the next tune began. "Would you spare a kindness and help me to a seat, dear? My hips are growing suspicious that I'm having far too much fun, the traitorous things."

With no way out, I smiled and twined my elbow with his, catching my breath, walking him over to one of the nearest hearths, where a merry fire crackled. I helped him into a free chair.

"And your master is well?" he said.

No, he appears to have lost himself in the Demonmere. The stifled laughter from earlier threatened to tumble out. I smiled instead. "At home with his books, sir. He has rather strong feelings about social events. And his desire to be as far from them as possible."

"A man of acumen. I'm rather jealous, between you and I, Miss Finch." He spared me a wink. Over his shoulder, I spied Francis—and nearly stopped breathing. The spell I'd cast might be good enough to fool the cream of Boston's society, but Doctor

Rush himself? I realized it would be like expecting Swaine to not notice a demon lurking nearby.

I took the empty seat next to Rush, hoping to draw his gaze as far from the direction of Francis and Clara as possible. "Have you had much luck, sir—with the demon you spoke of to my master?"

He put his liver-spotted hands upon his knees and nodded, appearing unsurprised at my question. "A pernicious difficulty, under the best of circumstance—as your master would surely attest, given his youthful research. And, as is the way with demons, a comforting end to a story appears elusive."

A servant appeared with a tray of tiny cakes, and Doctor Rush took one, motioning for me to do likewise. I barely tasted it.

"The bodies of the young girls haven't been found," he said, a pair of crumbs clinging to the corner of his mouth. "But there appears to be no sign of further demonic presence."

"Well—that's somewhat comforting, at least."

"More so if I had the slightest idea why."

"Might you have driven off the demon, sir?"

"I would seem to have unbridled success at driving off the Governor whenever I broach the subject, but demons around ponds seem quite another matter. I found no signs of an infernal presence when I investigated again, just two days ago—to which I credit myself nothing more than good intentions."

"Could it have been something else, sir?"

"Would that I could answer that very question, Miss Finch. While I found no infernal entity, I measured a significant shift to the flow of the unseen planar energies in the region. An unevenness that's difficult to fathom." He wiped the crumbs from his mouth. His spectacles shone with the light of the fire in the hearth. "I trust you've seen nothing amiss, living in the general vicinity, as I understand."

I thought of the resonance clock, the temporal disruption it caused, the appearance of the Demonmere. *An unevenness that's difficult to fathom.* "Amiss, sir? Oh, with the poor girls you mentioned. It's weighed on my mind, sir. Horrid. And frightful. But, no—it's been quiet."

"I see." He smiled, and yet something in his eyes hinted at seeing my lies for what they were.

I sat up as straight as Mary Whitelocke, confident and forthright, all the while fighting the urge to fidget and slouch under the weight of the nonsense I was babbling. "What might cause such shifts in the—what did you call them? *Plain* regions?"

"*Planar* regions." He rested his hands on the head of his walking stick and launched into a brief description of the planes that relied heavily on Emelie Du Marien's work. I noted that he didn't touch upon Thomas Wexler's concept of intraplanar confluence, which my master felt offered a more accurate depiction of the phenomena he'd observed in and around Salem. Perhaps being a more controversial theory, Doctor Rush put less faith in it. Then again, he may have been leaving such nuances out of the discussion for my benefit. Nothing he said, however, touched upon the Demonmere—which I was loathe to bring up.

"How fascinating," I said when he finished.

He smiled. "How rarely do I hear such words, these days. One would think I was forcing the Governor to discuss the various aromas that arise from Bostonians' shoes to see his curt responses to my briefings for him."

"It mustn't be easy, being the Royal Governor."

"And bound to become significantly less so, should my advice not be heeded."

"What of General Whitelocke, sir? Surely he values your wisdom."

Rush's jowls shook as he rocked his jaw back and forth. "The General is, in fact, attentive, though hardly less busy, of late. Put upon by London. Bedeviled by Rattlesnakes."

He gave me a tight smile and kept his gaze on me. I was at last thankful for the suffocating bodice and gown, for its armor-like tightness kept me from flinching. "I'm—I'm sure that General Whitelocke will bring them all to justice."

"Perhaps he shall. It's not in his nature to give up. He reminds me of his grandfather, in temperament and carriage—a fact that girds my heart when I ruminate on my worst fears. He will no doubt hear me out, but as with all such matters one must use the proper channels first."

"Is he here this evening? The General?" I said.

"I'd imagine so." He leaned forward. "Now tell me how you came into the service of your master. I imagine it a story worth hearing."

Did the dead bodies show on my face? Silas Wilkes? The demon who stalked me? After perhaps a moment too long, I opened my mouth to speak, unsure of what exactly was about to come out when a figure appeared next to me.

"Might I have this dance, Madam?"

I looked up to find Grayson Whitelocke smiling at me, wearing a waistcoat and jacket on the small side. His hair was ridiculously powdered and his cheeks flushed. He bowed, extending a hand. He turned to Doctor Rush. "You'll forgive me if I steal away your companion before you rob her sleep with more of your frightful tales, my good Doctor?"

Rush didn't appear ruffled. "Only if you promise to behave."

"Restraint is the Whitelocke way, is it not?"

"God help us all." Rush turned. "We shall speak again, Miss Finch."

"I look forward to it with pleasure, Doctor Rush." I stood, gave him a polite curtsey, and walked with Grayson into the start of a waltz. He took my hand as I fought to locate Francis and Clara in the crowd.

"I'm not sure why everyone I speak with this evening feels the need to extract a promise of *behaving* from me," Grayson said. "Is this not a ball? Are we not being festive?"

I could smell the ale on him. "Perhaps you've misbehaved in the past."

"All a matter of perspective. I've found my behavior to be entirely within the realm of reasonable." We executed a convoluted move that Grayson pulled me through. "And you're welcome."

I held his arm as we twirled. "Welcome?"

"The good Doctor would have prattled on until he nodded off, a point in time that may well have been shockingly far off for someone so ancient. Trust me. I've seen women gnaw off their own limbs to escape that snare."

As we danced, I spotted Clara mid-way across the dance floor. "He's fascinating."

"You must get out more. The book glue is obviously affecting your judgement."

"Behave." I turned back to him, following his steps in time with the string players. "Did you powder your hair yourself?"

"Finally. Someone acknowledges my statement."

"And what statement might that be?"

"The absurdity of it all."

"Of all the powder?"

"Clever, but no. The absurdity of pretending we're all not pretending, all the time." He raised my hand, and I executed a semi-respectable spin, finding that the girth of my skirts assisted the motion.

"How does half a tin of powder in your hair say that, exactly?"

"It wasn't half a tin. And the thing about an unspoken statement is that it's unspoken."

"Or an un-statement."

"Ha. You're on the right track, Miss Finch." The steps shifted, taking us across the parquet floor, one-two-three, one-two-three. "Are we not all, really, at a masquerade?"

"Hardly ever."

"Oh, but we are, all the time. Isn't that all we're really doing, in life? Hiding behind this mask, or that? One costume, or another?"

If he was about to make a comment about my eye, I would stop dancing.

He continued, no barb launched. "We all have a mask and a costume given to us. Forced on us. And then there are those that we put on ourselves, the ones we grasp at. Clutch tight. What is a uniform if not a costume? The attire of an apprentice, likewise?"

"An over-powdered head of hair," I said.

"Now you're catching on. For the tragedy of it all, the sublime ridiculousness, the appalling foot-stomping, scrunch-faced tantrum-inducing manner in which we deny it—all points to one thing. Care to guess?"

"I haven't the faintest."

"I suspect you do—but let me illuminate it anyways. The fact is that we're all committed to pretending that our costumes aren't costumes at all. That our masks aren't masks. Our real selves aren't the ones the world sees us as, or what we are. Do you see?"

"If this is a pretext to in some fashion peer beneath my dress, I will have to ask you to behave, yet again. And we know how sensitive you are to that guidance."

A broad smile crossed his face. "Heaven help us, you've almost struck me speechless. No, no, no. My intentions are philosophical, entirely—unless you're bolder than I'd had you pegged for, in which case let's see where this conversation might lead."

The number ended, and the couples broke apart, filling the air with the soft patting of gloved hands clapping.

"I'm not so bold, Master Whitelocke," I said. "Nor am I curious about such a conversation."

"Nor are you as dull as the other geese of my sister's gaggle, fine plumage notwithstanding." He swiped a pewter mug of ale from the tray of a passing servant and tossed half of it back in one long chug. "As for my point, look about."

"We're at a ball. People don't go about their days like this. I don't."

"Don't they?" He sipped at his beer. "Sadly, I've spent my life cursed with an excruciating awareness that everyone else is confoundingly *unaware* they are, in fact, costumed. So when I refuse to wear any costume whatsoever, I am dismissed, and I get nothing but scorn by the costumed fools all around. That's the problem, isn't it? The genuine is mocked while the superficial is praised to the heavens. And pity the person who's not what they've always been told they are."

Not that there wasn't sense to what he was saying, but I grew suspicious of what he was getting at. What did he know? "So that's why you over-powdered your hair."

"Well done."

"And this is in reality about the officer's uniform you're being forced into."

"You may be the colony's most insightful apprentice."

Another tune started, but we'd missed the beginning, and watched as two rows of dancers passed by one another, stepping in time.

"You don't want to be like your brother?" I said.

"I'd rather be pressed to death. He adores making men march in little circles. Drawing lines on maps. Speaking of cannon ad nauseam. Saluting our father."

As he spoke, I noticed General Whitelocke enter the crowded room, pausing by the doorway and regarding the spectacle. He was amongst the tallest men in the room and his presence drew the eye of many of the guests. "Does he enjoy balls?"

Grayson smirked into his mug. "No doubt a question the eligible young ladies of Boston have only wondered a thousand times."

As I realized what I'd said, a flush bloomed on my cheeks and throat. Behind the General entered the Governor, deep in conversation with a shorter man dressed in muted browns and blacks, trailed by a number of similarly dressed gentlemen. Grayson followed my gaze.

"Do you see that dour man next to my father?" he said. "Lionel Sackville, the Earl of Middlesex, just arrived from London. To torture us, apparently. I doubt the muscles of his face are even capable of calling forth a smile. A man for whom laughter is bookended by sin on one side, devilry on the other. Dry. Utterly cheerless. His eyes sweep everything crossing his path with a delightful blend of paranoia and religious mania— but since he has His Majesty's ear, being married to one of the King's cousins or other, my father and brother are yoked to him for much of the evening. London's grown a tad jealous and the Earl has been sent to make sure the ancient Doctor Rush isn't tilting the scales of trade with generous applications of the infernal. Ridiculous as that sounds, my father and brother have no choice but to smile and bear it. *That* is my future, if I let it be. Duty. Obligation. Joyless forbearance."

He shuddered and took a deep draw of his ale. Mary White-locke sauntered up next to him. She looked at his hair.

"You look idiotic," she said. "Did you get dressed in the dark?"

"Miss Finch can explain."

"Father expects you to behave."

"Oh, joy. Another." He drained his mug. "What father expects is for me to do the impossible. And I'm sorry, but the thought of tactics and drills and another grim meal trying to keep a stray dollop of soup from hitting my lapel for fear of revealing the black hand of Satan at work in our colony doesn't hurl me out of bed in the morning as though fired from a cannon."

"You get out of bed in the morning?"

"If life's passions occur after midnight, who am I to question?"

"It's not the *when* I question, but the *where*," she said. "At the bottom of bottles and glasses?"

"Well, I've yet to find them in dressing rooms and dressmak-ers' shops, but by all means keep up the search and let the rest of us know." He stopped a servant, glanced at the tray of drinks, and reached for one. Mary tried to block him. Grayson stretched past her. He tossed back a glass of sherry and put the empty glass on the tray while grabbing a fresh mug of beer in his other hand. "And I don't think I'm divulging any secrets to point out that there's not a single one of the rapacious Abbots, the self-serving Quincys, stiff-backed Earls from Court, or the rest who would take me seriously in any event."

"I can't imagine why not." She looked at me. "I apologize for my brother's—well, for my brother. I hope he's not been a bother."

"He's been delightful."

"Thank you, Miss Finch," he said, bowing and spilling a splash of ale on his shoes.

Mary frowned. She took him by the sleeve and led him to the food, then piled a pewter plate with chicken legs and potatoes cooked up with onions. She handed it to him. "At least put food in your stomach."

She took the mug from him and pointed to the plate. He dutifully took a bite. Looking past him, I spotted General Whitelocke again. He stared at me from across the ballroom, giving me a shock. I looked away, pretending to smile at something his brother and sister were saying. Mary turned. "Now enough of my brother. There are a few young men with more manners and less liquor inside them whom I will introduce you to—one of whom has already asked about you."

I spared another glance toward General Whitelocke and saw he'd straightened, his gaze still fixed on me. A moment later, he started off across the dance floor, cutting through dancers, apparently heading right for where I stood. My pulse found a tempo faster than the lively number the musicians played. I grabbed Mary's arm. "Your brother—he's coming this way," I whispered.

She saw him and nodded, shoving me along with her free hand. "I'll slow him down. Go."

As I tried to disappear into the crowd, one word rang clear in my head: *trap*. Had I walked right into one? Where were Francis and Clara? And why had those two survived, while the other Rattlesnakes had been caught and hanged? And why did General John Whitelocke, the man who'd hanged the Rattlesnakes, decide to suddenly attend the ball?

I fled through a sea of satin limbs, embroidered torsos, and rum-infused breath.

Desperate.

28

TWISTS OF SHADOW

I pushed my way through several gentlemen gathered by a punchbowl, begging the pardon of those whom I displaced. Beyond a gilded pillar, I spotted a narrow doorway used by the servants. On the other side was an empty hallway of plain plaster walls, lanterns hung every ten paces. Distant kitchen sounds reached me over the dull roar of the crowded ballroom. Lifting my skirts, I broke into a sprint. At the corner, I glanced back, only to see General Whitelocke's form filling the doorway I'd come through.

I sped past the corner and spotted the kitchens opening ahead of me. Two regulars loomed just inside the door. Coming to a stop, I looked forward and back. No hope of getting past anyone unseen. To my right, I found another door and yanked it open. A set of stairs led down to where a lone lantern burned. I closed the door behind me and hurried down as quietly as I could manage. At the bottom, a floor of packed earth stretched off to my left. Casks of ale lined one wall, while opposite them stood shelves stacked with sideways wine bottles. The air held the scent of hops and spirits. Beyond the wine, the cellar was dark.

As I felt my way forward, the door above opened. I darted

behind two casks, pulling in the overspill of my skirts and crouching. After a few moments, the door closed. I held my breath, listening, telling myself that General Whitelocke hadn't seen me come this way and had no reason to suspect that I had. Perhaps he'd only checked? Just when I'd nearly convinced myself of it, boots descended. I inched back farther between the casks. The steps reached the bottom of the stairs, took a few paces, and stopped.

"You might have outrun me if you'd kept going," General Whitelocke said. He stepped to the end of the row. "Get up."

The expression on his chiseled face was unreadable. He was a handsome man, tall, with a penetrating gaze, and a hint of dark stubble on his fair skin. The resemblance to his siblings was there, as well—he was a virile male version of Mary, and (frankly) a masculine version of Grayson. I stood.

He looked me over. "Well aren't you something?"

"I'm sorry, sir—I must have taken a wrong turn."

"As you fled. The moment I looked in your direction."

"I was just looking for the—privy."

"Wrong way. Finch, is it? The eye-patches. The dresses."

I grabbed at my skirts with trembling fingers and curtseyed. "Yes, sir."

He put a hand to his chin. "The only trouble I'm having here, if you'll forgive me being blunt, is with the description 'plain looking.'"

"Sir?"

"One-eyed certainly fits. Tall, likewise. But I'm not sure about plain-looking."

"I'm afraid I don't understand, sir," I said, though I was beginning to.

He opened his hands in a gesture of agreeable candor. "We don't need to play at this, do we?"

"Play at what, sir?"

"The magic. The spells."

The cellar tilted and I reached out to steady myself on a cask. I struggled to find a reasonable-sounding denial, but only a thin sigh escaped my mouth.

"But I wouldn't call you plain-looking, in truth," he continued. "The words of a Rattlesnake, mind you. Not mine. There are any number of young men who would no doubt trail after you from one end of the evening to the other. Still, you weren't at a ball when you set those lads' clothing afire. And, to be fair, perhaps what you did to them colored their impressions of your looks— who could blame them, really?"

"I didn't do anything with magic, sir. I don't know anything about it."

"Of course not. That said, I will suggest that if you're thinking of casting a spell on me, don't bother." He held up his left hand. A signet ring rested upon his index finger. "Doctor Rush fashioned these for my family a generation ago. No magic will work on me. Allegedly. How it works, I'm not certain, but the good Doctor would no doubt be happy to expound upon the theory behind it at some length. You can ask him from your jail cell—I'm sure he'll wish to speak with you soon enough."

I shook my head. "This is all a misunderstanding, sir."

"I suppose your master is in on this. He's made a name for himself, I will say. Anyone who's been to London over the past year heard all about him. Of course he has to come *here*. Become *my* problem—as though I hadn't enough already. Yet having him in custody will buy me and my father a good deal of relief. In short supply, believe me. If the Governor of Massachusetts can't convince his people he's protecting them from the infernal on an ongoing basis, he won't be Governor for long. Not these days." He motioned. "Come along. Let's go make my father happy."

I stepped back.

"Miss Finch, please," he said. "Look where you are. Look who you're with. Why not make this easy for the both of us. Put your arm in mine, no one needs know any better. We'll walk up the stairs, start a few rumors, I'll have the men escort you out the back. All very reasonable—if you come right this moment. If not, my patience—already down to the nub—may well escape me."

He held out a hand to me. I nodded, reaching out as though to take his hand. Before I made contact, I turned my hand toward the wine bottles in their racks. I had no time for a proper incantation, nor to reach the appropriate state of mind.

But I had my witchcraft.

It had been there in the sensation of power passing through me when I'd slammed Clara backward with my spell during our first encounter. And the fire, so much more intense—so much so that I'd questioned which fire spell I'd actually used. And when I'd cast de Burgh's *Grave Raven*, the extra power I'd experienced. Witchcraft.

I couldn't let myself be jailed, not with Swaine missing. Not ever.

The strength of my will surged forward from my hands, tracing crystalline pathways across the cool floor, touching soil, stone, rack as it followed my intention. Through the casks and shelves, carried by the wood itself—until I felt it touch the glass bottles, one after another. I felt each sloping shoulder of the bottles, each seam within, the beauty of the pressures and temperatures that had formed them, the taste of mineral and ore and fire, their crowns of cork and wire.

Now.

All it took was the gentlest winding of my will, a twist, a counter-clockwise collision with its mirrored opposite. One bottle shattered with a loud bang, followed by another, then another, then a fourth, a fifth, a sixth, and more. A dozen bottles burst into shards, each sharp *crack* reverberating in the chill cellar. Wine gushed to the floor in sopping falls of crimson, filling the cellar with a heady scent.

When General Whitelocke turned in surprise, I hauled myself over the nearest cask, hoping to get beyond it and outrun

him. Sadly, I hadn't counted on him being as well-trained a
soldier as he was. Before I could get down on the other side of the
casks, his hands grabbed at me, one pulling at the shoulder of my
gown, the other catching my pendant. I pulled away from him,
and my pendant ripped free.

"You've just made things so much harder for yourself," he
said. Even though I'd slipped his grasp, I turned and clawed at his
hand, where my pendant dangled. I couldn't pry it loose. He
punched me with his other hand, catching me in the side, driving
the wind from my lungs. Worse, a wave of icy air crashed over me,
shocking the flesh of my neck, throat, and hands.

A demon.

And I'd lost the protection of the pendant.

Whitelocke grabbed my wrist so hard I cried out. I struggled
to get in a breath, raking at his face to get him to release me.
Before he could punch me again, I rolled sideways, yanking my
wrist free. He lunged for me. I scrambled backward, out of his
range. The air between us darkened with the demon's presence,
causing us both to recoil. I got my feet under me and stood,
reaching for the words of the strongest ward I knew. A ripple in
the air pressed in at me, deadening the sounds of Whitelocke's
breathing. He'd dropped my pendant and it lay on the earthen
floor next to him, catching the light from the lantern.

I dove for it. Whitelocke tried to wrap me with his arms, but I
elbowed him in the eye as my fingers closed over the chain of the
pendant. Frigid air brushed the back of my neck. Rolling up into
a crouch, I curled my hand into the gesture that accompanied the
most potent ward I knew from Hume's *Srávobhiśśravasíyas*.
Thrusting my hand forward, my ring finger snugged by my
thumb, my remaining fingers touching tips and arching forward,
I shouted: "*Heimsks ertu, lyyche, hugar eigandi, er þú at augum í eld
hrapar! Liggr mér und herðum dymyn bani, allr er hann útan eldi
sveipinn!*"

The air whipped about, fluttering the skirts of my gown,

filling with smoky trails and a wretched stench. Casks of ale rocked, broken glass whipped about. General Whitelocke raised an arm to protect his face, even as he dragged himself to his feet.

"Stay back, sir." I backed off toward the stairs.

He shook his head. "Do you see what being reasonable gets me? I'm starting to wonder if that isn't half of my problems."

"You need to run—there's a demon about."

The door at the top of the stairs opened. Whitelocke ignored me. Instead, he looked up and motioned. "Get down here, arrest this woman."

I spared a glance over my shoulder. A soldier of the Governor's Own started down the stairs, others behind him. I tried to spring to my right. Whitelocke blocked me. The soldiers rushed down the stairs—leaving me no room to escape. Desperate, I readied a fire spell and spun on them. The first soldier stared at me, eyes wide.

Francis and Clara followed him, each with a pistol trained on him. They were clear to me, just as I'd last seen them, skimmed here and there with hints of faint blue light. I realized that to General Whitelocke, they likely appeared to be soldiers, as well. Francis shoved the real soldier forward, sending him sprawling next to the cellar floor. He walked straight to General Whitelocke, the pistol pointed at his face.

Whitelocke stepped back, his boots crunching broken glass in the spilled wine. "What is this?"

Clara stood next to me, pointing her pistol at the weaponless soldier on the ground.

"This," Francis said, "is what happens when you tread on a rattlesnake, General."

Whitelocke looked back and forth between Francis, Clara, and the soldier on the floor.

"Miss Finch," Francis said. "Our good General is confused. Please release the spell."

I nodded, still winded. Whitelocke had already seen me use

my powers—another display could hardly make for more trouble. I lifted my hand and recited the relinquishing incantation. With a flaring of the blue lines of magic, the enchantment of the *Deflected Guise* surrendered. Whitelocke's eyes widened.

The soldier on the floor spat. "Bloody shoved a pistol in my ribs, sir."

Whitelocke ignored him, staring at Francis. "What do you want?"

"The same thing any reasonable citizen of the colony has always wanted, General Whitelocke." Francis kept the pistol steady. "Justice for the people of Boston. An end to the greed. The corruption. It's time for the pigs to leave the trough."

"It must be invigorating to wake each morning with such self-satisfaction," Whitelocke said. If he had a sliver of fear, he didn't show it.

"If you must know," Francis said, "I wake each morning under a pall. Friends of mine, dead. The ramparts built by your richest friends to keep out anyone else with thoughts of prospering, higher. Knowing the bounty of the labor of so many will never benefit them, but rather will fatten the purses of your family and all those who praise and slaver and genuflect in your direction. Not much of that makes me satisfied, General. Not even a little."

"You'll be even less satisfied when I see you hang, Rattlesnake."

"William Harber. Alfred Graham. Samuel Van Horne. Those were their names, the ones you—"

Whitelocke swung his arm up, deflecting the pistol, shoving himself at Francis. Francis stepped back with a grunt. The pistol's muzzle flared. The shot drove the ball into the fleshy bit of General Whitelocke's throat, just above his collar and below his Adam's apple, where it lodged. He staggered back, his hands to the wound. He tried to dig the ball out with his fingers, and when that failed he appeared to try to swallow the burning chunk of lead, anything to clear it from his throat. Gun smoke drifted through the cellar. Francis lowered the pistol as General White-locke fell to his knees, unable to even gasp. The front of his uniform darkened with blood. In desperation, Whitelocke slammed his forehead to the floor, evidently trying to jar loose the ball from the puckered, bloody hole. He couldn't. The ball had sealed his windpipe. Shudders wracked him. His face went pale, his lips blue, and his fingers clawed at the earthen floor, where they soon stilled.

"Jesus bloody Christ," the soldier said.

Clara stood over him, pointing the pistol at his head. "What do we do with this one?"

"He's going to lead us right out of here," Francis said. "Or we'll kill him, too." He reached down and grabbed the soldier by the upper arm, heaving him to his feet. The soldier stared at the blood spreading out from Whitelocke's corpse.

So did I.

Looking up, I locked gazes with Francis. "You never said anything about killing anyone."

"You saw what happened."

"Meaning what?" I said.

The soldier shook off Francis' grip. "Meaning not a one of you is going to walk out of here alive," he said. "The entire Governor's Own is here tonight. And if you think they don't know the sound of a pistol, you're mad."

Clara put her pistol in his face. "You're going to walk us out of here, out the back, just like we came down these stairs. Or I will shoot you in the head. You'll be the one not walking out of anywhere ever again. Do you understand?"

The soldier shook his head. "What? Right past the others?"

"Exactly. And if you so much as raise a pinky as some sort of signal, the back of your skull will get blown off."

Francis reloaded his pistol, looking up toward the door, then into the darker portion of the cellar. "There's got to be a servants' door that way. Let's go."

My neck shivered. As they'd spoken, the temperature had plummeted. "We need to go—now," I said.

Back by the stairs, the flame in the lantern fluttered.

"I feel you, so near," came a choked whisper.

No one had spoken: not Francis, not Clara, not the soldier. I turned. The corpse of General Whitelocke stirred, hands clasping and unclasping in the blood.

"You can help me, can't you? Stop all the thunder, the storm in my head?"

General Whitelocke rolled onto his back, staring at the ceiling. In the light of the lantern, his face had gone pale as alabaster, dark smears of blood streaked on his chin and throat. His hands trembled as one reached the wound in his throat and dug into the flesh, working around with wet sounds until it emerged with the lead ball, which he dropped to the floor. When he spoke again, his voice was stronger, but thick with blood. "You're shining. All the others are lost in shadows. Cobwebs. Under sacks. I only hear mumbles."

His face twisted up in a horrid grimace and a retching sound tore from his throat, his shoulders heaving as a roll of dark blood spilled out of his mouth. A groan rose in his throat. "I've seen Hell." Each word grew louder, more desperate, until the words dissolved in a barren cry. He sat up, staring at me with bloodshot eyes.

"God in Heaven," the other soldier said.

"What's happening?" Francis said.

"Get back." I put myself between them and Whitelocke. "It's a demon."

I steadied myself against a sturdy set of shelves holding dusty bottles.

"No demon." Whitelocke put his hand over his mouth and smothered his words, glaring at me with his desperate eyes. He dropped the hand. "That's what it sounds like. All of it. And the fumes. The oils, the discharge. The rotten souls. Maggots crawling from the corners of their eyes. Thin, thin worms protruding from their gums and beneath their tongues."

He rolled forward, getting to his feet like a toddler. More blood strung from the hole in his throat.

"But not you," he said, his voice dropping to a whisper. "You glow like an angel at dusk. Your eyes shine with the precious gleam of evening stars. I see the coils of beauty as they wind around you. You have the power to fix me—have you not?"

I didn't let him get close. I moved past one aisle of wine, then another, not turning my back on him.

"Miss Finch," Francis said.

"Get ready to run."

"But we need the spell—the one to hide our appearance."

"Then you shouldn't have asked me to end it." I blocked them from Whitelocke. "Tell me your true name."

The demon kept coming in Whitelocke's corpse. "August Swaine," he whispered.

"Your name, demon." I raised my voice.

He cocked his head, and spoke several grotesque words of one of the six known tongues of Hell, a language best never written out, or seen. Raising my hands, I shouted another of Hume's wards at him.

"*Sá var aukinn jarðar megni, svalköldum sæ ok sónardreyra! Helzt þóttumk nú heima í millim, er mik umhverfis eldar brunnu!*"

The force of the ward knocked the corpse of the General back a dozen feet, sending him crashing into a rack of wine bottles and pinning him there. Several of the bottles fell and smashed open. I walked toward him, my hand in front of me. His body trembled and his limbs flailed as though attempting to snuff unseen flames. As I neared him, he howled in pain. Every muscle in the General's body strained, the tendons and veins of his throat bulging. A rank stench rose.

The air in the cellar shifted. Cracks crawled across dozens of wine bottles behind the General. Twists of shadow flowed from his mouth and nose, his ears, the corners of his eyes. The temperature plunged. I closed the distance between us and repeated the ward, holding my hand inches from his face. The shadow of the demon pulled itself free of Whitelocke's body, stretching and tearing. The mass of it coalesced around him, a scratchy collection of blurs and shadow that showed ghastly glimpses of its true nature: tendrils with cruel barbs, scorched flesh, glistening teeth that lined misshapen limbs, orifices that discharged unpleasant matter.

When I spoke the ward for a third time, the demon fled, smashing as much as it could as it did so. A wooden cask split, a shelf collapsed, and the plaster along the wall cracked and fell off in large uneven pieces. The stench was unbearable. I covered my nose with the material of my sleeve. Whitelocke's body slammed to the floor like a side of beef dropped from a butcher's hook. Dead, motionless.

"How did you—" the soldier said.

Before he could get another word out, the pistol spun out of Clara's hand and cracked against the wall, spilling its powder. Both she and the soldier staggered and crashed up against the wall where the pistol had hit, pressed by a ferocious, unseen presence. A grunt escaped Clara, while the soldier cursed. Both of them tried to free themselves, but neither could so much as pull an arm off the bricks.

Behind us, the door to the cellar opened. "What on earth is that smell?" Someone started down the stairs. "Check down there."

I raised my hand and tried a third ward from Hume's *Srávob-hiśśravasíyas*. Clara squeezed her eyes shut in pain as I spoke, and the air snapped with energy. The demon pushed back at me—but the ward gained force. Two channels of golden light poured forth from the tips of the twined fingers on my right hand. The floor shuddered as a swelling pressure grew. The soldier groaned.

Footsteps banged down the stairs, and a man cried out "Major!"

I ignored the voice and concentrated on completing the ward. Before I reached the final phrase, the wall where Clara and the soldier were pinned fell in on itself in a proliferation of cracks and plaster dust. Both cried out as they tumbled inside. I looked inside, seeing a dimly lit corridor of unfinished slats and a wooden floor stretching out toward the center of the manse.

The lifeless quality was immediately apparent: the Demonmere.

Clara slid down the length of the corridor, dragged by the collar of her cloak, raising a cloud of dust behind her, yelling all the while. The soldier got halfway to his feet before he was yanked cruelly backward, too. At the far end, stairs descended, and in the dim light I saw both of them hauled down into darkness. A thin female scream reached me, followed by distant bumps and thuds, then silence.

Off behind us, a lantern descended. "Wait a minute," a voice said.

Francis stepped into the Demonmere, rushing after Clara. I reached out and grabbed him by the collar, holding him back. "No," I whispered. "You can't go after her."

"But she's—"

"It doesn't matter—we'll never get out if we follow her."

He spun on me. "I'm not leaving her."

I yanked him back to me. "No choice. Come, now—run."

"What *is* this?"

"I'll explain later."

More bootsteps banged down the stairs. A voice called out, "It's General Whitelocke."

Taking Francis by the arm, I lifted the hems of my skirts with my other hand and darted around the corner, into darkness. A guard shouted for someone to stand aside. A thin line of light revealed a door down along the wall. I shoved it open and Francis and I found ourselves outside. Light spilled out of the many windows, and the sound of music floated in the night.

For a moment, I paused, my breath frosting the air. "Where to?"

"This way." Francis still clutched his pistol. The bravado he'd shown General Whitelocke had all but vanished—his face was drawn, eyes narrowed. As we traced the long edge of the manse, the music inside came to an uneven stop, replaced by a tide of raised voices. News of the murder had made its way up from the wine cellar. Francis and I came to a pair of privies, then passed through a splash of warm light that fell from the tall windows of the ballroom. Not much farther along stood a set of doors leading back into the manse, lit by a pair of lanterns.

Francis went ahead and checked that there were no guards at the doors yet, then motioned for me to follow. Before I could get more than a few steps, a shadow flew up from beneath a snow-draped hedge next to the path, flying up into my face with a scorched smell, battering me with smoky wings.

A shadow raven.

As I stepped back from the sooty bird, the sole of my shoe shot out from under me, hitting a patch of ice dusted by the fresh snow. While the billowing fabric of my gown cushioned my buttocks, one elbow and one wrist smacked the cobblestones. My pendant, still clutched in my hand, slipped from my grip and carved a sinuous line in the snow. I leaned over to retrieve it. Before my fingers touched it, I saw the shadow of my hand emerge, crisp on the snow. A pale glow, silver-tinged and clear as moonlight, brightened above me. I froze, confused as I stared at my silhouette as it pooled around me. I turned my head, squinting. A bright lantern shone atop a tall pole of black wood, at its base, iron chains and posts: a witch-pole, filling the night with a glow not seen in half a century. A witch-pole, designed to protect the colonists from—me. From my mother, as meek and compassionate and quietly exuberant and well-read as a person could be.

From women stalked by demons for no other reason than the composition of our blood. The absurdity of it was as clear as my own shadow, filling me with an indignation I'd never known.

I stared at the glowing lantern, ignoring the snow that fluttered into my lashes, ignoring the cries that rose from inside the manse.

My eyes widened. Atop the lantern perched the shadow raven.

My heart leapt beneath the cage of the corset, a terrified rabbit. The raven lowered its head, staring at me with obsidian eyes, cloaked in shadow. With a chuffing *caw*, it took wing, trailing wisps of black smoke. I watched as it disappeared into the night sky. I followed its path: north-east.

Francis stared at me, his mouth open.

I turned and snapped up my pendant. The moment it was in my grip, the lantern light of the witch-pole faded. From back along the side of the manse, guards shouted from the cellar entrance. Francis sprang forward and helped me to my feet. I clenched my pendant in my fist. We cut down a path between hedges in the snowy lawn. Behind us, the doors from the manse opened, and people streamed out, a mass of color and wigs and hurried chatter and warmth, the look on their faces confirming that word of the General's murder had erupted across the soirée. With one final glance back up at the darkened lantern overhead, I turned and ran with Francis.

The path ended at a gate in a stone wall. A guard lay sprawled in the snow, gagged, bound, and blindfolded. Francis sped through the opening, turned left, and headed for a trio of thick chestnut trees that marked the far edge of the property. A wagon stood beneath the farthest tree, a pair of horses filling the air with rolling clouds of their breath. At the side, Francis turned and helped me up, lifting me by the waist. A man in the wagon took my arm and pulled me the rest of the way.

Once inside, I got a good look at the other man, starting with recognition: Ethan Knox, Iris' husband, Francis' brother. I recalled Iris' words, her certainty that her husband had nothing to do with the Rattlesnakes: *No, of course he's not. He has a family.* Francis climbed in after me.

"Where's Clara?" Ethan said.

Francis shook his head. "Just go."

Ethan nodded, took up the reins, and started the team forward. With a gentle hand, Francis pulled me down, out of sight.

He leaned in to me. "How are we—"

"North," I said.

"What?"

"To Andover. Fast as we can."

Behind us, the lights of the Whitelocke manse disappeared behind night-black trees, banks of snow, and other buildings. I put everything else from the evening out of my mind, thinking only of the shadow raven, flying north-east.

29

FOUL PERILS, BOTH SEEN AND UNSEEN

The moon stared at us as the miles passed, accusing with its pale glow, not altogether different from the lantern atop a witch-pole. Midnight found the house in Andover quiet and dark, fresh snow tracing the angle of roof, sill, and lintel. I scanned the sky and house for ravens, but spotted none. No signs of passage marred the lane as Ethan pulled the wagon to a halt. No soldiers, no riders had come that way—yet. Ethan lit a lantern and took care of the horses once I pointed him in the direction of trough and feed. Francis followed me inside and helped me with a fire and lights. While he crouched by the hearth, I took a candle to the copy of Fletcher's book I'd used in the raven spell.

"You lied to me," I said. "You planned on killing him all along."

"I didn't."

"You're lying now—and if you keep doing that, I'm not helping you with anything. Not Clara. Nothing."

"You don't know what I planned."

"Your speech wasn't impromptu."

"It's what I believe. No rehearsal needed."

"I have enough problems on my hands." I put the candle down and lifted the raven feather. "And now murder?"

Francis stood as the flames took to the fresh wood. "He'd have hanged you. He'd have hanged me."

"Or we needn't have been there in the first place—I didn't volunteer, if you recall. Now shut up, please—I need to concentrate." The look I gave him emphasized my point. He crossed his arms and watched me. With a minute of careful focus, I narrowed my attention on the phrasing of the spell. When I felt ready, I spoke the incantation. The mixture of ink shuddered before I even reached for it. Once I did, I dipped the raven feather into it and once more flicked it over Fletcher's map. This time, drops of ink landed just above the page, hovering over Salem. To my surprise, they shifted, spinning in small, irregular spirals, yet remaining in proximity to the old town. It wasn't what the spell was supposed to do, but at least it was telling me something—confirming what my intuition had lighted upon when I'd seen the shadow raven on the witch-pole.

Swaine was in—or near—Salem.

After seeing little change over the course of several minutes, I ended the enchantment and took the ingredients, book, ink, feather and shoved them into a satchel.

"You're a witch," Francis said.

"I don't know what I am."

"The witch-pole seemed fairly certain."

"Then you must be thrilled to have yet another way to extort me."

"Do you know what it will mean to the Governor to have a witch in the colony? This could take him down."

"I know what it means to *be* a witch here. I know the history. They know I'm here now."

"That's my point exactly. If they can't—"

"I'm not interested in politics."

"Well politics is interested in you. Don't you see?"

I grabbed a warmer cloak and put it on. "I see nothing but trouble."

"The one thing every Governor of this colony has relied on for eighty years. What if you could—"

I stepped in front of him. "I'm not on *your* side. I'm not on *their* side. I'm on *my* side. My *master's* side. What do you think is going to happen now? You've killed the Governor's son—that's more than a bit of political theater. A sign. A bushel of manure. A pamphlet. Do you think that's going to win over hearts? Or lose them? Do you think you'll have more young lads and lasses lining up to join you? I'm not inclined to—and I'm probably more sympathetic than most, given my nature. No. They're coming after you. Which means they're coming after me."

"We escaped. Who saw us?"

"Do you think they didn't line up every guest at the ball and question them? Didn't do a little survey of who was there before the shooting and who was there after it?"

"They were spilling out of the manse," Francis said. "You saw it. Do you think the most influential Bostonians were going to stand around in the snow for very long?"

"If the Governor's Own told them to, yes. Muskets have their own influence."

"Your spell hid us."

"*You*, it hid *you*. Not me. I was there. I spoke with his brother and sister. I spoke with Doctor Rush. Do you think he'll miss the signs of what happened in the cellar? Trust me: he won't." Even as I spoke it, I wanted to retch. "Do you know how his witch-poles work? Because I honestly don't. For all I know, I'm marked—and he's riding here right this minute with a company of regulars."

The thought filled me with terror. Biting the corner of my lip, I spun and crossed into Swaine's study. I picked up the *Occultatum Ostium* and shoved it in the satchel. I descended upon my master's collection of books, rifling through them until I found Doctor Rush's own *On the Principles of Planar*

Cartography, wherein he detailed the workings of the witch-poles:

Thus harnessing the central transferent principles with the alchemical blending of recombinant energies, the application of such efforts to the object-based binding of the witch-poles throughout the Colony render them critical in the detection of witches. A lantern of silver and pewter and steel, forged and shaped (by the noted silversmith Apollos Rivoire), imbued with a sequence of spells that work to redirect the forces and energies of a second-order plane into a pattern that loops in on itself in seven folds, creating an effect as though curving mirrors expand outward in such a fashion as to tune the witch-pole to the specific currents of planar force that all witches, by their nature, must possess.

I read it and reread it. There didn't seem to be any mention of tracking—but that might well have been by design. The theory was sound. I had no reason to suspect that the witch-pole hadn't worked precisely as intended.

All witches, by their nature.

And what was *my* nature? Did I know—had I *ever* known? A child, a daughter. A Finch of the well-stationed Finches of Mayfair, weaponsmiths to Kings. Were those my nature, or were they costume of the sort Grayson Whitelocke insisted so many mistook for their authentic selves? Certainly, when those labels were torn from me by a murderous demon, they'd been revealed to be every bit as fragile as a mask of paper-maché. Orphan, indentured servant. More horrid conditions thrust upon me by chance. Apprentice? Student of the unseen arts? Yes, closer, I supposed, having taken those on of my own volition.

But underneath, who was I?

"What about Clara?" Francis said from the doorway he'd watched me from.

I put Doctor Rush's book aside. I'd have to risk carrying my master's most precious book with me. "If I can find my master, I can possibly find her."

"How are you going to do that?"

"I'm not sure."

"Surely you must have some idea?"

"Must I? How about you? Do you have any ideas?" My patience had burned away.

He waved his hand at all the books. "You're the expert."

"Then let me think." I paced the room, looking from one book to another. No, I wasn't going to find the answer in any of those: maybe I'd only been delaying what I knew I needed to do. I shouldered the satchel once more and headed for the door.

"What now?" Francis said.

"Now, you take me to Salem."

"Sa—I'm sorry, what? Salem?"

"Yes. Salem. And if you're too frightened, I'm going on my own."

I pushed outside into the frigid night air. Francis followed. "Fine. If that's what it takes," he said.

Ethan, however, wasn't quite as enthusiastic. "I don't know about that." He stood by the wagon, having gotten feed for the horses. "Whitelockes are one thing. The Devil is another. My life has gotten fraught enough without bringing a curse down upon me and my family."

I didn't have time to explain where he was right and where he was wrong. "Then just take me to the edge and no farther. I'll do the rest."

The wind rattled the trees, shaking off curtains of fine, fresh snow to glint in the moonlight. Francis and Ethan exchanged a look, then Francis nodded. "We'll do it."

Ethan raised a hand. "But only to the edge."

"Fine," I said. "The edge will do."

I remember little of the ride beyond fatigue and the steely cold as I guided Ethan to the most secret of the backways into Salem. The woods to either side of the roads passed by in moonlight, twisting branches lined with snow giving it the flavor of an unsettling dream. I dozed off more than once, jolted away by a bounce of the wagon, and a final time by Ethan bringing the team to a stop. A pair of white-washed boulders blocked the road, past which stood a faded sign that read:

Here ye, all who would cherish their Souls. Beyond this point dwell Foul perils, both Seen and Unseen. By order of His Most Faithful Governor William Cabot, such roads, lanes, paths, vales, fens, and forest as lead to the Accursed Towne of Salem are forbidden to Trespass on account of the Various and Vile Devilries and Witchcraft that infest it.

Neither of the brothers said anything.

"You can go around it," I offered.

Ethan fidgeted with the reins. "I don't know about this."

"I've done it scores of times—but if you can't go any farther, at least lend me one of the horses. There are miles to go before the real edge."

"Come on," Francis said. "We owe her. I owe her."

Ethan shook his head. "I don't like it."

"She's done it before."

"Is that supposed to be a comfort?" He looked around, screwed his face up tight, and released the brake on the wagon and set the team off at a trot. The silence eventually filled with the wide exhalation of the sea, its presence just beyond the hills making itself felt. I watched for ravens, not spotting any against the scraps of clouds speeding eastward, nor against the stars showing clear between. Glimmers of queer light flashed across the horizon, but elicited no remark from Francis or Ethan. Magic. I grew uneasy, thinking about what had gone wrong with the resonance clock, how time itself had looped across sections of the property. The absurdity of what I was trying to do left me feeling tiny indeed: pitting myself against all of the hidden secrets in Salem.

As the water came into view, the folds of land around it resembling a gown tossed carelessly into a puddle, the eastern sky lightened, a pale band revealing the line of the ocean. I spotted the manse on its rise off to the north. My chest tightened: home. The pang surprised me, for I hadn't felt that way about any place in years.

We approached a thick grove of alder and birch trees. I gripped the side of the wagon. "You can let me out here."

"I'm coming with you," Francis said.

"No. It's too dangerous." I lowered myself to the ground once Ethan stopped the horses. Francis climbed down beside me. "And I don't have time to worry about you."

"I can worry about myself."

"Sorry, but you're not in charge." I didn't wait, heading off. "Unless you want to threaten to turn me in to the Whitelockes if I don't listen? Or maybe you don't have that card to play any longer."

He followed me. "What if you need my help?"

"What if I don't?" I passed into the trees. The snow was light, but grabbed at my calves. I realized with annoyance that I still wore Mary Whitelocke's gown. I stopped, turning to Francis. "Listen to me—this is dangerous. For me. And it's more dangerous for you. I know you want to help, fine. I also know you want to give me a speech. You want to weave a little magic of your own with your golden words. But I'm telling you to listen. To me. You need to leave." He tried to speak, but I raised my hand. "And if you don't leave, right now, I'm not helping you with anything. You have your expertise, I have mine—and this is mine. Please, go. Now."

"I need to find Clara."

"I'll find her."

"Promise me."

"Fine, I promise—now just go."

He stared at me in the faint light before dawn, then nodded. "Do you need this?" He held out his pistol for me.

"You'd better keep it. It won't help for what I'm after."

"Right." He looked around, then down at me. "Good luck."

All the luck in the world might not be enough. I kept the thought to myself. Francis turned and left. It was possible he believed in me, had confidence in my judgement. It was also possible he was frightened. Or all of it. I didn't get too much farther, however, before I heard him cry out, a wordless yell. I ran back along the trail in the snow I'd made. He knelt by the side of the wagon. Both horses flung their heads and rolled their eyes.

Demon.

Sprinting across the snow, I gasped. Ethan lay on the ground, a terrible fan of blood steaming in the snow. His severed head lay on its side a dozen paces away. I thrust my hand in my pocket, making sure I still had my pendant: it was there. I readied a ward, wary of the demon. Francis was oblivious of the danger, kneeling beside his brother's body, his hands to his mouth, rocking back and forth. I came up next to him, my stomach wanting to empty itself, my knees threatening to drop me to the snow.

No, of course he's not. He has a family.

Iris. As much as I wanted to cry out, there was no time. I grabbed Francis under his arm and heaved him to his feet. "Come on—you have to leave. Now."

He yanked his arm from my hands, looking at me as though I were a demon myself. "Ethan—I saw his—his head—"

"Francis, it's a demon. It's still here—you really have to go. Now!"

"But what am I—"

"There's nothing you can do. I'm so sorry, but there's not. But if you don't go, the same could happen to you—I feel it near." And I did. Even in the growing dawn, shadows lingered and my skin prickled. I pushed Francis toward the driver's bench of the wagon. "Get up there."

"Ethan—"

"Leave him." I tried to shove him up. A blast of icy air wrapped us. Long gouge marks erupted along the side of the wagon, racing to where we stood. I spun and called out Hume's powerful Fourth Ward, *"Geata dryhten! Gryrefahne sloh incgelafe! Brun sio ecg gewac, brun on bane, bat unswiðor!"* The side of the wagon exploded in shards and splinters of wood, snow and frozen earth burst skyward as the demon flailed back from my ward. As it retreated, the shadow of its passing swept across the headless body of Ethan and dragged it off through the snow, setting it tumbling and cartwheeling, staining the snow with bright blood. Francis screamed. I reached out and put my hand on his shoulder, turning him toward me.

"Listen to me." I shoved my pendant into his hand, closing his fingers around it. "Take this—it will keep you safe. Don't let it go, don't let it off of your person. Don't lose it—I'm going to need it back. But take it with you. Don't stop for anything or anyone you see. I'll find you."

He nodded, but I saw his gaze following the bloody trail left by Ethan's body.

I shook him by the shoulder. "Francis! Do you understand?"

His eyes focused on me. He made of fist of his hand with the pendant. "Will you kill it—the demon?"

Demons couldn't be killed, only banished—but there was no time for the finer points. "If it comes near me again, yes."

"Good." Trembling, he turned and lifted himself onto the wagon. His voice wavered as he shouted at the horses, getting the wagon to lurch forward. I stepped back, giving him room to turn the team around. As one of the horses passed me, I smacked its haunch with the flat of my hand, adding urgency to its equine mind. The wagon banged over hidden ruts, but got back into its tracks from earlier. Francis whipped the reins and headed back along the lane, soon moving into the trees.

Whatever else might happen, we now had each other's most dangerous secrets—a thought that gave me precious little comfort.

30

A GREAT REALM

F rom the top of a nearby ridge, I scanned the sky, searching for shadow ravens as the sun crested out of the Atlantic. I tried to put Francis out of mind. And Iris. Ethan. The dead Rattlesnakes. General John Whitelocke. Another wake of death and loss, trailing me—this time, of my own making. I didn't know how much more ruin I could bring down upon the lives of all those around me. For a time, despair threatened to choke me.

Maybe that's who I was, really and after all: touched by the grave, fated to bring an end of days to all who crossed my path. Maybe that's the truth I didn't want to embrace. Maybe my time with Swaine had been no more than a corpse-filled respite—and look what had happened to him. Was that my fault, also? Maybe the best thing I could do would be to stand up, arms wide, no pendant, no wards, no protection. Let the demons finally take me, shred me, lob my head clear of my shoulders, free the world of the bane I carried with me.

But, no. I couldn't. Wouldn't.

Would my mother have wanted that for her only daughter, even knowing she carried the same curse of witch-blood?

Would my father—fearless, tireless, meticulous—have given in to despair?

Would Swaine—a man who begrudged sleep, hunger, exhaustion in the pursuit of the impossible—wanted me to give in, to let the demons triumph?

No. No. No.

Shoving all else from my mind, I focused solely on the task at hand: shadow ravens.

Across the expanse of Salem, the first rays of dawn grabbed hold of the tops of trees, gilding the roof of the manse, five hundred yards from where I crouched. As I watched, I saw one of the windows on the second floor, Swaine's room, shine with fire-light, then go dark. Shine, darken. Shine, darken. For a moment, hope flared—and then I remembered the disastrous repercussions of the resonance clock, the strange temporal displacements and loops. If only we'd never attempted to create the resonance well. I glanced over to where the distortion in the sky was—and my breath caught.

Above the ruins of the orchard, a towering column of light and energy filled the air, made up of thousands upon thousands of strands of magic in every hue imaginable—twisted, twined, patterns within patterns, all alive with an undeniable energy that filled my senses. Some glared like permanent lightning. Others shone as molten silver, gold, iron. Still others twisted in dark and brooding shades of night. The entire array shimmered and turned, rising three times higher than the hemlocks by the edge of the meadow. The glare from the magic lit the snow and trees in shifting colors that spiraled up in an unbroken pattern, glinting as though inset with metals and gems, while others shone with the deep glows of sunset.

The pendant: I'd never seen Salem without the pendant on me. In an instant, I realized that as it had cloaked my presence from demons, it had also cloaked the energies of Salem from my vision. The more I looked, the more I saw the strange intricacies, spires and wreaths, buttresses and coils that spanned the growing edge of daylight, glowing against the retreating night. As I traced the towering cables of energy, I froze.

Ravens, circling the spot we'd activated the resonance clock, six of them. And farther afield, a pair on the Rivers house. Up by the barn at the manse, three more. One circling high above the bridge.

But where was Swaine? He couldn't be in all those places.

I tossed the satchel from my shoulder, untying the straps and pulling out the contents. I grabbed the bottle of ink and the raven's feather, ready to try again with Fletcher's map of Salem— but I stopped when my gaze landed on the *Occultatum Ostium*.

What might the raven spell tell me that I couldn't see with my own eye? And without my pendant to protect me, how might I concentrate on casting the incantation without making myself even more vulnerable to all that stalked Salem, eager to catch my scent as a witch?

The book had pointed me in the right direction once before.

I glanced back at the ravens, still circling or perched as before. I needed more help. Grabbing the book, I pushed the other materials aside, kneeling in the snow. Nothing stirred nearby—but I didn't trust the stillness. Almost without thinking about it, I tapped into my witchcraft and found a particular energy, subtle as wind, unseen and cold. I raised it like a cloak about me in the hopes of recreating the protection of my pendant. Not quite the same, but enough, I hoped, to hide my presence from the stray demons of Salem. Once I felt it was stable, I turned my attention to the book.

The cover felt colder than the snow on which it lay. I opened it to the first page: blank. The second, same. As I found one blank page after another, I bit back rising panic.

Don't do this. Not now.

The last page was blank. I flipped once again through the

entire book and saw not a single marking, not a letter, not a word, not an answer. Taking in a long breath, I closed my eye, determined to pry an answer from the book—the most powerful book in all of the unseen arts. I placed my hand on the cover. Allowed my witchcraft to roll from my palm. That's when I felt the book shudder. I opened my eye and lifted my hand.

When I opened the book a third time, I stopped at the first page. An outline of a hand was traced in golden ink in the center of the page. The ink shimmered. I waited for more information, but saw nothing. A gust of wind ruffled the skirts of my gown.

I placed my hand over the outline on the page—it fit exactly. The moment I pressed my hand to the cold paper, a chill spilled across my back and scalp, my flesh broke out in bumps. *Demon*. I snapped my gaze up, a ward already on my tongue, my other hand raised.

"*Finch*."

A spinning gust of wind rose before me, dragging up drifts of snow, rust-colored pine needles, clumps of moss and earth from the hilltop. As I watched, the whirling flotsam assumed a familiar shape: Swaine's face, a yard in height from chin to crown, resembling a glass casting of his head filled with debris. His expression intense.

"*Finch?*" the cold whisper emerged from the spectral mouth. "*Where are you? How are you doing this?*"

I glanced back in the direction of the ravens. "I—I'm not sure, sir. The book. You can hear me?"

"*For the moment. I daren't risk more sorcery beyond this, certainly not where I am.*"

"But where are you?" I whispered.

"*Stairs. Hallways. Dreamscapes. Worlds. Little of it makes any sense to me.*"

"You're closer than you think, sir." I stared past the strange image of his face. "The ravens seem to indicate you're nearby—I cast a spell. They've led me to Salem. Where we did magic, but across several spots. Can you see anything familiar?"

"*Salem? Of course. There appear to be three—*" The form of his face dissolved, swept sideways. Needle, snow, and twig pattered to the ground.

"No!" I yelled. A malign will pressed against my thoughts.

A demon—or more than one—flew at me.

I spun around, breaking my connection with the book. Shadows surrounded me, shapes, eyes, mouths, claws, and worse. Ghastly presences flocked toward me. Lines of bright light sparked along the edges of the stone wall. From every direction came tattered monstrosities, foul stains, desolate wisps of doom.

I curled my hands in the complex gestures required and spoke Hume's Twenty-Third Ward: "*Feorrancundum, reste hine þa rumheort. Reced hliuade geap ond goldfah. Gæst inne swæf, oþ þæt hrefn blaca heofones wynne. Bliðheort bodode!*"

My ears filled with a roar as the ward boomed out from my hands, crashing into the onslaught of demons as they surrounded me. They fell back before swarming me again. Stunned by the shifting energy, my feet stumbled. Foul energy and brutal cold crashed over me.

From the snowy ground, I swung my hands at the demons. Bright strands of magic rose in a tight series of weavings from my palms. The demons shrieked and tore at the air with claw, tooth, limb, and ghastly appendage, but their attacks failed against the glimmering filaments of witchcraft.

By instinct, I concentrated on one of the thickest streams of color before me, blue as the base of a flame, fading into a deep red of sunset. It ran from my hands like flowing water and grew more powerful as I focused. The brilliant light that surrounded me painted the snow and shone on the nearby trees, shifting and turning, prisms from a thousand chandeliers.

Many of the shadows fled before me, while a handful of the

bolder entities howled and barreled straight for me, only to be knocked back when they reached my witchcraft. Above, around, behind—the frenzy continued. A power I'd never known welled up inside me. Without thinking, I repeated the potent words of the Twenty-Third Ward, letting the magic wrap my hands as I gestured. Filling my mind again with power of the incantation, I lifted my hands and let fly a wordless explosion of fury, the full force pouring out of my hands. A whipping, spiraling explosion of witchcraft spilled from my hands, coursing along my arms, circling around my head in a crown of lightning. Streaks of blood-red wrapped in molten gold flew in every direction—only to crash and ricochet against the demons, and send them flying off into the fields like stunned birds, falling to the ground before the trees, by the snowy stone walls, in the far meadows, the magic bouncing around them, bright and fearsome. For several long seconds, the morning filled with light and motion, and a zipping hiss that accompanied my heaving breaths. Demons cried out and fled.

Panting, I got to my feet and rushed back to the book, only to find the pages all blank once again. I tried what I'd done earlier—my hand on the cover, but my witchcraft slipped and wavered, spent from having pushed back the demons. I slipped the book into the satchel, and hurried down the hill. Snow fell down before me in thick tufts and I had to steady myself with my hand. I looked at the ravens. More gathered on the manse itself. Others circled the field. Pausing, shading my eye with my hand, I counted them—realizing that far more than thirteen filled the air above Salem.

No, there weren't more ravens: they were temporal reflections, temporal distortions, something of the kind caused by the rift the resonance clock had initiated. I had no way of knowing which ravens were the real ones. Energies upon energies looped through the air. Presumably the ground, as well.

The thought struck me that if Doctor Rush had noted a shift to the flow of planar energy in and around Andover, he'd have been horrified at what engulfed Salem. And how could he not know? He was, after all, the man who invented the witch-pole. He mentioned nothing of Salem to me at the ball, but as the colony's third Doctor of Magickal Sciences, he'd hardly be unaware of the perilous state of the planes centered in Salem. I stopped at the bottom of the hill, out of breath, my mind racing.

I looked to the manse. The fields. The Rivers house. Ravens, dozens, near them all. Pairs of ravens in other spots.

But where was Swaine?

Turning to the manse, as there seemed to be more ravens there, I slogged about a dozen paces through the snow before stopping.

Doctor of Magickal Sciences. Fletcher. Archibald Fletcher had been the first. His explorations of Salem had formed a keystone to my master's own understanding of the perilous nature of the area. His verbose style had earned my master's scorn—as he'd once quoted to me.

Something in what he'd quoted had always seemed strange. I spun the satchel around, keeping a wary eye out for more demons, and dug inside it until I came up with Fletcher's book. I whipped the cover open and paged through the beginning.

There, the exact paragraph Swaine had read aloud to me on my first night in Salem.

Tis when autumn eventide sets this feral forest a'smoulder as with the glow of Hell's infernal chambers that one begins to apprehend the discorporal touch of the darkness in this land, the soul and the nerves preyed upon by the blackest currents of Witchcraft and Sorceries of most insidious origin, whose reach extends from beyond the borders of midnight to reveal a Great Realm winding unseen, beyond sill and threshold, beneath Rivers.

Rivers.

Beneath Rivers.

I glanced up at the Rivers house, home of the one of the original settlers of Salem, a warlock.

A Great Realm winding unseen, beyond sill and threshold, beneath Rivers.

Ravens flapped above the canted roof.

31

GAZING INTO A MIRROR

I dashed along a wooded slope, steadying myself on the branches and saplings that were handy. At the bottom, a wide meadow leveled out. I stopped at the edge of the trees. The curious magic grew faint in the daylight, tracing old stone walls in spots, rising over buildings. Stretches of field appeared empty of all but the smallest coils of shifting light.

As I neared the dark bridge over the river, the sound of flowing water filled the air. Beyond, I saw the shimmering expanse of the harbor, and the straight where it opened into the mighty Atlantic. The water stretched out to the horizon, a line that cut the heavens in half, a blade that had cut my life in half by way of a storming, wave-tossed, miserable voyage when I'd fled London. I hurried across the bridge, the planks knocking with my steps, the river muttering around the pilings.

Nearing the heart of the town, the silence grew heavy. The wind sighed around an old well, a rotted pier, across the snow blown against the leeward side of a slanting barn. I hurried past an uneven row of weathered gravestones, past the exposed doorway of a moldering house. I reached a slight rise upon which stood the ruins of what had been the old town meeting house.

Blackened stones and the vestiges of burnt timbers littered the ground, half buried in the snow, hiding glimpses of faded weeds and cold earth. As with much of the town, it bore faint traces of magic.

So far, the demons kept their distance, though the back of my neck rippled with their presence.

Leaving the lane, I climbed over a snow-lined fence and cut across a white meadow, nearing the house once occupied by Thaddeus Rivers. The shadow ravens watched me in silence from their perches on the roof. A dozen paces from the faded walls, I found thin filaments of magic penetrating the ground like roots, spreading out in complex webbing. As I examined them, I sensed a tension—like fine netting with strength enough to support a ship. I knelt and closed my eye. It differed from the rest of the magic I'd sensed so far, with a pensive energy, unsettled and shifting. Looking around, I got to my feet and approached the open doorway. The wind gusted, blowing a plume of snow from the corner of the roof. I rested a hand on the canting doorframe, the wood made gray and splintery from decades of exposure. The interior was black, stabbed here and there by a fall of sunlight through windows and chinks in the walls and ceiling. I stepped inside. The boards underfoot creaked and let loose the scent of dust. I sensed a pressure to the air that struck me as unnatural, felt it weighing on my cloak. It wasn't a demon, I was sure of that.

I passed through to the main room with its flagstone hearth and tumbled chairs in the corner, their bannister backs cracked and broken. The wind chattered around the eaves, through the missing windows. I sniffed back the tickle in my nose and brushed aside cobwebs that hung from a warped joist overhead. I paused. Again, the pressure increased, yet it wasn't the deadening sensation of sorrow that had permeated the location when we'd first investigated it, nor was there a hint of the infernal tainting the house. I grew uneasy, looking for the source of the sensation.

Near the spot where we'd put the planar clock, floorboards

were missing, a few askew atop the remainders. In the center, an opening exhaled chill air. Kneeling by it, I pried at one of the loose boards. Bits of wood crumbled between my fingers and a breeze streamed out over my hand. I got on my knees and held the flame over the opening. The air smelled wrong—not the faint salt-tang of the harbor, not the scent of aged resin or dust. I leaned forward. There was no earth beneath the floor, nor the foundation beams, as one would expect to see. Instead, I peered down into a narrow corridor.

I pressed my face to the opening and lowered the flame cupped in my hand into the emptiness. Beneath the remaining floorboards, I glimpsed space and faint light. The floor rippled beneath me. I felt it in my knees, my palms. Where the ground should have been, a stone corridor opened, and as I listened, a hint of distant sounds rose from the depths: faint rattles, peculiar noises, a low humming, reverberations extending into nothingness. It was the same sensation I'd had when I'd looked into the opening in the wall of the Andover house—the same queer emptiness.

The Demonmere.

A chill passed over me. The sense of distance and depth overwhelmed me, made the whispering house around me seem a thing in appalling miniature. A shift in my awareness focused my gaze on something in the middle of the floor beneath me. A ring. I leaned in, staring. A silver signet ring. In a moment, I recognized it as the one I'd seen the night before on the hand of General John Whitelocke. Before I considered it any further, the ring rose onto its edge. It rolled off away from me, into the darkness, the metallic tinkle of its passage dwindling. I watched in horrified fascination.

A presence pulled my attention away from the Demonmere, a presence within the walls of the Rivers house. I yanked my arm out and sat up, knocking a loose board down into the peculiar corridor below me. It clattered on the stone—and the sound echoed off into the distance, growing longer, continuing to repeat until it seemed to fill an entire world beneath me.

Nothing moved in the house, save for the dust motes in the sunlight, kicked up by my passing. I wasn't sure how many more times I could cast a ward and have it be effective. Even the slight witchcraft I'd raised around myself trembled from exertion. I turned back to the hole in the floor and tore away one board after another until I'd widened the opening large enough to slip through. The dark floor was a good ten feet below me. Looking around, I searched for something to help me down—rope, a ladder, anything. The best I could come up with was a tattered mattress of straw, moldy and desiccated, but at least something to cushion my fall. I shoved it down into the opening and watched it thump down to the corridor floor. My nose filled with dust as I tightened the satchel and hung my legs out into the hole in the floor.

A chill washed over me—and hands grabbed at my shoulders, dragging me backward as I cried out in surprise. The woman from Swaine's study, from the first time we'd entered the Rivers house, loomed over me, her face turned down in a grimace. Pale skin shone with splotched patches of sunlight and shade. She clawed at me, whispering words I couldn't understand. I shoved her away from me, finding her to be no heavier than a scarecrow. I rolled out of her grasp and shouted another ward.

It did nothing. I'd exhausted my strength too much to cast anything potent.

The woman leapt at me, sending me sprawling as I lost my footing. Her slender fingers wrapped around the strap of my satchel. I pressed my hands into the center of her chest, trying to push her away. She pulled me in closer, her face showing the strain. I lifted one hand to her chin, straightening my arm, peeling her off of me. In an instant, she let go of the satchel and instead grabbed me by the legs, dragging me across the splintered floor toward the door. My head banged on the boards and I cried out.

Something unseen knocked her sideways, sending her flying into the stones of the central hearth. She tried to right herself, but the demon—for the presence was unmistakable, likely one of Swaine's somehow summoned to aid me—bore down harder, scraping her around the corner and heaving her into the far wall. The few remaining panes of glass in the window shook and pitched forward, shattering on the floor. With a cry, the woman lifted her hands. A burst of silvery light exploded in the air and the demon tore across the far wall, dragging loose boards, a rack of warped wooden utensils, a mildewed curtain with it. A joist from the ceiling collapsed at one end. The woman flew from the far wall, colliding with the demon in the midst of the room, filling the air with strange magic.

I scrambled back to the opening in the floor. The woman and the demon hurled themselves into the doorway to the back room, sending dust feathering down from the ceiling. I rolled to my side and got my feet into the opening in one smooth move. With a glance back at the battle tearing apart the far side of the big room, I twisted myself, scooted backward, and lowered my legs into the Demonmere. Hips. Stomach. Wriggling, I got my hands on the edge and slid down until I hung by my fingers. Only for a second. Closing my eye, I let go, landing with a grunt on the old mattress, sending up a shower of musty hay. The thud of my hitting the mattress echoed off in both directions. From overhead came crashes and flares of light—but no sign of who might emerge victorious.

Not risking being delayed further, I stood and started off in the direction I'd seen the ring tumble. After just a few paces, the light from the opening in the ceiling dimmed and I cursed myself for not bringing a lantern with me. A candle. Anything.

I held my palm out before me and whispered, "Ignis." A small flame flared to life in my hand. Moments later, candles in glass sconces sprouted flames, one after another on either side of the corridor, marching to life two at a time before me, revealing fifty yards of corridor. Well-set maple floorboards ran beneath darker baseboards; walls of ivory-colored plaster rose to delicate cornice work by the ceiling. No doors or openings broke the run of the walls between the sconces. At the far end of the corridor stood a door of what appeared to be mahogany. Halfway to the door, a small table with a drawer stood against the right-hand wall, spindly legs rising a yard or so.

From the opening I'd come in from, the rampage within the Rivers house continued, sounding as though the ceiling was crashing down. Behind me, more candles in sconces bloomed flame, running an even longer distance in the other direction, but ending at a similar door. Nothing else stood in the corridor.

Looking back and forth, I decided to move in the direction of the table. As I neared it, I saw the ring on the floor, glinting with the light of dozens of candles. I crouched next to it. There on the face was an engraved letter: W.

The table had but a single drawer, with a delicate hasp of black metal holding it closed. I flipped over the hasp and slid the drawer open. It moved evenly, lightly. Within, a thin velvet pillow of deep scarlet filled the drawer, the center fastened down with a matching button. The pillow looked as though it'd been designed for one thing only: to hold the signet ring.

I closed the drawer and left the ring where it was.

My footsteps filled the corridor as I approached the door. The sounds coming down from the opening in the ceiling behind me ceased. I paused and bent my head, listening. Nothing. The corridor remained empty. I continued on to the door, only to find it smaller than I'd thought, no more than five feet in height. Examining the walls and ceiling, I realized the geometry of the hallway had narrowed as it neared the door. I placed a hand on it. Cool to the touch, the surface was smooth and, as with the materials I'd found in my first trip into the Demonmere, bereft of anything resembling the mark of humanity, bearing only the impression of age, stillness, and abandonment. The materials themselves held a blandness to the eye, yet touching them delivered sensation that was almost too real. Wood that had never lived as a tree, seen sunlight, drank rain. Stone never quarried. Plaster never mixed, smoothed, imbued with a fundamental otherness, a peculiar expression of magic that had taken on a life of its own.

The handle—brass in appearance—turned without protest and I was able to swing the door outward with little effort. Cold air washed over me and I confronted a dark room. Reaching back, I lifted the nearest candle from its sconce and carried it with me, releasing the spell in my palm. The flame fluttered queerly, stretching, looking in various moments as more than a single flame, casting off a light that extended with more brilliance than might be expected of a lone candle. Uneasy as I was with the strangeness, but unwilling to attempt any further magic, it was all I had.

I ducked my head and passed through the doorway. Unlike the corridor, the room I found myself in appeared to have unfinished walls, slats and studs open to the interior, with angles that made little sense to me. A triangular section like the prow of a boat extended out from one side, while several thick beams ran from floor to ceiling at nearly a forty-five degree angle. There was no ceiling per se, only a collection of unmatched surfaces meeting around various wooden rafters. The floor, rough boards with notable gaps between them, appeared to be an afterthought, occupying a haphazard geography that wound its way between the strange walls. The feeling was of a long-abandoned garret, but in purpose it seemed to be a side-effect of the intersection of numerous architectural features unseen from within. Stairs, angled hallways, corners, chambers: implied on the opposite side of the construction I examined. Keeping my head low, I avoided knocking myself against studs and beams, making my way forward. Shadows leapt and loomed as I passed from the door, losing sight of it within a dozen paces. Not much farther, I almost stepped straight into an opening where the boards were missing, not seeing it among the shadows that preceded me.

I held the candle out over the void. Along the sides ran rough slats, dried plaster squished through their gaps. Dust and cobwebs. The longer I looked, the deeper it appeared to go. The effect was dizzying, and a strange light fell in from one side. Two-hundred feet? A thousand? It was impossible to tell. I stepped across the gap, mindful of the depth beneath. Angled segments of plaster wall appeared, cutting across the space, forcing me to crouch beneath them to get by.

A sound reached my ear.

Overhead—footsteps. For a moment, my heart lifted, thinking I'd found my way to Swaine. Before I called out, however, I listened more closely, a tension building in my chest. Rising with a heavy tread, shoe on wood. The steps passed over me at a perpendicular, beyond the strange angled sections. I held still, didn't even breathe. Step by step, a low, indistinct muttering accompanying them, creaking the wood in the ceiling overhead, and then rose away, not pausing. The word *murderer* kept repeating in my mind, intrusive in origin as though whispered into my ear by a stranger. I didn't move until the last of the steps had faded, up and to my left. I knew only that it wasn't my master, without question.

Trying to remain silent, I edged my way around angled corners, beginning to wonder if the area would crowd down into nothing more than a crawlspace. Just as I was starting to consider giving up and backtracking, I reached the first flat wall I'd seen in some time, rising in my path. While the wall itself was of the same craftsmanship as the rest of the strange eaves, a rectangular opening stood in the center of it, rising from the floor to a height of no more than three feet.

When I reached it, I felt a breeze blowing in through the

opening, strong enough to almost gutter the flame of the candle. I shielded it with my palm and squatted in front of the opening. The rough wooden boards changed over to what looked to be hewn stone and as I peered out, I saw a much wider space revealed. I crawled through. Wind rippled my cloak and skirts, sent my hair streaming back over my shoulder.

The space over my head opened up as I left the cramped passageway behind. Standing, I found myself on an elaborate balcony. Stone arches opened up, one to the left, the other to the right. Before me rose an iron railing at waist height. Intricately laid stonework formed the floor, a mosaic of light and dark marble, forming a circle with a radius of nearly a dozen paces divided into smaller circles inset with symbols of alchemy that I recognized from my studies. The symbols looked like they were made of various metals, though of the strange Demonmere variety.

I looked up from the floor. My breath left me. Beyond the balcony gaped a wide space, rising and descending out of sight. The scale was dizzying, larger than anything I'd ever seen. On all sides rose a complex of structures, all seeming to open into the chasm. Looking across and along the sides, I could make out vast mazes of rooms, hallways, stairways, catwalks, foyers, chambers. Distant sections of rooms revealed themselves to be upside down, or on their side, chandeliers standing up like decorative bushes of glass, cornice, frieze, and head-jamb lining the bottom. Doorway after doorway along strange landings. Wide windows that shone with strange colors of sunset. Walled gardens of dead flower, shrub, and tree. Bridges of stone, wood, iron, spanning precipitous drops between further rooms, balconies. Glimpses into rooms filled with walls of books, shelves of scrolls. All of it stretching both up and down to unseen depths, a thousand palaces stacked one upon another, every dwelling in the world that had been touched in some fashion by magic.

Staircases twisted in tight spirals, others extended out in

graceful arches out over moonlit ballrooms, bedchambers, or glass observatories. I traced the passage of one staircase of wood, the steps of which grew in size until each reached five feet in height, yet no wider than two feet.

My determination fluttered away with my breath: how would I ever find Swaine? I could search each visible room and passage and stair, and it would take half a year; what I couldn't see and what extended out, up, down, and away from me—and who knew how far it all went—would take years. Decades. Centuries.

The candle blew out on the gusting wind. No matter, for pale illumination seeped from windows and doorways, peculiar angles of ghostly moonlight spilled across the way, coming from nowhere yet everywhere. I dropped the candle next to me and grabbed the iron railing.

"Master?" I cried out. My call echoed after a few moments, repeating and reverberating off into the Demonmere. "Master?"

I heard no call in return. I saw no movement. Ten minutes passed, then ten more. Taking a reassuring glance back at the small opening I'd reached the balcony from, I inspected the arches to either side. Both were blocked by heavy doors of dark wood bound in iron, neither with a handle on the side I stood on. Attempting to shoulder or pry them open didn't work, they didn't yield a hair's width. Over the balcony's edge were a set of three windows, framed in iron, open to the air—and twelve feet down, with no way to reach them. I could barely look at them without a massive tide of vertigo carrying me back from the rail for fear of pitching headlong into the chasm. Craning my neck, I searched for an indication of what was above me, but could only make out the lower edge of a stone wall twenty feet or more above the balcony.

Sweeping the satchel off my shoulder, I dumped the contents onto the stone mosaic and went straight for the *Occultatum Ostium*. Keeping well away from the drop-off, I knelt, holding the book on my thighs, putting both my hands on the cover. A shiver ran along the backs of my arms and neck, for the book had gone cold as a slab of granite in winter.

"Please," I whispered. I opened the cover.

Expecting a blank page, I squinted as a golden illumination flooded the dim light of the balcony. I stared at what appeared to be my own reflection drawn in fine lines of shimmering gold. Even more shocking was the image's movement: as I turned the book, leaning closer, the lines shifted, bringing the image to life. I stared at the reflection of my own surprised face as though gazing into a mirror. I turned the page this way and that, confused. I reached my hand to the page, only to see my hand in the drawing near the surface. I placed my palm on the page, but the cold forced me to lift it right away for fear of frostbite.

I turned to the next page, but saw the same shining image of myself. Every page of the book was the same.

"Tell me what to do." The glow of my image in the book flared then began to fade, the lines thinning, dimming, until the only faint smudge of color I saw came from my own eye as I frantically scanned the page. "No, wait!"

In the faint light, the pages stared back at me, blank once again. The cold left the pages, but no matter how I ran my hands across them, not a mark nor letter appeared, no answer to my quandary.

Unless I'd already received the answer.

Me. It'd shown: me. Shining, glowing, flaring.

My witchcraft.

I stared off into the space beyond the railing. Could I use my witchcraft to shine? To reveal myself to Swaine? To act like a beacon my master might spot from wherever he was lost? I closed the cover to the *Occultatum Ostium* and placed it back into my satchel. It had given me the answers before, twice now.

And what other hope did I have?

I stood. Pushing the other materials off to the side, moving the satchel to the small doorway I'd crawled through, I moved to the center of the mosaic. Raised the crown of my head. Let my arms hang. Inhaled. Closed my eye. I pushed everything else out of my mind—where I was, what it had taken to get there. Instead, I breathed. Inhale. Exhale. For some time, that's all I did.

As I did, I felt a stirring in my chest. Was it witchcraft, or emotion—both?

More than anything, I found a sudden ache inside, thinking of my mother. Could she have done what I was capable of? Had she known? Had she ever wondered? Or, as I believed, had she lived her life a prisoner to her own nature? Fearful, with no answers. Different from everyone around her, with no explanation. Stalked by demons, never understanding. She may well have gone to her early grave never knowing who she really was, never having a name for it, never having anyone explain why she felt and saw the things she did.

Such a lonesome struggle. My heart broke for her.

Terrifying as the turns of Fate had been for me, at least I finally knew. And, better still, I had someone who could guide me, someone who cared about me learning as much as I could about myself, who—in his own cerebral way—cared about me. Who could help me make sure that I would never live in the shadow of ignorance and fear my mother was forced to endure. Who could help me make sure that no demon would ever take anyone else close to me—or even just physically near to me—again. Too late for my father, my brothers, my other masters, good and bad.

But not too late for the rest of my life.

August Swaine.

He was out there—and I was going to find him.

32

FATE'S SERVANT

I stepped to the rail of the balcony and raised my hands. As I did, I let my witchcraft rise up from my chest and out my palms. Spirals of moonlight-colored magic spilled out, thin as cobwebs at first, thickening into strands as the energy increased. I thought of Swaine, and the magic transformed into dozens of hues of blue, forming a stunning pattern that extended out a dozen feet or more, and I felt a calm comfort run up my arm. I relaxed and let more of my magic pour out, feeling the expression grow even more powerful.

I turned my attention to the Demonmere beyond the railing. Focusing my mind on the breath passing in and out of my lungs for a few moments, I increased the power. The witchcraft rose from my feet, surging through my legs and middle. A satisfying release of intention expanded outward from my bones. The air crosshatched with slender lines of magic, turning counter-clockwise.

I swung my gaze to the structures across the way and below. Stairs met at an apex, and I directed the magic I channeled to it. Loops of glowing magic spun out over the stone, across the chasm, to the other side. The sensation was like the other times my witchcraft had fueled my spells, but more potent; a result, I guessed, of tapping the forces that rose around me in the Demon-mere. As the witchcraft reached the stairs, I sent it into half a dozen flights, where it spun like ivy, following balustrade and top rail, from runner to landing. From there, it followed each step. The line of stairs shone with pale fire, shimmering. The space between me and the stairs blazed with a bridge of witchcraft, a web of lightning.

The stones around me lit up with golden lines, as though revealing cleverly inlaid ribbons of metal, setting them to glow with the heat of a forge. All around, witchcraft crackled with my intention. *The connection between the will of the maker, and the materials at hand*, as my father had once described his craft. Well, it was what I had at hand, and my will.

"Finch?" The voice, rising from somewhere in front of me, sounded small indeed.

I didn't falter, didn't let the energy subside. "Master? I'm here —can you reach me?"

"I'm not sure how to get there—do you see a route?"

Gazing down, I looked across the way and saw Swaine— wearing no shoes, no coat, his shirt tails hanging loose over his breeches—standing in a thin doorway at a stone landing. As I was about to shout down to him, I saw movement above him.

And saw him emerge from a passageway next to a crumbled wall of stone and mortar.

Over to my right, I saw a third instance of my master appear in a tall window backlit by a shifting firelight. Each version of my master raised his hand and called out my name, the timing off by less than a second. The echoes jumped around the massive space. *Finchfinchfinchfinchfinchfinchfinch.*

As I looked, I spotted three more instances of Swaine. "Master —which one is you? I see a number of you. Is it—"

"Those aren't me," Swaine shouted—though I couldn't tell which of the Swaines had done so. "Nor is this another temporal distortion. They've been pursuing me, and I've only just stayed ahead of them. Demons, Finch. Rather unpleasant ones, I fear."

"But which one are you?"

"The one who knows the proper gestures for Hume's Thirty-Second Ward."

Even as he said it, I watched the various doppelgängers move their hands and fingers. How the demons knew to even attempt to mimic a ward, I wasn't sure, but if he'd been pursued by them throughout the time he'd been lost, anything was possible. He'd no doubt used more than a few wards to keep them at bay.

But of course, there was no Thirty-Second Ward from Hume: he'd only documented thirty.

Only one figure of Swaine stood still, below me and to the left, the first I'd seen. I grabbed the railing, scanning the warren of structures between where he stood and where I was. "If you can lower yourself down, there's a walkway leading off to your—your right. It connects with a bridge. Follow that, sir." The bridge arched out over the empty chasm, stone and without railings. It looked horrifically narrow. Swaine didn't hesitate. He ran to the edge of the stone landing he stood upon and wriggled himself down over the edge, hanging. The distance was greater than it had looked to me.

"Finch?" he called out.

"It's—below you. Four feet, no more." It might have been a little more.

He let go, landing in a crouch on the walkway. His grunt reached me. "Keep your eye on my friends. They're not very nice."

Already, the other versions of Swaine moved in my direction. One of them leapt from rail to ledge. Two others hurled themselves down and onto the nearest promontories, feats of physicality well beyond my master's abilities. I tried not to let my witchcraft falter so Swaine wouldn't lose sight of where I stood.

"Finch?" he called out as he sprinted across the bridge.

I scanned the area. Panic gnawed at my concentration. "Your left. That walkway. It passes through three arches—and there are stairs after the third one." From my vantage, I only saw the stairs —stone things with no rail, protruding from an otherwise empty stone wall—and not where, precisely, they led. Still, it was the only path I saw leading in my general direction. As Swaine reached the walkway, I turned back to the demons in his guise. Two of them reached my side of the great void. One spidered his way along the outside of thin windowsills that lined an eighty-foot-tall battlement to my right. Another scaled the wall beneath the balcony. They whispered my name, filling the dim space with hissing repetitions of *Finch*.

By guiding Swaine to me, I also guided them. I couldn't find several of the shadow-Swaines. That bothered me even more.

Finch. Finch. Finch. The whispers fluttered and bounced off stone, off wood, out into space. Leaning over the rail, I watched Swaine pass through the second of the three arches—and then another Swaine step out of the third one, moving in the opposite direction.

"Master—there's one ahead of you!"

Swaine slowed. "Where?"

"Just out of the final arch."

"Good. I've had more than enough of their nonsense, thank you." Swaine lifted his hands and kept moving forward. For a moment, I lost sight of both of them in the shadows—but a massive eruption of white light revealed them a moment later, Swaine's spell lifting the demon off of the walkway and out over the void, where it spun out of sight, a wailing cry trailing off into the depths. "Keep watch for them, Finch—I haven't too many more of those left in me."

As I eyed the other demons, it occurred to me that I might better point them out to Swaine. Redirecting my witchcraft, I sent strands of blinding blue lightning, slender fissures in the air, down to the demons, my energy splitting into half a dozen branches. "There! There they are, sir!"

"Excellent." Swaine's reply was a breathless huff. He reached the staircase and started up, running one hand along the stone wall and leaning away from the bare edges of the runners.

One strand of my witchcraft curled up around my wrist and arm, leaping from my elbow to the door to my right, tracing the planks moments before the door slammed open, booming outward on hidden hinges. A demon simulacrum of Swaine burst through, eyes narrowed. Not entirely taken by surprise, I shouted Hume's Fourth Ward, the ward I felt most well-versed in, which I'd been saving for when I needed it. The demon loosed a guttural scream before breaking apart into dozens of scraps of shadow that curled into the air like sooty filaments and disappeared.

"Finch—I can't see you!"

With a yell, I forced the energy out of my hands once again, watching the jagged blue light spin out into the air, whirling and curling down to the other demons. It didn't feel as strong as before. *I* didn't have too much left in me, I realized. "Here, sir!"

"Try to hold them off—I'm not sure I see the best way to you."

I leaned over the rail, spotting him twenty-five yards below me. The angles of stone and wood occluded any details about what lay between us. "There are windows below me, sir—if you can find a way in—"

A hand grabbed at my wrist, yanking me off the railing and dragging me up and over. With a cry, I pulled back, bracing myself against the metal. Swaine's face leered up at me, distorted and not quite right, eyes wide, teeth showing in a snarl. Without time to shout a ward, I released the same energy I'd used in the fields outside. The demon released my wrist, filling my ears with a shriek, crawling off to the side. Rather than fleeing, it scrambled up over the railing and clung to the shadows at the side of the balcony. It rushed past me, reaching for the *Occultatum Ostium*. I spun and heaved forth another stream of witchcraft. It hit the demon, sending it sprawling to the wall. I stepped toward it, hands extended, shouting the Fourth Ward a second time. The demon tore apart into scraps of shadow, filling the air with a vile stench.

I snatched up the book, shoving it along with the other book and spell ingredients into the satchel and tossing the strap over my shoulder—I wasn't going to leave the book or anything else unattended again.

"Finch—help me!"

Leaping back to the railing, I leaned over and saw Swaine—the real Swaine—reaching out from the second of the windows below me. Even with me reaching down to him, our hands were half a dozen feet apart, nothing but rough stones along the wall in between.

"It's too far," I said.

"Rope?"

"Nothing. Is there another way up?"

More of the demon Swaines neared us. Swaine saw them. "A doorway and a passage, leading down. I won't risk it. No. Stay where you are."

With that, he climbed out onto the edge of the balcony beneath me, his knuckles white as he gripped the stones to the side. I could barely watch as he clung to the wall, the enormous gulf opening up beneath him. Searching out one hand-hold after another, he straightened. His arms shook as he pulled himself up by half a yard, his right foot scrabbling for purchase on one stone after another. Finally settling, he shifted and reached higher.

"This was a terrible idea," Swaine said through gritted teeth. His arms and legs stretched in awkward angles. "I can't go any farther. I don't think I can even go back."

"Hold on, sir." I stretched over the railing, reaching. Our hands were still several feet apart. I straightened and slipped the satchel from my shoulder. The leather strap might reach.

Lowering myself once again, I dangled the satchel by one end of the strap. The other end almost reached Swaine. "It's four inches above your right hand."

"It might as well be four miles. I don't think I can let go to grab it without slipping."

Bracing my knees on the rail, I stretched as far as I could. The strap grazed his fingers.

"I feel it," he said. "But I'm afraid I'm only going to have one chance to grab it."

"I have it, sir. I won't let go."

"Don't try to lift me—just steady me. Pull gently once I have it. If I have it."

"Yes, sir."

He took several deep breaths, then grabbed at the strap, stretching as far as he could. He caught hold of it, slipping in the process. I tugged at the strap with all my strength, holding him in place. Leaning back, I kept him from falling.

"Up," I grunted.

His kept his feet on the rough stones, pressing against the wall. I pulled. The satchel started to tear. Without pausing, I allowed my witchcraft to flow down through the tough hemp and leather, tracing the fibers, the hidden strengths of the fabric— toughening it, giving it more strength than it actually possessed. I pulled as hard as I could, lifting Swaine, letting the power do some of the work for me. He ascended more quickly, now grabbing the strap with both his hands, his feet hopping from rock to rock, nearly walking his way up. As I got him to the top of the rail, he grabbed for it and held on. I slid my hands over his shoulders and grabbed him by the shirt, pulling, getting a grip under his arms. In a moment, he wriggled over the rail, landing on the stone floor in a heap. I slung the satchel down next to him.

"You're here. You did it, sir."

"Well done, Finch." He sat up, opening and closing his fingers with a grimace, eyeing the depths beyond the rail. Up close, he looked stricken—pale, underfed, frightened. One of the demons neared the rail, another not far behind.

"Wards, sir."

He shook his head. "You know the way out?"

"Back through that opening, sir—it's not far."

"Then let's go, before they reach us. I'm down to the end of my wick."

I helped him to his feet and picked up the satchel. The demon Swaines drew closer. "This way." I led him to the back of the balcony and pointed to the opening in the wall. "Follow me, sir."

I got onto my hands and knees and crawled through the opening. Leaving the strange illumination of the larger space behind, the darkness grew complete. With no other choice, I held out my hand and whispered "Ignis," whereupon a small flame sprouted in my palm. As I did, more lights flared around me. I gasped. The strange unfinished eaves I'd followed to the balcony had changed: no longer raw slats and studs, smooth plaster covered the walls, even as they retained their peculiar angles. Moreover, candles in sconces shimmered with calm flames.

Swaine crawled in behind me. "Best hurry."

"I—yes. It's changed, sir."

"You might tell me as we hurry."

"Of course." After crawling for ten feet, we were able to stand. I helped Swaine. We hurried back through the curious angles, our shadows sliding over the tilted walls. Cast by dozens of candles, we appeared to be a crowd of nightmare figures, stretched, squat, looming. At the far end of the space, I reached the door into the corridor. Still open, thankfully. Hurrying into it, I was startled to see a deep scarlet carpet, stitched with golden threads in a pattern at the edges: galloping stallions. The walls, formerly plain plaster, now wore intricate wainscoting along the top edge, carved to look like vines, replete with blooms of flowers, bunches of berries, and tiny songbirds. The slender table had become a tasteful armoire. The decrepit mattress I'd tossed down had transformed into a four-post bed. Still, the opening in the ceiling remained, and that was all that mattered.

Swaine followed me, the both of us jogging past the strange finery. As we approached the opening, we both heard footsteps resounding out from the crawlspace. I turned and helped Swaine up onto the bed. "Up, sir." I interlaced my fingers and boosted him up high enough to grab the edge of the ceiling. Lifting his foot to the height of my shoulders, he got his arms fully onto the floor of the Rivers house and crawled free. Looking back over to the end of the corridor, I saw one of my master's doubles peering out from the doorway. I hopped off the bed and shoved it sideways by three feet, then jumped back up.

"Sir—a hand, quickly please!"

Swaine's head appeared above me. He held his arms down. I grabbed his wrists, he grabbed mine, and he lifted me free from the Demonmere, with the help of me shimmying up one of the bed's posts as he did. Once up, the scent of dust and sea air and mildew filled my nose in a rush, in contrast to the scentless spaces below. I dragged myself away from the opening in the floor, panting. The interior of the house showed signs of the fight between Swaine's demon and the figure of the woman: cracked joists, shattered glass, broken cabinets, blazes of gouged wood. I sensed neither the demon nor the woman.

"One of the demons is coming," I said.

Swaine nodded, the exhaustion clear on his face. He looked around the inside of the room, hurrying over to the old hearth, wiping his hand on the stones only to come up with dust.

"Sir?"

"No ash. I need something for a glamour."

I slid the satchel around and opened it. My fingers closed around the bottle of ink. "Ink?"

"Yes, that will work." He hurried back and took the bottle, eyeing how much remained. Flipping off the stopper, he circumambulated the opening in the floorboards, carefully sprinkling ink as he went. When he'd completed the circle, he tossed aside the bottle and raised his hands. Closing his eyes, he spoke, "*Gearofolm searobendum gegyrwed. Deofles cræftum ond dracan fellum. Unsynnigne dædfruma, gedon wolde manigra sumne!*"

The ink hissed, a flume of steam racing around the circle, leaving it shining a glaring silver.

Swaine put his hands on his thighs and leaned over, exhaling.

"Will that—" I began.

My master raised his hand. I closed my mouth. Demons arrived, darkening the doorways, sliding through the walls, shadowed and menacing. Glimpsing them, I reflectively extended my witchcraft again, holding them off. I sensed their unease: obeying their master, only to confront my protection.

"I don't have my pendant," I whispered.

Swaine looked at me. "How are you doing that?"

"Witchcraft, sir. I'm not sure—I just know."

"And is that how you knew to reveal yourself to me in there?"

"Well, not exactly. The book, your book—the *Occultatum Ostium*, sir. It told me. Or suggested it. It's strange."

"The book told you?"

I pulled it from the satchel. "Yes—I have it right here. I'm sorry, sir. I had no other choice. At least, I didn't think I did. And I don't know how else I would have found you."

If my master hadn't been pale already, he'd have gone so at the sight of the book. He reached out and took the book, turning it over in his hands as though to make sure it was authentic. "Good Lord. You brought this into there?"

"I'm sorry—I didn't know what else to do, sir."

His hands shook as he tightened the grip on the tome. I expected his fury, to see his brow lower. Instead, he stared at the book in his hands. "It saved me. You saved me. One would have done nothing without the other." He looked at me. "I thought I was done for, Finch. Every turn I made grew more confusing than the last. I couldn't find my way back after the first ten minutes. I lost my shoes within the first hour. What magic I attempted fizzled. I couldn't reach my demons. No—you did the right thing, and at great peril to yourself. But the *Occultatum Ostium* isn't to be trifled with. Do you understand?"

"I'd be happy never touching it again, sir."

"Good." He tucked the book under his arm. "That is the proper instinct. Now, how long was I in there?"

"Two days."

"Then I'm doubly impressed at your newfound facility with your witchcraft." He nodded. "But let's not have you harassing my servants. We should leave."

"Yes, sir." I followed him out through the wreckage of the Rivers house. "Was there... anybody else in there?"

"Besides the demons? No. It's a realm unlike any other, Finch. One that doesn't get many visitors."

Clara's final scream as she'd been hurled down into the Demonmere hadn't left my mind. If my master had barely survived his journey, I couldn't see how Clara might.

When we stepped outside, I was shocked to see that the morning had spun to late afternoon. How long had I been in the Demonmere? It'd felt like an hour at most, but the day looked long. Still, I saw my footsteps in the snow from my approach earlier, some of them still crisp. Swaine shivered. I took off my cloak and gave it to him. He looked at the gown I wore, from the top where I'd torn one of the sleeves, through the still-lovely middle, down to the stained and trampled skirts.

"Why on earth are you dressed like that?" he said.

"For—a ball, sir."

He put the cloak over his shoulders and started walking. "I see. I disappear into a deadly realm of interstitial planar residue, and you seize the opportunity to play dress-up."

"No, sir—it's not—it's a longer story." I followed after him, blushing.

Swaine lifted his hand. "Of course it is. It's always a longer story. We both ought to know that by now."

The winter sun neared the horizon to the west. My fingers ached. The frigid breeze whipped my hair into my face. All around, I caught glimpses of the strange intricacies of the witchcraft, spires and wreaths, buttresses and coils that spanned the trailing edge of daylight, glowing against the coming of night.

Swaine stopped. "You did well, Finch. You've done things I couldn't teach you in twenty years—which is good, because our biggest challenges are ahead of us. This place." He swept an arm out over the town and harbor. "This place holds *everything*. I've seen it. I understand it in a way I hadn't dared to imagine. The future of mankind will be forged here. Untapped power. The connections. The promise and potential. All we have to do is stabilize it. Harness it. I have ideas. Good ideas. Ideas to help us wring every drop from what Fate has offered us."

His eyes reflected the light of the first stars that kindled to the east. I knew he meant what he said, and more. Somehow I'd spared him from the Demonmere. I knew I couldn't have done any of it without all that he'd shown me. So perhaps that's what I was, after all: an apprentice. An apprentice to a great man. As we crossed the snow-draped countryside beneath a fiery western sky, I thought back to poor Silas Wilkes. Perhaps not a great man— but a good one whom I hadn't been able to save.

Our fortune is here, if we're lucky. His words came back to me.

As Swaine and I made our way toward the snowy lane, I realized that luck was a fickle thing. Fate's servant, really.

33

TALES ARE USUALLY JUST TALES

And what of secrets? Those unstable posts and hastily thrown-together beams out of which we build a facade for the world to see. Some built slapdash from lies that fly from the lips before a considered moment might argue otherwise; others sketched out with a cool deliberation. Do they not inevitably become a prison? Worse, one that promises to collapse and reveal the cowering liar within at the slightest prodding? Even sturdy lies, laid one at a time, forever bricking up a room—even then, they can't be forgotten. They will always whisper: *Here I am.* One doesn't spend all that time laying brick after shameful brick only to forget what's inside, as much as one would like to.

To live so, to fill your days with innumerable rotted trapdoors, ready to give way with the wrong step—and for what? Fear of hurting others, upsetting them, worrying them? Perhaps those are no more than more lies, foisted on oneself. Dig deeper, and one might scratch the true surfaces of vanity, of esteem, of reputation, all those imagined pillars of the self so susceptible to the corrosive nature of shame.

Put so, it seems ridiculous, yet I found myself dwelling more and more in just such an unstable edifice, one that threatened to

grow in time to rival the Demonmere with its mismatched structures, hallways, arching spans, pointless windows, upside down
rooms; for, you see, I'd told Swaine some of what I'd done in his
absence.

But not all.

Of Rattlesnakes and generals, I said nothing. Of Mary Whitelocke's desires to learn the unseen arts, no word. Of witch-poles,
silence. And I made no mention of my foolish promise to rescue
poor Clara from the Demonmere, yet another secret that gnawed
at me with the passing of each hour—for as much as I disliked
her, and she me, I could only imagine the terror of her plight.

As for Doctor Rush's hints and intimations at the ball—well, I
only needed to transfer the comments from the ball in Boston to
the inn in Andover, and the recipient from me to Iris Knox, who
could quite believably have relayed the rumors on to me. Swaine,
more consumed than ever with the planar forces around Salem,
paid close attention. To my surprise, he didn't outright dismiss
Rush's concerns. To my further surprise—and great relief—he
carefully posted his demons along the roads leading both into
Andover and Salem itself, set to observe any comings and goings
of the good Doctor.

Within two days, just such an excursion occurred. Notified by
the gentle ringing of a brass bell—one of seven located in the
study in the Andover house, its handle daubed with blue paint to
identify the demon as positioned near the old Boston Road
leading to Salem—Swaine and I huddled over a polished mirror
he'd enchanted and linked to the demon in question. A wide
winter sky stretched over fields of snow by the edge of the forest.
A trio of soldiers on horseback wound along one of the abandoned roads. Sunlight glinted on their bayonets and set their
scarlet uniforms ablaze. Behind them rode Doctor Rush himself,
unmistakable in girth, his white hair fanning out from beneath
his tricorn, his spectacles topping the scarf wrapped around his
lower face. I watched, horrified, convinced my terrible mistakes

had caught up with me. All that Swaine had worked for, all that he'd accomplished, the efforts I'd assisted with, and made on my own, all of it stood on the brink of ruin.

And it was my fault.

Swaine sniffed, folding his arms as he watched the surface of the mirror. The quartet's passage between shadows and snow brought them ever nearer to the fork in the road that led straight up to the property, and all our secrets.

"He does love his devices," my master said. "Look. His right hand."

Leaning in, I saw Rush holding what looked to be a lantern made of silver. As he rode, he occasionally lifted the lantern, then held it close to his face.

"Planar readings, no doubt," Swaine continued. "He should detect very little in the way of disturbance, thanks to my spells."

On hearing of Doctor Rush's investigations, my master had draped the approaches to Salem with a series of potent enchantments designed to compress any fluctuations in the harmonic shadow orders, guessing that Rush's approach to such investigations would almost certainly rely on his work within that discipline, as catalogued and documented in his own writings for decades. The real disturbances would be dealt with soon enough, Swaine insisted.

That, in any event, was the gamble.

The riders neared the fork. Every so often, they halted while Rush took another reading. When they reached the turn-off that would take them to the manse in another three miles, they paused once again. The road into Salem, blanketed in white, was crisscrossed with the shadows of trees. Gusts of fine snow curled from their tips as the highest branches swayed in the wind. Rush raised the lantern, north, south, east, west.

I held my breath. Swaine might have held his, staring intently at the mirror. Rush lowered the lantern and the riders gathered. After what appeared to be a brief discussion, they turned around, heading back the way they'd come. Beyond the line of trees, Rush and the soldiers soon dwindled. Man and horse, glimpsed through the spaces between trunk and bough, none sparing a glance in the direction of Swaine's manse. They moved off, into the shadows beyond the dell where the old lane snaked into the woods.

With a final glance at the lane leading into Salem once again deserted and forgotten, I looked up at Swaine. He smiled. "One hates to use the word *genius* too liberally—but feigning humility can be an equally disappointing affectation, wouldn't you say?"

"I'm not sure I'd recognize that particular affectation, sir." My pulse was only starting to slow down.

Swaine barked a laugh. "Fair enough. Well in any event, words aren't actions and actions need no words—so, onwards. I shall fuel my actions with the proper harvest of words, the ignition of which we shall use to forge the hitherto only-imagined into reality, what say? Tea, Finch—lots of tea. We've work to do."

He returned to the stack of notes and books at his writing desk. A pleasant fire snapped in the hearth, the chill of a cold winter's day held largely beyond the windows. I looked for a moment longer at the mirror as the spell faded, catching my own eye as my reflection returned.

My master was certainly a genius.

Yet I wondered, silently, what the lantern in good Doctor Rush's hand was designed to search for.

SOME SECRETS WERE MORE painful to bear than others. Excruciating, in one case.

That afternoon, I left Swaine to his work and drove the wagon into Andover to meet Mr. Robert Twelves at Knox's Inn & Tavern, where his ride up from Boston was to leave him. I'd barely eaten at noon and my stomach threatened to double me over as the wagon passed over rutted roads. I took my time. Still, I couldn't stop the clock. I couldn't not fetch my master's clockmaker. Whatever resolve to maintain my composure I'd worked up vanished as soon as I pushed open the door to the inn.

Iris sat before the fire, her hand on her mouth, a shawl over her shoulders. Bertram leaned against the mantle, his expression grim. The public room was otherwise empty. Iris looked at me with red eyes.

"Iris? Is everything all right?"

Her hand still on her mouth, she shook her head. "Ethan."

I stood in the open doorway, half a second from turning and running out. Guilt welled up in my throat. In my eye. All over my face, I was certain.

"He's dead," Iris said.

"What?"

She nodded, tears spilling. "They shot him. The Governor's men. A misunderstanding. Francis told me last night. In the chaos. After the murder of—of General Whitelocke."

I closed the door, on fire with shame. "Shot him? For what?"

"There was a meeting. At a tavern in Cambridge. Raided by the Governor's Own. Half of them were cut down by guns. Bodies dumped in the harbor. It was all a misunderstanding. Ethan had nothing to do with a plot against anyone." The last phrase came out in a whisper.

Bertram watched me. He looked as though he hadn't slept.

Thinking myself the worst wretch imaginable, I crossed the room to comfort her. As I took her in my arms, as her hot tears stained the shoulder of my dress, as she sat back and told me in a hitching voice how Francis had blamed himself, of how she had yet to tell her own son, of how many times she'd warned Ethan to be careful, of how she'd failed as a wife to protect him, of the ache in her heart that she didn't know how she'd bear, as I sat and listened, holding her hands in mine, her raw grief flooding the room around us—I thought only of demons, and why they stalked me. And in the guilt, and shame, and sorrow, beneath it all, rose an anger. They'd taken so much, my own family included. Why? Because of who I was. Because of the secret in my family bloodline.

And, in that moment, I vowed no demon would ever kill someone I cared for ever again.

Of course, I couldn't breathe a word of it to Iris. The secret was mine to bear. I simply held her hands, wondering what kind of friend I truly was.

Soon after, her sisters arrived, along with two of the town's pastors. Friends and family filled the public room, talking quietly, adding to the weight of mourning. I sat off to the side waiting for Mr. Twelves to appear. Bertram brought me a mug of cider. I thanked him.

"It's bad business," he said. "Murder. Guns. Killing. Worse than tales of spirits."

"You're not wrong."

"A lovely man. Fine brother-in-law."

"I'm so sorry."

"You're not the one to be sorry." He spoke more quietly. I stared into my cider. "Naught but trouble could come from that brother of his. Saw that early on."

"I don't think Ethan had anything to do with what happened." Another lie for me, another secret to carry. "Iris doesn't think so."

"She might not. Or she might not want to see it. Hard to say, what goes on with brothers."

"Where is he?"

"Francis? Blew in my front door last night like the wind, dragged me along with him, frightened my poor grandpa half to death. Needed me to stay with Iris. Said he was leaving. Off to New York. Said he'd been falsely tarred. Pretty sure he tarred himself, but no matter. Gone now. Maybe for the best."

I wondered if Bertram wasn't right. For a moment, a guilty thought filled my mind: since Francis had left, I wouldn't need to keep my promise to him to save Clara. Then I recalled the terror on her face as she'd been dragged off down that darkened stairwell. I didn't care for her, true—but I hated to imagine her suffering at the hands of a demon. No, my promise wasn't just to Francis.

"Did he leave anything?" I said, thinking of my pendant.

"Besides his broken-hearted sister-in-law and her two children, do you mean? No. He was naught but apologies as he left. I spent the rest of the night waiting for the Governor's Own to storm through the door looking for him. Maybe shooting as they did."

The door to the tavern opened and Mr. Twelves stepped in, taking his hat off to avoid knocking it on the upper edge of the doorway. I handed my mug back to Bertram and surprised him with a quick hug, whispering another *sorry* into his ear. I waved to Twelves, who spotted me.

"Mr. Twelves," I said when I reached him.

"Miss Finch." He nodded his head, looking around the room. "An ale might go down well after the coldest and bumpiest—"

"No time, let's get your things." I led him straight back out the door. "My master is beyond eager to get you settled in. We have ale at the house. Cider, tea, victuals. A meat-pie I baked this morning. Fresh bread. Cakes."

We crossed along the front of the inn. Wind whipped down from the gables. The sky was blue and unbroken by a single cloud.

"I won't say no to good food," he said, working to keep up with me. "You cook?"

"Among other things, I do. Our wagon is that one."

He put his hat back on. "My tools are these ones." A stack of trunks and a crate stood near at hand.

"Of course." I thought of Silas Wilkes again. "Your tools. You'd have a few."

"More than a few." He squatted down and hefted one of the

larger trunks. I helped him load the back of the wagon after ignoring his pleas that he could do it all himself. He appeared grateful, nonetheless. I latched the back of the wagon closed and joined him at the driver's bench. Within a few minutes, I had the team on the lane to the Andover house, passing orchards of bare apple trees, fallow meadows slumbering beneath drifts of snow, dappled with blue shadows of covered stump, stone, or fence.

"The other driver told me this all used to be part of Salem." Twelves warmed his hands by sticking them beneath his armpits. "Trying to frighten me, I think."

"I'd never heard that, Mr. Twelves."

"Nor had I. But it's a fright that used to keep me awake as a lad, hearing tales of Salem."

"You do know who you're going to work for, don't you, Mr. Twelves?"

He smiled. "Oh, I do. Course I do. I'm not a frightened eight-year-old any longer. Just thinking of the tales. Witches appearing. Spirits waylaying travelers. The Devil leaving his mark on children."

"I'm sure you don't still believe in such tales."

"Well, no. Tales must have come up from somewhere true, at one time. And I'll never close my mind too tight to get anything in or out of it—but you know how people are, love to put a fright into the gullible, Miss Finch." He nodded. "Do you?"

"Believe in the tales, Mr. Twelves?" My own fingers were cold. I remembered the feeling of the witchcraft that had poured from them. I believed in that. I believed it mine, as much a part of me as my own hands. I also believed in the intention I'd brought to bear, that it connected my past with whom I was becoming. The wind snapped at my coat and skirts. "Well, I think I'm with you—tales are usually just tales."

I followed the lane back through the bright afternoon, tracing the tracks I'd left earlier.

Ah, secrets.

The story continues in Volume Two of The Books of Conjury

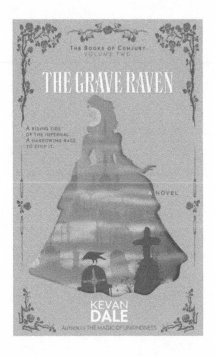

The Grave Raven is out now.

A WORD FROM KEVAN

Thanks for reading *The Magic of Unkindness*—you rock! I hope you enjoyed getting to know Finch and Swaine.

If you'd like to join my private newsletter for updates on what I'm working on, upcoming books, novellas, and stories, you can sign up at my website. I'll also send you a free copy of the prequel novella to the Books of Conjury, *Sorcery of the Stony Heart*.

Find out more at kevandale.com

ENJOY THIS BOOK? YOU CAN MAKE A BIG DIFFERENCE

Reviews are super important for me as an author. They get the word out and help potential readers decide if this book might be for them. If you enjoyed the book, would you do me a favor and take a few minutes to post a brief review?

A million thanks!

Kevan

ABOUT THE AUTHOR

Kevan Dale grew up in a Massachusetts home full of books, next to a winding patch of woods full of stories (in his already vivid imagination). Books and stories eventually pointed him to a degree in English. That degree in English inspired him to pursue a career as a professional guitar maker (long story.) A decade of luthiery led to a second career, this time in video games (another long story) where he remains. It all made sense at the time, honestly.

Throughout all, a new crop of books and stories made their way out of his head and onto paper: after a day spent woodworking, before the dawn and a long day making games, wherever a free moment unwittingly strays, to this day. History, fantasy, horror. All of them tug at his imagination, and he happily follows.

Kevan is once again in Massachusetts, glad to live in his own home full of books, next to a winding patch of woods full of stories.

kevandale.com

ALSO BY KEVAN DALE

The Grave Raven

The Halls of Midnight

Sorcery of the Stony Heart

Revolutionary Dead

The Devil's Key

Learn more at kevandale.com